SHE
TOO

EVE THOMSON

SHE TOO

echo

echo

Echo Publishing
An imprint of Bonnier Books UK
4th Floor, Victoria House, Bloomsbury Square
London WC1B 4DA
www.echopublishing.com.au
www.bonnierbooks.co.uk

Echo Publishing acknowledges the traditional custodians of Country throughout
Australia. We recognise their continuing connection to land, sea and waters.
We pay our respects to Elders past and present.

This is a work of fiction. Names, characters, businesses, places, events,
locales and incidents are either the products of the author's imagination or
used in a fictitious manner. Any resemblance to actual persons, living
or dead, or actual events is purely coincidental.

First Nations peoples are advised that this book
contains the names of people who are deceased.

First published 2023

Printed and bound in Australia by Griffin Press

Cover designer: Lisa White
Page designer and typesetter: Shaun Jury
Editor: Kate Goldsworthy
Cover image: Side view of redheaded young woman
covering her face, by Jen Grantham/Stocksy

NATIONAL
LIBRARY
OF AUSTRALIA

A catalogue entry for this book is available from the National Library of Australia

ISBN: 9781760687625 (paperback)
ISBN: 9781760687632 (ebook)

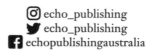
echo_publishing
echo_publishing
echopublishingaustralia

About the author

Eve is a lawyer specialising in commercial litigation and defamation, providing regular pre-publication advice to some of Australia's leading print and online publishers. Eve's debut novel was developed at the Curtis Brown Creative (London) selective six-month novel-writing course, followed by mentorship from Commonwealth Book Prize winning author Lisa O'Donnell. Eve is mother to two young children and lives with her family at the beach in Adelaide, South Australia.

For Mum and Dad

Prologue

'It's only me!' Mrs Forsyth called as she nudged open the door with her good hip. No one answered. They never had. She wondered if they disappeared on purpose, embarrassed to come face to face with the help.

Although she had barely met her employers, Mrs Forsyth didn't like them. She knew they were beautiful from their pictures on the mantel and in the newspapers. But the woman was always posing, so aware of her best angle. And the little boy was chubby and indulged; his toys, in shapes impossible to dust, covered every surface of his bedroom. In the hallways, white walls were hung with paintings of nothing in particular – some resembled huge naked breasts, others ghastly animals. A dopey dog deposited hair onto every surface. The house had no personality, nor any sign that its occupants were interested in anything outside of themselves.

She arrived at 10.30 a.m. every day except Tuesday. Her nephew, who seemed determined to pack her off to a retirement village, disapproved, but that only made her more determined to stay on. With the extra money, she could maintain regular donations to her local church. Father Matthew called her a saint.

On arrival she strode towards the darkened living room, intent upon opening the wall-to-wall blinds. Like a pair of sulking teenagers, her employers never thought to let in the morning light. Had the girl not been lying precisely where she usually placed her bag, Mrs Forsyth may not have noticed her at all.

The girl was curled up like a cat, in a grey puffy jacket so large it was surely borrowed. From beneath the jacket's hem, Mrs Forsyth could see the shimmer of a gold cocktail dress and a pair of pale bare feet. On the floor next to the couch lay two uncomfortable-looking strappy shoes. Dark hair fell across the girl's face, but Mrs Forsyth could make out a bolt of red lipstick and the twinkle of a delicate gold cross flipped upside down and resting on her chin. She must have fallen asleep while sucking on it. A child of the Lord.

Mrs Forsyth cleared her throat noisily. 'Rise and shine, my dear. Morning has well and truly broken.' When the girl didn't stir, Mrs Forsyth walked to the window and opened the blinds with a flourish. 'Let there be light!' Twisting back, she saw that the girl was not only pale but very nearly blue. Her feet were stiff, her toes stretched awkwardly to attention.

Mrs Forsyth started to apologise, although it was obvious there was no need. She reached for her rosary beads and, without knowing it, let out a soft wail.

Chapter One
A Change of Heart

A light rain began to fall as Romola Cross rounded the corner. By the time she had reached the doorstep, her hair was frizzed and her shoulders damp. She instinctively started to knock before remembering that this was her home, at least for now. She fumbled through her bag for the ugly plastic 'Melbourne' key ring. Shaped like a sun, it had been an ironic welcoming gift from her godfather.

Romola had been foolish to leave the house without an umbrella, but she was still unaccustomed to the city's relentless cold and wet. At least her new clothes were safe and dry in their tissue wrap and thick glossy cardboard. Never before could she have afforded clothes like them, but she had bought them on credit earlier that day, safe in the knowledge that her new wage would cover the cost and more.

She was due to start tomorrow. A chill scaled her spine with the thought. Her stepmother, true to form, had called it the worst decision of her life. As she stood on the doorstep, the cold shaking her bones, it was hard to remember exactly what had been going through her head on that morning in Sydney two months earlier, when the morning air was so warm she'd started sweating even before taking her seat in the courtroom.

*

Romola had overslept and skipped her usual coffee. She was feeling the absence of caffeine in the same way she would have felt the loss of her trademark tortoiseshell glasses – everything was blurry.

The judge shuffled his papers. 'Will your client be entering a plea today, Miss Cross?'

'He will, your Honour.' She hoped to get it over with quickly.

The judge cricked his head towards her client, a skinny, pockmarked man with faded jeans and a smirk. He had beaten his wife senseless earlier that month, and he'd barely attempted to hide his disgust when a brown-skinned woman was appointed to represent him.

'How do you plead?' the judge asked him.

He grinned. 'I plead that my lawyer is fucking hopeless.'

The judge raised an eyebrow and grunted, but didn't bother looking up. 'How would you like to proceed, Miss Cross?'

I wouldn't like to proceed at all, was what she wanted to say. Her face burned with anger that she knew would be taken for embarrassment – or worse, sadness. The judge might even expect tears. To look at her client was unbearable, so it wasn't until the warm droplets fell on her skin that she realised what he had done.

His aim was perfect. A shower of spittle covered her face and obscured her glasses. A larger ball of phlegm landed on her chest and dribbled down her right breast. She jumped up, sending her chair crashing to the ground.

Moments earlier the courtroom had been full of the sounds of murmuring lawyers. She'd felt invisible when she walked in, aware of the partial, hazy sort of recognition she normally received. Now the room fell silent and, at precisely the wrong moment, she became visible.

An elderly barrister tapped her on the shoulder and offered a neatly folded handkerchief. Two thoughts occurred to her as she dabbed her face. First: This is my fucking favourite blazer. Second: I've had enough.

As security officers led her client away, she finally managed to speak. 'An adjournment, your Honour. I seek an adjournment. To … clarify my client's instructions.'

But Romola left the courthouse without speaking another word to her client. She shrugged off her blazer and stuffed it in her ragged wheelie bag. She took the first left and started down Pitt Street, intent on reaching the water's edge. There was a slight limp in her gait caused not by pain but by the exposed broken heel of her left shoe. These shoes were normally her 'workhorses', as she liked to call them, because they could take her from her Park Street office to the

Downing Centre local courts several times a day without causing pain. Now she felt as though one leg was slightly shorter than the other, while the shoe clacked on the pavement with every step. She'd been meaning to get it fixed for weeks.

Lopsided and noisy, she walked until the lawyers and cigarette-sucking clients of the courts precinct were replaced by the tourists and traders of Circular Quay. Summer had reached its end, but its heat and humidity lingered. Her shirt clung to her back, and sweat ran down her temples. She spared a single thought for her boss, who right now would be pacing the office while dictating a letter to his long-suffering secretary, the smell of nicotine suspended in his wake. Romola bought herself an icecream, of all things, and sat on a park bench, taking in the beauty of her city with its oscillating ferries and striking white sails. She had almost forgotten it was there.

For months, Romola had known that her career as a criminal lawyer must end. She'd been full of hope at the beginning but, as in a bad relationship, things had turned sour. She couldn't displace the heavy lump in her stomach every time she introduced herself to a client, knowing that despite her best intentions and impeccable legal knowledge, she was probably precisely what they did not want. Most of the clients who came to Fowler & Page wanted attack dogs, a rottweiler or a staffy that they could let loose on the prosecution, not a beagle like her.

As she sat on the bench, she allowed herself to imagine leaving the city she had always called home. Her best friend Louise had left for Melbourne nine months earlier, and Romola missed her desperately. Maybe a change would make everything feel right again.

She finished her icecream, fished out her phone, and with a sense of resignation called her godfather Cliffy, otherwise known as Heathcliff Garner QC. Despite the cacophony of string instruments in the background, Cliffy said that it was a good time to talk. Without further delay, she told him that her answer was yes.

*

Autumn had set in, a balm to Sydney's long summer, when Romola arrived in Melbourne six weeks later. She had accepted Cliffy's offer of a spare bedroom while she found her feet. His beautifully appointed terrace home felt more like a boutique hotel than a refuge. But on the Saturday before her first day at the law firm Bassett Brown, she felt nothing but a sense of foreboding as she pushed open Cliffy's big blue front door and came in from the rain.

It was 6 p.m. and the house was empty but still warm, filled with the scent of fresh baking. She dumped her shopping bags next to an antique umbrella stand and went straight to the kitchen, where the large picture windows were fogged and a fresh brown seeded loaf sat on the black marble bench. Beside it was a short handwritten note:

> *Romy, I am experimenting with a new recipe involving chia seeds. Apparently they are <u>super</u>. Please give me your honest opinion! I'm off to the opera, but there's an open bottle of pinot that should go nicely with the duck rillettes in the fridge. Help yourself. Heathcliff.*

Romola cut two thick slices of the loaf and smothered them with butter and jam. She sat at the kitchen island and gazed out the windows into a darkening courtyard filled with statues and sculpted plants. The sound of the rain created that special kind of melancholy reserved for a Saturday night with no friends. She was reminded of being a teenager on those rare occasions when her parents left her alone. What would a normal teenager do now? she would ask herself.

Her laptop lay closed on the bench where she had left it that morning. She opened it, keyed in her password, and was met with the homepage of the news website she had been reading. She was momentarily struck by a black-and-white photograph of a beautiful young woman. Her prophetic sad eyes stared from underneath the headline: 'Tragedy strikes Payne family: Tributes flow for Hana Vukovic. Dead at 28.' The same age as Romola.

The link was opening when her phone rang – her stepmother, again. Every day since Romola's move to Melbourne, Judith had called with tales of corporate wrongdoing and of commercial lawyers either burned out or dead as a consequence of their demanding work schedules. Romola had given up trying to explain her decision to work at Bassett Brown. It was like dealing with an idealistic teenager.

She rejected the call. Not tonight, Judith Jones Skin and Bones.

The phone sounded again immediately. That damn woman was on a mission. Romola slammed the laptop shut and answered. 'Hello, Judith.'

'Sorry? This is Imogen Trigg.' The woman spoke quickly. 'Who is this?'

Romola stood to attention. 'Romola Cross. I thought you were someone else. Sorry.' Her mind gradually caught up with the unfamiliar number on the screen, the name of the caller.

In preparation for her job interview she'd studied every partner's online profile. Bassett Brown was a top-tier firm that acted for the big end of town; its clients were bankers, mining magnates, politicians, and sports stars. On its website, the partners' images were set against a pitch-black background. Each face stared down the barrel of the camera with a look of fierce competitiveness. From memory, Imogen Trigg was an expert in high-stakes litigation, with a no-nonsense approach to managing the most complex of disputes.

'How can I help you?' Romola offered. Hearing herself sound like a sales assistant, she felt ridiculous. She needed time to prepare for conversations like this, to plan out precisely what she would say.

'Have you read the email I sent you?'

'Email? Hang on – I'll look now.'

'I don't have time for that. It's about Patrick Payne, our client.'

'That's funny, I was just reading about him. His girlfriend died?' She desperately flicked through emails before pausing to add, 'I don't mean it's funny about his girlfriend. I just mean it's a coinci—'

'An overdose. Patrick's distraught. To make matters worse, the press are reporting he had something to do with it. That he was, I don't know, fucking abusive or some such thing. Which is plainly an outrage.'

'That's not great.' Romola banged her head silently on the kitchen bench, cursing herself for her clumsy words.

'It's *defamatory*, is what it is. Patrick's reputation will be destroyed.'

Romola called to mind an image of Patrick Payne, the prized only child of the retail and property mogul Malcolm Payne. Patrick was often in the press, mostly with a frown on his face. Her lasting impression was of a thirty-something man with his hands stuffed in pockets, his eyes on the ground, standing next to his more glamorous father. But recently Patrick had been going it alone in the hope of winning a seat at the next federal election; he'd been popping up in political debates and events, and on a broad cross-section of television offerings from the ABC's *Q+A* to Sky News. Grim-faced and awkward, and always dressed in an impeccable suit, he dismally failed in his attempts to relate to the everyman.

'You need to check your emails more often, Romola,' Imogen said. 'I've arranged to meet Patrick at his place tomorrow to take further instructions. We need to get on top of this before all hell breaks loose. You're coming with me. You have criminal expertise, which frankly I don't. If this gets ugly and the police become involved, we will need you. And when you start in the office on Monday, you're not to take on any other work. This is going to be big, and I need you on board. Understand?'

'Of course.'

'Sorry?' Imogen Trigg spoke like a football coach giving a half-time dressing-down.

'Yes,' Romola said, louder. 'Understood.'

The phone went silent. Romola was released. She felt as if a door had slammed behind her, giving her no way to go but forward.

Chapter Two
The Client

Imogen Trigg was instantly recognisable, her dark pixie haircut and startled expression familiar from her website profile. She was taller than Romola had expected, and her pointy face began with wide eyes and ended in puckered lips. Squirrel-like, thought Romola. A tall, very loud squirrel. As Imogen stood at the counter, she alternated between speaking on the phone and barking a lengthy coffee order at a cheerful waitress. The whole café had half an ear on Imogen.

Romola had been unsure how to dress for a Sunday morning client meeting. She'd decided upon her new black pantsuit, slim fit with a tuxedo stripe. Her only nod to the weekend was the choice of flat brogues rather than heels. Her dark curls were barely contained in an antique golden hairclip, a cherished and completely out-of-character Christmas gift from her father years earlier.

When she'd assessed herself in the mirror that morning, Romola had been impressed – she looked exactly like someone who belonged on the Bassett Brown website. But on seeing Imogen, Romola saw she'd made the wrong call. Imogen was effortlessly casual in denim and a trenchcoat, AirPods in her ears. She rolled her eyes when she saw Romola, then turned her back and kept on talking. Romola's heart sank at the thought that she'd got it so completely wrong, and worse still that her new boss was the type to notice.

The café was a short walk from Patrick Payne's house. She and Imogen had met early to prepare for the meeting, but thirty minutes in Imogen had spent the entire time on her phone. Romola perched on a high stool, waiting among lycra-clad cyclists, willing her stomach to calm while she aimlessly checked her own phone. Her attention kept being drawn back to the article on Rabbit Hole, one of her favourite news websites: left-leaning and at times controversial, it touched upon subjects that other journos wouldn't dare go near. She must have read it ten times over.

History repeats: The inexplicable deaths of Patrick Payne's lovers
By Jonathan B Wise

Patrick Payne is a grieving man. Last Sunday his girlfriend, influencer and blogger Hana Vukovic, was found dead in their luxury Toorak home following what is believed to have been an opioid overdose. Late yesterday Payne issued his first tweet since her death was confirmed: 'I have no words #heartsforHana'. But in the wake of her death, Rabbit Hole can reveal that their relationship was not as flawless as their social media would suggest. Nor is Vukovic the first of Payne's girlfriends to have met such a desperate fate.

When they first met, Vukovic was nanny to Payne's only son from his ill-fated marriage to socialite Sonia Kirk. At the time of their much-publicised divorce, it was widely speculated that Payne's alleged affair with Vukovic was behind the separation. The pair confirmed their relationship, after his separation from Kirk, in a series of intimate Instagram posts. Rumours of their engagement have been swirling for months.

But Rabbit Hole's sources have revealed that the night before Vukovic's death, she and Payne had a serious argument at swanky Malvern eatery Costello's, after which he was seen forcefully grabbing her arm. Friends also claim that Vukovic, who had over 250,000 followers on her nannying blog 'thebabygame', became withdrawn and nervous as her relationship with Payne progressed, their suspicion being that she felt she was no longer free to do as she pleased.

For those who knew Lisbeth Janssen, Vukovic's story is eerily familiar. Janssen had the world at her feet when she met Patrick Payne at age 17 while still in high school. A gifted rower and pianist, she hoped to one day become a lawyer. But the pair split when she was 19, and within months she was found dead, having taken a massive quantity of painkillers.

Those closest to Janssen claim the contrast in the bubbly teenager before and after her relationship with Payne was remarkable. They never received any explanation from Payne as to her transformation. 'She was gradually taken from us,' her sister Lara says. 'There was Lisbeth before Patrick and Lisbeth after Patrick. They were different people. I'm shattered to hear this has happened to another one of Patrick's girlfriends. Everything has been brought to the surface again.'

Meanwhile, online tributes continue to flow in for 28-year-old Vukovic, described by friends as 'gentle and selfless'. Having now heard of Janssen's death, those same friends are seeking answers from Payne as to how history could have repeated itself, and why the girl they describe as formerly 'loving life' would ultimately be so careless with her own.

The defamatory meaning – or the 'sting', as the defamation lawyers would call it – was there for all to see: something that Patrick Payne did was making his girlfriends kill themselves.

The story was gaining traction, with Twitter handles multiplying like bacteria. While some focused on the tragedy of Hana's death, Romola knew that others, like #Paynemustpay, were only the beginnings of the baying for his blood.

*

Eventually Imogen approached Romola, ignoring her outstretched hand and pointing to the door, muttering, 'How the fuck long does it take to make a soy motherfucking latte?'

On the walk to Patrick's house, Imogen issued her instructions. She walked fast. Her eyes barely left her phone screen yet she was able to avoid every puddle on the wet footpath. Even when she was met with red-faced children leaning into their scooters, her pace and laser-like focus did not waver. Romola, meanwhile, was working hard to manoeuvre the busy footpath, barely registering the impressive mansions lining the streets.

'I'll do the talking,' Imogen said. 'You listen. Make notes.' She flicked her phone as she spoke. 'Tell me what you know about Patrick.'

'I know he's Malcolm Payne's son.'

Malcolm Payne was one of the country's wealthiest men. The son of a pastoralist, his landholding had more than quadrupled his father's by the time he was thirty. His corporation, Payne Corp, was the biggest property developer in the country, having ventured into everything from department stores to luxury goods and hotels.

Imogen stopped. '*Please* tell me you know more about Patrick than that he's Malcolm's son?'

Romola silently thanked her lucky stars she had stayed up half the night cyber-stalking her new client. 'He's thirty-two. He studied arts at uni, majoring in politics, but until recently had been focused on running the family's charitable trust, including the breast cancer research fund set up after his mother died. In interviews he's suggested he's not interested in joining his father's business, and he was thought of as a bit of a lost soul until he announced that he was making a run at politics. He's in the Liberal Party but considered to be a moderate. He has no criminal history to speak of, apart from being photographed ten years ago in a nightclub bathroom with a suspicious white powder. He sued the photographer, claimed it was a set-up. He is an only child. He's divorced and has one son: Max.'

Romola didn't need to talk about the other material she'd found online. The memes of Patrick speaking at political fundraisers, fumbling over his words or looking hopelessly lost when asked the simplest of questions. Or that time he'd forgotten to turn off his microphone and been caught using a flurry of obscenities.

'Gold star for you,' Imogen said as they kept walking. 'But none of that will help us today. Patrick can be prickly. He doesn't love dealing with lawyers, and he's not at his best right now.' Romola wondered what his best was. The Patrick who found his way into the lives of young women was obviously at his best. But what happened next? Who was he at his worst?

'Do you think there's anything in it?' Romola asked. 'What they're saying about him?'

Imogen stopped again, so suddenly that Romola had to retrace her steps to be back at her boss's side. 'I don't *think* there's nothing in it – I *know* there's nothing in it.' Imogen pointed at Romola. 'You'll see that when you meet him. Patrick is harmless. He's rich, he's stepping on some toes trying to get preselection, and he has a massive target on his back because of who his father is. End of story.'

They walked on in silence before turning a corner to find themselves approaching an enormous Georgian-style home behind ornate security gates, two black Range Rovers in the drive. A small group of photographers stood in a loose group near the gates, some leaning against cars, vaping or drinking coffee, while others stood off to the side talking on their phones. Despite their apparent target, none of them took any notice of the two women approaching.

'This is him,' said Imogen.

*

On arrival they were directed to a pool area overlooking terraced gardens. The morning was so cold that steam drifted off the water. Patrick was sitting on the edge of a sun lounger. He was staring intensely into the aquamarine, as if he expected the Lady of the Lake to arise. Dark sunglasses were suspended on his face like it was the middle of summer, but he wore the woolly jumper of an Englishman, jeans and R.M. Williams boots. As they approached, he raised an arm and removed an earbud but did not get up.

Imogen spoke first. 'Darling. How are you feeling?'

'How would you expect I'm feeling?' He spoke quietly before raising his head from the lounger and turning it in Romola's direction. 'You're new.' He lifted his sunglasses to take her in more clearly, revealing his puffy grey eyes and creased face. It was a face disposed to frowning, not handsome but not unattractive either. He had a sharp gaze and a large gap between his front teeth, which she was surprised he'd never had fixed. He had the perfect face for an extra in a movie or suspect's line-up, the kind of face that wouldn't have stood out in a crowd had it not been for the family he was born into. She could see now that his hair, which appeared brown in photos, was flecked with grey; the silver hair that so defined his father was beginning to show through.

'Romola Cross.' She reached out to shake his hand firmly, determined to be different this time. She had told herself she would be confident, strong. 'I'm new to the firm, but I've been practising for a number of years in Sydney. Criminal, mainly. A bit of civil. I'm very sorry to hear about Hana.'

Patrick turned to Imogen. 'There's a show of confidence, bringing in the criminal lawyers already?' He sounded miserable as he sank back to lie on the lounger, leaving his hand up in a weak wave. 'Welcome aboard.'

Imogen shot Romola an icy glance before continuing. 'I know what you're thinking, but she is an excellent lawyer who just happens to have experience in criminal law. That could really help us here, Patrick.'

He peered back out over the pool. 'Can we get this over with?'

The setting could not have been more inappropriate for the task at hand: Patrick lying prone, with Romola and Imogen sitting low on loungers, handbags at their feet. The air smelled of snowdrops and chlorine, with a scent of pancakes wafting over them from a neighbouring house. Romola was reminded that she was ravenously hungry and that for other people this was an ordinary Sunday morning. She never normally skipped meals but had been unable to stomach breakfast today. Now her guts moaned at their neglect. She covered her tummy with her hand, hoping no one else could hear its protestations.

All night she'd thought about what she would ask today if she were allowed to speak. Patrick was different from her previous clients but not for obvious reasons. Romola normally acted for defendants who had been charged with specific offences involving precise elements that would need to be proved by prosecutors. It was formulaic. Driving under the influence equalled alcohol over the 0.05 limit, plus taking control of a vehicle on a roadway. Murder equalled an act causing death, plus intention to kill. The path to a not guilty verdict was usually clear enough, and if it was muddy that was generally a good thing – the more mud the better. By contrast, Rabbit Hole's accusations against Patrick were vague: he was not a good partner; he had cheated on his wife; but even worse, he had a tendency to drive his girlfriends to drug addiction and death. To assess whether Rabbit Hole could prove that, Romola would need to understand Patrick as a person. How had he made Hana and Lisbeth feel? Had they withdrawn from friends (and in the case of Lisbeth, her family) because they desperately wanted to be with this man, or because he wouldn't let them out of his sight? But how could Romola learn the truth when both women were dead?

Imogen began speaking to Patrick as though she were dictating a letter. 'By way of an update, we wrote to Rabbit Hole last night demanding they take down the story and issue an apology. They haven't done either, nor have they responded. We should assume they're not backing down. I don't expect them to. You've probably seen that the story's starting to escalate online. It could soon do some real damage if it hasn't already.' Imogen paused, clearly waiting for Patrick to fill them in as to how much damage had been caused to date, as most clients would. But he seemed nonplussed and remained silent. 'We need to understand what we might be fighting here, Patrick. If we sue for defamation, they're likely to rely on the truth defence. They'll say the article was justified because everything in it – including all of the possible defamatory meanings – is true.'

Patrick stretched out his hand to cut her off. 'This is inconceivable to me. I loved Hana. And I thought I loved Beth too, at the time.'

'I understand,' Imogen said, 'but like it or not, in court Rabbit Hole will say that you made these women deeply unhappy, scared even. We need to make sure they can't prove that.'

He didn't respond, and Imogen's words hung in the air. Romola remained silent as instructed by Imogen, but the hair on the back of her arms rose as a magpie crowed overhead, urging the conversation forwards.

'Maybe you could start by telling us about your relationship with Hana?' Imogen asked. 'How did you first meet?'

Patrick pointed his face to the sky. Romola saw the muscles in his neck pulse as he gulped down any second thoughts. 'She started off as an employee. She was Max's nanny. Sonia found her, actually. She was good with Max, and, if I'm being perfectly honest with you, she was beautiful. Hana made our house a nicer place to be. I wasn't going to complain about that.'

'How old was Max?'

'I guess around four or five? Sonia and I weren't getting along, although we were ostensibly "together" for another couple of years.' He continued staring out over the pool, lazily shaping his fingers into quotation marks.

'Were you and Hana together when Sonia left?'

'I'm certain that Sonia was sleeping around by then. She likes to think I wasn't faithful to her – it makes her feel better about herself. But I didn' cheat. Hana was focused on Max and her blog. Admittedly, we probably both knew it would happen eventually.'

'And so when did it, eventually, happen?' Imogen prompted.

'Not long after Sonia moved out. But we kept it to ourselves. Hana was worried Max might find it difficult to adjust, and Sonia and I were still sorting out the custody arrangements, as you'll recall.' Patrick spoke in monotone and avoided looking at either of them directly. Romola found it hard to assess the truth of his words.

'If Rabbit Hole is wrong about the affair, that's another way they've defamed you, Patrick. I know it's been reported in the past, but that's not to stop you from suing on it now. We can look at adding that to the claim.' Imogen directed her last comment to Romola, reaching across and tapping at the notebook balanced on her lap to ensure she was getting it down.

'You remember it was a messy time, Imogen,' said Patrick pointedly. 'Everything is fuzzy from that period. The media ran with the cheating story back then, and I denied it. I knew Sonia was probably their source, but I didn't want to take it further, given what was on the line with Max. The last thing I want right now is to get dragged back into that old territory. And why would I, when what they're saying about me now is so much worse?'

'Okay, understood. We won't go there.' Again Imogen gestured for Romola to take a note, though she now had more questions than answers.

Imogen continued. 'You went public with the relationship with Hana when?'

'Here.' Patrick wriggled on his lounger as he drew out his phone from his jeans pocket, then began scrolling through images. 'It was the New Year's before last.' He turned his phone to face Imogen and Romola, the screen showing a photo of him with Hana aboard a yacht in Sydney Harbour, fireworks behind them, kissing passionately. Her face was in profile, and her eyes were closed. The photo had been posted on Instagram and was captioned 'New year – new love'. 'My thought process was – I love this woman and I want people to know it. Max was happy about it too, in the end.'

'How old is Max now?'

'He'll be nine in December.' A suggestion of a smile vanished as quickly as it had come. 'I haven't told him about Hana yet.' Patrick cupped his face in his hands.

'What was she like?'

Patrick paused for thought, releasing his face from his hands and blinking hard before speaking. 'She was perfect. Intelligent. Charming. Incredible with Max. They were like two peas in a pod. She was absolutely, completely, perfect.' Tears began to run down his cheeks, but he didn't wipe them away. Only when clear liquid came from his nose did he reach for his face again, grunting in frustration.

'Sorry, Patrick.' Imogen placed a hand on his shoulder, then withdrew it and pressed on. 'Did you fight?'

'Sometimes. Like anyone.' He looked to them for confirmation that 'sometimes' was an acceptable level of conflict. Imogen gave nothing away; Romola concentrated on her notes.

'Were you ever violent with her?' Imogen asked.

Patrick sat up, the life kicked back into him. 'No. I never would have. To even suggest that –'

'You don't have to convince us, Patrick,' Imogen reassured him. 'But we have to ask you these questions because that's where Rabbit Hole is heading with this.' She reached towards him like she was taming a wild animal before she went on. 'I have to ask about the night before Hana died. This journalist – Jonathan Wise – wrote that the two of you argued in public, but also that you were seen "forcefully grabbing" her. We need to know what could come out.'

Patrick sighed. 'Fine, here it is.' He began to speak in short, controlled sentences. 'We had dinner at Costello's. It was Hana's favourite. We were there until late, maybe around eleven-thirty. Then we came straight home. She said she wasn't tired. She wanted to watch a movie. I went to bed. I woke up in the middle of the night. She wasn't in bed. I thought she must have fallen asleep in front of the movie. I decided to let her be.' He paused. 'I slept in the next morning. Our cleaning lady woke me up, screaming. I ran down the hall, and ... and Hana was there. We called an ambulance, but it was clearly too late. They said she'd been gone for hours.'

He'd managed to remain composed as he recounted the events of that devastating morning. Romola wondered how many times he had told the story. Repetition of an answer normally meant less emotion in its delivery.

'How was she when you left her?' Imogen asked. 'Did you notice anything wrong? Had she been depressed?'

Too many questions at once, thought Romola.

'She had a headache. She was quiet. I'd had a bit to drink. I didn't notice anything different.'

'And before then? Was she depressed, different?'

'I don't know – I don't think so. Quiet sometimes but happy enough, or at least that's what I thought.'

'Did you fight that night?'

'We had a disagreement, at dinner. Nothing major – relationship stuff.' He again remained steady. Behind the sunglasses, his eyes were still set upon the water, and Romola found it difficult to know which questions, if any, were getting to him. She wanted more details. So they had argued, but about what? And why had that argument been Hana's last?

Imogen took her time before asking the next question. 'What happened to her, Patrick? Did you have anything to do with it?'

Romola expected fireworks from Patrick but got the flicker of candlelight. 'The police told me she overdosed. They only gave me the basics. I don't even know what she'd taken. I'm still ... I still can't believe any of this is actually happening. If only I'd gone down to check on her that night, things might have been different …' His voice finally faltered, and he let out a ragged breath.

'I'm sorry, Patrick.' As Imogen spoke, she subtly checked her phone. Romola saw her expression change, distracted already. When she raised her head, it was clear she had moved on from the conversation with Patrick. 'That should be enough on Hana for now anyway. Other things will come up once we confirm that Rabbit Hole is going to defend the article, and on what basis.'

Romola felt as though she were sitting in the audience of a movie and the screen had gone blank at its climax. She raised her hand like a schoolchild and cleared her throat.

Imogen was moving to pick up her bag, but Patrick noticed and urged Romola to speak up. 'What is it?'

Romola looked to Imogen for permission, and she smiled through gritted teeth but nodded her assent. 'I wondered if you had any idea who might have spoken with Rabbit Hole. Who would want to spread these sorts of stories about you?'

Patrick sat up and pointed a finger at her, animated for the first time since they'd arrived. 'Good question! Finally someone who thinks this is a set-up. I wondered if it might be one of her followers? Online, I mean. Some of them really hate me. The comments are appalling. I'll forward you some examples … Or maybe one of her old schoolfriends? Hana had done well for herself. They didn't exactly like her moving on and doing better than them.'

Imogen was smiling now, proud that her new associate had elicited such a positive response from her difficult client.

Romola went on. 'And, going back a step, who would have seen you argue that night?'

'The restaurant was pretty much empty by then. And honestly, it wasn't a big deal. I don't think anyone would have even noticed. Emir was there – he can tell you. He drove us home.'

'Emir?'

'Emir's my security guy. He's also Hana's brother. Poor guy – she was his only family. He's taking it pretty hard.'

Romola wrote 'Emir' and double circled the name. Her list of remaining questions was long, but because she didn't know how much longer she would have the floor, she decided to ask the sort of simple question that often was the best chance to assess a witness's honesty. 'Which movie did she watch?'

'Pardon?'

'Which movie was Hana watching that night?'

Patrick stared, confused.

'You said she wanted to stay up to watch a movie and you wanted to go to bed?'

'Seriously?' Patrick's eyes moved from Imogen to Romola and back again. 'Hana is dead, and this is what you want to know?' He stood up and shook his head. 'I don't have the foggiest idea. Not a clue. What do you make of that, hotshot?' He put his earbuds back in and stomped off to the house.

Imogen stood and turned on Romola, squirrel eyes wide. 'What the fuck was that?' With immaculate timing, the phone in her hand buzzed again. She swore profusely as she read the screen. 'I have to make a call,' Imogen said as it began to drizzle. She swore again and dug into her large Louis Vuitton for an umbrella, which she opened and held awkwardly between shoulder and ear as she wrestled with her phone.

Romola stood unmoved, unsure if Imogen intended her to bear witness to the call.

Imogen seemed to have the same thought at the same time, as she stopped what she was doing to deal with Romola. 'We'll talk about this more later. Wait for me up at the house, and if you see Patrick try not to say something so bloody idiotic this time.'

She waited, hand on hip under the umbrella, for Romola to leave. The magpies had quietened down, and the deep hum of the pool cleaner seemed to be getting louder. Imogen's angry breaths were visible in the cold.

As Romola slowly made her way after Patrick along the cobblestoned path, the drizzle turning to a light rain that obscured her glasses. Her supervising partner's voice echoed up the hill towards the house. 'It's me ... Calm down ... Yes, I can talk now, but you're going to have to calm down, darling ... Is Daddy there? Good ... Now tell me exactly what's happened.'

Chapter Three
Tears and Television

Romola reached the house's back verandah, where she waited for Imogen and dried her glasses, unsure of what to do with herself. The rear of the Georgian home had been renovated, and she stood in front of an enormous sliding door of spotless glass. Her reflected image was different from the one she had seen in the mirror that morning. Her shirt was now crumpled, and her hair, which earlier had been the perfect amount of dishevelled, now simply looked untamed, with wet curls escaping the clutches of the pretty gold clasp.

She had fixed her curls back into place and begun rubbing at smudged mascara when her vision shifted from her reflection to the scene inside the house. Patrick sat not three metres from her in a sunken lounge room. He was slouched in the corner of a modular suite facing an enormous television, an ageing golden retriever sprawled next to him. Patrick had obviously been watching her for some time, his earlier anger replaced by an expression of barely contained amusement. Romola waved as her face reddened, and he beckoned for her to join him.

The dog lifted its head as Romola pulled open the heavy door, raising itself up. 'It's okay, Jessie.' Patrick rubbed her belly, and the dog seemed to decide Romola wasn't worth the bother. She settled back down, shuffling as she found a comfortable spot on Patrick's lap.

With Romola inside the house, Patrick's eyes returned to the television, which was showing what appeared to be a documentary about World War II. Emaciated prisoners of war were being marched along a dirt track. The sound was down low, so Romola couldn't make out the words. Patrick turned to her. 'I'm sorry about before.' His broad-set grey eyes seemed to search her face and meet her gaze at the same time. 'I'm so up and down at the moment.'

Romola sat at the opposite end of the deep lounge. Her legs were too short, her feet dangling awkwardly. She still felt a lingering embarrassment, both at Patrick's earlier outburst and at the uncomfortable way in which she had found herself invited into his lounge room. Nevertheless, she also sensed an opportunity to be alone with Patrick.

On the adjacent wall to the television hung a huge abstract canvas – a geometric pattern of electric pinks and blues. Patrick followed her eyes. 'Hana chose that. I keep seeing her things everywhere. I don't know what I'm supposed to do with them.' Patrick's forehead creased, and his eyes were pleading.

Revealing personal information went against her better judgement, but something told her that with Patrick there would need to be some give in order for her to take. 'My dad died. It was almost a year ago, but it's taken me a long time to get used to the idea he's not here. I kept sending him texts for about six months afterwards. I know it doesn't necessarily help for me to say this, but I understand.'

'I'm sorry for your loss.' Patrick looked genuinely concerned, shaking his head emphatically. 'Was he a good man?'

'The best, actually,' Romola said quietly. Having endured a year of these conversations, she knew that her voice would not break. Still, the reminder of what her father had been like – her earnest, thoughtful father – made her heart rise and fall.

'You should feel lucky to have had him,' Patrick said, then added, as an afterthought, 'Have you met my father?'

'Not yet.' She conjured up a mental image of Malcolm Payne from her years of reading about the man. White hair, a pinstriped suit. Like Patrick but taller and paler, as though he'd been stretched from top to bottom and projected in black and white.

Patrick rubbed the dog's ears, his fingers moving tenderly back and forth. The veins on his hands were raised, and his fingernails were short; they were hands less manicured than she would have expected for someone like him. Jessie the dog dozed off, practically smiling.

Romola thought carefully before she spoke. 'Are you sure you want to sue them for this?'

'Dad's determined, which means it's happening. It's not like that journo at Rabbit Hole doesn't deserve it.' From the speed of his answer, she could tell he hadn't given it any thought.

She persisted. 'I agree that you have to hold them to account. But if this goes ahead, they'll be saying terrible things about you in open court, probably that you're a controlling, possibly violent partner. Even if you're not charged with anything, it will be like you're on trial. You could become one of those men, Patrick – blacklisted.'

He stared at her like she was missing something obvious. 'And? You think I don't know what people are saying about me? I'm already on trial. They'll believe what they want to believe.' He shrugged. 'They always have about me, no matter what I do.'

'Let's assume for the moment that's right. Why sue? Why not let it be?'

His eyes returned to the dog. He looked at Jessie differently to how he looked at people, free of suspicion or fear. 'Maybe you're right. Fuck – I don't know. Dad's pretty adamant.'

'What about Lisbeth?'

Patrick gazed up at her again. Even though she was his lawyer, it seemed to Romola that he was assessing whether she could be trusted. 'Beth was my first real girlfriend. We were at that age when a relationship still seemed novel. We thought no one could have possibly loved each other as much as we did. But things changed ... she wasn't well. As bad as it sounds, no one was surprised by what happened to her in the end.' He rubbed his face, forgetting himself. 'God, that's a terrible thing to say, isn't it? I don't even think she loved me. She hated herself so much, there wasn't room for anything else. It was different with Hana.'

Romola could normally spot a lie a mile off – and if a client was about to tell one in court, she prided herself on being able to bring them around, convince them to be either truthful or silent. But with Patrick, she was unsure. She'd met clients who were illiterate, who had never known a real home, who had fended for themselves since primary school. Yet despite all his privilege, Patrick Payne seemed just as vulnerable as they had.

A loud knock on the glass door interrupted Romola's train of thought, and she turned to see Imogen shaking out her umbrella and banging on the surface with her elbow. Imogen then opened the door a little, her startled eyes taking in Romola on the lounge. She didn't move to enter the room, instead calling through the gap, 'We'll get going now, Patrick – no need to see us out, we'll go through the side.' Imogen's eyes urged Romola upwards. 'Thanks for today. I know this is difficult to talk about, but it's been very helpful. We'll be in touch.'

Romola seized her bag and made for the door before turning back to Patrick. 'Good to meet you.'

'And you. I'm sorry again about your dad.'

'Thanks.'

Imogen shot Romola a quizzical frown as she squeezed through the door, then slid it shut with a thunk before any more sympathies or thanks could be exchanged.

Chapter Four
Bassett Brown

Romola had already given up on the prospect of decent sleep when the sounds of Rachmaninoff and a flamboyant banging of pots and pans became impossible to ignore. She would have taken it for a deliberate attempt to wake her, had she not already become accustomed to Cliffy's morning ritual. She'd been drifting in and out of sleep since 4 a.m. anyway, incessantly roused by memories of the prior day's meeting with Patrick and Imogen, uneasy about the day ahead.

Cliffy started each day at five a.m. Accompanied by Rachmaninoff or Schumann, he would cook himself a breakfast of buttered blueberries, steel-cut oats and strong black tea, his first of many for the day. He would open his brief and fill his daybook with last-minute strokes of genius using a steel-blue Montblanc fountain pen, before meticulously cleaning the kitchen and then setting out on foot for his chambers, a brisk thirty-minute walk away. Romola normally woke around seven and caught the tail end of his routine, scraping the porridge pot and adding lashings of golden syrup and butter.

This morning Cliffy was gathering his things as she entered the kitchen in her second-best suit, her best having been entirely wasted on Imogen and Patrick.

'So,' her godfather said, 'the big day has arrived.' He held his arms wide like he was greeting the guest of honour at a surprise party.

'Nope,' said Romola, dropping crumbs over the clean bench as she cut herself a large chunk of bread. 'It's been and gone. I had a client meeting with Imogen Trigg yesterday.'

'Ah – the indomitable Imogen Trigg.' Cliffy raised a bushy eyebrow as he found a cloth and wiped away the crumbs. 'I remember when she was fresh out of law school. I was in a negotiation with her. She must have been the youngest lawyer in that room and had the audacity to tell me my submissions were a load of bollocks. She was completely wrong, of course, and she must have known it was so, but she said it with such bloody conviction that half the people in the room believed her. She probably made her client thousands more that day – and with absolutely bugger all legal basis for it. You need to tread carefully with her.' He pointed, giving more of an order than a suggestion. 'Who's the client?'

'Patrick Payne,' Romola said in the manner of a confession, careful not to say what the meeting had been about, but knowing that the firm's representation of the Payne family would be well known among Melbourne's legal profession. She also knew, without a doubt, that Cliffy would never repeat their conversation, and that he was sure to have an opinion on Patrick, as he did on everyone.

'Is that so?' Cliffy said, with a curious half smile. 'Back in the day I acted for his father, until we had a falling-out over a completely ridiculous point he wanted me to pursue. Malcolm was always one to get so emotionally involved. Not a desirable trait in a client by any means.' Cliffy picked up his creased brown leather holdall and began filling it with the documents he would need for the day, before he paused. 'I once had the misfortune of sitting next to him at a Roman Empire-themed dinner party. They plonked an entire suckling pig down in front of us, teeth intact, curly tail – you can imagine. Malcolm made such a point of eating the poor creature's head. He sat there next to me, carrying on like he was the emperor himself, sucking out the brains with a rigour that turned my stomach.' Cliffy closed his holdall and shook his head. 'I don't think he'll be briefing me any time soon. I clearly recall him saying as much to me. "Heathcliff, you will never see a brief from me again," were his exact words. Always so dramatic.' He laughed as he produced a handkerchief and began wiping the last remnants of breakfast from his face. 'Imogen Trigg and Malcolm Payne – what a combination!'

'You might have warned me –'

'And what might I have warned you of, exactly? That you might have some challenges ahead. What a wonderful position to be in! I have not a shred of doubt that you are capable of besting all of them, my dear. And you should relish every moment.' With a flourish, he grabbed his bag and left.

*

Before Romola's move to Melbourne, Louise had gushed to her about the city's incredible coffee, but in her first week in the city she had struggled to find a place where the baristas didn't ascribe her and her coffee order an undeserved level of importance. She longed to be disregarded, to sink into the bowels of a café and enjoy a strong coffee without a side of personality. When she stumbled across a narrow Turkish café named Azra's on a street close to Cliffy's, run by its namesake – a terse, big-boned lady named Azra – Romola knew she had found her place. Azra made the strongest coffee Romola had encountered in the Western world, and spoke no more than three or four words at a time, even to her regulars. After breakfast at Cliffy's, Romola walked to the café and sat at a small table in the furthest corner, where Azra's pudgy son Mohammed, dressed in the local school uniform, was slumped in a beanbag. Wearing headphones and huddled over a screen, he hardly counted as company.

The café was dark and warm, and it smelled of Turkish delight. Romola imagined remaining there all day, drinking coffee and eating burek, a novel on her lap. Then she would return to Cliffy's place at 6 p.m. and tell him a tale of her disastrous day at Bassett Brown: 'I can't believe they asked me to falsify documents either! I had no choice but to resign on the spot!' She would never have to encounter Imogen Trigg again.

But the notion was a fantasy. Romola Cross would never be late to her first day at the office, or to an interview, an exam, even a dentist appointment. And she never, ever lied. The fact she was even dreaming of it was extremely out of character, although it seemed to be par for her course these days.

She took out her phone and googled 'Hana Vukovic'. A link appeared to the Rabbit Hole article, along with a number of reports of Hana's death. Some had now picked up the Rabbit Hole story and were either running with it or trying to distance themselves from the allegations made by the left-leaning website. There were also Hana's own social media accounts, now suspended in time, as well as myriad other images of her in the social media pages of others. In colour she seemed different. Romola hadn't appreciated the piercing green of her eyes, the smattering of freckles across her nose, the dimple in her left cheek, or her tendency to raise her right eyebrow.

In a post from Hana's Instagram page, she appeared with a chubby dumpling of a boy on her lap. He was clapping his hands and beaming a chocolate-coated smile, while she laughed, holding him at a distance. As Romola delved further, she found selfie upon selfie of Hana with the dumpling boy, who grew in size as the years passed. They were captured peering out of ball pits, licking cake mix from wooden spoons, proudly presenting craft creations, and roaring like tigers next to zoo enclosures. This must be Patrick's son, Max.

Romola opened 'thebabygame', the blog where Hana had offered child-rearing tips. Scrolling through, Romola wondered what sleep-deprived parents had seen in the blog – surely many were infuriated by images of Hana rocking babies into peaceful slumber. Had some of the parents heaping praise on Hana for her 'lifesaving' advice done so with secret disdain?

Then there were the Instagram pictures of Patrick with Hana. She was bikini clad and sandy on the beach; in evening dress with champagne in hand and glittering lights beyond; sipping coffee on a European rooftop while wrapped in a fluffy hotel robe. Patrick's expression was always stuck somewhere between a smile and a grimace – except when it seemed he was genuinely caught off guard. When he admired Hana with wonder, and the gap in his teeth became visible, then he looked like a man in love.

Romola found the whole display a little sickening. She would never profess her love so publicly – in fact, she struggled to profess her love at all. With Tommy, the bespectacled history major, she had stumbled over, 'I think I could really like you,' in response to his confession of love. The relationship had lasted another week.

Based on their social media presence, one was certainly left with the impression that Hana and Patrick were a happy couple. But that didn't mean anything. In Romola's days of using social media, she'd been guilty of posting gorgeous photos of some of the worst food she had ever tasted. Recently she had sworn off socials altogether, after defending a man accused of the stalking and assault of various women he'd met online. 'Easy targets,' he'd said.

She scrolled back to the photo of Hana at the beach, laughing as she held down a straw hat and squinted into the sun. Romola wanted to ask, What happened to you? She stared into the laughing green eyes, imagining them cold and hard in the corpse on the mortician's table.

*

The morning was chilly but sunny, and Romola was soon treading a popular route to the city centre, enjoying the silent company of other commuters. Since arriving in Melbourne she had grown used to the cold, grit and grime that gave the city its 'cool'. But the grey of the place was inescapable. Sunlight was so hard to come by that she'd begun to crave it like chocolate, and its presence on her morning walk seemed a good omen.

She almost felt relaxed by the time she reached the foyer of the Collins Street building, with five minutes to spare. She switched from trainers to heels, then shared the elevator with a pair of young men wearing navy suits and trendy glasses, their hair perfectly dishevelled, morning coffees at their hips. She assessed them as being about her age, and they were travelling to the same level as her, but they didn't seem to notice her as she watched the lift numbers climb. When the doors opened, the men exited first, then strolled past a minimalist stone reception area and into the depths of the office. Romola's nerves returned as she introduced herself to a frosty receptionist, who directed her to a group of people stranded in the middle of the room making small talk.

Bassett Brown's recruitment manager had explained that Romola would be starting on the same day as an intake of articled clerks. They had just finished law school and were about to begin the months of practical experience they needed to be admitted to practice. There were ten of them, and they stood together collectively fidgeting like a bunch of golden-ticket holders outside the chocolate factory door.

A diminutive girl with strawberry-blonde hair turned to greet Romola, extending her arm with enthusiasm. 'Hiyee, I'm Gretchen. I love your shoes.' She pointed to Romola's burgundy suede stilettos. 'Is it just me, or are you so nervous you could bring your breakfast up right here on these beautiful tiles?' Gretchen beamed. It turned out she was exceptionally enthusiastic about everything, especially the 'opportunity' to work at Bassett Brown. 'Maybe we could have a girls' lunch together sometime?' she asked happily.

'That would be nice,' said Romola, wondering how long she could politely avoid it.

Besides Gretchen, none of the clerks offered Romola an introduction. She was reminded of being at law school, where she had constantly been mistaken for an international student – not worthy of the attention so steadfastly bestowed on the rich girls with their silky blonde hair.

Soon the group were ushered into a large glass-panelled boardroom with views to the MCG, where the seven of them sat staring at a platter of sugar-dusted pastries. A tall, dark-haired man with a condescending smile and a basketballer's bounce entered the room. He vigorously shook hands with each of them, repeating their names and introducing himself as Derek Russell, managing partner.

He sat at his place at the head of the table and began. 'First, let me say welcome to Bassett Brown, and congratulations. We had over one thousand applicants for these positions, and you were the cream of the crop. I'm sure each one of you deserves the opportunity, but now's the time to show us what you're made of …' As he continued his speech, he regularly ran his hands through his hair, and he removed and replaced his glasses so frequently that Romola wondered what purpose they actually served. 'I'm just going to be straight with you. We don't suffer fools at Bassett Brown, because our clients don't. You'll be dealing with household names here. Companies you've seen on the television all your lives. Individuals whose net worth is, frankly, staggering. Our clients are sophisticated, and they expect sophisticated, hardworking lawyers. That's not to say we won't support you. You'll be given all the tools and support you need. We're big on collaboration, we're big on teams. We're not about eat or be eaten here.'

His talk was full of catchphrases, but the main message came through loud and clear: You had to work hard, and be great, in order to progress at Bassett Brown. The clerks all nodded along, lapping up Derek's every word. Gretchen scribbled furious notes. Romola was trying to let the words float over her, having recognised within Derek's first few sentences that if she listened too carefully she would feel compelled to leave.

She was trying to mask a tummy rumble and weighing up the pros and cons of being the first one to take a pastry, when the door swung open and Imogen wandered in as if she'd stumbled across the room while looking for the bathroom. 'Derek! *So* sorry to interrupt. I need to take Romola.' Her eyes searched until they landed on Romola's shrinking form.

'Imogen Trigg, everyone,' Derek said, raising his arm as if he were announcing the next performer at a comedy evening. 'One of our very best litigators.' He assessed Romola with raised eyebrows. 'I believe you've been summoned. I'll ask my secretary to email you the notes for the remainder of the session so you don't miss anything.'

'Thanks,' Romola said quietly as she seized the writing pad that had been placed in front of each of them and followed Imogen out of the boardroom, equal parts concerned as to what was to come and relieved that she wouldn't have to hear another word about the firm she'd sold her soul to.

Chapter Five
Instructions

Imogen walked with large strides as she led Romola past the reception area and into a maze of offices. In glass-walled rooms, lawyers sat staring at screens or huddled over documents. A murmuring quiet settled across the place. At Fowler & Page there had been only four lawyers, and every Monday morning they'd shared doughnuts and compared weekend notes. But there were no light-hearted catch-ups in Bassett Brown's corridors. Romola sought out a nod, a smile, any sign of welcome from one of the labouring lawyers, but no one paid the slightest attention to her. Behind the glossy introductions, the offices of Bassett Brown were as cold as the Melbourne winter.

'What were you doing in there with Derek?' Imogen asked, looking ahead, oblivious to the bevy of secretaries avoiding her gaze.

'Oh, that? Training for my first day. Background information on the firm – that type of thing.'

'You've worked at a firm before, yes?'

Romola nodded, clutching her notepad and pen.

'So you don't need it. We have more important things to do.'

Romola thought of the ancient systems at her old firm, and she imagined things would be run very differently at Bassett Brown. Some training would have been helpful, but already she knew better than to quibble with Imogen.

'About yesterday,' the woman continued, not adjusting her volume for the quiet of their surroundings, 'I told you how sensitive Patrick is, and I specifically said that *I* was to do the talking. *You* were to be the silent observer. I don't know what you were thinking, asking such a pointless question. You weren't there to cross-examine him, for fuck's sake. He's our client. Lucky for you it seems you managed to patch things up with him afterwards, but –' She stopped walking and faced Romola. 'I need you to follow my instructions more closely from now on. Yes?'

'Yes, Imogen.'

As they kept walking, Romola's heart began racing to a familiar beat, one she'd thought was behind her. In childhood she had lived in constant terror of being told off. She'd barely slept for a week after her grade 3 teacher Mrs Anderson accused her of stealing an eraser and made her stand in the corner of the classroom for a whole lesson, her back to the students, tears streaming down her face. Since then, her father's death, along with years of being chastised by judges, had shown her there were worse things in life than a telling off. But something in Imogen's voice – and in being reprimanded in front of her new workplace – brought back the memory of old Mrs Anderson and the terrible injustice of the eraser incident.

Imogen stopped outside a corner office, in front of which a red-faced brunette was seated at a desk. She was staring into space, visibly sweating, her fingers hovering over her keyboard. Her workspace was covered in photos of two smiling young boys and a heavily tattooed man.

'Victoria!' Imogen snapped. 'Where have you been?'

The brunette jumped. 'Sorry, I was in the bathroom.' Victoria spoke with an English accent, and her voice had a husky tone, a smoothness that was instantly reassuring.

'I couldn't find you anywhere,' Imogen continued, 'so *I* had to go and *interrupt* Derek's session to find Romola here.' Imogen waved her arm in Romola's general direction.

She began to extend her hand as she offered a sympathetic smile, but Victoria almost imperceptibly shook her head, eyes locked on the screen in front of her. Her blotchy red fingers shook slightly as she typed.

Imogen, meanwhile, seated herself in her office, chair to the window, back to Romola. 'We've received a response.' She clutched a piece of paper and waved it behind her for Romola to take. It was a short response, all of two paragraphs, from a Finnigan Price.

Dear Colleagues

Article entitled 'History Repeats: The Inexplicable Deaths of Patrick Payne's Lovers' (the Article)

We refer to your letter of 18 May 2019. We act for Mr Jonathan Wise, journalist, and Rabbit Hole Pty Ltd, the publisher of the Article.

To the extent that the Article, also dated 18 May 2019, contains imputations that are defamatory of Mr Payne (which is denied), those imputations are substantially true. Alternatively, the defence of qualified privilege applies. In circumstances where your client is seeking preselection for a seat in Federal Parliament, the public has an interest in receiving the information contained in the Article. Our clients make no offer of retraction, apology or compensation.

Yours faithfully

Imogen turned her chair to face Romola, red with rage. 'I don't know who the fuck this Finnigan Price is, but he must have some big balls.'

'Perhaps he's calling our bluff?' Romola felt like the mother of a child teetering on the edge of a tantrum. 'He doesn't think Patrick would want to damage himself any further by actually suing.'

'Ha!' Imogen spat. 'Well, they don't know much about the Paynes then. Suing people is what they do.'

Romola couldn't think of a sensible response.

'Have a seat, for goodness sake.' Imogen motioned towards a small stool in the corner, upon which Romola balanced, her pencil skirt forcing her knees together while her calves stuck out like chicken wings. Imogen stood and started pacing. 'I'm going to forward Malcolm and Patrick this letter and speak to them about it. We're going to draft a media release. I expect we'll be instructed to file proceedings as soon as possible.' She tapped her pen on the notepad on Romola's lap. 'Take this down.'

She needn't have asked – Romola was a scrupulous note-taker. Imogen dictated a series of tasks for her, which included preparing a first draft of defamation proceedings against Rabbit Hole, its journalist

Jonathan Wise and editor Eddie Moss; preparing Patrick's witness statement; and, most importantly, briefing counsel to settle everything they did and to appear in court. Solicitors like those at Bassett Brown didn't present arguments in court but rather briefed barristers to do so. Imogen suggested Neville Desmond QC, a senior barrister at the Melbourne bar, along with a junior named Tom Painter. Romola had heard of neither man but was instructed to speak to them urgently. She wasn't to take no for an answer.

Imogen checked her watch. 'Unless there's anything further, we're done. That was five units. Close the door on your way out.'

Melbourne and Sydney alike, lawyers charged for their time in units of six minutes, always rounded up. But Romola was used to offering discounts or occasionally taking on work pro bono or with limited legal aid funding. It felt luxurious to be at a firm where she could put down her time on Patrick Payne's file with no fear of financial difficulties.

She closed Imogen's door and looked around. Having not been allocated an office or computer as yet, she loitered like a child lost in the playground on the first day of school. She could see Victoria on the other side of the office, but the secretary was busy eating a custard tart and speaking in hushed tones to a lady with a trolley of cakes. Victoria's back was to Imogen's office and to Romola.

*

An hour later, a reluctant Victoria had shown Romola to a small internal office close to Imogen's, its walls entirely obscured by document boxes. 'Apparently I'm working for you now too.' Victoria moved a box so that the door could close. 'Just so you know, I leave at 5 p.m. and I don't do overtime. Let me know if you need anything.'

The door thudded shut, leaving Romola surrounded by cardboard. She dropped her head onto her desk three times, calmly repeating 'What have I done?' with each knock, before she inhaled deeply, straightened her back and switched on her computer.

She'd only just lifted the landline phone to call Neville Desmond QC when there was a loud knock on the door. Before she could say anything, it swung open. 'Is this a bad time?' Derek Russell, managing partner, was leaning against the doorframe, head bent to one side, arms and legs crossed as if he were about to burst into a jazz number. He surveyed her office. 'Surely they could have found you somewhere better than this. I'll ask my PA to move these boxes.'

'Honestly, I don't mind.' Romola was speaking the truth; she didn't mind being surrounded by boxes, or hidden from view for that matter. What she didn't admit was the creeping fear that she was in completely the wrong place, one where she did not belong.

Oblivious, Derek perched on the side of her desk, picked up a pen and started twirling it in his long fingers, regarding her with a smile. He had the manic energy of someone addicted to life's highs, but she suspected he was also prone to its lows. As a teen he would have joined lots of clubs and worn blazers. He already exhausted her. 'I'm sorry you missed out on the rest of my presentation this morning. I always think it's important to give our new lawyers a sense of our firm. It's a unique place. I didn't realise Imogen already had you working hard.'

'I'm sorry to have missed it.'

'Have you worked everything out? Can I lend a hand?' The twirling pen flew out of his hand and across the room. He picked up another and carried on.

'All under control – thanks,' she said, attempting a smile.

'Well, you let me know if I can be of any help.' He spoke as if he were wrapping up, but stayed seated and looked at her sideways. 'I hear you're helping out on Patrick's defamation matter?'

'We met with him yesterday. That's why Imogen wanted to see me this morning. There's a bit to get on top of.' Romola felt sick at the thought.

'Tell me, how was he when you saw him?' Derek asked, ceasing his pen twirling.

'Upset. As you'd expect.' She spoke with confidence but felt unsure as to what exactly Derek was getting at or expecting her to say. Of course Patrick would be upset after the death of his partner, let alone being accused of mistreating her. Was Derek expecting her and Imogen to have made life any better for their client over the course of one meeting?

'Poor man. One can only imagine what he's going through. The press can be savage. It went okay, though? Imogen managed to calm him down?'

'Yes, all fine. Actually good – I'd say good. I'll make a start on the claim documents now.' She was hardly going to mention to Derek, her new managing partner, that she had been the only one to upset Patrick at yesterday's meeting, particularly when she seemed to have patched things up with him in the end. Instead she turned to her computer and placed her fingers on the keyboard, hoping he would understand that from her perspective there was nothing more to say.

But Derek was unmoved. 'Excellent.' The pen twirling began again. 'I handle most of Malcolm Payne's work, so I'll be interested to follow your progress. I know Malcolm isn't happy about the coverage Patrick is getting. The sooner you can put a stop to it, the better. I'm surprised Rabbit Hole went ahead with a story like that. They better hope they have their sources lined up.' He stood to leave before turning back. 'I'm really happy you've started here, Romola. It's great to mix it up a bit, have some diversity in the office.' He paused, staring at her as if he was seeing her for the first time, before stammering on, 'By which I mean your criminal expertise, of course.'

'Of course.' She was accustomed to this phenomenon: the casual retraction of a comment after the speaker was struck by a sudden fear that their words might be construed as racist. It normally made her laugh, but she also knew it meant that she'd been marked as different – that she was someone to watch your words around.

'You be sure to keep me in the loop,' Derek said. 'If things aren't going to plan or if there's anything you're concerned about, anything at all, you can come to me.'

In that instant, she knew he was happy to have the protection of all those boxes too, because Imogen would have been in there in a second if she'd seen them talking.

'Of course, Derek,' Romola said, feeling queasy, 'happy to help any way I can.' There I go again with the lying, she thought.

*

Media Release from the Offices of Mr Patrick Payne

In the past week there has been speculation about the death of Patrick Payne's partner Hana Vukovic. Mr Payne strenuously denies any involvement in Hana's tragic death. Mr Payne has instructed his lawyers to commence civil proceedings against Rabbit Hole Pty Ltd and its journalist Jonathon Wise, who have seriously defamed him in the publication of false, baseless claims concerning Mr Payne's role in this tragedy. We ask for understanding and privacy at this difficult time as Mr Payne and his family grieve for Hana, whom they loved dearly.

Chapter Six
The Other Side

The small bar was warm and bustling, with a '70s Italian restaurant vibe. Though the lights were low, the walls were unmistakably lined with loud orange-and-green wallpaper, along with horizontal bottles of wine that seemed to amplify the Friday night chatter and '80s soundtrack. The noise was a welcome contrast to the silence that had engulfed Romola during her first week at Bassett Brown. She and Louise were seated at a busy bar overseen by a proud barman with a hipster beard. He showed mild disappointment when they ordered two glasses of pinot to accompany their veal ragout, rather than one of the aperitifs he was preparing with flair.

Romola raised her glass. 'To Fridays!'

'To Fridays,' said Louise, her face lit by one of the many small lamps dotting the bar, 'may they always be filled with red wine and happiness.'

Romola closed her eyes, one sip loosening the tightness that had been gripping her since the meeting on Sunday. 'I can't believe I made it through a whole week. It feels like I've been at that place a lifetime.'

'In a good way or a bad way?'

'I fantasise daily about my supervising partner dying a horrible death. That can't be a good way.'

'Gosh, that's extreme for you, Romy. I always thought I was the one with murderous fantasies.'

'Imogen does have small children, so maybe murder is a step too far. A flesh wound, perhaps? One that would need a few stiches and leave a permanent scar.'

'Subtle. I sometimes like to imagine my editor's brains on the floor – if he had any.' Louise laughed. 'Aren't there any redeeming features?

Is the work interesting at least? Or any gorgeous eligible men?'

A tortured writer at a gossip magazine, Louise had learned over the years to extract the good from any bad situation, a skill necessary to exist inside the tabloid machine. She also liked to say that her happiness was directly linked to her distance from the nearest handsome man, but Romola knew that couldn't be further from the truth. The two of them were happiest on Friday nights like this, when they could unload anything and everything that had happened to them in the past week, knowing it would be received with total and utter acceptance.

As Romola drank her first glass with ease, she searched her first week at Bassett Brown for redeeming features. No one other than Imogen, Derek and Victoria had spoken to her beyond the blandest of introductions. Victoria the secretary was guarded and seemed to expect Romola to behave like Imogen. Romola found herself apologising when asking Victoria to do even the smallest of tasks. The articled clerks thought her too senior to join them for their daily lunches, while the lawyers at her own level eyed her with suspicion. Every day she had smiled tentatively as she made cups of tea in the kitchen, but they'd just stared back with blank faces or muttered 'hi' before returning to their desks. She felt silly for having hoped, and she was reluctantly beginning to feel stabs of nostalgia for her old firm – for the secretary who was always trying a different diet, and the first-year lawyer who had just come out to his family and would regale them with stories of his weekend dates, and even her clients, whose lives were filled with such difficulty she had to admire them just for showing up.

She set down her glass and raised a finger. 'One good thing, and it's a biggie, is the tea lady – fresh scones, muffins and cakes delivered to your door every day at 10.30 a.m. like clockwork. And there's a cocktail night coming up. I'm dreading it, but you would be in heaven.'

'Boozy nights and a tea lady, how very 2019 of them!' Louise laughed. 'And you're right, that sounds like it *would* have been right up my alley. *However*, I have become very clean living of late.' She demolished a forkful of pasta and washed it down with a swig of pinot. 'Johnny's into all this healthy-living palaver. I haven't had the heart to tell him I think it's a load of shite. Speaking of which, you need to give me the yea or nay on him. You remembered he's dropping in for a drink tonight?'

Romola had indeed forgotten and was disappointed to realise that they would soon be joined by this Johnny. Not only had she been looking forward to dinner alone with Louise, but she was also feeling too tired to make an effort at conversation with a stranger – all those obligatory introductory questions.

But Louise seemed so excited that Romola faked enthusiasm. Hand on chin, she put on her best listening face. 'Quick, tell me everything before he gets here.'

'He's a journo. We actually sort of knew each other at uni, but not properly. Then we met up at this industry thing a few weeks ago. We were the only ones on the dance floor when they started playing Eurythmics. You can imagine. We danced for a while, exchanged details, and we're now on our fourth date. I haven't even made an idiot of myself yet.'

'And you said he's already seen your dancing?'

'Ha-ha, very funny. Like you're a regular Beyoncé.'

'Who's a regular Beyoncé?' A man had approached unannounced and was now planting a kiss on Louise's pink freckled cheek.

'Hello, stranger! Romy, Johnny – Johnny, Romy.'

Johnny had a manicured scruffiness to him. He had messy hair but had gone to the trouble of tucking in his greying band T-shirt, over which hung an impossibly trendy vintage bomber jacket. Louise was slightly taller than him, and her long ginger curls seemed to merge with his dark ones. They made a handsome couple, and both appeared genuinely delighted, though embarrassed, to be seeing each other in the company of a friend for the first time.

'Nice to finally meet you,' Johnny said. 'Lou talks about you a lot.' He kissed Romola's cheek like they were the best of friends.

She flushed. She hated cheek kisses, particularly from strangers, and took note of his use of Louise's nickname.

He hung his arm casually over Louise, waving his credit card to get the bartender's attention. When he did, he ordered a Sanpellegrino mineral water, using an extravagant Italian accent.

Romola couldn't help feeling suspicious of him. She was almost entirely dependent on a Friday night drink to smooth the passage from week to weekend, and to dull her response to the week's turmoils. Maybe he was a recovering alcoholic rather than a health nut? Though she wasn't sure which was worse.

'How was the food?' He popped a bar snack in his mouth. 'They do an excellent mushroom tagliatelle here.' Again with the accent.

Romola stole a look at Louise's bowl of ragu, which had been pushed to one side, her elbow surreptitiously covering the evidence of the veal she had just devoured.

Johnny turned to Romola. 'How are you finding Melbourne? Settled in?'

'The cold has been hard to get used to.' She knew weather was a popular topic among Melburnians, who liked to think themselves stoic for withstanding the chill each year. 'I don't know how you can stand it.'

'Easy – winter means footy. It gives us southerners a reason to live.' Johnny smiled broadly through his curls, and suddenly Romola could see precisely what Louise saw in him.

'You been to a game yet?' He asked the question in a way that made her think if her answer was no he'd be on his phone booking tickets to tomorrow's game.

'Louise and I aren't exactly sports nuts, are we, Lou?' Romola instantly remembered how a mutual hatred of sport had brought them together in that first year of high school. They'd both feigned period pain to get out of a beep test and instead sat in the library, hugging heat pads supplied by a compassionate school nurse and comparing terrible illustrations of Napoleon Dynamite. She met Louise's eyes, waiting for her to smile with the same memory, but her friend was instead shrinking in her seat.

'Come off it – really? That's so interesting ...' Johnny raised his eyebrows and held Louise a little closer. 'And yet you seemed to be having such a good time last weekend cheering on your "beloved" Magpies?'

Only then did Romola pick up on her gaff. She'd known Louise to tell some tall tales in her time, but Romola twigged that her friend must really be keen on this boy if she had feigned an interest in sport.

Romola mouthed an apology to Louise, whose face was now glowing red. 'Sorry, Johnny,' Louise said. 'I know you really love your footy, and black and white has always suited me, so I thought, why not go for the black-and-white team?'

Romola thought he should laugh. She couldn't help but giggle herself, despite Louise's embarrassment, because the mental image of her old friend attempting to understand the game of football and cheer at appropriate moments was hilarious. But Johnny didn't laugh, nor make any effort to lighten the mood. Instead he stroked Louise's hair and spoke gently about how they needed to be real with each other. Romola knew then that despite his winning smile, she would have to fight every one of her instincts not to dislike this Johnny character.

'So, Johnny, you're a journalist too?' she asked.

'Correct. I was freelance for a few years. Then I started craving something different – a little more structure, a new challenge, I guess. I've recently started on contract at Rabbit Hole.'

Romola's body made the connection first, her face bristling with heat. Then the sweat set in as her brain caught up with her predicament. She saw what would follow, like a semitrailer travelling towards her in the wrong lane.

'You've probably read his stuff, Romy – he goes by the name "Jonathan B Wise",' Louise said mockingly in a posh accent, but her eyes were full of affection as she glanced towards Johnny.

'The B stands for Bertram,' Johnny said. 'I put it in one of my early pieces as a joke, and now my editor makes me use it. Sadistic arsehole.'

Romola's pulse pumped audibly at her temple, drowning out the restaurant noise. Fuck, fuck, fuck, she thought. My client is suing my best friend's new boyfriend for all he's worth. She gulped the remainder of her wine, trying to mould her thoughts into a familiar shape so that she could say something intelligible. Johnny had said at the outset that Louise had talked about her. He would have seen that the letter of demand was from Bassett Brown. It didn't say her name, but Louise would have told him she was a lawyer, and perhaps where she worked. But if they already knew about the connection, this surely wasn't how they would break the news about Johnny's job.

Romola was confident that if Louise had known, she would certainly have mentioned it before his arrival – in fact, she would have called Romola about it before now and hashed it out.

But Louise now beamed with pride. 'You know he broke the story about Patrick Payne last week?'

'Sure did,' Johnny said, venom in his eyes, 'and it's only the tip of the iceberg.' He straightened up, seemingly struck by his own viciousness. 'I mean, those poor girls. Apparently he just tears them down. It's the sort of thing we can't tolerate any more as a society. Now he's trying to bully us into taking it down, getting his lawyers onto us. I guess I shouldn't talk about that, though. You're a lawyer, yeah?'

Romola desperately tried to make sense of what he was driving at. If he did know about her involvement, then was this diatribe intended to make her squirm, or did he genuinely not know?

She was reaching for the right words when Louise rescued her. 'I've told Johnny all about the work you used to do in Sydney. I couldn't remember the name of the firm you've moved to, though. Don't kill me, I know we've talked about it so much, and I should definitely know, but they all sound the same to me – something and something? You haven't updated yourself on LinkedIn, you know. All I know is you're working for the bad guys now – according to Judith, that is.' Louise grinned at Romola, obviously expecting her to enjoy some light-hearted criticism of her stepmother.

Romola felt simultaneously relieved that Johnny didn't already know, and panicked that she would now have to give herself away and that they would all have to adapt to the discomfort the news would create. Because Romola was certain of a few things. She could not discuss Patrick's case with Johnny. She could not become friends with Johnny. If she got any closer to Johnny, she would risk being hopelessly conflicted out of her first big file for Bassett Brown. Imogen would probably fire her on the spot.

'I studied law for a while,' Johnny said to her. 'Before journalism. I got the marks for it, but the other students were such a bunch of wankers. I realised that if I wanted to make a difference, law was not the way to do it. So I switched to journalism.' He began tracing a line along Louise's arm with his fingers, making Romola feel even more uncomfortable. 'Remember old Bruce Bladdernock, and that first-year lecture he used to give about the potential for journalism to shift societal norms? That got me here.' He thumped his chest with his free arm.

'Oh, I remember him!' said Louise. 'The one who always carried a thermos? Rumour was it was filled with whisky.'

'Well, I can tell you for a fact that it was filled with whisky, because the old bastard offered me some after a tutorial one day. In fact, I was the one who started that rumour.'

'No!' Louise pulled away. 'You should have reported him!'

Johnny was laughing, obviously enjoying her outrage. 'Give the dude a break, Lou – he'd been teaching at that place for more than thirty years. I'd need some seriously heavy liquor as well. You know he was in the box seat to be editor of the *Herald* and then got blacklisted for an opinion piece he wrote on the Soviet Union?'

'I never heard that! Poor man. His lectures were fantastic, though – Romy, you would have loved them.' Louise was clearly trying to draw her friend back into the conversation. 'He made you feel like you were entering such an honourable profession.'

'How far you've come, hey.' Johnny laughed.

Romola cringed inside, knowing how much that comment would have stung her friend, who had so desperately wanted a job in serious journalism when she left university. After numerous rejections, she had ended up accepting the job with the women's magazine, determined to write impactful articles, but had been stuck on the entertainment desk with an editor who liked to keep her there.

Louise paused, blinking, but then joined in Johnny's laughter and spoke in an exaggerated manner. 'I'm offended! I've seen those lifestyle pieces you used to write when you were freelance – it's not like every piece you've ever written is winning a Walkley, thanks very much.'

The two indulged in an exchange of light-hearted insults while Romola sat uncomfortably, questioning whether there was now any way to subtly work Patrick Payne back into the conversation so that she could tell Johnny the truth.

Her question was answered for her when, a short time later, she was bumped on the shoulder by a large man trying to slide his way through the tightly packed bar towards Johnny. 'Johnnaaay!' the man called as he passed Romola, his voice so deep that it cut easily through the music, which had switched from '80s pop to '90s electronica. He wore a dark double denim, yellow-and-purple high-topped trainers, and a number-two all-over shave.

'Maaate,' Johnny said as he reached across Louise to shake the man's hand, leaving his other arm resting on her shoulders.

'Been too long, mate,' the man said. 'Where you been?' His eyes shifted from Johnny to Louise, obviously waiting for an introduction. 'Let me buy you a drink, man. Negroni?'

'Nah, mate, I'm good. This is Lou and her friend Romy.' Johnny pointed to each of them in turn. 'And this is my mate Catch. We used to DJ together back in the day.'

'DJ?' Louise pulled back in surprise. 'Okay, I need to hear about this.'

What sort of a stupid name is 'Catch'? thought Romola. And clearly Johnny had drunk alcohol at one point, so maybe she was right that he was recovering from a problem.

As the nostalgic conversation with Catch progressed, it became clearer that the night wasn't going to circle back to the point of introducing jobs or discussing the boring facts of their everyday existence. Romola would have to call Louise later and tell her. It was probably better like that anyway, without Johnny around to muddy the waters. After another half an hour, Romola masked a yawn and half-heartedly rubbed her eyes before bending to pick her bag off the floor. 'I'm so tired, guys. I'm going to make tracks if you don't mind. You stay – enjoy yourselves. So nice to meet you both. Lou, I'll call.' She mimed a phone.

Happily, Louise and Johnny were engrossed in conversation with Catch, and their relationship was still at a stage where they enjoyed any opportunity to be together regardless of the company. Romola weaved through the restaurant and tripped out into the frigid winter night like it was her salvation.

Chapter Seven
The Slug and the Hare

The conference room was uncomfortably warm, but Neville Desmond QC refused to turn off the heat. He had a cold, and every few minutes he would noisily fill a tissue before throwing it to the floor. One had landed on the toe of Romola's shoe, and she couldn't stop thinking of her beautiful patent Mary Janes. She could still feel the clamminess of his weak handshake. There was no question he was a Slug.

As instructed, Romola had engaged Neville Desmond and Tom Painter as barristers to represent Patrick. It was Monday morning of her second week at Bassett Brown, and Romola and Imogen were having their first meeting with the pair, at their chambers on Lonsdale Street in the CBD. They were to finalise the court papers to officially begin defamation proceedings against Rabbit Hole, its editor Eddie Moss, and its journalist – Romola's new problem – Jonathan B Wise.

The room was reasonably sized but windowless, walled on three sides by ancient hard-back books, and carpeted in red paisley. The four of them sat around a large oak table inlaid with black leather. Imogen was at one head, and the Slug at the other. He had directed Romola to sit near the corner closest to him, with the fidgeting Tom Painter sitting opposite her.

'So, what's this all about?' huffed the Slug, his question directed at his junior barrister rather than his instructing solicitors. Romola had in fact sent the Slug a detailed brief of background documents so that he would know in advance what the matter was all about; he obviously hadn't read a word.

With much ado, Tom produced a copy of the article and handed it to the Slug. Tom was tall, with buckteeth and pockmarked skin. His eyelids fell half closed in a superior manner, and his deep voice was slightly obstructed, perhaps by the large Adam's apple sticking out from above his collar. His looks were offset by what many in the law considered to be an incredible mind – he was said to be one of the best and most hardworking young barristers in Melbourne. Unlike the Slug, he had read the brief and was keen to show it. 'We have a defamation claim,' he said. 'There's arguably a number of defamatory imputations arising from Rabbit Hole's article about Patrick Payne.'

Romola had researched defamation law extensively since that first phone call from Imogen. In order to succeed, they would need to establish that the article was defamatory: that the meaning or meanings it conveyed would lower Patrick in the estimation of reasonable members of society or hold him up to hatred, ridicule and contempt. The critical question was whether Rabbit Hole had a defence for the defamation. Finnigan Price's letter had talked about both 'truth' and 'qualified privilege'. Rabbit Hole would try to rely on justification: to prove the substantial 'truth' of all the defamatory meanings in the article. 'Qualified privilege', otherwise known as the reasonable journalist's defence, was a little trickier. That defence, sometimes used for government and political matters, applied where there was a social duty to report on a matter, and where the readers had an interest in knowing; the catch was that the journalist must have acted reasonably in publishing the material and cannot have been motivated by malice.

Whatever happened from here on in – and especially if there was eventually to be a trial – Johnny would be in the thick of it. She thought back to Friday night, to meeting him in that darkened bar. He had said something about Patrick heading for a fall – and he'd seemed happy to be the one to push him.

Tom continued. 'The real sting here is the suggestion that Patrick treats his girlfriends in a way that makes them want to harm themselves, withdraw from friends et cetera. A 'coercive control' sort of inference. The article suggests that he was at least emotionally, if not physically, abusive to these two young women, and that, on at least a macro level, their premature deaths can be attributed to his conduct.' Tom picked up the draft court documents that Romola had prepared, now covered in dramatic red annotations. 'The draft claim papers were in relatively good shape, but I've made some edits.' He stuck them under the Slug's nose.

The older man sniffed before speaking directly to Imogen. 'And we are certain, before we embark upon what I can assure you, from previous experience with Malcolm, will be an absolute shitstorm, that his son did not do these things? Firstly, do we know the grounds upon which this journalist says Patrick is so offensive? And secondly, are we confident that those grounds cannot be proved? Because if the answer to either of those questions is no, this could get embarrassing quickly, Imogen, both for yourself and for Patrick.'

Before Imogen could answer, Tom chimed in. 'I was just about to ask that, Neville. How confident are we in Patrick?'

Romola had been in the room with Tom Painter for less than ten minutes but already felt repelled by him. What made it worse was that he continued to glance across at her, his arrogant eyes blinking. How she wished for him to slip up so that she could correct him. But it seemed there was very little she could add to the conversation other than to take her notes, which was again all that Imogen had told her to do.

'I know that perfectly well, Neville,' Imogen said. 'Patrick denies everything, and he seems credible to me. Romola here has been doing some digging on his relationship with the other girl – Lisbeth.'

The three of them turned to Romola as she was finally granted permission to speak. She cleared her throat and shifted her papers. 'I'm preparing a memo that I'll forward to you later today, but I haven't found anything significant to date on Lisbeth. It's all very tragic, really. She was clinically depressed at the time of her death. There's not a lot of evidence to suggest that Patrick was responsible for her depression, other than that's what her sister says, and these unnamed friends say, but as you know a relative will be very compelling for a jury. I'm trying to get in touch with schoolfriends, teachers, other relations, anyone who might shed a different light on what happened and help explain that Lisbeth's condition was independent of Patrick.'

'It's vital that we learn everything we can about this girl,' said Tom. 'Anything that could discredit her – any hint that she was a liar, a fraud, a whore – you need to uncover it. Same with her sister. If the jury is sympathetic to the family, we've all but lost. And what about Hana? Did she have a drug problem or was she depressed before she knew Patrick? Was she taking drugs at all? We need to be on to this. A week has gone by already.' He clicked his fingers three times as if beckoning a dog. The Slug was blowing his nose again but gave a faint nod of agreement.

Imogen put her pen down pointedly, her squirrel eyes fixed on Tom. 'We have taken a preliminary statement from Patrick. He's distraught, and he needs more time, which I intend to give him. From all accounts he loved those girls and treated them well. We are exploring all of the things you have mentioned, but for now we have instructions to proceed with the claim, and there's no reason to question that. You and I both know that Patrick has more than reasonable grounds to issue.' At this she turned to the Slug. 'And frankly I don't appreciate the suggestion that we're somehow lacking here, Neville.'

'Okay, Imogen, no need to get your knickers in a knot …' Neville said with a wink in Tom's direction. 'I'm sure they're much too nice for that.'

Romola cringed, but Tom began banging his fist on the table and snorting with laughter that sounded like loud hiccups. His lips drew back to reveal his buckteeth.

And you are a hare, thought Romola. The Slug and the Hare.

She was accustomed to this sort of carry-on from the criminal barristers in Sydney but had been hoping for more decorum from Melbourne's elite commercial bar.

Imogen had her arms crossed. 'Please, boys, can we leave the schoolyard behind us just this once?'

The Slug cleared his throat and motioned for Tom to settle down. 'I understand the position, Imogen. I don't see any problem with filing the action, but you need to get more out of Patrick. Find out what happened with this "girlfriend" of his. And put in a call to the police to see if they are taking an interest.'

Romola thought of telling the Slug that she had called the investigating officer six times throughout the previous week. He hadn't answered any calls and had not called back. But she didn't want to needlessly prolong the torturous meeting.

'And what about the ex-wife?' the Slug continued. 'What does she have to say about all this? Is there any prospect of her supporting Patrick? An ex-wife who can testify to his good character would be very compelling.'

Romola had thought the same thing, and said as much to Imogen before, but Imogen had brushed off her queries, telling her to draw a line through Sonia's name without further explanation. She was thankful her boss couldn't so easily avoid answering the Slug's questions.

'There's not a chance she'll help, Neville.' Imogen shook her head. 'The woman's a mess, the marriage was a mess and so was the divorce. I expect Patrick would rather be eaten alive by the press than have to fall on his sword and crawl to Sonia for help.'

'What do you mean by a mess?' the Slug asked, again mirroring Romola's own thoughts. 'Are we facing a risk that Rabbit Hole will call her as a witness? Or perhaps we'll see a feature story on *her* next? This is all heading down a very unsavoury path, Imogen.' The Slug noisily blew his nose again, before exploring each nostril with his pointer finger. This time he placed the tissue on the table, centimetres away from Romola's writing pad.

Imogen was shaking her head. 'I'm not going to go into the gory details today, Neville, but I'm confident Sonia won't speak to the press. She's got too much to lose. It became obvious in the divorce that Sonia had some big issues, not the least of them being that she has a huge dependence on alcohol. I mean, she was hardly able to look after her own son at times.'

'Well, that's nice and consistent with their case theory, isn't it?' said the Slug with a cough this time. As much as Romola was repelled by him, she was agreeing with everything he said. She was also feeling more uneasy about Patrick's case by the minute – and wondering why Imogen was seemingly so confident in pressing ahead with a claim.

'The public doesn't know anything about Sonia other than that she's the perfect wife, seemingly hard done by because Patrick had an affair with the nanny – which, by the way, isn't true. Sonia's not going to want to put her relationship under the microscope – believe me. She's got her son to think of, after all. Plus she signed a non-disclosure agreement when everything was finalised.'

'And how long before she decides she's got more to gain by breaching it?' the Slug pressed.

'She's got too much skin in the game here. Please – just for now – take my word that we can rule her out as a witness, either for or against. Unless they subpoena her, but there'd be too much risk for them in doing that if they don't know what she's going to say.'

'Your client's not paying me twenty thousand a day to take your word for it, Imogen. But I will for now – only because I like you.'

The Slug winked at Romola, before something caught at the back of his throat and he hacked into a tissue. Romola felt both uncomfortable and grimy – possibly because of the barrage of germs being shed next to her, or maybe because of the unspoken understanding that Sonia might have stories to tell about her marriage that would, they hoped, never see the light of day. Either way, Romola wanted this meeting to end.

'Now let me read this draft,' said the Slug as he tapped his fingers on the paper. 'Can someone please find Linda and ask her to bring me in some tea? She knows how I like it.'

*

Twenty minutes later, Romola and Imogen had left the building, a light drizzle embracing the women as they walked down Collins Street towards their offices. Now used to Imogen's height and pace, Romola managed two strides for every one of her boss's. She felt like a pony trotting alongside its mother. But for once she was relieved to be alone with Imogen, glad to have left the Slug and the Hare in their dreary lair.

'I need coffee.' Imogen made a beeline for a small café where aproned staff leaned over every cup like priests administering Communion.

They sat at a tiny round table, and Romola noticed for the first time how tired her supervising partner looked, as she practically fell into her seat. 'They're all the same,' Imogen said, rubbing her eyes. 'Barristers. Without exception they think they're the smartest people in the room. What they don't realise is how much easier it is for them only dealing with the law. They're not the ones having to manage the clients, figuring out what the fuck is going on when a matter comes in the door. We are.' Imogen pointed to her chest and then to Romola, who felt a surprising bolt of collegiality at being part of a 'we'. 'I normally let it go, but it kills me every time. Tom Painter needs to learn a thing or two about where his instructions come from.' Her coffee arrived, and she downed it like a stiff whisky. 'Oh god, I'm so tired. Take my advice: do not have children.'

Romola savoured the first of two deliciously sweet cubes of chocolate that the barista had placed on her coffee spoon, a complimentary treat. It was hot and steamy in the little café. Imogen removed her suit jacket and rolled up her sleeves. Her forearms were all muscle and bone – she was strong in every sense of the word.

'How old are your kids?' Romola knew this was the kind of question to ask people with children, even though she felt she would have almost nothing to contribute to a conversation on the topic.

'Three, and eighteen months. I thought it was an efficient choice having them so close together. God knows why. They don't sleep, ever. Little fuckers.' She said this with a smile, placing her phone facedown on the table. Romola hadn't imagined Imogen's children to be so young; she had put her at well over forty with kids at least in primary school. She imagined Imogen being woken at midnight by a baby's cries and telling the kid to 'Fuck right off back to sleep!'

'How did you come to start acting for Patrick?' Romola asked casually.

'I was in the right spot at the right time. When Patrick and Sonia announced their separation, the firm was desperate to keep the business. In a previous life I practised family law, so I was the only one with any relevant experience, even though Derek didn't want me to have it. He was, and still is, worried I'll infiltrate the Payne dynasty and steal his most prized client.' Imogen smiled sardonically.

Romola nodded, making sense of Derek's visit to her office. What didn't make sense was that Imogen was sharing high-level gossip with her, a new associate. But Imogen seemed to be short on allies at Bassett Brown, and maybe she saw something in Romola, united by their common disdain of the Slug and the Hare.

She bit her lip. 'Imogen, there's something I need to tell you. Something I want to make sure you're okay with.'

Her words chased the smile right off Imogen's face. She stared down her straight nose at Romola. 'Yes?'

'It's pretty funny, actually.'

'Spit it out.'

'Well, I was having dinner the other night with one of my good friends, my best friend really, and she introduced me to her new partner. I'd never met him or heard his full name before.'

'That's generally what it means to be introduced to someone.'

'Yes. That's right. Ha – funny. Anyway, it turns out he's Johnny Wise, as in Jonathan B Wise ... as in the journalist from Rabbit Hole.' Romola braced herself.

But Imogen's face was unchanged, her frown having set in at Romola's first mention of having something to tell her. 'Right. And, what? You're worried about a conflict?'

'Yes. But I've thought carefully about it, and I'm satisfied there isn't one – a conflict, I mean. I met him for the first time on Friday night, and I don't expect I'll have much to do with him from now on, not until the trial's over anyway. I'll just avoid seeing him. I don't owe him anything. But I thought I at least needed to tell you about it.'

'I agree you needed to tell me.' Imogen paused, running her finger over the rim of her coffee cup. Romola got the feeling she was being assessed. 'This doesn't need to be an issue unless you make it one, Romola. Of course you shouldn't talk to him about the case.'

'No. I wouldn't.'

'What the fuck is your friend doing dating someone like that anyway?'

'Lou? Oh, she's notoriously bad at choosing men. It probably won't last long.' As soon as Romola had spoken those words, she wished she could swallow them back in. Louise deserved happiness. And who was Romola to talk about men and choices, or to judge anyone who was at least giving it a chance?

'So what did you make of Johnny?' Imogen asked. 'What are we dealing with here?'

'To be honest I left not long after I found out who he was. Before then he seemed nice enough. A bit of a tosser, I guess – takes himself too seriously. He did seem happy to have been the one who exposed Patrick. But any journalist would, wouldn't they? It's a big story.'

'I bet he's happy.' Imogen licked her lips. Using her tiny teaspoon, she picked up the chocolate cubes from her plate and slid them onto Romola's. 'So he doesn't know you're involved at the moment?'

'I don't think so.'

Imogen turned to her phone, as if her attention had been diverted, but it was clear that her mind was still ticking away. As Romola went to review her notes of the meeting with the Slug and the Hare, her boss got as close as she would get to the point. 'You may not have to mention to him, or to your friend for that matter, your connection with the case for now. Just keep your distance from him, to the extent that you can. We wouldn't want him getting sensitive and ruining the romance, would we?'

Romola recognised Imogen's efforts to stretch the outer boundaries of ethical lawyering. She wasn't instructing Romola to breach her duties – to obtain information from the opposition without his knowledge – but she was certainly not discouraging it either. Whether Romola would do it was another thing. Louise was her most precious friend in the world, her one shoulder to cry on now that her father was gone. And Romola prided herself on her ethics. She wouldn't jeopardise either of those things lightly.

Without thinking, she picked up one of Imogen's chocolate cubes and popped it in her mouth. But the sweetness had all but disappeared, replaced by a sourness that settled on Romola's tongue. Even when she lay in bed that evening, her teeth freshly brushed, she could still taste the bitterness of her afternoon coffee with Imogen.

Chapter Eight
The Stepmother

The sky was clear as Romola walked home from the tram stop later that week. The smell of the day's heavy rain lingered in the air, the grass underfoot was still sodden, and the roads were slick with water. The streets of East Melbourne were well lit, with the windows of homes glowing as families sat around dinner tables.

Romola preferred to be on the phone while walking anywhere after dark, as if that would somehow defend her against a would-be rapist. '*Stop! I'm on the phone!*' she would call out, like that would help.

She would normally have called Louise but had avoided making contact since that night with Johnny, worried she might accidentally blurt out that she was acting for Patrick Payne. Nor could she call any of her old workmates, who hadn't forgiven her for leaving their firm on such short notice. Having spent nearly six years with the same group of lawyers, she'd thought their friendship extended beyond the office walls, but it seemed their spite trumped everything. To have left them to prosecute would have been acceptable, or to go to the bar. But to choose corporate law over criminal was an unforgiveable sin in their eyes.

Judith was her next best option. Since the move, Romola had spoken with her stepmother twice. Each time she had prematurely ended the call after hearing the condescending, nurturing tone in Judith's voice, as though Romola had entered a world of drugs and sex work rather than big business.

Looking at her stepmother objectively, though that was hard to do, Romola could understand where she was coming from. Though Judith was a child of the '70s, she had come late to a life of social activism, and for as long as Romola had known her she seemed to be making up for lost time. Romola had lost count of the stories her stepmother had told of her youth spent in a small country town, and how she had felt short-changed when – at the tender age of thirty-five – she'd moved to Sydney and realised that the '70s and '80s had passed by without her so much as burning a bra strap. Judith had confessed to Romola (in the manner of a cautionary tale) that she put up no resistance when her father had suggested she leave school for the local secretarial college at age fifteen, and how she'd then worked at the town real estate office with no appreciation for all she could have achieved if she'd seen her education through.

Romola had been a stubborn twelve-year-old when Judith – by then ensconced in city life – had met her father Don, a professor of anthropology. A short time later they married without fanfare at the local registry office. Her father had taken the wedding photos himself in front of the big camellia bush in their garden, putting his old camera on a timer. Romola's face was partially obscured by the broad bunch of sunflowers that Judith had made her carry, but the utter misery she'd felt on that day was plain in her downturned eyes. Before Judith had come along, Romola couldn't have been happier with the life her father had created for the two of them. Both calm spirits, Don and Romola stuck together like barnacles, laughing at the silliness and calamity of the world around them. Judith blew into their home like a polar wind – she was all drama, light and activity. From the moment she arrived, and despite making every effort to repel her, Romola felt like she was nothing but a cause for Judith. The woman was insistent Romola would grow up to know right from wrong; she never failed to remind Romola that she would not allow her 'daughter' to stand by like she had. The word had caused Romola something close to physical pain the first few times she had heard it, and even now she cringed when Judith described her as her 'daughter', feeling that she was no one but her father's girl.

'It's so nice to hear your voice again, sweetheart! Tell me, how *are* you? Are you cold? You sound blocked up.'

'I'm fine, Judith.' In fact, Romola had been sniffling all day, and her throat was scratchy. She suspected that the Slug had passed on his cold, but would not concede as much to Judith, who had always been unnaturally concerned about flus and chills. Romola would never live down the skivvies that Judith had insisted she wear underneath her school uniform, just like the other South-East Asian kids whose parents were accustomed to a subcontinental climate.

The story of Romola's birth mother had been told many times over by her father during her childhood, though never in enough detail to satisfy her curiosity. Eventually Romola had stopped asking questions; she'd decided it was better not to ask at all if there were to be no answers – that imaginings were better than blank space. What she did know was that her birth mother had been Sri Lankan and her name had been Ishanvi. She had met Romola's father while he was researching in her village one summer. The pregnancy had been unplanned, and Ishanvi had died in childbirth, the hospital in the small municipality no match for the massive haemorrhage. Don had brought the tiny Romola back home with him to Australia, an unplanned but welcome byproduct of his study abroad.

Romola often wondered if Judith's obsession with the cold was her subconscious attempt to channel the young woman who had lost her life so that Romola could have hers. But Judith's fussing only made Romola contemplate the alternate universe that might have existed if things had turned out differently. In these moments she would fill in the blank spaces with everything she dreamed her mother might have been. For one thing she was sure her mother wouldn't have been compelled to think about Romola's wellbeing every moment of every day. She would have left her alone, having more important things to think about. How Romola longed to be taken for granted.

Faced now with Judith's prodding about her wellbeing, she had flashbacks to all those times as a teenager when her only wish was to feel miserable in peace. But she'd been the one to call Judith, after all – she could hardly finish the call here. Instead she tried to deflect the conversation away from her job, like a goalie protecting the net. 'How's everything with you? Keeping busy?'

'Don't worry about me, darling, I'm busier than I can cope with. Plus of course your Dad's anniversary's coming up, so that's on my mind.'

'Oh.' Romola recoiled. 'Have you thought any more about what you might do?'

Don's death had been like a bolt from the blue, the explosion of an aneurism enveloping his brain in a matter of moments. The surprising nature of his death made its anniversary even more notable, the day sticking out like a sore thumb. The first anniversary was only weeks away.

'I wanted to speak to you about it,' Judith said, 'I thought I might come down to Melbourne. I could stay for the weekend. Dad would have wanted us to be together, don't you agree?'

Romola broke out into a sweat despite the chill. The anniversary was a Saturday. She had planned very precisely what she wanted to do: absolutely nothing. She would sit by herself, do some work, speak to no one, and wait for the day to be over. Seeing Judith would only remind her of everything she missed about her father. He had been the meat in the little sandwich that was their family. He was the only reason Romola had pretended to get along with Judith, and with him gone there was none.

'I'm not sure if that's best,' Romola began. 'It's so cold down here … with your arthritis. And I'm working on this new matter, which is going to keep me flat out –'

'Surely you're not too busy to remember your father, Romola? And what kind of an employer would make you work on a Saturday, especially on the first anniversary of your father's death?'

My kind of employer, thought Romola, but would never admit that to Judith.

'How *is* it there, darling, really? You can be honest with me. We can work out the next step together.'

'It's fine. It's more than fine. I have a really interesting new matter – a defamation claim.'

'Ooh, tell me about it?'

Bugger, Romola thought, there I go again, walking into things; Judith would probably hate that she was acting for Patrick Payne. But the proceedings had been filed. It was now public that Patrick Payne was suing Rabbit Hole, in one of the country's most high-profile legal cases. Maybe she'll be proud, Romola thought.

'You know Patrick Payne?'

'As in, the son of Malcolm Payne, the scourge of the Australian landscape?'

'The very same.'

Judith breathed in sharply. 'Patrick Payne is meant to be an abomination, Romola. The things I have read about him would keep you up at night, especially as a woman.' Her voice was growing shaky. 'Goodness, I actually feel a little sick about you having to meet him, sweetheart. Let me sit down.'

'I've already met him, so you can relax.'

'And? Is he as bad as they say?'

'He doesn't seem so bad to me, Judith,' Romola answered truthfully. 'I've met worse.'

She thought of her former clients, many of them accused murderers and rapists. She'd sat across from them for hours in interview cells. While Judith had sometimes expressed worry for her safety, Romola had always had the overwhelming impression that Judith was proud of her work. Or perhaps her dad had been the proud one. He had encouraged her to practise criminal law at the start of her career, and had loved hearing about the complex legal aid matters she had taken on. If Judith had privately expressed concern or disapproval to Don, Romola assumed he must have cooled her off before she could make her feelings known to Romola. But now Romola no longer had her father as a buffer.

It wasn't until after Romola had made an excuse and said her goodbyes that it occurred to her: people like Judith would be the real jury. She believed everything she read in the places she chose to look, even more so if it was presented in a cloak of investigative journalism. If Romola could find enough evidence to convince Judith that Patrick was a good man, then the case could be won. But as she continued walking, the task seemed an impossible one. She swallowed, the pain in her throat now sharper. She reached the corner where Azra's café stood dark and empty, a surge of icy air hitting her and blowing open her puffer coat (her second major Melbourne purchase). A shiver broke over her body like a current of electricity. She longed to lie down with a cup of her dad's 'cold buster', a mix of honey and lemon and a mystery salty ingredient that he had taken to his grave. She called a 'hello' when she reached Cliffy's, but the place was pitch-black and her voice echoed back to her. Once again, she was alone.

Chapter Nine
Cocktails

Late the following Friday afternoon there was a buzz about the office, along with the waft of warm hors d'oeuvre and the sound of glass clinking as cocktail waiters polished champagne flutes. Men congregated with beers in hand, while women bunched in the toilets reapplying make-up. Romola had never seen so much life in the office – it was like the place had risen from the dead.

The Bassett Brown Annual Art Auction was one of the most important nights on the firm's social calendar. Significant paintings were displayed and sold, with the proceeds going to the Paynes' charity. The event attracted the wealthiest clients and made junior lawyers appreciate the circles in which they moved.

Romola was in her office, the door closed, her brow furrowed. She was trying to ignore the fuss outside as she finished an advice to Patrick. Gretchen, the young clerk with whom she had started three weeks ago, passed by and raised her eyebrows, pointing to the champagne flute in her hand and mouthing, 'Come on.' Romola shrugged, unable to muster any enthusiasm for a night of small talk with other lawyers and clients. She was thankful her nose had stopped dripping in time for the festivities, but her head continued to pound. Balancing hors d'oeuvre and a drink was hard enough without a brain fog. She dug out two aspirin and plopped them into the glass of water next to her keyboard.

Twenty minutes later she arrived in a large space that had been created by opening the removable wall separating the firm's two largest board rooms. The usual bright meeting lights had been turned to their lowest setting, so one's eyes were drawn to the glittering city beyond and to the pools of light hovering over each of the paintings on display. The air was thick with the odour of sweat, freshly applied perfume and alcohol. A string quartet played in a corner. The paintings were hung sparingly, with downlights highlighting their texture and vibrancy. There were landscapes, still lifes and portraits of Melbourne identities, along with some Indigenous pieces that she could have got lost in for hours. She chose a red wine and entered the throng, hoping to spot a familiar face in one of the groups milling about the paintings, or at least a circle of people with an opening wide enough to slide into.

She soon found herself drawn into a group of young lawyers who appeared relatively harmless. Emmett was holding court. He was eminently handsome, with windswept hair and gold cufflinks pressed with a private school crest. 'Romola, right? Come and join us.' He beckoned. 'Have you met everyone here?'

Emmett had introduced himself to her earlier that week as the head of Bassett Brown's Young Lawyer's Social Committee. His office was a few doors along from hers, and she often overheard his loud conversations in aid of his committee duties.

'What's been keeping you so busy, Romola? I've seen you in with Imogen Trigg. Still in one piece? You haven't pulled "the Trigger" yet, have you?' He laughed loudly at his own joke. 'You know that's what people say about her? That you haven't worked in litigation at this firm until you've "pulled the Trigger". Hilarious.'

'Imogen's great, actually,' Romola said bluntly.

'You've been working on Patrick Payne's defamation case, haven't you?' He again spoke a little too loudly. She glanced around, conscious of the presence of other clients, aware of the sensitivity of Patrick's case. But Emmett seemed oblivious. 'So tell me, did he kill her? I read something about how maybe he'd drugged her – in a jealous rage? Come on, give us the low-down.' Emmett playfully elbowed Romola.

Her grip on her wineglass tightened with anger. 'I don't think it's for us to speculate, especially in this setting.'

Emmett recoiled and clutched at his chest in mock horror. 'Ouch! Remind me not to cross you, Romola.' He laughed, and the others followed suit, giggling at her seriousness. She felt as though she were back at high school; the taunts of 'Can't you take a joke, Rolly?' were ingrained in her brain.

She was hatching an escape plan when she felt a large hand on her shoulder and looked up to find Derek Russell towering over her. 'Romola, Emmett, just the two I've been looking for.' He was flushed with excitement, his bouncing irrepressible now. 'Malcolm Payne has arrived. Come and I'll introduce you.'

Derek adjusted his glasses, and Romola noticed the embroidered initials on the cuff of his shirt: 'DNR'. Those letters stuck in her mind. She had once acted for a nurse accused of allowing one of her patients to die prematurely. Her defence was that the patient had in fact, and to no one else's knowledge, declared themselves 'DNR' or 'Do Not Resuscitate'. Romola had needed to intensely research the law surrounding the term. In Derek's case, the 'N' probably stood for a middle name like Nigel. Still, she found it funny that these were his unfortunate initials. A man defined by his drive to never give in, Derek would surely opt for resuscitation even when death was singing its most beautiful lullaby.

He led Romola and Emmett through the close-packed crowd to where a semicircle of people stood facing a window. Their attention wasn't on the view, but rather on a short, stout bald man who stood in its way, telling a story that he obviously found supremely amusing. Gretchen stood next to him. His short arms, every now and then wildly gesticulating, intermittently came to rest on her hip, ever so close to the top of her bottom. She had a drink in her hand and a smile on her face, but – at least to Romola – she was emitting an energy of terror.

There was no mistaking the tall silver-haired man who stood on Gretchen's other side, staring over the crowd. He held a glass of water and was clearly searching for someone better to speak to. Derek led them across to him. 'Malcolm, I'd like you to meet Emmett DuPlessis and Romola Cross. Emmett is helping me with your new acquisition –' he raised an eyebrow '– and Romola here has been working on Patrick's case with Imogen.'

She extended her hand, which Malcolm shook with a weakness that men sometimes reserved for women. His hands were cold. He said hello, but his voice was so low that his words became lost in the laughter of the crowd when the bald man's story reached its climax.

Malcolm shook Emmett's hand firmly, and as the noise died down Romola could finally hear him speak. 'I've heard good things about you, Emmett.'

The bald man finished his story and removed his hand from Gretchen's hip, extending it to Romola, his eyes wandering downwards before meeting her own. 'I don't think we've met …?' He spoke through wet lips, spraying those in his direct line of speech, and had round, frog-like eyes.

'And this,' Derek placed a hand on the bald man's shoulder, 'is Barnaby St John, our head projects partner. You behaving yourself, Barney?' Derek glanced from him to Gretchen.

'Me? I'm always trying, Derek, always trying …' He slurped his drink and moved his eyes from Romola to Gretchen and back again. 'Good to meet you, Romola,' he spat. 'I trust Patrick is in good hands with you and Imogen on board. I certainly don't envy your opponents!'

Laughter ensued, and Romola tried to look elsewhere, annoyed that these were the circumstances of her introduction to Malcolm Payne – being drooled over by this toad of a man.

'I agree with you, Barney,' Malcolm said with a frown, 'this is exactly what we need for a case like this.'

She hoped he was referring to her and Imogen's expertise, but knew he was referring to having two female lawyers defend his son against these particular accusations.

With Barney at the helm, the conversation moved quickly, from football, to skiing destinations, to boat trips, to wine. Gretchen stood awkwardly next to him, laughing at appropriate moments while her eyes scanned the room.

'Gretchen,' said Romola, 'I saw someone looking for you over by the drinks table.' Romola pointed to the opposite side of the room, and the young woman flashed her a grateful smile as she left.

While Barney endlessly spoke, Malcolm gradually moved closer to Romola. The room was loud, but slowly she started to feel him breathing above her, a warm, stale cloud of coffee and tobacco. She could smell his body too, the musky sandalwood scent of a grown man. He wasn't touching her, but Malcolm Payne's presence was suffocating in its own way.

It seemed as if they were standing there for an age before he spoke. His voice carried to her in the deep tones of a late-night radio host. 'Tell me, how's it going with Patrick? How are we looking there?'

She sipped her drink and cleared her throat. 'It's difficult to say. It's still early. We don't know what evidence Rabbit Hole will be relying on, or whether they might be open to a negotiated outcome, for example.'

'No.' He shook his head emphatically, and his voice grew louder. 'There will be no negotiated outcome. You're not to think that way. This poor excuse for journalism has already taken its toll on the business, both Patrick's and mine. It's not about resolving this quickly. I don't need to save costs.'

She felt she had apologise, though she knew she hadn't spoken out of turn. 'I didn't mean to give the impression we were actively looking to negotiate. I only meant we don't know how hard they're going to fight. There's always a chance they won't have the stomach for litigation. Maybe they'll make an offer to avoid it going further.'

'Any offer would have to be well north of a million dollars for us to even consider it. And there would have to be a public apology – I won't take anything less. This is nothing short of a witch-hunt.' His words were angry but he spoke calmly, still staring out over the top of the crowd.

She was torn. Part of her wanted to excuse herself and walk away, because Malcolm's intensity was stifling, especially when combined with the heat in the room. But another part of her wanted to stay by his side, to find out as much as she could while she had the chance.

'Did you know Hana well?' she asked, peering up at Malcolm and trying her best to make him make eye contact.

His focus remained fixed on the room. 'I'll never understand what Patrick saw in her – but, yes, I knew her well enough, I suppose.'

'Were you surprised by what happened?'

'Well obviously I was. No one expects these things to happen. But of course they do …' He shrugged, as though her death was just one of those things.

The crowd was becoming more raucous as the night wore on. Jackets had been discarded, and random hoots of laughter cut across the steady buzz. She could see Derek standing with the art dealers, who – now that the alcohol had loosened everyone's wallets – were preparing to step up to the podium and begin the auction.

Malcolm finally turned towards Romola, his eyes the same flinty grey as Patrick's. 'Hana obviously got in over her head with drugs. You know she came from a very different background to ours. Who knows what she might have been caught up in.'

Romola nodded and swallowed, her throat still tender.

'You might think I'm cold,' he continued, sipping his drink like he was talking about the weather, 'but you have to be honest about what works and what doesn't. The truth is, Hana never worked well for our family. She wasn't good for Patrick while she was alive, and she's certainly not good for him now. That much is as clear as day. Now you'll have to excuse me – I'm supposed to say a few words.' He pointed up to the lectern, then passed his empty glass to a waiter and strode away.

No sooner had Romola exhaled, glad to be rid of his company, than she saw Gretchen weaving towards her through the tightly packed people. The room quietened just as the young woman leaned over and whispered in her ear. 'Sorry about the timing, but Imogen asked me to find you. She's in the foyer waiting. I'd get over there if I were you.'

Chapter Ten
The Third Woman

Romola found Imogen with Patrick in a dark corner of the reception area, where soft leather couches provided rest for the weary. The auction was now in full swing, jeers and whistles sounding as the city's money makers outbid one another. Imogen and Patrick appeared oblivious; they sat hunched together, deep in conversation.

As Romola drew nearer, the look of panic in Patrick's eyes made her want to run in the other direction. But she balanced on the couch beside him, awkwardly waving a hello. It was hot in this corner, and her armpits were clammy with sweat. Ordinarily she would have taken off her jacket, but she was wary of being seen in her camisole top, especially with the likes of Barney floating around.

'Good, you're here,' Imogen said. 'Patrick had just arrived when we saw it.' She held out her phone. 'Rabbit Hole have a third woman – but this one's alive, unfortunately. One of Patrick's exes is saying he … sorry, Patrick, but to put it bluntly, she's saying you abused her.'

Patrick flung himself back onto the couch, shaking his head.

Romola tried to show the right amount of surprise and outrage at Rabbit Hole's reporting while remaining a reassuring presence for her client. But she was feeling nothing but surprise and outrage at her client: she had almost convinced herself that Rabbit Hole had unfairly treated Patrick in its first article, plus he should have told her and Imogen that there was a possibility of a girlfriend coming out of the woodwork.

'When?' Romola asked. 'As in, when are they saying this happened?'

'Years ago, before Sonia.' Imogen held out her phone for Romola to read the story.

Johnny's smug face appeared in the top corner of the screen, above an article claiming that one of Patrick's ex-girlfriends, Matilda 'Tilly' Klein, had come forward to tell the story of their doomed relationship. Romola's mind was working fast as she read, devising the ways in which the story could possibly be wrong, as well as how Rabbit Hole could prove it to be true.

'I never knew what he would be capable of in the heat of an argument-'

Ex-partner makes allegations against Patrick Payne

Tilly Klein was an aspiring model when she met Payne, their tumultuous relationship lasting a little over a year. Klein paints a grim picture of her time with the heir to the Payne fortune. 'Patrick could make me feel like the most special person in the room. He was kind and caring, different from the other men I knew. But it wasn't long before I saw another side to him. He would check my phone and accuse me of flirting, he would want to know where I was 24/7. He even became jealous of my girlfriends.'

Klein claims that Payne also frightened her physically. 'He was intense, and strong. I never knew what he would be capable of in the heat of an argument.' She says that her mental state deteriorated to the point where she saw no way out.

Her saviour came in the form of the glamorous Sonia Kirk, whom Payne met through a mutual friend. When Payne soon afterwards dumped Tilly unceremoniously, she felt as though she had been spared. She was too scared to come forward with her story until she read about the deaths of Hana and Lisbeth. 'I know that Hana would have been suffering in silence. I couldn't sit by anymore – not now that we have lost another beautiful soul.'

Romola finished reading and looked up at Patrick, still slouched on the couch. He searched her face pleadingly. 'You have to believe me that Tilly's a mess. She lies. It's what she does.'

Imogen took her phone back from Romola and tapped its screen. 'You're saying this is a total fabrication?'

Patrick turned up his palms as if to say there was nothing more he could give. 'I swear to you. I didn't know compulsive lying was a real thing until I met Tilly. It's why we broke up. Although I didn't expect her to stoop this low. I thought maybe she still liked me ...'

Despite the apparent sincerity of Patrick's plea, in her mind Romola baulked at the suggestion that Tilly was telling lies. She'd heard that excuse countless times, normally in the face of a heart-wrenching first-person account from her client's victim. She considered it to be both a lazy and an egotistical excuse. It also caused the most distress to victims and gave them the least credit. Romola had never been convinced of any credible motive for lying about abuse – other than in exceptional circumstances, why would a woman who hadn't being abused have a motive to say otherwise, or to put themselves through public cross-examination on the topic? Yet Romola had run this argument on instructions from clients before, and knew she was required to do so unless she absolutely knew them to be guilty, which was rare. The first thing her supervisor at Fowler & Page had taught her was to never ask a client if they're guilty.

Rabbit Hole putting words into Hana and Lisbeth's mouths was one thing, but to be up against a first-person account was another. Romola had thought she would be leaving that world behind her when she moved to Bassett Brown, but here she was, sitting beside a man who was asking her and Imogen to believe that the woman claiming to be his victim was a compulsive liar – and staring up at Romola as though he could tell she didn't buy it.

Imogen threw her phone down on the couch. 'Well, if she's making this all up, we should add her to the claim. She can bloody well pay up.'

Patrick shook his head, obviously confused. 'Sue Tilly too?' He sounded surprised. 'Just let me think about that. This is all happening so fast. I mean, Tilly hasn't had an easy life. I don't know if I want to drag her to court. I'm sure people will work out she's lying, once they hear a little more from her.' He shifted in his seat like he wanted to be anywhere else but here. His chin wobbled, and his eyes were brimming over.

'What's happening here?' said a deep voice. 'Looks like some sort of war council.'

Romola followed Patrick's gaze to the tall figure standing behind her. 'Dad.'

'Everything okay, son?'

Patrick thumbed away his tears. 'Tilly's up to her old tricks. She's talked to Rabbit Hole.'

'For Christ's sake, I thought we'd seen the last of her.' Malcolm's eyes were boring into Imogen. 'You should be able to discredit that girl without much trouble. Add this story to the claim. Get a letter out tonight. Put them on notice that she's not to be trusted as a source.'

The auction was coming to its pinnacle. Two clients were in a bidding war for the most prized painting of the evening: a Brett Whiteley oil of Sydney's Lavender Bay. It had reminded Romola of home. Already the price was in the hundreds of thousands.

Malcolm stepped closer to his son, briefly glancing back to the room filled with his associates and peers, cheering and goading as they backed a bidder. 'You know what Tilly's like, son. It won't come to anything.'

'It's not that. It's this whole bloody situation. Anton called me before. He "respectfully" said he's withdrawing his support for me in the preselection. "Nothing personal," he said, just "bad optics".'

'Stand up, son.' Malcolm offered his hand, and Patrick clung to it firmly as his father pulled him from his seat. Malcolm placed his other hand on his son's shoulder, speaking quietly. 'You must not let this affect you, not here, not now. The lawyers are going to deal with it tonight. They'll make this disappear. And these bastards at Rabbit Hole will not get away with it, I promise you that. Now get yourself home.'

His hand stayed on Patrick's shoulder as he guided him towards the bank of lifts. Romola and Imogen saw the men out, walking with them until they met a black-clad security officer who tapped the lift button and called down for a car. The man was so huge that he intimidated Romola without saying a word. As the lift doors opened, she remembered what Patrick had said about Emir, Hana's brother, working security for him. She met the tall man's eyes, green like Hana's, and the sadness in them reached out to her like a drowning man.

Emir placed a hand on Patrick's other shoulder, so that he was comforted on both sides by the taller men. The lift doors closed without another word being said.

Chapter Eleven
Silence is Golden

Romola arrived early to Louise's apartment, armed with a box of cannoli from the local Italian bakery and a bottle of red. The tiny loft studio was more stylish than functional. Romola, who wasn't convinced it was possible to prepare a dinner for two in its kitchen, was relieved to discover that Louise – not famous for her cooking anyway – had arranged for a delivery from her local Indian restaurant.

They had both missed the television phenomenon that was *The Sopranos* when it originally aired. Since Romola's arrival in Melbourne, they'd been working their way through the series. Before long they became blissfully lost in the life and times of Tony Soprano and his family, eating in front of the television in their tracksuit pants like an old married couple who had long ago given up trying to impress each other.

'I would have made a good mob wife. Keeping the other wives in line.' Louise crunched her cannoli as she spoke, icing sugar wafting onto her lap.

Romola stole a sideways glance at Louise's red hair and freckles. 'You have the personality but not the looks, I'm afraid. The Irish mob might have you, if there is such a thing?'

'Hmph. Why always so practical? Let a girl have her dreams.'

'Dream away. But I think you might be heading in the wrong direction – with Johnny, I mean. He doesn't seem the mobster type.' Romola had intentionally raised Johnny, unable to keep enduring the space that he had created between them in the month since she had met him. She had resolved to discuss Patrick with Louise tonight, before things got any more awkward. In fact, she supposed that Louise and Johnny had joined the dots by now, it being three weeks since the claim was filed. She was surprised that Louise hadn't yet asked her about it. 'How's it going with him, anyway?' Romola asked, testing the waters.

'Well, now that you ask … it's going superbly!' Louise's face lit up. 'I think this could be *it*. He's so different to all the other men I've dated.'

'Different how?' Romola tried to sound nonchalant as she bit into the pastry and oozing custard.

Louise guffawed like the question was ridiculous. 'He's intelligent, for one. All my past boyfriends have, I think you'll agree, been beautiful douchebags. Johnny's not like that. He cares about things. He's always supporting one charity or another, exposing a fraudster, sticking up for the underdog. I really admire that in him. He's strong – noble, even.'

Seriously? thought Romola. Louise had never seemed to particularly admire her when she'd been fighting the good fight for her downtrodden clients. She'd never been called 'noble' before.

'We should catch up again,' Louise said. 'I really want you to meet him properly.'

Romola felt uneasy. The last thing she wanted to do was be stuck in a room with Johnny Wise.

'We need to get out more,' Louise continued. 'He's seriously stressed, worried about his job – you know he's getting *sued* – so he likes to stay low, which has been really nice actually because we've got to know each other more than we would have. We're so comfortable together.'

It was clear to Romola that, somehow, Lou still didn't know who her client was, and also that now was the time to say something. 'About him, Lou –'

But Louise didn't seem to hear. Instead she turned to Romola with a huge grin on her face. 'I actually have some news, Romy. We're thinking of … of moving in together! Isn't that *crazy*?!' She started bouncing up and down on the couch, knees tucked beneath her.

Romola stared at her friend, plate of cannoli balanced on her lap, completely lost for words.

'What do you think of that, Miss Romy?' Louise urged. 'Surprised, I know. But I really think he's the *one*!'

Louise seemed so happy. Happier perhaps than Romola had ever seen her.

'Well? Hello?'

'What do I think?' Romola chose her words carefully. 'I think it's *extremely* early to talk about moving in with this guy, Lou. What do we really know about him? He might be a total psychopath.' She gently put her hand on Louise's forearm, trying to instil some calm into the bundle of energy next to her.

'His lease is about to expire,' Louise explained, 'and as it happens so is mine. The universe is bringing us together. He's not a psycho. And if he does turn out to be one, you can always get me out of there. I trust you, Romy. I know you're not necessarily –' Louise's eyes shifted as she searched for the words '– *looking* for someone. But please, can't you just be excited for me?' She'd now seized the hand Romola had offered, clearly willing her friend to give her blessing.

'I don't know, Lou.' She stared into her friend's puppy-dog eyes, taking in the pouting lower lip. It reminded her of the time Louise had a crush on a surf instructor and begged Romola to start classes with her. Romola had known it was absolutely the wrong thing to do: she was terrified of ocean swimming, and Louise got sunburnt with the windows open. But Louise begged, Romola gave in, and the whole thing ended in tears. She and a red-raw Louise were dumped by both the waves and the surf instructor, then left on the beach absent bikini tops. Back then the tears had ended in hysterical laughter. It had been one of the funniest things they had ever done together.

'If you're absolutely sure, then. I think it's great.'

Louise tugged Romola's hand in closer, pulling her in for a hug. Romola drew away quickly, anxious to rescue the plate of cannoli that was now teetering on her lap. 'Can't you look a bit happier, Romy? Why always so serious?'

How Romola hated being called serious. She configured her face into a broad smile and hugged Louise again, her gut churning with the knowledge that the situation was about to get a whole lot more complicated. She couldn't tell her about Patrick now – not tonight.

After looking through some potential rentals, they turned their attention back to the television. Before Romola knew it, Louise had fallen asleep, her head resting on the arm of the couch. Romola tucked a throw rug around her, smiling fondly at the animal-like snorts emanating from her beautiful friend. *The Sopranos* was still playing, and Romola pondered what Tony Soprano would do in her position. He would probably have Johnny killed, single bullet to the head, and buried in concrete. If only it were so easy.

Chapter Twelve
Little Smiles

The Tuesday of the following week, Romola was seated in the back of a black Mercedes that smelled of leather cleaner and, faintly, women's perfume. Romola was feeling mildly sick as the car made its way onto the crowded three-lane Monash Freeway. There was something about being alone in the back seat of a stranger's car that gripped her with a special kind of terror. It had been that way since her first year of practice, when she had defended a cab driver accused of sexual assault. He'd been frank with her, admitting that he enjoyed breathing in the scent of lone women in the back of his cab, knowing their vulnerability. That sensation was enough for him, he said – he didn't need to touch. His passenger, who had a nervous and flighty disposition, did not perform well before the jury, and he was acquitted. Romola had avoided cabs ever since, and – to Louise's amusement and eternal frustration – hadn't even downloaded the Uber app when it became a thing.

But today Imogen, who was interstate with another client, had insisted Romola use one of the firm's drivers for the forty-minute journey to Deer Park in Melbourne's outer suburbs. It was the type of place that city dwellers like Imogen may have never stepped foot in. 'Practically a ghetto,' she had said.

The car raced along at a steady pace, passing B-doubles, cement trucks and buses slugging their way towards the factories and depots of the outer suburbs. Romola followed the car's path on her phone as they passed by fast-food outlets and superstores, before the driver turned off the Monash and snaked through sad-looking streets of untended weatherboard homes. The Little Smiles Childcare Centre stood on the corner of Wall Street, but the GPS announced that they

had reached their destination when the car pulled up to a street sign
that had been spray-painted to read 'BALLS ST', a large flaccid penis
springing from the letter B.

The centre was painted in faded primary colours and had military-
level security around its perimeter. Romola pressed a rusted intercom
button and was surprised to hear a friendly girl on the other line. The
girl buzzed Romola in without further ado when she announced she
was there to meet Storm, the manager.

She had found Storm through 'thebabygame' blog. An old friend
of Hana's, Storm had commented on what had turned out to be
Hana's final post:

> Hi babygamers. I can't believe how long it's been since
> I posted! Eeek – sorry! To be honest, I'm working
> through some issues, and I have to do that with the
> time, patience, space (and chocolate!) that I need. I will
> be back again posting soon. In the meantime, love to
> you all and thanks for your patience. It is a gift. Be kind
> and be happy, Hana x

Storm had been the first of many of Hana's followers to respond:

> Hey sis. Long time no speak? Don't forget I'm always
> here for a chat if you need. Like old times. Miss you x.

Romola pulled open the heavy door to the centre and was confronted
by the faint odour of soiled nappies, bananas and disinfectant. Frantic
children wailed. A large Pacific Islander woman came to meet her
with a red-eyed, snotty child attached to her hip. Storm had a wide
smile, despite the chaos around her, and a happy energy that relaxed
Romola immediately.

After handing the reluctant child off to a co-worker, Storm led
Romola into a quieter, windowless room where cushions, walkers and
books were scattered across the floor. At the end of the room stood
a line of cots, each holding a blanketed small lump that rose and fell
with the regularity of deep sleep.

'Nap time,' Storm explained. 'Peace.'

Romola checked her watch; it was a bit after 11 a.m. 'Already?'

'The younger ones have to sleep early, otherwise you're screwed. You sit down and I'll get us a cuppa.' She pointed to a child-sized chair, then ducked out of the room.

Romola bent and sat, her knees knocking the underside of the matching tiny table. With Storm gone it dawned on her that she was the only adult in a room full of sleeping babies. What if one woke up? Should she cuddle it? Was that allowed? She was hardly authorised. In fact, she was certain there were regulations about the number of caregivers required to be present in a childcare setting. What if more than one woke? What if they all did?

By the time Storm returned carrying a tray with two steaming cups of tea and a plate of Milk Arrowroot biscuits, Romola was in a state. Storm plonked the tray in front of her. 'Sorry about the bickies. Not very exciting, but it's the only sugar we can get our hands on.' She sat down slowly with creaky knees and a sigh, wiping the sweat from her brow. 'I normally get in at least one cuppa before the first one goes off.' She looked Romola up and down, making her self-conscious about the formality of her suit, her back straight and awkward against the miniature chair. 'You like kids?'

'I don't have a lot of hands-on experience.' Romola gratefully sipped the hot sweet liquid.

'You wait.' Storm smiled softly, her eyes crinkling around the edges. 'I've got three. Piece of cake once you adjust to it.'

She certainly had a maternal wisdom about her, although she must have been around the same age as Romola and Hana.

'Thanks for agreeing to meet me,' Romola said, anxious to start speaking about Hana, aware of the ticking timebombs at the other end of the room.

'I thought you sounded nice, for a lawyer. And now look at you, a woman of colour! You've done well. And so pretty … like you're out of a TV show.'

Romola cleared her throat, embarrassed. 'As I explained on the phone, I'm trying to get an understanding of what Hana was like. It seems from your posts that you and she were quite good friends?'

Storm gulped down the steaming tea as if it were room temperature. 'We met at TAFE years ago, both of us studying early childhood education. We were totally different, like chalk and cheese, but something clicked. I always said she was like the little sister I never had, even though she was actually a couple months older than me.'

Romola fished out her notebook. 'What was she like back then?'

'Hana was the best. She was pretty, kind – a real nurturing type, you know? She had, like, an aura about her. One of those people all the kids wanted to be around.' Storm watched the babies, a smile on her face as she remembered her friend. 'Hana always looked after herself real nice. I used to tease her, because she was so beautiful but she was always getting one treatment or another, manicures, lasers, tans, injections, this or that. "You look so good already," I would say, "you may as well give your money to me, and I'll spend it on something better like booze and chocolates!" Didn't change her one bit, though. I don't think she believed me.'

'Back then, did you ever feel like she might have bigger problems?'

Storm rubbed her tired eyes, then moved her hand over her face, massaging her cheekbones. 'I never really thought about it like that. Not until now, with what's happened. I always knew she was a bit – how would you say – lost. She didn't have her mum, and her dad was old school, very traditional, very strict before he died. Her brother was a serious guy – quiet as a mouse – but they were close. She was the light in those men's lives. A lot of pressure on her, I always thought, but … never so bad that she would do this.' Tears had started to fall down Storm's face, which had blotched red. She wiped them away roughly with the base of her palm.

'What about drugs? Did you ever know her to take them?'

'Never. She always said no to anything like that. Booze … well, that was another thing. We used to love to go out on the town in our day.' She spoke as if at twenty-eight she were already middle-aged, her partying days long behind her.

'Did you know Patrick?'

'I met him once. She invited me over to his place for dinner, and she probably tried a bit too hard that night – she was stressed out of her head, I could tell. Everything was so different from where we came from. Patrick wasn't what I was expecting, though. He was okay. Quiet. With all that money I thought he'd be a bit of a prick, you know?' She laughed half-heartedly.

'I got the impression from your comments online that you weren't seeing much of Hana anymore?'

'We used to catch up every couple of weeks for a drink and a gossip. At first I liked hearing her stories about Patrick and that woman Sonia. But once Hana and Patrick got together, it was different. She'd talk about Max till the cows came home – she loved that boy. But other than that she left the talking to me, which I'm pretty good at. Then she started making excuses not to meet, and ... you know how it is. I got busy with the kids, it stopped being a regular thing.' Storm threw her head back as she finished her tea, then peered down into the warm mug cradled in her hands. 'She did message me recently, though. She texted me the week before it happened. Said she needed to talk to me about something, and sorry for not getting in touch sooner. We were going to have coffee on the Tuesday. I was looking forward to it ... but then on the Sunday night, I saw the news. It was such a shock to see her pretty face on the screen. I cried like a banshee. My partner thought I was mad.'

On cue, a baby started the hiccupping beginnings of a full-blown cry.

Hands on knees, Storm hauled herself up from the low chair. 'And it starts. Perfect timing as always. Sorry we'll have to cut this short. Could you call me if you have more questions?'

'Sure,' said Romola, also standing. 'Just quickly, though, did you have any idea what Hana wanted to talk to you about?'

Storm picked up the baby and began rocking it to-and-fro, a tiny boat in her arms. The crying stopped at once. 'No idea, sorry,' she said quietly. 'I'm guessing it had to be something important, but I couldn't say what. I thought perhaps she was breaking it off with him.'

Another baby started up. Storm bent to place her hand on its back, patting firmly as she continued to bounce the first. She began murmuring a lullaby in a beautiful deep voice.

'Thanks,' Romola whispered, 'I'll be in touch if I think of anything else.' She gathered her bags. 'I'll let myself out.' She headed to the door, anticipating the clean fresh air outside.

More babies cried out, and Storm's lullaby grew louder, more stirring than restful. Romola didn't look back.

Chapter Thirteen
The Club

When Patrick had said he would be at 'The Club' all afternoon, she had imagined velvet lounges and martinis. But the driver had dropped her instead at a turn-of-the-century red-brick clubhouse overlooking the Yarra River, surrounded by terraced lawn tennis courts. Players sauntered around in their whites as if it were 1920s England, while boys and men in beige chino shorts and polos handed them towels and cold water.

She found a seat in the near empty grandstand, where ivy grew on the walls behind her and she could look across the courts to the muddy Yarra and the city beyond. It was midafternoon, and the sun had chosen to make an appearance, the skyline glistening. She removed her stilettos and stretched her legs, the air clean and fresh, a welcome change from the car's suffocating heating.

Patrick was playing a game on the court before her. He seemed at home in his tennis whites, moving effortlessly across the lawn. She didn't notice his opponent until she heard the deep voice calling the score between points. Malcolm Payne, with his long white legs sticking out from underneath knee-length white shorts, was covering the court like a praying mantis. Dressed in a knitted vest over a polo top, he moved with remarkable speed, almost matching his son's depth of movement by virtue of the length of his arm span.

Patrick lifted an arm to Romola in greeting but made no move to finish the game, which was in the balance. Neither man was giving an inch, nor speaking to the other beyond Malcolm's blunt declarations of the score. There was an occasional grunt of effort, and every now and then Patrick clapped his racquet against his hand in acknowledgement of a good shot by his father, but Malcolm bestowed no such compliments – he nodded to himself when he won a point and turned his back when he conceded one.

It was five–four, Patrick's way, when Malcolm pulled up short, reaching for his side before attempting a stretch with a wince. Patrick jogged to the net. 'You all right, Dad?'

Malcolm was leaning over, hands on knees. 'Give me a minute. I'll be okay.' He stood up, still holding his side, before extending his back in the other direction and wiping his brow with a towel offered by a ball boy. 'Let's press on.'

'If you're sure.' Patrick grabbed a water bottle. 'Don't push yourself.'

Malcolm swatted away the comment, treading slowly back to the baseline. As clear as day, Romola saw the smirk on his face.

Four points later, Malcolm served out the game, Patrick having gone gently on his old man. The match was again for the taking.

'He totally faked that.'

Romola jumped, not having noticed that she had company. The boy had been slouched two rows down, but when he'd spoken he had shuffled up in his seat, revealing a round head and shoulders bouncing with repressed laughter. He turned around and smiled at her: Patrick's son, Max. The dimpled face, and the dark eyes, serious even through laughter, were exactly like they were in the photos. 'That's my dad,' he said, pointing to Patrick, and then Malcolm, 'and that one's my granddad.'

'They're good players,' she said, as Max continued to regard her.

He put his iPad down. 'You like Pokémon?'

'Not really.'

'Lego?'

'Not so much.'

'Hmm. You should give it a go.'

She checked the time on her phone. 'Aren't you supposed to be at school?'

'I felt sick this morning, so Dad said not to worry about it.'

'So are you sick?'

'Yeah – course I am.' He scrunched up his mouth and peered at Romola sideways.

'I remember when I was at school, sometimes I would have a rest day.' She did not meet his eye as she spoke. 'I convinced my parents I needed some time to myself, to rest. In fact, a couple of kids at my school were really awful to me. But I didn't want to say that, of course.'

He slowly nodded. 'Me too.' Something about Max made him seem a lot older than his eight years. 'My family's sort of famous. Some kids think that's funny.' His voice rose with the injustice of it all.

'That sucks,' said Romola honestly.

'Yeah.' He gave her another smile.

'Max!' She wasn't sure which of the men had spotted them first, but it was Malcolm who called out, standing at the baseline, hands on hips as he peered up at them.

Patrick jogged up to his father's end of the court. 'Okay there, Max?' he called.

'Chill out, Dad.' Max shrugged innocently. 'We're just talking.'

'It's all right,' Romola called to the men, 'you two finish playing, I can keep an eye on him.'

Max raised an eyebrow at her as if to say he was old enough to look after himself.

Malcolm tucked his racquet under his arm. 'No. I'm done.'

The men were thrown towels, which they draped around their necks, and joined Romola and the boy in the stands. Patrick ruffled his son's hair. 'Hope you weren't talking Romola's ear off there, Max? He has a tendency to do that.'

'Dad. Please.' Max rolled his eyes. 'Why are you always so embarrassing?'

Malcolm led them inside the clubhouse to a corner table overlooking the courts. The staff brought him a mineral water with ice and lemon. He crunched the ice audibly through closed lips, his breath coming loudly through his nose. He glanced from Max to Patrick, nudging his head slightly to signal to Patrick that the boy should be elsewhere.

'You can go on your iPad if you want, mate,' said Patrick.

'Yesss!' Max pumped his fist, then skipped to the furthest corner from the adults, clutching his headphones and iPad, in its faded Albert Einstein cover.

They sat in silence for a moment. There was something between the two men that Romola couldn't quite identify, something viscous – love, hatred, competition, ambition? She felt less like a lawyer sitting with new clients and more like a documentary filmmaker sitting among an unfamiliar species.

She could now see more plainly the resemblance between father and son. They both had sharp features and deep grey eyes, but Patrick's had a softness to them that Romola thought must have come from his mother. She had been an Italian beauty, which accounted for Patrick's slightly olive skin and fuller mouth. Malcolm, on the other hand, was a cardboard cut-out of a man, all triangles and squares – a five-year-old could have drawn a good resemblance.

He turned to Romola. 'So, how are you progressing?'

She wouldn't be caught out again by Malcolm's style of questioning. She understood now: it was all a confidence game with him. 'It's going well.' She pulled a pile of papers from her bag and placed them in front of her. 'I wanted to see Patrick to discuss our initial formulation of loss. To look at the impact of the articles to date.' She sat back, waiting to see if Malcolm would leave. She had assumed she would only meet with Patrick, but it was obvious that Malcolm was going nowhere, feet firmly planted and long legs spread wide.

'Show us what you have then.' He pointed at the pile.

She had asked Gretchen to gather all the news stories that referenced either the Rabbit Hole story or the allegations that had been made by Rabbit Hole about Patrick. The stack of paper was an inch thick. Short stories about Patrick had appeared in print and online news websites all over the country, and there were also deeper analyses of the situation: opinion pieces about the impact of concentrated wealth, background pieces on the Paynes, and discussions of what had led to Patrick's downfall. Was it the breakdown of his marriage or the early death of his mother, or was he simply a bad, misogynist, egg?

Romola walked Patrick and Malcolm through some of the more damaging articles, but she didn't need to show them the comments left on Patrick's social media sites. Those were filled with foul abuse. She also didn't need to remind father and son of the fall in share price of Payne Corp since the Rabbit Hole articles had appeared almost six weeks earlier.

Malcolm nodded as he listened, but Patrick stared out at a game being played on the court below. Nothing seemed to register with him.

'The party's dropped him too now,' Malcolm said. 'Have you told her about that, Pat?'

Patrick's jaw tightened, though he continued watching the game. 'I'm sure she would have found out soon enough – they're putting out a media release later today.'

'What's happened?' Romola shifted her focus from Patrick to Malcolm, willing at least one of them to explain.

'I've been told to withdraw my preselection,' said Patrick. 'Apparently I'm damaged goods. Too risky.'

Malcolm stood up to pace back and forth in front of the window, his voice growing louder as he grew more agitated. 'What sort of thanks is that? Our family has said nothing, simply handed over donations for years, while that party has been putting up hacks, simpletons and bigots. And now my son isn't good enough? Never in my life have we received this sort of treatment. You can put that in your statement of loss.' He now paused to stand perfectly still, towering over the table. 'And what about the other girl?'

'Sorry?' Romola asked.

'The other girl? Lisbeth. It seems to me that all your focus has been on Hana. What about Lisbeth? I understand that no one has even spoken to her parents. You did tell her, Pat?'

Romola again looked from Patrick to Malcolm, confused.

'Oh for Christ's sake, son.' Malcolm no longer sounded angry – he seemed saddened by his son's inability to deal with the situation at hand. He turned to Romola. 'It's very important that you speak with Lisbeth's parents. They are going to support us. They're even happy to testify, to say that Patrick had nothing to do with her death.'

'Really?' Romola couldn't hide her surprise.

'Patrick obviously hasn't mentioned that I know them socially.'

Patrick turned from the window and locked eyes with his father for a long moment, the two communicating in a language Romola didn't yet understand. She thought Patrick was on the verge of saying something, but instead he exhaled loudly, blowing away the unspoken words.

Malcolm came to stand behind his son and tenderly placed a hand on Patrick's shoulder. A dark cloud moved over the sun, turning the bright warm room to grey, like a technicolour film reverting to black and white. 'You're a good man, son. Don't you let them make you believe otherwise.'

*

A little over an hour later, Romola walked into Bassett Brown and was happily shocked to find a plateful of chocolate brownies sitting on her office chair. Victoria gave her a smile from her nearby desk. The brownies were Romola's favourite but were normally snapped up early in the day by the other secretaries; her heart lifted a smidgen to think that Victoria had noticed. She poked one into her mouth with a smile.

'You've decided to grace us with your presence then.' Imogen appeared in the doorway, her arms crossed and jaw clenched at the sight of her returned associate with her mouth stuffed full.

'Imogen.' Romola tried to swallow, but it took some time to wrest control of the thick sticky mess in her mouth. For an awkward moment there was little she could do but chew as Imogen waited. 'I thought you were interstate?'

'It was a morning meeting. I was back by three. Where have you been?'

'I told you how I was going out to meet Hana's friend Storm …? I'll think she'd be worth speaking to again. And then I met with Patrick to discuss his formulation of loss. Turns out Malcolm was there too and –'

'Malcolm was there?' Imogen cut in, her eyes wide.

'He was. And he –'

'Just you, Patrick and Malcolm?' She blinked quickly in disbelief. 'You should have got me on the phone straight away.' She was already checking her phone, as if she expected to find a message from Malcolm letting her know how Romola had cocked it up. 'While you were out gallivanting, we've been given a first directions date by the court. It's this fucking Friday. You need to be on the phone to counsel, make sure they have everything they need. Tell them we've got Justice Debenham. Clusterfuck.' Imogen started to stride out.

It had been almost a month since the claim was filed, and Rabbit Hole had filed its defence on time, relying as expected on the defences of truth and reasonableness. The defence was an annoyingly thorough document, leaving little room for interlocutory arguments about the adequacy of the defendants' pleas. Not that Bassett Brown had been asked to take technical points – Malcolm's standing instruction was to press for an urgent trial.

The thought of Malcolm reminded Romola of what he had said earlier. 'Malcolm was quite helpful today, you know,' she called to Imogen.

The woman turned. 'How so?'

'He knows Lisbeth's parents. He says they'll testify for us.'

'Is that so.' Imogen flipped her phone over and over in her hand. 'Make a time for us to meet asap. We're going to need all the help we can get.'

Chapter Fourteen
Grief

'I should warn you, I'm not good with emotions,' Imogen said matter-of-factly as she rapped on the front door of a graceful California bungalow two days later, on the eve of the first directions hearing. The sound of footsteps came almost immediately, then a porch light switched on. The door opened before Romola had the chance to register what Imogen had said or what it might mean for their meeting with Lisbeth Janssen's grieving parents.

A slender lady opened the door, her long grey hair held back in a loose low ponytail. She wore no make-up, the lines on her face revealing a sadness that could not have been concealed anyway. Severe but strikingly beautiful, she reminded Romola of a Nordic queen. 'I'm Carol,' she said softly, before gently taking their hands between her own and then motioning for them to follow her inside.

It was late in the afternoon, and the sky had turned a deep grey as both evening and rain announced their arrival. The wide hallway was lit by stained-glass lamps that threw the colour of rust over deep-green walls dotted with picture frames. The house smelled of the first scent of a home-cooked meal, onions and garlic sweating in a pan. A large fluffy white cat rushed to greet them, sliding between Romola's legs as they entered a spacious living room. She'd known there would be a cat as soon as she walked across the threshold, the familiar scratch already teasing the back of her throat and nose.

Lisbeth's father, Piers, stood awaiting their arrival, his hands set deep in his corduroy pockets as he stared into the flames of a wood combustion heater. The timber mantelpiece held an assortment of silver and brass photo frames. Most of the images were of three remarkably similar girls: golden hair, wide-set blue eyes, broad grins.

There were family portraits when the girls were toddlers, and school photos from prep to graduation. At the centre of the mantel stood a photo of Lisbeth alone in a rowboat, her ponytail tousled, face bright with effort and arms raised in victory.

'Let me turn the stove off before we start,' said Carol. 'Can I get you ladies a drink? Tea, coffee, wine?'

'I'll be fine,' said Imogen.

'Water would be great,' said Romola, before letting out a sneeze that could no longer be contained. Her eyes were itchy and beginning to run. Imogen frowned at her with something like disappointment.

'Please, take a seat,' said Piers.

Imogen and Romola sat on a dark brown chesterfield facing the fire. An antique grandfather clock stood against the wall to their right, and its ticking drew almost all of Romola's attention, although she was conscious that the rain had begun to fall and the fire was crackling.

After what seemed an age, Carol returned with a glass of water. 'Oh dear.' She handed it to Romola. 'Allergies?'

Romola realised her symptoms were plain to the two doctors. She'd read about the Janssens in preparation for today: they were neurologists who ran the Fournier Stroke Institute. It had been founded decades earlier by the wealthy husband of the late Ruth Fournier, who had died of a stroke aged forty-eight.

Carol assessed Romola with motherly concern. 'Stay here and I'll get you an antihistamine.'

After Romola and Imogen spent another agonising few moments alone with the silent and steadfast Piers, Carol returned with a small tablet and two large glasses of red wine. 'Pixie was Lisbeth's cat. We can't believe she's still with us. She must be over a hundred in cat years.'

'She's lovely,' Romola offered with another sneeze, louder than the first. She gratefully gulped down the antihistamine with a swig of water.

Carol passed one wineglass to Piers and kept the other for herself. She sat down and savoured a long sip, briefly closing her eyes.

'Thank you for seeing us today,' Imogen said. 'I'm sorry for your loss. Your daughters are – sorry, I mean they *were* – sorry, I mean to say they *are* very beautiful. Sorry.' Imogen hung her head briefly.

Romola had never seen Imogen fumble over her words, except in anger when the woman spat out expletives at too great a speed. She felt uncomfortable seeing her boss out of her depth and wondered how bad it would have to get before she stepped in. She steeled herself, knowing this was one situation where Imogen could throw to her at any moment.

Piers walked over to a photo of all three of his daughters, taken in their teens, long hair brushed smooth over their shoulders beneath paper Christmas-cracker hats, arms around each other. 'Lisbeth was our middle child,' he said. 'Our eldest is Peta.' He pointed to the tallest of the three, the one who Romola would have judged the most serious, her hair a darker honey shade of blonde and her nose more prominent, her smiles for the camera toothless and lacking the abandon shown by her younger sisters. 'And our youngest is Lara. There's almost exactly two years between each of them.' Lara had the broadest grin, the bluest eyes and a curl to her hair. She was holding tight to Lisbeth, giving the peace symbol with her free hand.

'Are they both still in Melbourne?' asked Imogen.

'Not our Peta,' Piers said with pride. 'She's in Washington, DC. Married an American. She's a surgeon, thoracic. Extremely successful.'

Carol stared at the floor.

'And Lara?' asked Imogen.

The grandfather clock ticked away. Piers stared back into the flames. Romola could have sworn she saw Carol flinch. 'She lives with us,' the woman said quickly, after taking a long sip of wine. 'She's still finding her way. She and Beth were the closest of the three.'

'Turning to the matter at hand,' cut in Piers, 'you wanted to hear about Lisbeth and Patrick?'

'Malcolm said you would be happy to talk to us,' said Imogen.

'I'm not sure "happy" is the right word,' Piers muttered as he finally sat down in a well-worn leather recliner, a book sitting open on its arm. His regular chair, Romola supposed.

Carol gave him the settling look of a long-term partner.

'Sorry about my poor choice of words,' Imogen said awkwardly. 'Malcolm thought you would be prepared to talk to us – that you might disagree with what's being reported about Patrick and Lisbeth's relationship.'

'Yes,' said Carol, before her husband could speak, 'we do disagree. I've been heartbroken to hear this has happened to him again. The poor boy – or man now, I suppose. I still think of him as he was in high school. He accompanied Beth to her year 12 formal. It was their first proper date.' Carol stood up and moved to a bookcase at the rear of the room. Crouching down, she pulled out a heavy burgundy photo album, kneeling as she flicked through its pages. 'Here it is.' She stood and approached them with the open album. Teenage Patrick stared out, his gap-tooth smile unchanged despite the silver braces on his teeth. His hair was gelled like that of a 1950s movie star. He wore rimless glasses, and Romola wondered if he now wore contacts or had had laser surgery. He emanated a composed confidence, a Ferris Bueller type of nerdy charisma, with no sign of his present-day intensity and sadness. He held his left arm around Lisbeth, who stood slightly slouched – she was a little taller than him – in a silk crimson slip dress, her blonde hair down and wavy. Red lipstick showed off her white teeth and aqua eyes. She looked happy. Romola would have guessed she was having the best night of her life.

'They were together for a couple of years after this?' Imogen asked.

'This photo was taken when they were seventeen,' said Carol. 'They split up when Beth was nineteen, not long after her birthday.'

'Did you know Patrick beforehand? Malcolm said you were family friends?'

'I wouldn't go that far,' said Piers. 'We'd met Malcolm at some of our work functions for the Institute, but we didn't socialise outside of that. I hadn't met Patrick before he and Beth started seeing each other.'

'And what did you make of him?'

Piers was silent, gritting his teeth. The clock's rhythm drew Romola's attention once more. There was a pressure deep within her nose as she tried to suppress a third sneeze.

'I've found it hard to like anyone who's dated my girls. It's difficult not to still think of them as my three little fairies running around the garden.' He cleared his throat again.

'Well, *I* liked Patrick,' Carol said decisively. 'He was always polite. He liked to talk. To me it felt as if he wanted company – or family, I should say. He seemed to enjoy being part of the family, don't you think, Piers?'

Her husband shrugged.

'He completely fell for our Beth,' Carol added.

'Beth was living with you at that stage?' Imogen asked.

'Yes. At first Patrick spent a lot of time here with us too. I had to almost double the amount of food I cooked. But as time went on, Beth spent more time at the Paynes'. I remember thinking it was such a change, because initially they seemed to want to spend all day here. I assumed it was because Patrick had the run of the place. They could do as they pleased unsupervised, if you know what I mean. They were at that age when you couldn't stop them.' She shot a cautious look at her husband, but he didn't interrupt. 'Towards the end of their relationship, we weren't seeing very much of her at all. It was probably terribly naïve of me, but I thought she was off enjoying the high life! People think we're wealthy because we're both doctors, but research isn't as well paid as other areas. We'd never been exposed to that type of wealth. I thought she was in good hands. It was only after they broke up that we found out she'd stopped going to university. She was out drinking a lot. I'd thought she was halfway through a law degree, and it turned out she'd only lasted a few months.'

Carol's eyes seemed to be drawn to Romola. Perhaps she was wondering if Lisbeth would have been sitting like her, interviewing clients, if only things had turned out differently.

'I remember having a conversation with Patrick after they'd broken up. It was when she was ill – once we all knew about her addiction. I bumped into him while I was out at dinner. He seemed genuinely concerned and insisted that he hadn't known she had quit university either. He said he was sorry, but it was more like he was sorry for the situation. Not that he was responsible for anything. I would have had every reason to blame him, but no … I believed him. And in those days it was so difficult to know who to believe, who to trust. But I did my best.' She shrugged apologetically, clutching her wineglass in her lap.

'Carol – these people are here to learn about Patrick. There's no point going over what you did or didn't believe,' Piers said, shifting in his seat. 'The outcome won't change.'

She stared into the distance, undeterred. 'The thing is, Beth was the one I worried about the least. She was always so capable, so composed. Things fell in her lap. Peta was always so driven that I worried what would happen if she failed. And Lara ... dear Lara. Where to start? She was always emotional, very easily led astray. Whereas my Beth, she was the mother hen looking after everyone else.' Carol closed her eyes again and sipped her wine without opening them. Clearly she was spent.

Imogen spoke tentatively. 'You said she had addiction issues – she got involved in drugs?'

Piers glanced at his wife, who with pursed lips shook her head, unable to continue. 'Yes,' he said in a low voice. 'I don't know if you've had much experience with ice, but it's a terrible thing. In a brief moment of clarity she once told me that some schoolfriends on the fashion scene had introduced her to it. But who knows? By that point it was hard to get sense out of her.'

'It was after Patrick then,' said Imogen.

'To the best of my knowledge, yes,' said Piers. 'It was as though she was possessed – she simply wasn't our Beth. And when she was clean she was ... just empty. We tried. We really tried. We knew people who ran the best clinics – the longest she stayed was a week. We needed her to want to sober up – and the fact is, she never reached that point. By the time we tried ... we'd already lost her!' His voice cracked. He let out a guttural cry and began to sob loudly.

Imogen sat straight backed and utterly still. She stared at Piers as though he had emptied the contents of his stomach into the middle of the room. Carol carefully placed her wine down, walked over to her husband, moved the book from the arm of his chair – folding the corner of a page to keep his place – and rested next to him. She rubbed his back and ignored the tears that ran from her own eyes.

Romola felt that she might burst into tears as well, her itchy eyes beginning to brim. She knew that grief could come suddenly and overwhelmingly, as it sometimes did for her. But she hadn't lost a daughter, and such outbursts weren't as acceptable for the elderly dead, especially not when one was attempting to appear a strong-minded lawyer. She regained her composure and, seeing that Imogen was speechless, reached for something useful to say. 'You know, it's almost impossible to help someone once they've reached that point. I'm sure there's nothing that could have been done. We honestly can't thank you enough for speaking to us.'

The sobs slowly subsided, a log in the fire sparked and popped, and the room fell quiet, the regular tick of the grandfather clock returning like a welcome old friend.

They all jumped in their seats when, a moment later, the front door opened and closed with a loud bang. Then came the jangle of keys thrown onto a table. Irregular footsteps thumped up the hall.

'Oh lord, not now,' muttered Piers. He and Carol exchanged a look somewhere between terror and shame.

In walked a girl who bore a passing resemblance to the youngest daughter in the photographs, Lara. Her hair was no longer blonde and curly but a lilac-grey and shocked straight, her previously bronzed skin pockmarked beneath a heavy layer of foundation. Black liner was smudged under her eyes as if applied by a kindergartner. She wore leggings and an oversized hoodie, which she began pulling off with great clumsy effort as she swayed to-and-fro across the room. 'God, it's hot in here, Mummy,' came her muffled voice. When her head eventually popped out, she was clearly affronted by the sight of the two strangers sitting awkwardly on her parents' couch. 'Who are *they*?' she asked casually as she began taking off her boots, again with the type of exertion not warranted by the task at hand.

'Nothing to worry about, darling,' said Carol. 'Just some work people. We were finishing up, actually.'

Lara stopped mid-action, one boot on, one boot off, obviously sensing something wasn't right. She began to fidget. Romola had seen that look many times before: the look of a client who had been put in the watch house – who was still off their face, outraged and unpredictable as hell.

Romola stood up and beckoned for Imogen, who sat wide-eyed and motionless, to do the same. 'Your mother's right,' said Romola, 'we were just leaving.'

'Have you been crying, Daddy? And Mummy?' Lara ran up to her mum and started to paw at her face, her dirty nails marring the pristine landscape of Carol's complexion. 'What have you been talking to my parents about? Who are you?' She started towards Imogen, who had turned white and was holding a lever arch folder of documents in front of her for protection.

Carol seized Lara's hand in an effort calm her, but the young woman had caught sight of the client label on the side of the folder. 'Patrick fucking Payne?! You work for Patrick Payne?' She pointed at her dumbstruck parents. 'You've been helping them? Oh my god, Mummy, what are you doing? You have no idea what you're doing!'

'Sweetie, it's fine. It's nothing really. They only wanted to have a chat about Beth and Patrick.'

'*You* wouldn't even know the half of what happened with Beth and Patrick,' Lara spat at her crestfallen mother. 'Both of you are living in some sort of fucking dream world. That family is evil! He killed her. He killed my sister.'

With that, Lara began following Romola and Imogen down the hallway, one boot held above her head, the other still on her foot. Carol and Piers trailed behind, offering helpless apologies. The time for niceties having passed, Romola pushed Imogen towards the front door.

Rain was belting down, and Imogen's driver flashed his lights as they emerged, before he raced out of the car with an umbrella, intent on ushering them to the safety of the back seat. Water splashed up Romola's ankles as she ran to the car, disregarding the umbrella offered by the driver, conscious of Lara's frenzied screaming from the bungalow's verandah – not even words now, just indecipherable cries. Imogen reached the car first, and Romola climbed in after her. The noise of Lara's sobs immediately concealed by the jazz playing from Bose speakers and the hum of the heater. The click of the locks safely sealed them in.

As the car sped off, Lara Janssen still raged, silhouetted against the orange glow of the hallway, her lone boot thrown to the wet footpath. Neighbours switched on lights and pulled curtains aside to bear witness to the scene playing out in their otherwise quiet street.

Carol and Piers came up from behind to take their youngest daughter in their arms, not prepared to lose her as well.

*

'That was intense,' said Imogen as they crossed the river, the comfort of the city lights now within reach, the car crawling to a halt in heavy traffic. She hadn't spoken for the first part of their journey, staring out the window, clutching her handbag. Her face was unreadable in the dark of the back seat. She turned to Romola. 'I did say I wasn't very good with emotions. That's just not my thing. I don't know what to say. Let alone dealing with a crazy fucking drug addict attacking me.'

'Poor Carol and Piers,' said Romola. 'I like them.'

'Me too. I hadn't appreciated they've effectively lost two daughters.'

'No. Me neither.'

'On the positive side,' Imogen continued, 'if Lara is Rabbit Hole's only source, they're pretty much screwed.'

'I suppose that's true. I can't see her holding up in front of a jury.'

Imogen looked out the window again. 'Thanks for before. How you stepped in. I was ... pretty fucking hopeless.'

'This may not necessarily be a good thing, but I have a lot of experience dealing with drug-affected individuals. And people who are grieving. They tend to go hand in hand.'

'Well. Good job. I think we might work nicely together, you and me.' Imogen smiled at Romola – a proper, genuine, grateful smile.

For a moment Romola forgot the fog of mourning that had hung over the Janssen household and the way it reminded her of her own improperly formed but ever-present sadness. She forgot the fright of the chase and the rain that had soaked through her jacket as she escaped a tortured daughter and sister. And she felt just a little warmer inside.

Chapter Fifteen
Seeking Directions

The grand courtroom was a cavernous space, with detailed fretwork on its high ceilings and towering arched windows. Its glossy wooden surfaces smelled of polish, and the rain that had been carried in on umbrellas and suited shoulders made the air smell of wet wool and morning coffees.

'I don't know why they bothered coming,' Imogen whispered, glaring at the bevy of journalists in the back rows. 'It's not as if anything interesting is going to happen. They can't have been expecting to see Patrick here, surely.'

Patrick had travelled to Sydney for the day. He claimed to be attending to some business, but Romola suspected he'd simply had enough of the paparazzi parked outside his house.

The Slug and the Hare were seated at the barrister's bench, the Slug sitting back comfortably, one hand resting on his belly while the other held a paper he was reading. The Hare, on the other hand, was hunched over, his face inches from a pile of legal authorities that he was marking with highlighter with great flair.

Imogen and Romola sat side by side, opposite the Slug and the Hare, their backs to the judge's bench. Romola was unaccustomed to this arrangement – in Sydney the solicitors sat facing the judge, perfectly positioned to assess whether things were going well; to witness every headshake or drooping eyelid from the presiding officer. Imogen hadn't stopped fidgeting since they had taken their seats, crossing and uncrossing her legs, checking her phone, frowning at the media pack.

Romola glanced across at their opposition. Finnigan Price, Rabbit Hole's solicitor, had a Nutty Professor air about him, with unkempt white hair, a bold stripe in his shirt, purple-framed glasses and a floral bow tie. He met her gaze with an unsettling smirk, like he knew something she didn't.

The barrister whom Rabbit Hole had briefed was more subdued. Annette Esposito was short and resolute, wearing a crew cut and a loose pinstriped pantsuit. She had dark round eyes and heavy brows, from under which she stared unflinchingly across the bar table to Romola and Imogen. Within minutes she had cemented her place in the menagerie in Romola's mind: the Bulldog.

Silence fell at the three loud knocks followed by the call to 'All Stand!'

Justice Debenham scurried in from a small door in the back corner of the courtroom and stood while everyone bowed to him. Romola knew of Justice Lew Debenham both from reading his judgments and, more helpfully, the background Cliffy had offered once she told him of the judge's allocation to Patrick's case. He was one of the most senior justices of the Supreme Court. In his final year before compulsory retirement he was clearly throwing caution to the wind, delivering judgments that raised the ire of the legal profession. For years his colleagues had nicknamed him 'the Diva'. Romola had heard Imogen joke that the Diva always enjoyed taking his seat at the bench because, standing at only five feet five inches in shoes, he spent the rest of his life looking up to other people. Romola, who was five foot three in heels and no stranger to tactless jokes about height, was trying her best to reserve her assessment of Justice Debenham until after she had seen him in action.

When the judge eased onto his seat, Romola positioned herself almost sideways in her chair, so she was able to turn around and see the man in control of her client's fate, but also the self-satisfied smiles of the Slug and the Hare as counsel announced their appearances. They knew very well that the country's media would be reporting every word from their mouths today. Both of them had worn their best suits and arrived at the courthouse in time to walk purposefully past the media pack, their embroidered red-and-blue damask bags containing robes that would never be needed for the directions hearing.

'Quite a turnout.' The judge nodded in the Slug's direction. 'Mr Desmond, I believe we have a defamation claim.'

The Slug stood slowly before he leaned forward on his lectern to address the judge. 'Indeed, your Honour.' He paused a moment for effect. 'My client, Mr Patrick Payne, has been most egregiously defamed by the defendants. And continues to be, I might add. Your Honour will no doubt be aware of my client's standing in the community. It's astounding – I would go so far as to say almost without precedent – that he should be defamed to this degree.'

The Bulldog got to her feet. 'Your Honour, I don't mean to make a habit of interrupting my friend so early in the piece, but is this really necessary? This is a first directions hearing. However "egregious" the defamation might have been, which is denied, it's none of your concern at the moment.'

'Please,' the Slug interrupted, 'your Honour has been given carriage of this matter. Some initial understanding of the background, and of the frankly shocking context to this claim, is only going to assist. This is no ordinary defamation case.'

The Bulldog rolled her eyes and muttered, 'Give me a break.'

The Slug let out a loud snort somewhere between a cough, a laugh and an indecipherable insult. The courtroom gallery murmured.

Justice Debenham, who had been reading a document in front of him, removed his glasses. 'Counsel, I do not need, nor do I want, chapter and verse on Mr Payne and the nature of the alleged defamation. I am simply not interested today. That's not to say I won't be interested at some point, but for today's purposes it's more than unnecessary, it's unhelpful. I would ask you to confine yourself to what is essential in terms of trial preparation. I assume – from what you have said, Mr Desmond – that your client will be looking to work towards the earliest possible trial date …'

Imogen nodded furiously, facing the barristers' bench.

'Yes,' said the Slug, 'there are grounds for a very urgent trial. My client is anxious that the continuing damage to his reputation cease and be remedied.'

But the judge hadn't finished his train of thought. 'And settlement discussions have failed?'

The Slug responded with some trepidation. 'There have been no formal discussions, your Honour.'

Justice Debenham leaned in, both palms on the bench, looking from the barristers to the instructing solicitors before fixing his eyes on the Slug. 'You're telling me, Mr Desmond, that you have come to my courtroom today, asking that we go to trial urgently, that we use up valuable court resources and cause both parties to incur no doubt hundreds of thousands, possibly millions of dollars on legal costs, when not even a single attempt has been made to settle this through without prejudice discussions? I find that almost inconceivable. It is most definitely unacceptable.'

'I understand that settlement discussions are not something the defendants are willing to pursue. A concerns notice was served, after all, to no avail.' The Slug waved with disdain towards the defendants' side of the bar table.

Justice Debenham swung his gaze to the Bulldog. 'Ms Esposito?'

As she stood to address the judge, Finnigan Price jumped up and whispered urgently in her ear. 'Your Honour,' she said, 'I am told that my clients are perfectly happy to engage in settlement discussions, and suggest a mediation is appropriate in this instance. Indeed, had the plaintiff waited the required period after issuing his concerns notice before bringing these proceedings, we might have been in a position to have already conducted one.'

'Un-fucking-believable,' Imogen muttered under her breath, then whispered a little louder so that the Slug and the Hare could hear her. 'They were the ones who outright refused any kind of apology.' She started furiously poking away at her phone, presumably texting Patrick for instructions on the prospect of a mediation.

Justice Debenham swung his head back to face the Slug. 'What is your client's position, Mr Desmond?'

'We'll have to take some instructions –' he met Imogen's eyes, and she pointed to her phone and whispered that she was awaiting a response '– and it could be a few minutes. Perhaps I can suggest a short adjournment while we do that. I apologise, your Honour. If the defendants' solicitors had told us of this proposal before rather than during the hearing, or had not sent my instructors correspondence to the effect that the parties were irretrievably at odds, this delay might have been avoided –'

'No,' said the judge, 'I will not allow an adjournment. There is no doubt a mediation is not only valuable but also necessary in a case such as this. In fact, I won't let you proceed without it. Unless you're going to tell me that Mr Payne's just been hit by a bus or had some other disaster befall him –'

'I simply don't know, your Honour. I couldn't say with absolute certainty that such an incident has not occurred. My instructing solicitors are trying to make contact with Mr Payne as we speak.'

'Don't be cute with me, Mr Desmond. As you can see, we seem to have representatives from half the nation's media here with us today. If your client had been hit by a bus, I have no doubt they would have known about it by now.' The judge scoffed, appreciating his own humour. 'So. We are going to have a mediation. If it's unsuccessful, then I'll look very favourably upon an expedited timetable for trial, given the seriousness of the alleged defamatory imputations here. Now, how long will you need to prepare to mediate?'

'Six weeks, your Honour, at the very least – eight to be safe.'

Romola began mentally listing off all the tasks they would need to get done before their case was ready for a mediation.

The Diva licked his fingers and flicked through his diary, taking his time before he peered over the top of his glasses at the barristers awaiting their fate. 'I'll give you *three* weeks. You can exchange key documents beforehand, including a formulation of loss. In the event this doesn't settle at mediation, the court will do what it needs to make sure the trial can be heard urgently thereafter. After all, you're the one who said this was urgent, Mr Desmond.' The judge closed his diary and folded his arms, a Cheshire cat grin on his face.

'I'm grateful to your Honour,' the Slug said, noting the date in his diary. He leaned very close to Imogen and Romola. 'Arsehole,' he whispered, before standing up and bowing his head to the judge in deference.

Chapter Sixteen
A Visitor

Judith's plane was due to land in thirty minutes, and Romola was still at her desk. She cursed herself for having agreed to meet her stepmother at the airport, which in Melbourne traffic at five on a Friday night was a good hour away. She had two lengthy emails left to draft before she could leave. Had she subconsciously left them until the last minute? She'd been feeling uncomfortable about Judith's visit all week, but she was unsure if it had more to do with the prospect of commemorating one year since that dreadful day when her dad died, or the thought of having to spend the weekend with Judith.

Romola could feel the energy change in the office and hear laughter as Friday night drinks kicked off in the boardrooms. For the first time since her arrival at Bassett Brown, she wanted to be in there with her colleagues, taking the edge off the week.

Two weeks had passed since the first directions hearing, and the office had been heaving with activity for days on end. The acquisition that she'd first heard Derek speak to Malcolm about at the art auction was now in full swing. Payne Corp was hoping to acquire Goodalls, the country's second largest supermarket brand. Still a privately owned business, it had a strong name but had fallen behind in the online shopping game. Malcolm had noticed its earnings drop and had been keeping his eye on it for some time. He was now swooping in for the kill, having persuaded some of Goodalls' larger shareholders that Payne Corp had the capital to re-enliven the brand. Derek, Emmett, Gretchen and a swag of other lawyers at the firm were pulling long hours as they undertook a laborious due diligence process and worked on the 'transaction bible', in which all the contractual documents for such a large deal were recorded.

Romola had also been working late nights. She was preparing for the mediation but had come up against a major stumbling block in the form of an absent client. Patrick had gone AWOL. Last they'd heard, he was still in Sydney, but he hadn't responded to her emails, texts and voicemail messages. The mediation was now only one week away, and the simple fact was that they couldn't settle the case without him.

Going through her handwritten to-do list for the hundredth time, Romola circled the bullet-pointed questions that she wanted to ask Patrick, pressing her pen down so hard that she tore a hole in the paper. She was hanging her head in exhaustion and frustration when her phone sounded with a text from Louise.

> Where have u been? All ok? Did u get my msgs? I'm
> moving on Tuesday (hurrah!). Johnny's away. I need u!
> Monday after work – can u come help me box up my stuff?
> I'll supply wine. Pretty pls?
> L x

Seeing as Johnny was away, Romola responded without much thought.

> Sorry been flat out. Count me in.
> R x

As an afterthought she sent a second text, though not to express the way she really felt.

> So exciting!!

*

It was 8 p.m. when Romola finally walked in the door of Cliffy's place and headed straight to the kitchen, red-faced after her run from the tram stop.

'Hello, darling,' Judith said with a sip of her red wine and a glance at the clock. 'Cliffy and I were just about to start without you.' Judith sat at the kitchen island, which had been set for three with geometric gold Wedgwood crockery. Small dishes of chutney and raita, along with a plateful of pappadums and a bottle of South Australian red, were set in the centre of the island. Towards the back of the house, Cliffy had a beautiful dining room with a grand table that seated fourteen, but – guest numbers allowing – he preferred to eat in the kitchen so he could cook and entertain at the same time.

'Sorry ... sorry.' Romola offered Judith an awkward kiss on the cheek as her stepmother stood perfectly still. 'I had a couple of urgent things that couldn't wait.'

Cliffy was standing by the stove in his 'What's Cookin' Good Lookin?' apron, stirring a big burgundy Le Creuset pot. He turned, and she nodded a hello to him; he offered a wink in return.

'How was your flight?' Romola asked Judith.

Judith rose from her stool and joined Cliffy at the oven, her back to Romola. 'It was terrible, thanks for asking. Don't even ask about the taxi ride.'

Judith absent-mindedly stirred another of Cliffy's smaller pots, clutching at her plentiful bosom to protect it from being scalded by the hot stove. Before Don's death she'd always had short hair, but she had let it grow in the year since, and it fell over her shoulders in soft grey waves. As usual she wore layers of brightly coloured clothes and was adorned with costume jewellery in deep amber and turquoise. Because her sense of style was coupled with her wide-eyed stare and predisposition for unwanted psychoanalysis, she reminded Romola of a washed-up fortune teller.

'Anyhow,' Judith said, 'I've settled in now. I've been watching dear Cliffy here cook up a storm. It's been so long since I've been treated to a meal. It's not worth the effort when you're only cooking for one.'

'Foods up!' Cliffy exclaimed, and gestured for Romola to hand him the plates that had been set. One by one he filled them with steaming white rice, chicken korma, dhal, and potato and spinach curry. The aromas of mustard seed, ginger and garlic were deliciously inescapable.

Romola took her plate and sat down opposite Judith. She grabbed a poppadum and crunched it, spraying crumbs sideways with a look of apology to Cliffy, who removed his apron and joined the women at the table. 'What's the plan for tomorrow?' Romola asked casually, as if tomorrow were a normal Saturday. She couldn't quite bring herself to say the word 'anniversary' – to put her father's death so firmly in the past when it still seemed like yesterday. She had no desire to keep track of the days, months or years that had passed without her dad.

'I thought we might go to the art gallery,' Judith suggested. 'There's a photography exhibition on. Your dad always loved photography, remember?'

'I remember how he liked to take photos,' Cliffy offered. 'I always felt as if I was being followed by the paparazzi when I was with Don. He didn't like to let a moment escape him. Quite admirable, really. It's funny to think he was so disdainful of the selfie generation, when really that's what he did for years!'

Romola had often thought the same thing. Her dresser drawer was filled with envelope upon envelope of photos of the two of them together on their adventures. Don would carefully set up his Minolta Maxxum 7000 on the tripod, and then the two of them would thoughtfully construct a pose. Whether they were on a country lane, on top of a cliff with the wind blowing a gale, or on a park bench with their faces obscured by overflowing gelati cones, Don would always have his arms around Romola, holding her up – not to show her to the world but to show the world to her. Sometimes he was looking at the camera, but more often he had his eyes on his daughter. Those were the ones she loved the most, when she could see him see her. He looked so utterly delighted.

'Did I ever tell you how I met your father?' asked Cliffy.

He had, but Romola never tired of hearing about the evening they'd met in the university bar, when they'd talked till four in the morning. She even had a black-and-white photograph of the night itself. The two young men had their arms around one another, each of them holding up a pint glass. Cliffy had been caught mid-word, his mouth an oval, while her father grinned widely with his eyes half closed, beer froth spilling from his glass. The framed picture used to sit on the desk in his office.

'And you were friends ever since?' Romola asked Cliffy, although of course she knew the answer. As long as Romola could remember,

Cliffy would visit them in Sydney at least once a year, if not more when he had a case running up there. Sometimes he would even surprise her by arriving at her birthday party with a brightly coloured but very badly wrapped package, always something completely inappropriate for her age – Scrabble at two, Dostoyevsky at ten.

As Romola reminisced with Cliffy, she noticed that a tear was running down Judith's face.

'Sorry, Judith.' Romola's voice was full of sympathy, but what she actually felt was fierce anger. Perhaps it was completely irrational and even cruel, but these memories of her father were her own, not Judith's. Romola should be the one in tears.

It was like being twelve years old all over again, when to her shock and fury Judith had moved in. Romola had never asked for a mother, and she wasn't going to accept one without making a fuss. She offered Judith nothing more than sulky silence for the better part of the year, and not much more after that. Before Judith had arrived, Romola had been the only light of her father's life, and she wasn't prepared to let anyone else share in it.

'I like hearing about Don,' Judith said sadly. 'No one seems to want to talk to me about him since it happened. It's nice.'

Cliffy nodded. 'It certainly is.' He raised his wineglass.

'To Don.'

'To Dad,' Romola said quietly, swallowing the words with a mouthful of red as she willed her tears away.

Nobody moved for a moment, so the room was quiet enough for the three of them to hear the vibration of a text on Romola's phone lying facedown next to her plate. She instinctively flipped it over and saw the message was from Imogen.

> Have you managed to track down Patrick? Please update
> me. If he's still in Sydney we need someone on the ground
> there asap. He needs to be on hand to give instructions
> this week and in the room at Friday's mediation. You can
> fly up Monday, first thing. Hold his hand until you get him
> back here.

Romola re-read the text and thought about her plans for Monday: drop Judith at the airport in the morning, and help Louise move apartments in the evening.

'Is that work contacting you?' Judith asked. 'Don't they ever leave you alone? Isn't that harassment?' The pitch of her voice increased with each question.

Despite the terseness of Imogen's text, the only person Romola felt harassed by was Judith. In fact, the message had lifted Romola's flagging spirits. She had been given something useful to do: she would find Patrick and return him to Melbourne. She had no idea how, but it would give her something to think about all weekend – something other than the fact a whole year had gone by without her father, the first of many.

Chapter Seventeen
Flight

'Can I give you a hand? It can be a little tricky if you've never sat up the front before.' The well-meaning flight attendant leaned over a grumbling businessman to help with Romola's tray table. Romola had searched for the table for a full five minutes before the business-class flight attendant had come to her aid.

It was 7.15 a.m. and Romola was still flustered. She had woken before sunrise to leave for the airport and found Judith waiting for her in the kitchen, face grim and creased from sleep, preparing to deliver yet another lecture on the perils of working for Patrick Payne. Romola had struggled to stay civil as she hurried out the door, forgoing breakfast in the interests of avoiding another argument.

Then, as she'd stowed her cabin luggage, she had received a call from the sergeant in charge of investigating Hana's death for the coroner. For weeks the sergeant had ignored Romola's calls, then he'd spoken to her as if 7 a.m. was a perfectly normal time to be calling – and as if he had nothing particularly important to say. He informed her that Hana's autopsy results were back; he would send them to her if she liked, but they contained 'nothing surprising'. A run-of-the-mill suicide, he called it. He said there had been a cocktail of drugs in Hana's system (she'd really 'thrown the kitchen sink at it'), but that it would have been the fentanyl that killed her ('something we've seen a lot of recently'), and that her death was unlikely to warrant a coronial inquest. Hana had ingested so much that she could never have expected to survive the overdose, he said. He'd likely want to speak to Patrick at some point, but he didn't see any particular rush – unless the family thought otherwise, of course. He noted that Patrick, as Hana's 'domestic partner', was the senior next of kin, so that was really a matter for him. With insincere regret the sergeant said the whole process was likely to take more than a year, if not two.

She could hear him sucking on a cigarette as he spoke, and she imagined him leaning against a wall in a cordoned-off smoking area. She was both grateful and alarmed at the thought that he wasn't a man the police would have put in charge if they'd truly wanted to get to the bottom of what had happened to Hana. He'd said he would call again with any updates, but Romola was left with the firm impression there would be none, then signed off with a casual 'condolences to the family'. Romola noted down everything he'd said and took a moment to hope that the police officer had been so brisk with her because she was a lawyer, and that if he'd been speaking to a family member he would have shown more tact. Her dad's death had never been investigated, as it was from a medical episode. She imagined the horror of dealing with such a cop if it had been her dad's death in his hands.

As the plane tracked towards Sydney and hopefully Patrick, Romola let her thoughts drift on. She finished her breakfast, flipped open her laptop and plugged in her earbuds. The music of her dad's beloved Herbie Hancock drowned out the plane's engines as she opened a file of screenshots of Tilly Klein.

Tilly was now thirty years old, but at the time of her relationship with Patrick she'd been barely twenty and something of an 'it girl'. She had appeared in ads for swimwear companies; there had even been talk of movie roles. Patrick, at age twenty-two, was already one of the country's most eligible bachelors, with speculation rife about every woman lucky enough to be dangling off his arm. Tilly had a Cinderella story: she'd been scouted by a modelling agent as a teenager at a Western Sydney shopping centre. The media lapped it up, and she became a darling of the social pages. That was until Patrick dumped her. Then the stories about Tilly simply vanished, her flourishing modelling career all but finished.

For a brief period in her mid-twenties, Tilly was in the tabloids again after she joined the cast of a reality dancing show. At the time she was dating an up-and-coming surfer named Jason Reznak, but he didn't have the face or apparently the inclination to be part of a celebrity couple, and what little attention she garnered from the show fizzled as quickly as it had come.

But now she was back. Her hair was still peroxide blonde but cut into a severe bob sitting close to the chin. She'd had her breasts and lips enhanced, and she promoted various fashion and swimwear labels on her Instagram, as well as offering make-up tutorials and motivational advice to anyone who would listen. Since her claims about Patrick had come out, she had launched a skincare range, Inertia, aimed at ladies who 'don't live to be held back' and started hosting empowerment seminars in Byron Bay.

Romola became aware of a slight pressure on her left side. The disinterested businessman seated next to her had all of a sudden become very interested in Tilly's Instagram posts – so much so that he had closed his newspaper and was holding it firmly over his lap, unwittingly leaning into Romola's shoulder.

She swivelled to look him straight in the eye, expecting him to burn with shame. But he just smiled goofily with no sign of embarrassment. She wondered if he thought her not worthy of it. To this middle-aged white man, was her brown skin acting as an invisibility cloak? Or did he think he might be in with a shot? Was he genuinely unashamed – maybe even proud – of his easy arousal, like it was a sign of masculinity that might appeal to her?

She snapped her screen closed and turned up the volume on her phone. The businessman huffed and stared straight ahead again. As she closed her eyes, she thought about how easily men deluded themselves.

*

Romola called Patrick the moment she was permitted to switch her phone from flight mode. There was no answer, nor when she called again minutes later as she made her way through the gates and past the morning's commuters. When she'd found a quiet gate to sit in, she called him a third time. Patrick answered on the fourth ring.

She could tell he was outdoors from the background noise. Voices yelled instructions in the distance. Birds squawked, and fog horns bellowed. 'I'm guessing you're going to keep calling me?' he asked flatly.

'Afraid so. I'm in Sydney. I've come to find you.'

'Is that so?' He sounded a little amused. 'Well, you're out of luck. We're about to launch.'

'Launch? Where are you?'

'The marina in Rozelle. I'm taking the boat out for a few days.'

Romola started walking towards the cab rank. She mentally acknowledged that she was about to hop into a car with a cab driver, a stranger, but she kept on walking. She felt almost proud that her fear wasn't strong enough to derail her from her mission of returning Patrick to Melbourne.

'Did you say for a few *days*?' she asked him. 'You need to be in Melbourne by Friday for the mediation, Patrick. And we need to meet with you before then.' She was beginning to get odd looks from strangers, her panic laid bare.

'If you make it here in the next twenty minutes, you might just catch me.'

She broke into a run.

*

Stepping out of the cab at the Rozelle marina thirty minutes later, Romola experienced a fleeting moment of bliss as she was enveloped in Sydney's winter sunshine. Something in her melted a little as she steeled herself for the task ahead.

She could just make out Patrick at the other end of the marina, standing on the deck of a boat with his back to her. He was at least fifty metres away. She raced over the wooden boards, waving her arms like a latecomer to a bus stop. 'Patrick! Patrick!' She'd had the foresight to change into ballet flats in the taxi.

His 'boat' was a superyacht: navy-blue, white, red, glossy and streamlined, with the word 'Honour' emblazoned on its bow. Patrick was on the side nearest to the marina, unfurling a heavy rope. It was the only thing tethering him to land, and to the possibility of returning to Melbourne with her.

Panting and sweaty, she had almost made it to him when he turned and saw her coming. 'Wait a second!' he called to a man in chinos who was drawing the gangplank towards him. 'Can't say I was expecting a personal visit,' Patrick said to Romola, standing to full height and shading his eyes from the sun. 'How much is this costing us?'

'I need to speak with you.' Out of breath, this was all she could think to say. 'Emails didn't seem to be doing the trick. I need you to come back to Melbourne with me.'

'Why?'

Romola had come prepared with a list of reasons, but faced with a rapidly departing yacht she couldn't call a single one to mind.

Patrick saw that she was speechless and started back at his rope. 'Dad's down there – he can deal with it.'

'But it's *you* we need. Not your father.' She dropped her bag on the ground and began to compose herself, hands on hips.

'You'll have to convince me of that.'

'Can we sit down and talk?'

He squinted out to sea, the glassy water of the harbour mirroring the blue skies. 'It's a beautiful day for sailing.'

'No. Can we talk here?' She pointed to the sturdy wooden boards of the marina beneath her. 'I'm not big on boats. And I have an afternoon flight to catch.'

She hadn't told Louise she was coming to Sydney for the day, hoping she would make it back to Melbourne in time to help with the move. It was only an hour-long flight, after all.

'Well,' said Patrick, 'if you want me, you're going to have to come aboard. Up to you.'

She noticed that he was beginning to enjoy himself, his usual intensity replaced by a teasing smile, the gap in his teeth peeping through.

She thought of Louise packing up her apartment all alone, bottle of wine in hand, getting angrier with each item stuffed into a box. But then Romola pictured Imogen's face when she reported back that she'd been unable to convince Patrick to return, that she had barely even tried – and Justice Debenham's face when the Slug told him their client hadn't bothered attending the mediation.

Romola lifted her bag and walked the plank.

Chapter Eighteen
Home Sweet Harbour

The lower deck was all golden timber and soft cream leather seating. It was so impressive she almost didn't notice the view as they navigated past other vessels, big and small. They glided under the Anzac Bridge and into the harbour, which glistened with morning sunshine. Patrick was speaking to a deckhand, pointing to different parts of the boat, while Romola wandered to the rear of the deck where stairs dropped down to a small pool.

It was almost 9 a.m. and the harbour was busy. The yacht sailed slowly past commuter ferries and water taxis, and under the Harbour Bridge as a train rumbled overhead. Romola felt uneasy but awestruck, muddled by the mixture of the familiar and unfamiliar. She was well acquainted with the bustle of Circular Quay, the beauty of the botanic gardens and the bays, but to experience them from this perspective was surreal. How many times had she and her father sat at Camp Cove and watched the yachts sail by, contemplating the lives of the people on board? And now she was on the other side – and in another way, so was her dad.

She felt daunted by the prospect of the day ahead with Patrick, and nervous as to how far they would sail. She'd been fearful of the open water ever since a treacherous crossing of the Bass Strait when she was a child. But as the boat approached Watsons Bay, she also felt cleansed. The air smelled of salt water, and of home. After the weekend spent remembering the worst day of her life, perhaps this was what she needed.

'You want to see inside?' Patrick asked. He had approached from behind and was beckoning for her to follow.

He led her indoors and down a set of stairs to a space that was bigger than the whole of her old apartment. The open-plan area was styled like a Hamptons beach house, the colour palette white, cream and navy. First they came to the lounge, where two white sofas faced one another, piled with cushions and throws. They passed a flat-screen television and entertainment unit, and then a twelve-seater dining table with rounded corners, in the centre of which stood an enormous fruit bowl containing only lemons. Finally they reached a kitchen of shiny white benchtops and dove-grey shelving. 'Coffee?' he asked, banging out the filter on a café-style espresso machine.

'Sure.' She continued checking out the interior. 'Just your average "boat" then,' she said lightly.

'Dad bought her years ago, then started suffering from vertigo. He gets dizzy on the water, so I've been taking her out.'

A deckhand – the third she had encountered – pottered around in the kitchen behind Patrick, stocking fridges, while Patrick, barefoot, shorts on, moved easily around him, grabbing a bottle of milk. His hair had grown since their first meeting; it had a slight wave to it and was now at a length where he had to constantly tame it back and out of his eyes, which were much clearer today than when they'd first met. He pressed some buttons on a remote, and soon music filled the room: Dizzy Gillespie. Patrick stood frothing milk and humming along to one of her favourite jazz pieces, looking like a man on holiday.

'I need to talk to you properly, Patrick,' she said, hoping to bring him back to earth.

He placed a coffee proudly in front of her, then weaved back through the dining and lounge area, his macchiato in hand, calling behind him, 'Let's talk about it later, shall we? We've got all day, after all.' He smiled. 'Come on, I'll show you the sundeck.'

She was going to have to play the long game.

The sundeck was up two flights of stairs and consisted of a semicircular booth, big enough to seat around ten, and a hot tub. The sun seemed brighter up here. She shrugged off the jacket to her black pantsuit, turned up the sleeves of her crisp white shirt, and switched her tortoiseshell glasses for big round prescription sunglasses – her 'Audreys', as she liked to call them because they reminded her of

Breakfast at Tiffany's. The air was cool, and Romola could feel her sweat begin to dry. Her hair still felt a mess after her run to the boat; she could sense the halo of it around her face, and she surreptitiously tugged a few loose curls behind her ears.

Patrick ignored her as he laid out the daily newspapers on a large coffee table, title by title, section by section, and began to read the first, page by page, sitting forward with a hand on his head, keeping his hair at bay. He made no sign of breaking focus when a deckhand climbed the stairs bearing a platter filled with chunks of fresh lobster, lemon, mayonnaise, and crusty bread. Before the deckhand descended, he gestured for Romola to help herself, but she didn't move, focused instead on Patrick and his determined disregard of her.

'Do you read the ones about you?' she ventured.

'I read everything.' Patrick still didn't look up. 'Force of habit.'

'Does it bother you?'

'Didn't used to.' He seemed to be scanning an article about the prime minister's latest gaffe, but a minute later he lifted his face and spoke with a frown and an accusatory tone. 'Are you going to eat anything?'

'I filled up on the plane.'

He considered for a moment, the sun reflecting her own image back to her in his Ray-Bans. Her face was a picture of determination.

Then he put down his paper and crossed his arms. 'Okay, let's get this over with. I can't relax. Tell me – why should I come back with you?'

'I don't understand what you're doing here ... I mean ...' She started again, slower, 'I understand why you would be here –' she motioned towards the ocean and the harbourside mansions '– to get away from things. But – haven't you seen our emails? What we've said, essentially, is that now that you've got proceedings on foot, you have two options. Your first option is to go to trial. But you must know that's not going to be pleasant – the media attention will be worse than it is now. There'll be a running commentary on the trial, and Rabbit Hole's lawyers will do their best to make you out to be the devil. Your second option is to try to settle this early and quickly, possibly get some compensation but more importantly extract an apology and a retraction. Why wouldn't you at least give that option a shot?'

Patrick had taken a piece of bread and spoke casually as he chewed. 'I'm more straightforward than you think. I only came up here because I've found it hard, being in the house where Hana and I lived together. Dad's in Melbourne. He's going to be better at dealing with this mess than me. He's experienced with litigation. He knows how to handle this kind of thing.' Patrick went back to the newspaper, though it was now open to the television guide.

Romola tensed. She wished she could wrestle the paper from his hand and pull off his sunglasses. 'But, Patrick, it's *you* that everyone's reading about, not your dad. Rabbit Hole is telling the world you're a terrible and, frankly, abusive man. And you're letting your dad step in to say otherwise? I'm sorry to say this, but it makes you look worse.' She fixed him with a stare, daring him to look away. 'You're the only one who's going to make them see they're wrong, Patrick – if they're wrong.'

She could feel his steely grey gaze behind his glasses as he popped a piece of lobster into his mouth. They had moved through the heads, and she suddenly became aware of the impending absence of nearby land. All she could hear was the sea breeze and the motor's thrum deep below. A flutter of fear tickled her stomach at the prospect of the open water.

He swallowed his mouthful and reached for a napkin. '*If* they're wrong about me?' His forehead creased. 'You don't believe me, do you?'

An imaginary Imogen screamed in her ear – *Say you believe him, right now for fuck's sake!*

Romola had been surprised when her boss had given her the responsibility of coming to Sydney alone. When they'd spoken over the weekend Imogen had said it was because Patrick may see her as less threatening. Imogen had been firm in her direction not to poke the bear – Romola was to get him back gently. But Romola's instincts told her that she shouldn't try to reassure him now. Part of her was switching on, the part that knew she was good at dealing with clients when they believed in her. She felt the adrenaline of being the expert that her client needed to listen to, for his own good. 'You have to understand where I'm coming from. In my last job I never so much as turned my mind to whether or not I believed my clients. I pulled together their evidence, and I put it to the court. It was for the judge or jury to decide their guilt or innocence. If I started to believe or not believe, it would make it harder for me to do what I had to do for my clients.'

'Right.' Patrick shuffled forward in his seat, elbows on knees. 'I get that. But that's criminal cases, right? This is *me*.' He tapped his chest. '*Me* against some journalist who's gone out on a limb trying to make a name for himself, and the trash publication that's supporting him. Surely it's not against the rules for you to trust *me*?'

'So give me more of a reason to do so. You're running away, and you haven't told us everything we need to know. It doesn't add up. Was everything really okay with Hana? What were you arguing about that night? I've spoken to a friend of Hana's who said there was something Hana wanted to tell her in person. And what about Sonia? We're not supposed to talk about her, but it seems to me she could be a ticking timebomb – a first wife who you're apparently on very bad terms with, and we're crossing our fingers won't speak to the media.'

Patrick leaned back, his hands behind his head, readjusting his legs, reassessing Romola. 'You've been doing your research.'

She straightened her back, affronted by the condescension in his voice. 'This is my job. It's what you pay me for, Patrick. I'm not here in the faint hope of getting you back to Melbourne, for the fun of it. I'm terrified of sailing, I hate lobster, and I should be doing about a million things back at my desk. The least you can do is take me seriously.'

Patrick lowered his hands. 'I'm sorry. I don't mean to sound like I'm not taking you seriously. But you can't possibly understand what it's like – when everybody thinks they know you, but inside you know the reality is something else. All I want, and especially with Hana, is to keep some things, some memories, to myself. Why is it that I have to share everything in order to prove that I'm not a monster. The onus is on them, right?'

Romola was surprised that with all his years in the public eye,

Patrick could be so naïve. 'Technically that's right, but you're the one suing, and you know they'll try and dig up as much about you as possible to justify their reporting. We need to be ready to counter it with what we say is the truth. If you're pressing ahead with this, you can't just ignore it – you can't have a defamation trial and expect to keep anything private. If you don't want to be fighting this in court, now is the best time to settle, before this gets any more air. We can use the mediation to show Rabbit Hole that their defence is shaky. And if we can extract an apology, the public might start to see you differently. But to do all that, you'll have to be full and frank with me and Imogen, warts and all. You'll need to commit to this.'

'Is that what Imogen told you to say to me?' Patrick asked, his forehead creased, bringing Romola's mind back to the stern orders of her boss to go gently on him.

'Honestly – no,' she said, matter-of-factly.

Patrick turned his head to look back at the green heads of land still showing in the distance. 'Okay,' he said quietly.

'Okay?'

'I'll come back. I'll come to the mediation.'

Romola froze, then slumped a little, like a child in a game of chasey whose opponent had given up too easily. 'Well. That's good to hear. Good decision.' She suddenly felt embarrassed by the way she'd spoken to him, but now that she was done, the ocean seemed less threatening. She saw that it was actually a calm day out at sea, and that the boat was as steady as an ocean liner.

Patrick continued leaning back in his chair, now gazing beyond her. 'In the interests of full disclosure,' he said, still speaking softly, 'and I'm sorry, I should have told you this before – I don't think anyone else knows, other than the police ...'

She urged him on. 'Yes?'

'Hana was pregnant. Eight weeks. We hadn't told anyone yet.'

Romola's brief moment of calm ended as fast as it had come on. Her heart clenched. So, Patrick had lost both a partner and child. His obvious grief morphed into a new shape, encompassing the loss of a family to be. As much as she felt for him, her primary thought was for the potential impact on the case. What had happened to Hana would become all the more inexplicable to a jury.

Patrick continued, no longer hesitating, seeming almost anxious to explain things properly to her. 'Having Max is the best thing I've ever done, but things were hard with Sonia before she was pregnant. As she got further along I knew my marriage wouldn't last – it's strange bringing a child into that scenario. Whereas to think of having a baby with Hana, who I loved, and who I felt confident would have been a good mother, was something else.'

'How about Hana? How did she feel about it?'

'That was the thing,' he said, like she had hit the problem on the head. 'I thought she would be ecstatic, but she was flat. I wanted to talk about the pregnancy, make plans, but she seemed to switch off when I did that. I didn't know what was wrong. I thought of asking her to see a psychologist – obviously I should have.' He held out his palms and exhaled.

'So you did notice something was wrong?' she asked gently. She could see he was fragile and changeable, and she knew that one question too many could close him up like a clam.

'I noticed she was different then, with the baby. That's what we were fighting about that night. We had dinner at her favourite restaurant. She said she didn't feel like eating, but morning sickness had kicked in so that wasn't unusual. And then after dinner –' He paused again, but then seemed to decide he was too far in to stop. 'I proposed.' He wove his fingers together in his lap, his face reddening.

'What did she say?' Romola encouraged, though she suspected the answer already.

'She said no.' He was grinding his fingers together now, staring down at them. 'She said it wasn't going to work, that the baby didn't deserve to have her as a mum, that type of thing. But even as she was saying it I didn't believe her. She couldn't even look at me. Then she said she was thinking of putting an end to it – to the pregnancy, I mean – and ... I lost it.'

Patrick met Romola's eyes again as he made his confession. She could see he wanted to leave it at that, but she needed him to explain, and to see what happened to him when he did. If he needed to repeat this in court, he would do so after being fully prepared for the hearing by counsel. But this could be the first and only untarnished time he was speaking about it. It was her best chance to assess what he might be like as a witness.

'That's when you got angry?' she asked.

'Furious. I was furious.' He clenched his jaw, as though his fury hadn't diminished even with all that had happened since.

'And did you grab her arm, like Rabbit Hole's sources have claimed?' She braced herself for the impact of this more specific question, knowing how Patrick had baulked when Imogen had asked him a similar question when they first met.

But Patrick did not flinch. 'Not that I can remember.' He shook his head. 'Of course I didn't want to lose her or our baby, but I would never have threatened her. I would never have hurt her. That's not me.'

Romola paused, feeling grateful for his honesty but also the weight of what was to come. It seemed that Johnny had at least one source close to Patrick and Hana. If that source also knew of the pregnancy and the reason for the couple's fight before Hana's death, Romola could only imagine what Johnny would give for, and make of, that information.

'Okay. I understand.' She felt she had almost reached his limit, conscious that he'd already agreed to come home and that if she pushed him too hard he could easily change his mind.

Her instinct was correct – a few moments later, Patrick started folding up his papers. 'This isn't easy,' he mumbled as he stood up. 'I'm going to need a minute.' His back to her, he disappeared down the stairs into the cabin.

'I'll be here,' she called after him, before falling back onto the lounge. She tilted her face up to the bluest of blue skies, feeling the pleasant prickle of the sun warming her skin.

Chapter Nineteen
Progress

After about ten minutes, Romola understood Patrick wasn't coming back any time soon. She wandered to the lower deck, where she had left her bag and laptop inside. She would use the time to take a detailed file note of her conversation with Patrick, and call Imogen with an update. With a grumble in her stomach, Romola realised they'd now been on the water for a couple of hours – it must be nearing lunchtime.

Inside, the shades had been pulled and the television screen was lit up with an image of two animated cars tearing across a colourful racetrack. Lying on adjacent couches, controllers in hand, were Max and Hana's brother Emir. Max's whole body was shifting as he manoeuvred his imaginary car. 'I've got you now, sucker!' he cried.

Romola had to stop herself from saying, 'I didn't know you were here!', realising that she was in fact the stranger who had unexpectedly joined their journey. She coughed to reveal her presence, but the two only turned their attention to her once the race was completed in a flurry of twists, turns and jeers, Max having won by a small margin.

'You're here,' he said, pointing at her. 'I remember you.'

'Yes, I remember you too,' she said, 'but I don't think we were properly introduced. My name's Romola, I'm helping your dad.'

Max peered up at her quizzically. 'Romola. What sort of name is that? Are you from here?'

Romola was used to these questions, although normally they were asked in a long, drawn-out fashion, as though the questioner thought the question would be more appropriate if they just happened to stumble into it. 'Well – my name actually comes from an old Italian king. Have you ever heard of Romulus? He founded Rome.

My dad was a big fan.' She had tried to keep the explanation simple, as opposed to the lengthy explanations of Roman folklore that her father would embark upon when asked the same question.

'So you're Italian? My grandma was Italian. But you don't look Italian.' Max put his thumb and forefinger to his chin as he considered her.

'Quite right, I don't. My mum was from Sri Lanka, but she died when I was born. So I grew up in Sydney.'

As she spoke, she noticed Patrick sitting at the dining table further into the cabin, probably listening in. His knee was bouncing, but his arms were steadied on the table as he read something on his phone.

Emir had also sat up. He was again dressed in black, with a five o'clock shadow and his hair shaved close. His olive skin was made darker by the dim cabin, but his green eyes, outlined by the black of his lashes, were still striking. They were Hana's eyes. He sat with his legs apart and his feet firmly planted.

'I don't think we've been introduced either,' she said to Emir, reaching out her hand.

He hesitated before taking it in a weak, brief shake. She thought he was probably unaccustomed to being personally introduced to Patrick's guests.

'I'm Romola Cross, one of Patrick's lawyers. I'm so sorry about your sister, Emir.' Romola didn't like mentioning Hana around Max, but felt as though she couldn't meet Emir without expressing some condolences.

'Everyone's sorry.' His voice was deep and his gaze darted from Romola to Max as he spoke. 'Thanks, though.'

'Why are you here, anyway?' Max broke in.

'Max – manners, mate,' Patrick said from the dining table. 'She's just here to talk to me about work stuff.'

'Oh,' said Max, deflated. 'Boring.'

'We were talking about some things I need to do back home.' Patrick stood up, tucked his phone into his back pocket and came over to Max, ruffling his hair. 'We're going to head back tonight, mate.'

Romola thought about telling her client that technically he just needed to be contactable throughout the week and back in Melbourne by Thursday for Friday's mediation, but she wasn't going to push her luck now – getting Patrick back tonight was better than she'd hoped.

'Seriously, Dad? You said another week up here.' Max pushed his dad's hand away.

'I know, but things have changed. And don't forget, Jessie's back home waiting for us. She'll be missing your walks. I bet the sitter doesn't spoil her like you do.'

Max hunched over, not falling for his dad's attempt to cheer him up. 'Does that mean I have to go back to school?'

'Afraid so, bud. Hey, how about you give me a game? You remember I'm still undefeated at this, right?'

With a dramatic flip, Max threw himself back on the couch, still clutching his controller, and grinned at his dad. 'Bring it on, old man.'

Father and son played a frenzied game while Romola grabbed her phone and notepad out of her bag. Emir had forfeited his place on the couch to Patrick, and he now stood a little apart from the group, watching the race as he leant against the doorframe.

Romola chanced a careful step towards him and lowered her voice. 'Emir, we were actually hoping to speak to you.'

He put a hand on his chest. 'Me? What, right now?' He shot a nervous glance at Patrick, who was still absorbed in the game.

'Sorry, no, I didn't mean right now.'

Emir seemed to relax a little.

'How is tomorrow or Wednesday?' Romola was conscious that Emir had a front-row seat to his sister's relationship with Patrick. He could therefore make the perfect witness. While his ongoing employment by Patrick meant he was in a difficult position to speak out, surely the fact he was still prepared to work for the man spoke volumes. Emir had been in the prime position to protect Hana if he'd felt she was being mistreated by Patrick. But he appeared to remain loyal to his employer. Romola wanted to speak to him before the mediation on Friday so she could firm up all the presumptions she was making about him. The alternative – that he was remaining with Patrick but as a witness for Rabbit Hole – would be disastrous.

Emir fidgeted, flipping his phone over and over in his hands, and glancing at Patrick again. She was uncertain if his uneasiness stemmed from the fact she was a lawyer – it wasn't abnormal for witnesses to feel uncomfortable talking to her – or from the possibility of Patrick overhearing their conversation. She hoped it was the former.

'Wednesday might be all right,' Emir said, 'if we're going back to Melbourne now anyway.'

'Wednesday's perfect.' She jumped at the chance to lock him in. 'Shall we say 10 a.m.?'

'Um. I'll need to check the schedule with Patrick, but yeah, that should be okay.' He put his phone in his pocket.

'Excellent – thanks for that. Give me your number, and I'll text you mine.'

After Emir and Romola exchanged numbers, the big man slunk off to a different part of the boat, leaving her to witness Patrick's crushing victory over his son, which he celebrated loudly before shaking hands with a sulking Max.

*

Half an hour later, once Romola had sent an email update to Imogen, lunch was served. Max and Emir ate inside, while the table was set for Romola and Patrick back up on the sundeck. A large platter had been laid out, heaped with cheeses, meats and breads. There were two salads, one of witlof, apple and candied walnuts, the other of broad beans, tomato and basil. A broad silver ice bucket was filled with frosted white wine and champagne, Italian beers, and small bottles of Italian mineral water. The music of Otis Redding drifted to Romola from speakers below.

Patrick sat down first. 'Help yourself. You said you don't like lobster, so I asked them to give us a bit of everything. And we're going to start heading back to the harbour soon.'

'Thanks,' she said, sitting down. He handed her a plate, which she began filling with prosciutto, mozzarella, salad and bread. She realised she was ravenous.

He held up a bottle of prosecco.

'Water's fine for me.'

'Well, there's plenty in case you change your mind.' He poured himself a beer. 'In my experience, lawyers like to wine and dine their clients.'

'I guess I'm different.'

He sat back, resting an elbow on the leather lounge and holding his beer loosely. His Rolex reflected the sun like a beacon. His feet were still bare, and as he sat back he crossed a hairy ankle over his knee, his legs already browner than they had been at the tennis club in Melbourne. 'I can't imagine you working in criminal law. You seem too nice.'

'I've never seen why you have to be an arsehole to be a good lawyer.'

He smiled knowingly. 'I used to feel exactly the same way about politics. But now I think maybe an arsehole is precisely what you need to be – only you can't let the public know about it.'

She crunched on a candied walnut, sweet, salty and delicious. 'Did you always want to go into politics?'

Patrick laughed. 'God no. I mean, I've always been interested in it, but if you'd asked me ten years ago, I wouldn't have dreamt I would end up running.'

'Why is that?'

'I've never been a great public speaker. It terrifies me, actually. When I was in primary school I had a stutter – a proper couldn't-get-my-words-out stutter. The teasing was ferocious. It embarrassed my dad. He got me into therapy, and it had disappeared by the time I was a teenager. But I've never really shaken it. I always worry it's going to rear its head again, especially now with all this public speaking. And the press are so savage every time I speak – it's like being back in primary school.'

Romola recalled the memes that made fun of Patrick facing the cameras at community events, with his constantly furrowed brow and downturned mouth, a manner that media commentators had labelled 'incompetence'. She felt sorry for him, knowing how hard it could be when perception and reality conflicted. So often she wanted to appear tough and self-assured, but people still perceived her as feeble and delicate. 'So what made you decide to run?'

'Someone from the party approached us,' he said, as he fastidiously stacked himself a multilayered sandwich. 'Dad thought it would be a good idea. In hindsight it's hard to see the appeal. Rose-coloured glasses, I guess – I thought I could make a difference somehow.'

They sat in silence for a while, Patrick looking over her shoulder to the water as he ate.

She spoke next. 'For me, I don't mind public speaking as much as chitchat. You know, filling the silence with colleagues, with clients. I don't really like talking for the sake of it, and then I sort of get … stuck.'

He gave her a lopsided smile. 'Right. So this must be killing you right now?'

Her face warmed. 'Oh god. I didn't mean it like that. This is fine.' Her mind helplessly searched for conversation topics as she felt her face blush.

Patrick adjusted his watch, and when he spoke again it was as if he had been figuring out how to broach the topic. 'I wanted to speak to you about the case again anyway. You mentioned Sonia before. You called her a "ticking timebomb", if I recall correctly.'

Romola placed down her fork with a clink, unsure where he was going with this. 'It's just – she's the obvious choice for Rabbit Hole to speak to, either as a witness or for another story. Imogen seems confident she won't do that, but … do you agree?'

He nodded enthusiastically. 'I completely agree. Not least because I'm confident she'd have nothing to say, other than to accuse me again of having an affair with Hana, which as I've said is untrue. But she wouldn't say I mistreated her in other ways. For all her faults she's not like Tilly – she won't tell outright lies.'

Given Patrick was clearly in the mood to share, Romola decided to venture further. 'Imogen mentioned alcohol abuse. Is there a risk she'll say her issues with that were down to you?'

'No way,' he insisted, sipping his beer and appearing to gather his thoughts. 'What you have to understand about Sonia is that she was always a bit wild. She's a couple of years older than me, and she likes to party. That was what attracted me to her in the beginning. She seemed to have such … abandon. Tilly was a real control freak, whereas Sonia – when I met her, at least – appeared so carefree. When we were dating that was an attractive thing to me, but once we were married and had Max, I gradually developed a totally different perspective on it.'

Romola's mind was ticking, assessing whether – based on what she knew of Sonia so far – this was credible. The trouble was she knew so little of the woman, who was most often seen on the social media pages of influencers, admittedly often with a drink in hand. Before marrying Patrick, Sonia had been in PR; she preferred heavy make-up and wore designer labels, with never a hair out of place in her ponytail. She'd given up her career when she had Max and had been quiet on her socials ever since the divorce. As with Tilly, it was like Sonia had fallen off the face of the planet when the relationship was over.

'Was her drinking why you ended up with custody of Max?'

'She has him one weekend a month,' Patrick clarified. 'But yes, that was the main reason. At the time we separated, I almost felt like I couldn't trust her alone with him. As you know, Hana was our nanny, so she was with him a lot regardless. But Sonia wanted to be alone with him more and more – obviously because she was suspicious of Hana. One night I got home after a dinner with Dad. It was past eleven and Max was still up watching a movie, eating junk. Sonia was passed out on her bed. I could smell the booze and God knows what else she'd taken. That was it for me.'

'It wasn't just alcohol?' Romola asked, feeling as though she didn't want to know the answer. Despite Patrick's assurances, instinctively she knew this would not look good before a jury.

'It always started with a drink,' Patrick said, drink in hand. 'But then she would take coke. I couldn't tell you what else, to be honest.'

Romola nodded, processing all that he'd said.

'You look worried,' he observed. 'Believe me, you don't have to be. Sonia knows the only one who will look bad, should the facts of our relationship come out, is her. Trust me.'

Again, Romola was being asked to trust her client, and she knew that she had no option but to do so. If she were in control of the case, she would be factoring Sonia into her advice to Patrick – telling him there was still a material risk that evidence about his ex-wife's substance abuse would make it in front of a jury, and that he should factor that into his assessment. But Imogen was the one in control. So Romola put a mental pencil mark through Sonia's name, one that could be rubbed out easily.

The two were silent a while longer, and Romola became aware that the boat was making a slow U-turn. She checked her phone and saw it was now close to 1 p.m. Based on how long they'd been sailing, she estimated it would be early evening when they disembarked, and well into the night before she made it back to Melbourne. Having almost forgotten about her promise to Louise, she now saw she would need to call her friend and beg forgiveness.

Patrick followed her line of sight and guessed her thoughts. 'Don't worry, we can get back faster than we came. This baby can move when we want her to. I've called to get the jet ready as well – should have you back in Melbourne by, say, seven?'

Of course the Paynes would have a jet. That made perfect sense, yet until that moment Romola hadn't imagined she'd be flying home on it that night. Her first thought was of Louise's reaction when she told her – a superyacht and a private jet all in one day. No sooner had the thought surfaced than it was squashed by the reality that she hadn't yet told Louise about Patrick, and she would of course need to keep the details of today's meeting private.

Romola was brought back to the present by Patrick, who held out his hands like a magician showing he had nothing up his sleeve. 'Anything else you want to ask me?'

Romola's full belly made the prospect of further questions seem tiring. What she felt like was lying down for a nap in the afternoon sun. But then she recalled one thing she wasn't meant to ask Patrick but to tell him: the call from the police officer that morning on the plane. She'd intentionally not mentioned it earlier, eager to get as much information from Patrick as possible, her rule of thumb being to obtain facts from clients before giving them.

'This morning I spoke to the sergeant in charge of the coroner's investigation. I know it's hard to talk about, but the autopsy results are available. He's confirmed that Hana passed away from an overdose – apparently there was a mix of drugs in her system. He said they might want to speak to you at some point, but they don't seem to be sharing Rabbit Hole's line of thinking – as in, there's no suggestion you played any part in her death. He called it a "run-of-the-mill" suicide.'

Patrick hung his head and ran his hands through his hair. 'Right. Sorry, I wasn't expecting you to say that. I don't know what to say. Where the hell did she get all the pills from? Are they going to look into that?'

Romola shook her head. 'I'm sorry, Patrick, he didn't say.' She could see the conflict that Patrick was facing: relief that the police weren't interested in him, mixed with dismay that they weren't more concerned about what had happened to Hana. Romola felt relieved that it was the latter concern that seemed to be consuming him.

'Run of the mill, hey?' Patrick sighed. 'Hana was anything but.'

'Strangely he didn't say anything about discovering the baby – in the autopsy, I mean,' Romola said, putting a voice to one of the many uncertainties that had been gnawing at her since Patrick's revelation of Hana's pregnancy.

'They already knew before the autopsy,' he said bluntly.

'How?' Romola asked, taken aback.

'Because I told them. I wanted them to be careful, during the autopsy. Even though I know the baby was so tiny there was no …' His voice trailed off, but then he spoke again, seemingly as an afterthought, 'Plus, I didn't know how it would look – you know – if they only learnt about it during the autopsy, and I hadn't said anything beforehand. I thought that would seem a little suspicious.'

Romola regarded him, unsure precisely how to respond. She was thankful that her client had been open with police and that she wouldn't later, in the coroner's investigation, have to deal with allegations of withholding information. But she struggled to comprehend how he could possibly think to tell the police but not his own lawyers, who were only there to help.

In the end, she couldn't settle on anything to say, and no response was needed, as it became clear they were both content to sit with their thoughts. Romola gradually became aware that the hum of the engines was louder, the yacht now surging towards the heads at some speed. A few minutes passed before Patrick reached into the ice bucket for a second beer, which he held on to for a moment, cooling his hands on the glass. 'I'm done talking about Hana for today, Romola. I know you don't like chitchat, but can we talk about something else?'

'Of course. Happy to.' And she really was happy to talk about anything else. She'd got more than she could have hoped for today. She would bring Patrick home with her, and also a greater understanding of the man himself, and of Hana and Sonia.

'Are you sure I can't get you a drink?' he asked, filling his glass with the amber liquid.

Romola glanced at the bottles, her muscles unwinding a little just at the thought of a drink. She knew that sharing moments like this with Patrick, getting to know him better, wouldn't be a bad thing for her case preparation.

'Sure,' she said, 'why not? I'll have what you're having.'

He poured her a beer. As she brought her glass to her lips, Patrick did the same, then tilted it towards her. 'Cheers – to going home,' he said, with a grim smile.

'To compromise,' she offered.

*

It was almost 10 p.m. when she arrived back in Melbourne, exhausted. Travel by private jet wasn't as efficient as she had hoped. With its usual runway out of action, they'd had to wait for another space to open up during the busy early evening period. After a couple of drinks with Patrick, followed by a long call with Imogen detailing the day's revelations as the yacht came into harbour, and then some time spent helping Max with his English homework in the limo, she'd been boarding the plane when she'd suddenly remembered Louise. After calling three times, she'd sent a hurried text as the plane taxied:

> I'm so sorry!! Unavoidable work trip to Sydney. Only just flying back. How I can make this up to you? I can come tomorrow?? Xxx

There was no reply by the time she landed, nor when she arrived at Cliffy's, where she followed the music to find his study door ajar.

A warm yellow glow elbowed its way into the dark corridor, along with the fragile bars of Debussy's 'Clair de lune'. She poked her head through the gap and rapped lightly on the door. Cliffy was leaning back in his leather armchair, hands folded behind his head, eyes closed, lips curled in a smile. His reading glasses were folded on his desk. Tentative piano notes, mournful but joyous all at once, filled the room.

When she cleared her throat he opened his eyes briefly, then put a finger to his lips as he waved her in, asking her to be silent for the song's conclusion. 'Clair de lune' had been one of her favourite pieces as a teenager, a song she'd spent years trying to perfect before abandoning the piano at age nineteen. Now she would barely know where to start.

As the next piece began, a melancholy cello number, Cliffy turned down the sound and gave her a tired smile. Early that morning when she'd told him about the purpose of her trip to Sydney, he had found it wildly amusing. 'How was the retrieval mission?'

'Very successful, thank you. Patrick should be tucked up safely in his bed any minute.'

'I'm sure you were very persuasive.'

'I appealed to his sense of responsibility.' Romola paused, then asked tentatively, 'Did Judith get off okay?' Romola didn't want to talk about her stepmother but was sure her abrupt exit this morning had been noted.

'She'll get over it,' soothed Cliffy. 'You know she loved your father very much. It was a difficult weekend for her.'

'I know – I know,' Romola said, the guilt returning, 'but she needs to let it go about this job. I'm all grown up now. I think Dad would have approved.'

Cliffy sighed. 'Of course he would have – you and I know that. But Judith's got your best interests at heart.' He took a sip of his cognac, rolling it around in his mouth. 'There are things about Judith that you may not appreciate. I think you'd be well served to keep an open mind.'

'My mind is wide open,' she said, drawing her hands out to either side, 'as open as the heavens.' It was an expression her father used to use, which made both of them smile. 'Night, Cliffy.'

She climbed the stairs to her comfortable room on the first floor. Her bed linen was the crispest of whites and always smelled delicious thanks to Cliffy's fabulous housekeeper. Every time she walked into the room, she had an almost uncontrollable urge to bury her head in the fluffy cushions, and tonight that was precisely what she did.

She checked her phone again for any messages from Louise, then turned her phone to silent and allowed her tired body to succumb. As sleep began to take hold, she could still hear the sound of lapping water and wondered if the room was swaying slightly. No, she decided, it was all in her head.

Chapter Twenty
The Outing

If Romola had expected more praise for the safe return of Patrick beyond the 'good job' that Imogen had offered on the phone, she was very much mistaken. As she knocked at Imogen's office door the next day, her boss stood, grabbed a large folder and thrust it into her arms. Romola, who was holding a takeaway coffee in her right hand, felt the hot liquid splash and begin to dribble down her wrist as she tried to grapple with the heavy folder.

'A present from our friends at Rabbit Hole,' said Imogen. 'Arrived yesterday. Key documents for the mediation. There's a statement from Tilly, photos, and I think there's some material on Hana in there too. Look for any holes. If we want any hope of coming out on top here, we're going to need more than a denial from Patrick.'

'I know. I've been thinking about it, and –'

'I can see you've been working hard, but we need more. There's only a couple of days before the mediation. It's all well and good that Patrick's back in the land of the living and communicating with us again, but I'm still furious he didn't tell me Hana was pregnant, for fuck's sake – in what universe is that not something you tell your lawyer? And now we need to press him for his responses on everything they've included in here.' She flicked a fingernail against the folder in Romola's arms. 'Malcolm will expect to see results, either through winning a trial or extracting a huge fucking settlement payout. Our position needs to be stronger than just putting them to proof.'

'Yes, but –'

'Now before you tell me so, I know that's technically the right position at law. They have to prove what they've published – it isn't on us to prove the opposite. But you and I both know that if Patrick's going to come out of this thing with a shred of his reputation intact, let alone win, we'll need to discredit their witnesses, call evidence to show he treated those women well, that there's no factual basis for the stories. You need to find us something we can use, for goodness sake.'

Romola was ordered out of the office with a flick of Imogen's wrist.

Victoria smiled sympathetically over the top of her computer screen.

'I think I'm going to need a brownie,' Romola whispered to her.

Back at her desk, Romola started carefully making her way through the massive folder Imogen had given her. A fifty-page written statement, signed by Tilly, described in detail her abuse at the hands of Patrick. She deposed that he would not allow her to see friends without his permission, that her clothes were cleared by him, that he checked her phone multiple times a day, that she had to explain any calls or messages he couldn't identify, that she was not to drink alcohol alone or with others. Textbook stuff. Horrifying stuff. And then there were her tales of his angry outbursts, the time he pinned her against a wall, the multiple times he pushed her forcefully onto beds, onto couches, into walls.

Patrick hadn't held back when defending himself against Tilly's claims. According to him, she was a compulsive liar who craved attention. But how to establish that? Romola had checked to see if Tilly had a criminal record, but she was clean. Old Facebook posts had given Romola the names of two of Tilly's exes, a man and a woman, as well as Jason Reznak – the surfer whom she had dated during her reality show days – but none of them had answered her calls or returned her messages. She'd managed to make contact with a friend of Tilly's named Trixie, who'd said that Tilly was now represented by a celebrity agent, but this agent hadn't accepted Romola's calls. Every day Tilly was getting more famous, and more out of reach.

Romola had felt buoyant about the case after her day with Patrick. When he'd spoken about Sonia and Hana, she had assessed him as being sincere – if he testified in court in the same way, he would make a credible witness. And what Lisbeth's parents had said seemed to support his recollections of his relationship with her.

But Romola had stupidly put Tilly to one side, and seeing her claims in a black-and-white signed statement made them even more real. It was one thing to tell stories about an ex; it was another to swear to them under oath. Add that to two dead ex-girlfriends – both of whom had apparently been happy, healthy women before starting their relationships with Patrick – along with an apparent witness to him manhandling Hana, and Romola saw afresh all the obstacles in the way of winning the case.

She called the number Emir had given her, anxious to firm up the details of their meeting the next day, but it went straight through to voicemail. She was scribbling over her to-do list, wondering how she'd felt so positive upon returning from Sydney, when her phone rang. The receptionist at the front desk spoke in her trademark clipped voice. 'There's a Louise McGovern here to see you. She says you know her. She's very insistent.'

Instantly Romola forgot the to-do list, focused instead on why Louise had come all the way into her office unannounced. Surely she couldn't be that angry about Romola's no-show the previous night.

'I'll be right out.' Romola shuffled her papers into some sort of order, closed the evidence folder, and retied the bow on her blouse as she headed out to reception. Her friend was always on her about looking presentable.

Louise stood at the window of the reception area, her back to the room, clutching her designer handbag to her chest as though she were about to be robbed. She was wearing tailored navy culottes and a chunky mustard cardigan, as though dressed half for work and half for moving day. Her curly hair had been hastily slung up in a messy topknot. When she turned and trained her eyes on Romola, her mouth was set in a determined frown. It was obvious she'd been crying.

Romola felt both hope and dismay. Louise and Johnny must have broken up. Louise had probably been lumped with the overpriced lease in her name, and she needed Romola's help getting out of it. As sad as she was that Louise had to endure yet another painful break-up, Romola was already feeling a weight lift off her shoulders at the prospect of not having her friend date the opposition any longer.

The receptionist showed them into a room, pointedly raising her eyebrows as she gently closed the door. It was one of Bassett Brown's most impressive meeting rooms, with a huge Minnie Pwerle artwork of fierce reds and yellows on one wall and a video-call screen on the other, cornered by enormous windows overlooking the city. Normal Louise would have been impressed – she would have cooed over Romola's fancy new workplace, telling her how far she'd come. But this woman was not Normal Louise. She was upset enough, or unhinged enough, that she hadn't even spoken a word.

Romola sat down at the large blond timber table, but Louise remained standing, eventually pulling out her phone and scrolling.

'Are you okay?' Romola began, deciding to keep up the pretence of Louise being mad about her no-show rather than to ask outright about the break-up. 'I'm really sorry about last night. I got stuck interstate. There was honestly nothing I could do. I've told you what Imogen's like – what she says goes, and I'm too new to rock the boat.'

'Hah!' Louise spat out, eyes still down on her phone. 'How ironic.'

Romola froze, understanding very clearly now that she herself was the object of Louise's anger. 'Sorry?'

Louise had stopped scrolling and was looking intently at an image on her phone as she began to explain. 'Some new pics came through this morning from one of the photo agencies we use. They're shopping them around to all the mags as we speak. This guy says to us that Patrick Payne has a new love interest, and that the images will move mags so we better make our offer quick. The gossip editor, Susi … You've met her a couple of times, remember?'

Romola shrugged, and Louise didn't wait for an answer.

'Susi emails the pics to me and then she calls me and is like, "This looks just like your friend, what's her name, that lawyer?" And I'm like, "There's no possible way that could be Romy." And then I take a look at the photos and I'm like, "What the fuck?"' Louise pushed her phone towards Romola as if she were brandishing a sword. 'Is this you? Because this looks exactly like you. But … how could this be you?'

Romola seized the phone. There she was – a little blurry but distinctly herself, on the upper deck of Patrick's superyacht, sitting opposite him. There was her crisp white cotton shirt with the sleeves rolled up. There were her Audreys balanced on her nose. There was the long glass of Italian beer in her hand and the laughter on her face. The photo must have been taken as they were sailing back into the harbour. Patrick was leaning towards her, his arm out but his hand invisible to the camera. He would have been helping himself to food from the platter on the low table, but from the camera's angle it appeared as though he was reaching to her. Romola ran through the other images, all taken within seconds of each other. They both gave the impression of being so happy, so carefree. Patrick looked so unlike a man who has just lost his girlfriend – so unlike a man with his lawyer.

She passed the phone back to Louise and put her head in her hands, trying to comprehend what the next hours and days could hold for her. Then she lifted her head to face Louise. 'I was going to explain this to you the next time I saw you. I've just been waiting for the right time. Which I guess is now … So, the thing is, I act for Patrick Payne. He's my client, and I'm working on the defamation case against Johnny.'

Louise snatched her phone back, sat down and slammed it hard onto the table. 'So it's true that you're the one suing Johnny? How could you not tell me? And why the hell would you be cruising around on a fucking yacht with him? You never even said you were going to Sydney.'

'I'm not personally suing Johnny – my client is. And these photos are not how they look. I had a meeting with Patrick, which just happened to be on his yacht.'

'Oh yes, just a meeting which just happened to be on a yacht. Can you hear these words come out of your mouth? Tell me the last time you met a client on a yacht. You think I'm completely clueless?'

'Of course I don't. I know it sounds crazy, but it's what happened. And obviously I can't tell you what the meeting was about, but it was important that I meet with him and, logistically, the yacht was the only place it could happen. That's all there is to it.'

'Please, Romy.' Louise shook her head. 'I know you. I've known you since grade 7, and I know when you're into someone. I knew it when you had that crush on that awful Mr McCarthy in English, and

I know it now. God, just look at your face.' She stabbed her finger at the screen. 'Even an idiot could see it.'

Of all the ways Romola had foreseen their conversation playing out, none had been remotely like this. 'What? No. Absolutely no. We were just talking. There was nothing enjoyable about that day, believe me.' Her face flushed with uncertainty as she examined the photo again, not even knowing whether she was telling the whole truth.

Louise sank into a chair, deflated. 'Jesus, I can't believe you didn't tell me this. I'm *living* with Johnny now. I *needed* to know this. You *must* have known that.' It seemed her anger was fading, her hand on her heart.

'I'm so sorry, Lou. I didn't want to have to tell you like this. I was just waiting for the right time. And part of me thought that if … you know, if it didn't work out between you and Johnny, then the problem would sort of go away.' As soon as Romola said the words, she saw the hurt they would cause.

Louise looked both physically ill and enraged. 'Poor Lou can't manage to keep a boyfriend, so I won't tell her that I'm the one taking Johnny to fucking court. Was that the thought process? How can you even represent someone like him anyway? Maybe Judith has a point.'

Romola tensed, feeling stung. 'It's not like I have a fricking choice in it, Lou. And even if I did, that shouldn't matter. I've acted for much worse in my time. It's what I bloody well do. And no one has ever had a problem with it before. I'm not supporting the Paynes – I'm not trying to justify their existence. Patrick's just as entitled to representation as anyone else.'

'If that's what you need to tell yourself.' Louise turned her face away, arms folded, sulking. 'I can't believe this.' She snatched a tissue out of the deep bag at her feet and dabbed at her nose, before meeting Romola's eyes again. 'For what it's worth, Johnny said to be careful – around Patrick, I mean. Johnny said he can be very charming.'

'You told Johnny?'

Of course it was a fait accompli that Johnny would find out, but Romola still wished she could somehow have retained control of the situation.

'What do you mean?' Louise stared at her like she was a fool, before laughing manically. 'He *already knew*, Romy. *I* was the one telling him it couldn't be true, like a prize idiot. Don't think he's not in my bad books too. I'm fucking livid with the both of you for not saying something earlier.'

'He knew?' Romola's stomach dropped.

'Yes. And he's known for a while, apparently.'

What a creep. He had probably enjoyed waiting to see how long it would take her to tell Louise – waiting for her to slip up. She wondered, with a shiver, what information Louise had given him about her during that time – not about the case, which Romola had never spoken about – but about Romola, her demeanour, how she approached matters, what Imogen was like. He'd been the one who was two steps ahead, and she hadn't even suspected it. She kicked herself.

'Lou, I know this is probably asking too much, but if there's anything you can do to stop your magazine running these photos?'

'Seriously?' Louise scoffed. 'If you think anything *I* say is going to make a difference in that department, then you don't understand *my* job. And the offer wasn't exclusive anyway. Those photos are going to be everywhere before you get back to your bloody desk, whether we like it or not.' She fixed Romola with an icy stare. 'Besides, it's all you in those photos, babe.'

Romola found herself frozen, and in that moment she became aware of her emotional gears shifting. At the beginning of the conversation she'd felt nothing but sympathy and guilt, but now what she felt was raging anger that Louise was taking Johnny's side over hers.

'You're right, Lou, it is me in those photos. But now you know without a shadow of a doubt, because I have told you so, that I am Patrick's lawyer, and that those are photos of a private, confidential client meeting. So if your magazine prints a story that says anything else, you're on notice that it's false.'

Louise stuck out her chin and glared at Romola. Her eyes, still rimmed with red, looked as though they were about to spill over again.

'It's your call, Lou.'

'Yes, it is.' Louise plonked her phone back in her bag and swung it over her shoulder as she headed to the door, calling out, 'Don't say we didn't warn you.'

The door edged to a close, leaving Romola in silence, aware of nothing other than the loud drumming of her heart and a sense of injustice.

Chapter Twenty-One
The Fallout

B y noon the photos were everywhere. Romola's image, dizzy smile on her silly face, appeared on news websites all over the country, beamed to hundreds upon thousands via Twitter, WhatsApp and Facebook. The websites all opted for a similar sell: an 'unnamed exotic brunette' had been spotted flirting with a carefree Patrick Payne on his father's superyacht. *Who's the girl? How quickly has he moved on? Poor Hana's body is hardly even cold.*

Romola had told her boss immediately, like ripping off a bandaid, but Imogen had been surprisingly relaxed about the whole affair. 'As long as you're not naked it's going to be fine,' she'd said without looking up.

Later in the day, Imogen also came to her aid when Derek called them both into his office. This was ostensibly to offer support but really to reprimand them for how the photos made the firm look, especially when the Goodalls acquisition was reaching a critical point – apparently Malcolm was fuming.

'Please, Derek,' Imogen said, 'if I'd sent up a male associate to get Patrick, we would not be having this conversation right now. You know that as well as I do. You yourself wouldn't have thought twice about getting on a boat with Malcolm or Patrick. There should be no questions asked, no inferences drawn. Now, can we put this behind us and go back to preparing for the mediation?' Imogen winked at Romola as they left Derek's office together.

Romola spent the remainder of the afternoon focusing on work rather than thinking about Louise's fierce face, or the incessant buzzing of Judith's missed calls and texts. She worked on finalising Patrick's position paper for the mediation, and was on and off the phone with the Slug and the Hare, and in and out of Imogen's office. Romola made repeated unanswered calls to Emir, and to Tilly's exes and ex-friends. She was looking for an angle, and the more she searched the more she forgot about her own problems. But the inescapable reality facing her client was that it would now be almost impossible to empanel a jury who did not have rusted-on impressions of him.

We need more, she thought. Something has to break the cycle. We need people to like him again.

When her mobile rang at five o'clock she went to answer it quickly, expecting it would finally be Emir. While he couldn't shed any light on Patrick's relationship with Tilly, it was imperative that she interview him about Hana, and his experiences with Hana and Patrick together. But her mobile showed that it was just Patrick calling. She felt a twinge of nerves, the angle taken by the media sure to make this conversation uncomfortable.

'Hi, Patrick,' she answered, hoping to sound nonplussed, like she dealt with being the subject of media speculation every day.

'I wanted to call before things got awkward,' he said briskly. 'And to check you're okay. I appreciate this sort of thing will be new to you.'

'It's ridiculous, really. Don't worry about me, I'm fine.' She started doodling on her to-do list, circling back to Emir's name and underlining it, before realising that Patrick himself had been the main target of the media today. 'What about you? Are you okay?'

'Don't worry about me. They'll need a fresh angle by tomorrow – probably have new pictures of me getting coffee with a friend or walking Jessie alone or something. I'll either be moving on too quickly or troubled, alone and close to a breakdown, depending on what suits the news cycle.' In fact, Patrick sounded as though he might be out walking Jessie now.

'Hey, Patrick, has Emir been with you? I'm supposed to be meeting with him tomorrow, but he hasn't been answering my calls.'

'He's gone away.'

Romola paused, dumbfounded. 'What do you mean?'

'He's on leave, on holiday. He wasn't coping well, with Hana not around. Last night he asked me for some time off – I told him I agreed that was best. I think he's going to head off road somewhere up north. I'm not sure how quick he would have left, though. I can see if I have any more luck making contact.'

'Please do that. I really needed to sit down with him.'

'Right. Sorry – I should have known.'

She wanted to say that yes, he definitely should have known. After their discussion on the yacht, she'd thought he would be in no doubt of the significance of her having access to any relevant witnesses. His nonchalance not only surprised her, but it troubled her as well.

But she just said, 'If you could get hold of him for me, that would be great. I don't need to meet him in person – even half an hour on the phone would be better than nothing.'

Patrick assured her he would do so, and they quickly ended the call. Romola immediately reported Emir's absence to Imogen, knowing that she'd wanted to be the one to interview Hana's brother. Imogen swore profusely and then said to leave it with her – she'd speak to Malcolm.

At eight o'clock Romola came up for air. Not having eaten since breakfast, she noticed the hollowness in her stomach, which had been unsettled all day. The firm would be offering dinner in the large kitchen on the thirty-first floor, but she couldn't face eating opposite Emmett and the others working on Malcolm's deal. Earlier in the day Emmett had passed her office, waved at her, and in a loud voice said, 'Hey, Romola, I see you've been papped! Nice photo.' A few muffled giggles had come from surrounding offices.

Romola opted instead for a bowl of borscht at a small and neat Russian bistro she'd found in one of the city's rambling lanes. It had good food but little else to attract customers, with the basic decor and fluorescent lighting of a cafeteria. It was raining hard, but the bistro was warm and blissfully empty. She put away her umbrella and chose a table set for one by a fogged window, thinking of the first time she had tasted the soup.

She and Louise were eighteen, just out of high school. They had saved up for a backpacking adventure and for some reason, which now escaped her, had decided it was imperative that they visit either former or current communist states. Russia was their first stop. In the freezing city of Saint Petersburg, it wasn't long before they discovered that borscht and vodka were the perfect cheap and warming start to a night out. These were nights when the snow meant there was nothing to do but settle in at a warm bar, take shots with other backpackers and – on a good night – attempt some Russian folk dancing, which would inevitably end with Louise at the centre of a heaving, laughing heap while Romola looked on.

The happy memories were soon replaced with thoughts of her current predicament, and then of Hana, with her Bosnian background. Perhaps her mother had cooked borscht, before her untimely death when Hana was eleven.

Soon the steaming bowl arrived, blood-red and topped generously with dill and sour cream. Romola spooned the soup slowly into her mouth. But although she felt its temperature and consistency, she could not taste a thing, her mind spinning with thoughts of Louise and Hana. To distract herself, she picked up her phone for the first time in hours, having made a point of ignoring its buzzing through the late afternoon.

The latest was a text from Patrick:

> R,
> Sorry again about letting Emir go. Hope you are still weathering the storm. They are savages, but it will blow over soon.
> P

Before that there were five missed calls, five voicemail messages and three texts from Judith. All were variations on a theme of 'Are you okay?' and 'Please call me'. There was nothing from Louise or from Emir.

Romola strummed her fingertips on the formica tabletop. She was conscious of the prying gaze of a pudgy old Russian lady who sat behind the counter, crocheting with a wry smile. Romola thought of Judith, pacing the wooden floors of her old-fashioned kitchen, fiddling with her colourful beads, waiting for Romola's call. Her stepmother would surely be feeling satisfied with herself, thinking she'd been right all along about the dangers of Bassett Brown, and of Patrick. She would also be out of her mind with worry.

And then Romola thought of Louise, probably blabbing to Johnny about her deepest darkest secrets, about her argument with Romola and all the hurtful things that had been said.

Unable to settle her thoughts or her strumming fingers, she reached again for the phone.

I'm all good. Thanks

She pressed send without hesitation. The reply came straight away, a thumbs-up emoji. From Patrick.

After putting her phone in her bag, Romola returned to her eating. Finally the flavours came to her: the earthy sweetness of beets, the sourness of vinegar, the delicate dill. She finished the bowl, soaking up the dregs with homemade bread until a smear of deep crimson was all that remained. When Romola said yes to dessert, the old lady offered a knowing smile from her perch.

Chapter Twenty-Two
The Mediation

H e winked at her, she was sure of it. They arrived at the same time, walking towards each other from opposite ends of the corridor. Johnny moved with a casual swagger, while her legs felt as collapsible as a puppet's. When he held the door open for her, no doubt about it, she saw the corner of his mouth curl and his right eye close. He'd dressed up for the occasion in a grey check suit with a floral pocket square, and his curls were held back in a ponytail. He looked like he was going to the races.

They had agreed upon a neutral venue: bland serviced meeting rooms that hadn't been updated since the '90s – the only space available in the CBD for a party of their size at such short notice. On arrival, each group gathered in separate rooms to prepare for the introductory joint session before the mediator, where counsel would make opening statements.

The Paynes' room contained only a small white table for a meeting of four, not the crowd of six in attendance, comprised of Patrick and his father Malcolm, the Slug, the Hare, Imogen and Romola. They seated themselves in order of importance, with Malcolm, Patrick, the Slug and Imogen taking their seats around the table, and Romola and the Hare left to wheel themselves chairs from the neighbouring room and squeeze into a corner. Square steel-framed windows revealed another miserable day. Romola didn't expect to play much of a role throughout the day, except to check the facts and figures when asked. But that didn't stop her from feeling trepidatious about the hours ahead.

Patrick and Malcolm greeted her when they arrived, Patrick in a stiff suit, clean shaven with his hair freshly cut, Malcolm in his trademark black-and-white pinstripe. But the Slug completely ignored her, flinging his bag onto the table with gusto. 'Who found this place?' he scoffed. 'I feel like I'm in some sort of East German government facility.' He plonked himself down on a chair, sending an audible squeeze of air from its vinyl cushion. 'I expect this will all be over by lunchtime anyhow. These pricks are just putting on a show for old Debenham at your great expense, Malcolm.' Romola noticed Patrick's face fall.

She should have known then that despite her best efforts, the day would end badly for Patrick. As it happened, it was all over and done with in three small words.

*

'Thank you all for attending today,' the mediator began, once the two sides had come together in a larger but equally stuffy boardroom. Blank whiteboards bookmarked each end of the table, and threadbare carpet emitted a musky scent of chemical cleaner. 'We all know why we're here …'

The mediator was Walter Kornitz QC, a wrinkled, gentle character who had long since given up the chest beating of advocacy. Instead he spent his time nudging adversaries towards out-of-court settlements. He reminded Romola of a turtle coming out of his shell. His watery blue eyes leaped from person to person as he made his introductions.

Malcolm sat opposite Rabbit Hole's editor, Eddie Moss. Eddie was well into his fifties but had a head of sandy hair and a wonky eye that gave him a juvenile look of excitement. Eddie and Malcolm mirrored each other's body language, leaning back in their chairs with their legs crossed. Both feigned comfort in the face of fierce negotiations. Patrick couldn't pull it off; he sat next to his father, back straight, elbows and forearms resting on the table in front of him.

Romola was seated directly opposite Johnny, whose eyes were trained on her. Sometimes in her peripheral vision she could see him smile, barely noticeable to the others. It was a smile that said, 'I know you.'

Instead of focusing on Johnny, she tried to focus on the windows behind him, squares similar to the windows in the other room. It was still pouring outside, the type of rain that doesn't look like it will ever stop, and in fact it hadn't for days. Normally she would have found it comforting, but today the weather felt as if it was conspiring against her, blurring out the world beyond the hot stuffy boardroom.

'It seems to me that both parties are at great risk in this case,' Kornitz continued. 'If Mr Payne is right and the defamatory sting is not proven to be true, he will receive a substantial payment of damages. On the other hand if Rabbit Hole proves that they have reported the truth ... well, I don't need to tell you the damage that will be done to you, Mr Payne.' The mediator peered at Patrick and then more pointedly at Malcolm, already understanding how things worked between father and son.

The Slug, as the plaintiff's senior counsel, spoke first. He held five fat fingers aloft, slowly counting off the reasons why Rabbit Hole should be making an offer of compensation to Patrick.

First, the articles were defamatory of Patrick; there was no doubt they suggested he'd played some role in the deaths of Hana and Beth or that he was a controlling, coercive, partner. Second, there could be no viable defence because, third, there had been no charges or convictions for offences against any of the women. Fourth, there was no evidence of abuse towards Hana or Lisbeth – no complaints to police, no domestic violence orders, no photographs, no texts, no emails. There was nothing but two girls who, for reasons no one could fathom, chose to destroy their own lives. Fifth, there were Lisbeth Janssen's parents, Carol and Piers; the very people who have every reason in the world to hate Patrick were he responsible for Lisbeth's breakdown, didn't blame him, and were even willing to support him and testify at the trial.

Rabbit Hole's barrister, Annette Esposito (aka the Bulldog), was seated opposite the Slug. Romola noticed the look exchanged between her and Eddie Moss at the mention of Lisbeth's parents.

The Slug had run out of fingers by the time he got to Tilly, the subject of the second article. He spared few words for her, dismissing her claims as barely worth responding to, so unreliable and uncorroborated was her witness statement.

'So your truth defence is going to fail. Then we have your alternative, qualified privilege, or let's call it the reasonable journalist's defence.' The Slug shifted his focus to Johnny, who smirked in return. 'And the obvious problem you have there is the conduct of Mr Wise. As we all know, the defendants must have acted reasonably in the publication, and Mr Wise's conduct was far from reasonable. These were serious matters to be publishing, and he didn't even reach out once for a comment from my client – not even once.'

Johnny raised his hand, but the Bulldog waved him down and the Slug went on.

'There was absolutely no urgency to the publication. He must have been certain the publication would be damaging to my client, so there is no excuse for the lack of any notice. You therefore have another untenable defence.'

'Okay, Annette, your turn,' said the mediator, with a tempering hand towards the Bulldog, who was gripping the edge of the table, raring to deliver her response. 'But keep to the essential points, please. I don't think anyone will benefit from dragging this out today.'

'I assure you, I'll be quick.' The Bulldog spoke a little too loudly. 'In both articles my clients simply reported on the facts. Two of Mr Payne's former partners are dead. Fact. They both died of drug overdoses. Fact. They were both happy, well-adjusted young ladies prior to their relationships with Mr Payne. Fact. Those closest to them saw immense changes in them while they were with Mr Payne. Fact. Both couples fought. Fact. Another of his girlfriends has come forward and put on the record that she was terrified of him – that is how she felt. Fact. It's all simple, and it's all easily proven.'

Romola stole a glance at Patrick during the Bulldog's speech, not wanting to be too obvious in assessing her client's reaction. She saw that he wasn't afraid to look the Bulldog in the eye as she delivered her assessment of his private life, though Romola detected a wince at the mention of the women being terrified of him. Patrick must have sensed her observing him, for his eyes darted to meet hers, then just as quickly shot back to the Bulldog.

'Oh come off it, Annette,' the Slug interjected. 'There are plainly other meanings in those articles. That Patrick made these women unhappy. That he turned them to drugs. That he was responsible for their deaths. That he abused Tilly. Any reasonable reader would come to those conclusions.'

'That's for a jury to decide,' Esposito insisted. 'And even if the stories did have those meanings, my clients can prove the truth of those as well. They have direct evidence from Tilly as to the way Patrick used to treat her.'

'Sorry, Annette –' the Slug coughed '– but where's your evidence about him mistreating Hana or Lisbeth? And how do you expect Tilly will go before the jury in this trial? She has an awful lot to say to the media now, but the fact is she had nothing to say when she broke up with Patrick. The police never laid any charges. Only now that she has a product and *an image* to promote, she uses my client to do so.'

'Honestly, Neville, do you always have to stoop? Defaming women in the interests of defending your client?'

'I'm putting my client's position, Annette, as I'm sure you are. Spare me the personal insults.'

'Counsel, can we please stick to the matter at hand?' Walter Kornitz waved his hand in the air; he was searching for authority but came off like a priest offering a blessing.

The Bulldog backed off with a knowing smile. 'I have only one more thing to say – something which points without doubt to Hana's troubled state of mind.'

She paused until she was certain she had the room's attention. The sun had come out from behind the rain clouds briefly, and Romola could see dust particles suspended, circling above the table, reflecting the tension in the air.

'Hana didn't only cause her own death that day. She also ended the life of someone who we can assume was more dear to her than any other. It has recently been confirmed to us that at the time of her death, Hana was pregnant.'

There they were: three words that spelled the end of any hope of a resolution. Simple words but said with such spite, so much cutting judgement, that two things occurred almost at once.

First, Patrick recoiled, then pointed across the table at the Bulldog. His lips smacked together as he struggled to speak. 'Be careful what you say there,' he eventually said, stumbling over the words.

The Bulldog arched her back like a cat but kept one eye on the mediator. 'Are you threatening me, Patrick?' She brandished his name like a piece of incriminating evidence, though all in the room could see Patrick was speaking in anguish rather than rage.

Second, Malcolm slightly lost his composure. He looked away from Eddie Moss. Romola could see his hand shaking as he put it to his forehead. His chin extended and his teeth clenched. He was containing himself. At first Romola thought she was the only one to have seen it, with everyone focused on Patrick. But then she saw Johnny's eyes were also on Malcolm – that was, until the journalist noticed Romola's gaze on him and reciprocated, his eyebrow raised in a sharp point as he stared her down. He was obviously taking some perverse pleasure in this moment, though Romola was unsure if he was relishing the bomb-like impact that the Bulldog's statement had made on the Paynes, or if he felt as though he'd manipulated Patrick and Malcolm into revealing their true selves. Either way, Johnny made Romola's stomach turn.

She briefly calculated the possible ways in which Rabbit Hole could have discovered Hana's pregnancy. She hoped it was as simple as Johnny having police sources who had divulged the autopsy results. More uncomfortable was the alternative but more obvious prospect: that someone from Patrick's inner sanctum had been playing informant all along. It hadn't escaped her notice that the most obvious culprit, Emir, still hadn't returned her calls.

'Okay, I think we've had enough,' the mediator said to Patrick, who was drawing in air like a cornered bull. 'I understand this isn't pleasant, but we need to clear the decks today. Everyone should feel free to speak their minds. Better here than in court. Ms Esposito, I trust you have a sound basis to be making these assertions?'

'A very sound basis.'

The mediator paused, clicking his tongue against the roof of his mouth as he stared at the ceiling. 'Well, the two competing positions are clear. There's not going to be much more achieved by sitting together and firing shots across the bow. I suggest each side go to your respective rooms, and I'll visit you in turn to see where you are sitting in terms of a possible compromise.' He shuffled his papers in a move to stand up, and the room began to stir.

'Can I say something?' asked Eddie casually. He'd been sitting with his arms crossed, observing proceedings with wry smile, but now he uncrossed them to raise a lazy finger, a signal to everyone that they were not done yet. Everyone paused as he spoke with the slow pace of a television journalist and the lisp of an English public school boy. 'You *know* this is good journalism, Malcolm. You know the work that has gone into making sure this is right.' He bent forwards, his wonky eye growing larger with every sentence. 'A trial will make this even bigger. And Piers and Carol Janssen? You're really going to call them? *We know* you bankroll their institute. That poor couple have been through enough without having to lie to save their livelihood. It's time to back down, Malcolm.'

Malcolm stood, towering over the table. He balled his hands into fists. 'This is not good journalism, Eddie. This is hysteria. This is a witch-hunt. This is exactly what's wrong with today's media, and it's exactly why you no longer work for a credible publication, and you never, ever will. And you, boy ...' He turned to Johnny. 'I *know* you. I know your secrets. You may have a score to settle, but don't you think the tables can't be turned one day. Because they can in an instant, and when they are you won't know what's fucking hit you.'

With that, Malcolm left the room, banging his thigh heavily on the corner of the table as he passed. Romola flinched, imagining the pain radiating from the point of impact, but Malcolm simply walked on.

*

Malcolm had arrived in their private meeting room by the time Romola, Imogen, the Slug, the Hare, and Patrick lumbered in. Payne Snr was standing by the window with his back to the room, staring through the glass to an old slate church rooftop, its spires covered in pigeons and their white droppings. All but Patrick returned to their seats, leaving only father and son standing – Patrick in front of the closed door, the table separating him from Malcolm. 'You might have told me she was having a child,' Malcolm said to the window.

Everyone except for Romola and Patrick focused elsewhere. 'She was only eight weeks,' he said quietly, his eyes on his father's back. 'She didn't want to tell anyone yet. Can we talk about this later, Dad, in private?' Romola stole a look at Patrick, expecting that, given they had spoken before about Hana's pregnancy, he might seek her out for whatever form of moral support she could offer. But he was entirely focused on his father's broad pinstriped shoulders.

'Now is fine,' Malcolm said calmly. 'The press knew before me, so I don't see why having this conversation in front of others should bother you.' He spun around to face Patrick. His face was grey as he snapped. 'What were you going to do about it?'

'What do you mean?'

'Were you going to have my grandchild?'

'Of course we were.'

'And what about her? Were you going to do the appropriate thing and marry the woman?' he demanded.

'This isn't the '50s. And we weren't exactly fifteen.' Patrick pressed his back against the closed door exhausted. 'Are we done now?'

A silence settled over the room. Romola instinctively felt sympathy for Patrick, knowing of his joy about Hana's pregnancy and wondering what conclusions he would be drawing from his father's reaction. Would the baby not have been welcome if Hana had lived? Or would his father have regarded his offspring as a second-tier member of the family? Romola thought back to the cocktail party at which she'd first met Malcolm – his barely disguised disdain towards Hana, whom he'd said wasn't good for the family, alive or dead. Romola's mind again grasped for a better understanding of this father–son relationship. The two were like magnets with alternating poles, one moment pulled together by an invisible force, and the next repulsed.

Imogen was staring at the floor, her jaw clenched and her lips pursed. Romola was waiting for her to fill the silence, and wondered if she was holding her tongue, before Imogen finally shook her head and straightened up. 'I'm sure there's a lot for you to discuss between yourselves, but today we are best served by reminding ourselves why we are here. Let's see if there's any chance we can settle this thing. They should be making the first offer – after all, they're the ones who suggested this mediation. We're not going first.'

She turned from Patrick to Malcolm. But Patrick's head was down, and Malcolm was facing the window again. When Payne Snr spoke a moment later, it was to the Slug, as if Imogen had said nothing at all. 'What do you think, Nev? Are they going to play ball?'

'That depends on what you mean by playing ball,' said the Slug, slowly turning a page from the brief in front of him. He'd been reading it as the conversation between father and son played out.

Malcolm turned back. 'I mean, are they going to make us a good offer, one that reflects the damage that's been suffered as a consequence of their reporting? North of 500k for an opening position, I would have thought. They're going to need to feel some pain over this. And we need an apology, of course.'

The Slug leaned back in his chair, hands clasped around his gut. He inhaled and then exhaled loudly and licked his lips. 'They think they're onto a good thing here, Malcolm. And we haven't exactly come up with anything concrete to convince them otherwise. I can't see them making an offer anywhere in that vicinity today. You will need to think about accepting less if you want to avoid a trial.'

Malcolm stayed at the window, hands clasped behind his back. 'Who said anything about avoiding a trial? If we have to go there, we will.'

Romola tensed, knowing she had spoken at length to Patrick about the benefits of avoiding a trial; indeed, it was how she'd managed to get him in the room today. Nor had she been completely open with Imogen about her methods of persuasion. As she waited for Patrick to call her out, to say she'd advised him about all the cons of going to trial, she mentally prepared to back herself up to the room if necessary. In front of her was her notebook, where she'd noted down the key points of the Bulldog's address – a ready reckoner of all the reasons to settle.

But Patrick didn't so much as glance at her. He pushed himself off the closed door and directed his words to the Slug. 'What about me? I can give evidence. Why isn't that worth something?'

'Well, frankly – because it's just not,' Neville countered.

'Thanks, Neville.'

'Don't be so fucking sensitive, Patty,' Malcolm spat.

The Slug put up a palm towards Malcolm to indicate it was his turn to speak. 'The fact of the matter is that your word will not be enough, Patrick. That may not be right, but it's the way things are.' He closed his eyes briefly. 'Have you ever heard of the illusory truth effect? It means that the more times you hear something, the more likely you are to believe it's true. Apply that to the internet, and your word counts for less than nothing right now. That is in the court of public opinion, of course, and our job is to try and prevent that from bleeding into the court of justice. That may be a difficult thing to do here, Patrick. We can argue that the trial should be heard by a judge alone, but Justice Debenham may well not be convinced – in my experience he's loath to deprive defendants of their right to a trial being heard by jury, where of course they have that right.'

'So why the hell am I even taking them to court?' Patrick directed his question to both Malcolm and Neville, his pleading hands held out. 'I'm going along with you here, Dad. This was all your idea, but it's my reputation on the fucking chopping block.'

'Because we have pride.' Malcolm peacocked. 'And we have self-respect. I'm not going to let them get away with saying you hurt these women. It's not your fault you keep attracting these ... types. I won't let Eddie continue printing this garbage about us.'

'About me, Dad – it was printed about me. You seem to keep forgetting that.'

'This is about more than just you, Patrick. It reflects poorly on both of us. We are better than that. We always have been. If they think they can get away with this, there'll be no stopping them.'

Imogen, who Romola had seen attempt to intervene on a couple of occasions, finally found a break in the conversation long enough for her to speak 'Can we get back to the facts for a moment, everyone? Are they right about the Janssens? Do you fund their institute? We researched that and couldn't see any link.' Imogen had a folder of key background documents in front of her, which Romola saw was turned to a memorandum summarising all of the Paynes' commercial interests. Romola remembered preparing the document; she was sure she'd checked the companies down to their last shareholder, but perhaps she'd missed something.

Malcolm lightly waved away the question. 'I make a fair contribution to them, through various means. And so I should – they do important work. That's not why they're helping us.'

Romola thought back to the tennis club; to Patrick's face when Malcolm had told her the Janssens were willing to help. Patrick had wanted to tell her then, she could see that now.

Imogen rubbed her forehead with manicured fingers. 'It would have been nice to have known that before we got in the room with them, Malcolm.'

Romola was shocked that Imogen would speak so directly to Malcolm, the prized client, and waited for him to bite back. But he completely ignored Imogen's comment, switching his attention back to the church roof, where pelting rain had frightened the pigeons away. Imogen noticed she had Romola's attention and rolled her eyes with the hint of an exasperated smile. Romola wondered if her boss was also thinking back to that dismal afternoon with Lisbeth's parents, and, like her, calculating whether they would have bothered speaking to poor Carol and Piers had they known of Malcolm's financial support for their institute.

No one spoke for some time after that, as they waited for any sign of the mediator with news from the Rabbit Hole team. Malcolm finally sat down, but unlike the others he didn't read a laptop or phone. The silence was only broken by the Slug's occasional hefty, moist throat clearings, and the Hare blasting air from his nose.

Romola watched the windowpane behind Malcolm and played Raindrop Races in her head, a game she'd played as a child on rainy day car trips. She would guess which drop would be the first to reach the bottom: twenty points for a first place, ten for a second, five for a third. She would accumulate points in her mind, knowing that once she got to a thousand something magical would happen – maybe her father would take her on a holiday, just the two of them. But she would almost always pick the wrong drop. The ones that seemed to be most confidently falling at the start would end up with an obstacle in their path, and the slow and steady drops would come through for the win.

It was an hour after the close of the joint session before the mediator opened the door to the stale room. 'This hasn't been easy.'

He wiped sweat from his brow with an embroidered handkerchief. 'But I have managed to get them to the point of making an offer, of sorts. They will walk away from this with each side bearing their own costs. You drop the claim, they don't seek their costs from you, and you pay for your own lawyers. No apology.'

'That's an insult,' Malcolm pronounced, before anyone else could speak.

'I tend to agree with you,' said the mediator. 'But I'm not getting anywhere with them. If you want them to make a real offer, I think you'll have to go first. Give them something to respond to. I'll give you a moment alone to talk.' He began to close the door.

Malcolm held up a hand to stop him from leaving. 'We don't need time to talk about anything,' he said with his eyes on Patrick, whose face in that moment was unreadable, his eyes fixed somewhere in the middle of the meeting-room table. 'Tell them it's one million plus an apology, or we walk.'

'Why don't we take a few moments to talk this through with everyone, Malcolm?' Imogen said, standing up. 'We've got all day. There's no point jumping into things.' Again, Romola was impressed at Imogen's attempts to pacify Malcolm, particularly given that the Slug, the most senior lawyer in the room, was unmoved, clearly planning to stand by and let Malcolm give instructions on Patrick's case. If anyone had asked Romola her opinion, she would have suggested that Patrick make a counteroffer closer to $500,000, something Rabbit Hole might bite at by making a lower offer. They could use the prospect of a lesser payment to leverage an apology out of their opponents, which really – in Romola's view – should have been Patrick's endgame.

'We've all had enough time together, Imogen. Now will you please tell them it's one million plus an apology or we're all going home.'

The mediator shook his head in dismay. Before he walked out the door, he turned back. 'Patrick? Is this what you want?'

Patrick closed his eyes and rubbed his eyelids with the palms of his hands. 'What I want is for none of this to have happened.' He met Romola's eyes, and she thought that perhaps he was going to ask what she thought after all. But then he closed his eyes again, and when he opened them he was staring straight at the mediator, apparently certain. 'The offer is fine. Whatever he wants.'

The Slug heaved a knowing sigh, as if to emphasise that he had predicted things would end this way. 'Shall we make bets on how long this takes?' he asked, and Romola suspected he was eyeing off an early minute.

Roughly five minutes passed before the mediator rapped on the door. He almost appeared apologetic as he told them, 'Your offer is wholeheartedly rejected. I'm sorry to tell you they've left the building.'

The Paynes and their legal team followed suit, all making separate exits from the conference room like caged birds being freed one by one. Romola and Imogen were the last to leave. With no apparent hope of resolution, they were headed to trial.

The days leading to the mediation had been hectic, and Romola was bone-tired. On the walk back to the office her muscles ached despite her having not done the slightest bit of real exercise for weeks. The thought of morphing immediately into trial preparation mode left her both daunted and exhausted. At the same time, a part of her – the part that ardently loved the law – relished the thought of a trial. And as much as she'd hoped to avoid one for Patrick's sake, a trial meant the possibility of clearing his name, an opportunity to prove Johnny wrong, and a chance to win.

Chapter Twenty-Three
The Real Work

The week immediately following the mediation passed in a flurry of activity. On Monday morning there was a directions hearing before Justice Debenham, where counsel reported back on the outcome of the day. From her seat not a couple of feet away from the judge, it was plain to Romola that whatever mild disappointment he expressed about the failure of the mediation was overshadowed by his obvious delight in listing the matter for what would likely be his last trial.

The Slug was urged on by a phone call from Malcolm – who had bypassed Imogen and Romola – to press Justice Debenham for the earliest possible trial date. The Slug did as he was instructed, and the judge obliged by giving them a listing date a mere seven weeks away, thanks to another of his trials having settled. There was a truncated timetable set for the discovery of relevant documents and any expert reports. The timetable was one of the tightest Romola had ever seen, with the Diva urging the parties to pull out all stops to make it happen. As Romola frantically noted down the orders, she could hear Imogen next to her, swearing under her breath.

On the Monday afternoon, after that morning's hearing, Romola and Imogen spoke with the staff of Costello's, the restaurant where Hana and Patrick had eaten their last meal together. All of them were willing to assist and to give evidence if necessary, but none of them were particularly helpful. While three staff described Patrick as 'doting' on Hana in the early part of the evening, the same three had witnessed their argument at the end of the night; they described Patrick as appearing variously 'enraged', 'beside himself' and 'ready to explode'. Two of the waiters had overheard bits and pieces of the argument: Hana had repeatedly said she was sorry, while Patrick had said, 'There's something wrong with you', 'What's wrong with me?' and 'If you loved me you'd do it.' They struck all of the staff from the list of potential witnesses.

On the Tuesday she and Imogen spoke with the psychologist whom they had engaged as an expert witness to testify about the behaviours associated with coercive control in romantic relationships. She was able to give evidence about the sort of characteristics one would generally see in a person in the grips of an abusive relationship, but she had never treated Hana. Nor had any psychologist, according to the medical records that Romola had obtained with Patrick's consent.

The problem was, they were having a lot of trouble finding anyone to give evidence about Hana's behaviour before her death. While Patrick could testify, corroborating evidence was also essential. But it was all but impossible to locate any friends of Hana's who had done more with her recently than interact with her online. Those few who had seen her in person told Romola in no uncertain terms that they would not be helping Patrick's case, which meant they were probably lined up by Rabbit Hole to testify for the defence, either as one of their original sources or to shore up the truth defence by reference to other substantiating evidence. Hana's old friend Storm was still happy to testify for Patrick, but other than at the one dinner, she hadn't seen Hana and Patrick together – and her experience with Hana withdrawing from their friendship supported Rabbit Hole's version of events rather than Patrick's.

Patrick was bunkered down in his Toorak mansion. While he was taking calls from Romola and Imogen, he was unhelpful in responding to their queries and couldn't – or wouldn't – direct them to any helpful evidence. Emir was still incommunicado, with Patrick insisting that he had also tried to contact him multiple times but that he'd gone 'off-grid'.

Until they could speak with Emir, Imogen and Romola knew that the next best witness would be Max. But Patrick refused even to contemplate the prospect of putting Max in the witness box, nor of subjecting him to an interview with lawyers. Patrick was immovable on this point, and it was one area where Malcolm was either unable or unwilling to exert his usual influence. Romola didn't want to push her luck, knowing that Max was probably the only reason Patrick was remaining in Melbourne and available to give instructions. She had expected him to fly the coop again after the mediation, but he had told her that he needed Max to settle in at school, and so he was sticking around. While Romola admired his steadfast protection of his child, she couldn't help but think about whether Patrick was also worried about what Max would say. Kids were often unpredictable but usually honest witnesses – maybe Patrick had assessed the risk as being too great.

Then there was Patrick's first wife, Sonia, but Imogen and Patrick had both been insistent that she was not to be approached, and Romola was powerless to change their minds.

As things stood, at the trial they would be relying on Rabbit Hole's evidence not coming up to proof. The Slug and the Hare would have to cross-examine like their lives depended on it – they were stuck with Patrick's testimony, along with Hana's sunny social media posts, which didn't hold much sway when seen in contrast to the photos of her body in a glistening evening dress.

On Wednesday and Thursday, Romola and Imogen shifted their focus to Beth and Tilly but had no more luck with them. While Beth's parents remained prepared to appear as witnesses, whatever evidence they gave would be severely undermined by their financial connection to Malcolm. A decision had nevertheless been made on advice from the Slug and the Hare to persist with them, in the hope that any sense of their loyalty to Malcolm would be outweighed – in any jury member's eyes – by the implausibility that they would support the man involved in their daughter's downward spiral and untimely death.

A couple of Beth's friends were happy to give evidence to the effect that her downfall had only begun once she'd broken up with Patrick. But Romola wasn't convinced of their intentions – they seemed very enthusiastic to appear in a high-profile trial – and the extent to which they remained loyal to Beth's sister Lara was questionable. Romola believed their evidence wouldn't be as helpful as they made out, while Imogen had been even blunter in her assessment, declaring there was 'not a fucking chance in hell' they could be trusted.

Patrick's history with Tilly remained elusive. Of his three supposed victims, she was the only one he insisted was a liar. Romola couldn't escape the fact that Tilly was also the only one who was still alive. Romola had left more messages with those few people who appeared to be connected to Tilly, and none had responded. Patrick was unable to suggest any helpful witnesses to his alleged arguments with Tilly or to produce corroborating evidence for his version of events.

There was a nagging question that wouldn't let Romola alone: where were Patrick's friends? Surely he should have schoolfriends, uni friends, work friends, sailing friends who could back him up. Friends who could say he was a good guy, that they'd seen him with these women, and that he was a normal, loving man. But Patrick seemed to have no one other than his father in his corner, or at least no one that he was prepared to tell them about.

Romola had to catch herself before she judged him. After all, now that she and Louise were no longer on speaking terms, her own friends were thin on the ground. In the years since university, everyone had retreated to the core of their friendship groups, and she had failed to be at anyone's core. She also found it hard to infiltrate new groups: she played no sports and had no hobbies, and so far she didn't really like the people she worked with, other than Gretchen, whose bright-eyed enthusiasm had grown on her, and Victoria, who had gradually thawed. So Romola had some sympathy for her friendless client, though she wasn't convinced that the gregarious Justice Debenham would be quite as understanding.

The only person who was trying to contact Romola these days was Judith. She left messages almost every day. On Thursday, alone in her cramped office, Romola gathered the strength to phone her but was immediately infuriated when Judith answered by saying, 'Are you calling to finally apologise?'

'Oh, right, what for again?' Romola asked, having genuinely forgotten her mad rush to Sydney on the same morning she was supposed to be dropping Judith at the airport.

'If you can't remember then it doesn't matter, does it? Obviously you don't feel the need to apologise, and that's fine. I understand your priorities are elsewhere. It's admirable how you've thrown yourself into this job, Romola, but don't forget –'

Romola bristled at Judith's overt passive aggression. She had shown Judith a sign of life but couldn't face another sermon from her stepmother – her heart rate intensified just at the thought of sitting through it. 'I was actually just calling to see how *you* are, Judith, not to talk about me. I wanted to check everything's okay.'

'As I keep saying, I'm fine, but I'm worried about –'

'Good. Listen, I'm sorry to call and run, but a call's coming through on the other line, so …'

'Goodness, really. You literally just called me. Ring me back, won't you?'

'Yes, of course. Speak soon. Bye.'

Romola quickly hung up and closed her eyes, feeling like she'd just dodged a bullet. She had been mindlessly scrawling through Tilly's Instagram as she was speaking to Judith, and the computer screen's glow remained white behind her closed eyelids. She pressed her fingers to her dry eyes and rubbed hard, trying to bring them back to life.

'You okay?'

Opening her eyes, Romola saw that Gretchen had come in.

Romola didn't always hear people knocking. The sound was muffled because her office remained almost entirely covered in boxes, with folders now dumped over the desk and floor. And there was a noisy air-conditioning duct overhead, which meant that visitors could enter unannounced and be standing by her side before she even noticed them.

Gretchen had dark circles under her eyes and appeared a little gaunt. She was part of the group working on the deal between Payne Corp and Goodalls, and they'd barely left the office in two weeks, utilising the firm's kitchen staff, gym facilities and showers. Emmett, keen to make an impression, had even fashioned a makeshift bed in the corner of his office.

'I had a minute spare,' Gretchen said, 'and a coffee.' She held out a takeaway cup. 'I accidentally got one extra. Thought you might want it …?'

'Thanks. I was just about to grab myself one. How's it all going?'

'It's manic. Malcolm wants to bring forward the signing date, so now we only have, like, a week left to get everything done. Emmett's given me all these contracts to review and summarise but – don't tell anyone this – I hardly even know what I'm looking for. He's pretty sketchy when he gives instructions, if you know what I mean? Anyway, it's exciting, though. Good for me to see how it all works, I guess.'

Gretchen was talking so fast that Romola hardly had the chance to respond – to tell her that if she was reviewing contracts Emmett should really be giving her more guidance as to what exactly she was to look for.

'What about Patrick's case?' Gretchen asked. 'I hear it didn't settle? You under control?' Before Romola could answer, Gretchen's phone pinged. 'Oh sorry, that's Emmett. He wants me. Sorry – we'll catch up soon, okay?'

'Sure, Gretchen. Don't work too hard.'

'You too! See ya!' She practically ran out of the office.

*

By Friday afternoon, despite being entirely spent, Romola felt she had achieved very little. She was no closer to finding further evidence to discredit Rabbit Hole's claims, and she couldn't escape the suspicion that Patrick was continuing to withhold what could be valuable evidence.

As Imogen left for the night, she popped her head into Romola's office. 'Anything new to report?' she asked, looking harried, clearly not up for a long chat.

'Afraid not,' Romola replied.

'We must get some more resources onto this,' Imogen said, shaking her head. 'This Goodalls deal is soaking up the whole fucking firm. I'll speak to Derek about it on Monday.'

'Thanks – that would be great. We'll be getting more discovery in next week, so it's going to take a while to get through that, depending on how much there is, and I could really use a hand with the experts –'

'I get the point. Leave it with me.' She waved as she closed the door. 'Don't work too hard over the weekend,' she added, leaving no doubt that Romola was to work through. Romola had no plans anyway; there had been no contact from Louise, and Cliffy was in the midst of a trial so would be burrowed deep into his office. Plus her mind was constantly ticking over with possible angles and paths of enquiry, offset by the obstacles in their way, as though she was plotting her way through a maze.

By 7.30 p.m. Romola pulled up stumps. Her brain still tied in knots, she felt that familiar Friday night yearning for a release; she needed a drink, to unload her thoughts and to escape back to the real world. She decided to give the firm's regular Friday night drinks a try, but was disappointed to see that only a few unfamiliar tax lawyers were in attendance. They sat at a table around an enormous cheese platter, having an animated conversation about a recent ATO ruling. She stood by the drinks table, undecided as to whether she should attempt to join the group.

'Are you looking for something?' one of them eventually called, hardly an invitation.

'Me? No, just heading off for the night. Have a good weekend!'

As she left the room, half of them called for her to do the same despite having absolutely no idea who she was.

She walked the long way to the tram stop, feeling a bolt of loneliness as she passed laughing crowds jammed into warm bars. There was a big footy match on, and as her tram approached the Melbourne Cricket Ground she saw the winter fog illuminated over the enormous stadium.

Any hope of a drink with Cliffy was dashed when she arrived home to a cold, dark and empty house. She heated up some leftover quiche and ate it alone at the kitchen counter with a glass of shiraz, watching *Keeping Up with the Kardashians* on her laptop, suddenly too tired to register the sadness of the scene. She left her dish in the sink, headed upstairs to bed, and within minutes sank into a welcome sleep.

Chapter Twenty-Four
Breaking Deals

Romola's father was sitting at the bottom of the garden, reading a book. She could barely make out the back of his head over the bougainvillea that Judith was always at him to prune. He was on the bench seat Romola had made with Louise in tech class at high school: three railway sleepers screwed together, with the initials RC and LM carved into its leg. He must have forgotten his glasses, because he held the book at a distance.

'Dad!' Romola called as she tiptoed over the stepping stones in the sprawling garden. Don said that the garden would have cost them at least a million in today's market, but he could afford it on a university wage in 1988 after the market crashed. 'Dad!' she called again, but he didn't turn.

His head was cocked to one side to take in the sunlight. The book must have been funny – his shoulders bounced with laughter. If only he would turn around, she would see him smile. Why wouldn't he turn?

She shouted this time. 'Dad, it's me!'

His back straightened. He lifted his elbow and placed it on top of the bench next to him. At last he would turn. Any second now she would see his familiar face.

Then came the sound of a phone. The ugly noise wormed its way into the garden, into her consciousness. It came from afar at first, then closer. Soon it was as clear as a bell. With a dreadful thump she remembered she would never see her father's face again. Her heart raced at how close she'd come this time.

She reached for her phone, registering that it was only midnight; she had been so soundly asleep that she'd mistaken the sound for her morning alarm. Her stomach flipped when she saw it was actually a call, and that the caller was Patrick. She held her breath. There was never a good reason for a client to call at midnight.

'I think I fucked up,' he said in a wet, weepy voice, his words slurred.

She propped herself up on her elbows. 'Where are you?'

'Home. But I was out b-fore. At a bar.'

'And?' Now she sat upright.

'Hadda few drinks.'

'And?'

'What – I carn even havva drink anymore?'

'What happened, Patrick?'

'Bloody paps. Waitin for me ousside. Askin bout Hana, an Beth, an ... *you* too now.'

Romola hardly needed to ask what had come next. The fact he was at home and not in a prison cell gave her some comfort. 'And?'

'An I was angry. Swore. I dunno – I mightta pushed a guy. My driver got me out.'

'You didn't actually hit anyone?'

'No. I think no.'

'Did the police come?'

'No.'

'So why are you calling me?'

Patrick was quiet for a moment. 'I thought you'd wanna know. Not sure how the photos'll look. Could be bad for the case ... I dunno. I just wann-ed to call.' He was silent, perhaps waiting for praise that didn't come, before he continued, his voice breaking. 'When's this gonna end? All I wan is for this to end. Let-em say anything – then no one'll care anymore.'

'Okay.'

Romola threw her covers off and stood up, absent-mindedly pacing over to the full-length mirror in the corner of her bedroom, before catching her reflection. She wore the nightie Judith had given her for Christmas, ankle-length white French cotton with an embroidered hem. Fit for an Austen heroine, it was one of few gifts from Judith that Romola had loved immediately. She saw her wild black curls, her face creased and her eyes dark with tiredness. The blue glow of the phone under her face made her look like she belonged either in a horror movie or an asylum.

She turned away from her image. 'It's going to be okay, Patrick. We'll see what we can do. Thanks for telling me – I appreciate it. Now get some sleep, and I'll give you a call on Monday. Does that sound okay?'

'Yeah, yeah. I'm gonna sit ere for a bit. Listen to some music.'

She could hear the first bars of Portishead's 'Sour Times'. She would know it anywhere.

After hanging up, she held her breath as she checked the news. The story was already leading most websites: 'Payne hits out at reporters', 'Payne rears his ugly head', with images of Patrick leaving the club. Red-faced, bloodshot eyes half closed, lips curled back, gap-toothed and crazed, he was mid-tirade. The camera flash had caught his saliva floating through the air. A suited driver who carried himself like he was ex-armed forces was holding him from behind while pinning his arms.

There was also video footage. The paparazzo's questions weren't included, only Patrick's furious reaction: 'What the fuck did you say? Come out from behind the camera and say that to my face, you vulture! If you say one more thing about her, I'll …'

It wasn't clear which 'her' he meant.

The footage showed a brief tussle with the driver, who easily had Patrick's measure, before he guided Patrick, head down, into a waiting Range Rover. The pack of photographers fed off every last one of his dazed moments.

The video was trending on WhatsApp and Twitter. Memes were being created. Patrick's descent was almost complete.

Head aching and eyes dry, Romola was nearly overwhelmed by her need for sleep. She forwarded the links to Imogen with a short email, before turning off her phone.

Imogen,
Patrick called to warn this was coming. He wants to extricate himself from this. Perhaps we could focus more on an apology as opposed to compensation.
Happy to talk tomorrow,
R

*

The next morning Romola waited for a call, an email, anything from Imogen. But by 10 a.m. her inbox was empty save for the usual Saturday morning spam.

She was determined not to start work too early, walking instead to the café on the corner for a chat with Azra. In recent weeks Romola had begun to befriend the café owner. When Romola came in for her early morning coffee, if business was quiet Azra would often come and join her, and they would chat about Romola's struggles with Judith, or Azra's son Mohammed. It was the kind of friendship where they seemed to have progressed beyond small talk very quickly, each knowing that the other wouldn't ask too many questions. Every now and then, Azra would reveal something of her former life in Turkey, or Romola would talk about her father without fear of having to dissect exactly how she was feeling.

But today was unexpectedly busy at Azra's. Its owner was in action mode, her face determined as she stood behind the counter tersely taking orders and making coffees, giving Mohammed – who worked weekends – instructions as to which coffee belonged to which customer. When Romola arrived all the tables were occupied, so Azra gestured for her to sit at a small table near the counter that was stacked with envelopes and a calculator, where Azra normally did her paperwork. With a lift of her hand, Azra apologised for being too busy to speak today. There was a small smile on her determined face; she was obviously relishing the fact that on this wet Saturday, double the usual customers had chosen to venture to her corner.

Azra soon snuck away from the counter for a moment to bring Romola an espresso with a baklava nestled on the side.

'So many people!' said Romola.

'I know!' Azra exclaimed with a smile. 'It's the pogaĉa. They all want my pogaĉa!'

Romola sipped her coffee and watched strangers tuck into Azra's pastries with delight – but she couldn't stop herself from scrolling the news. The feeding frenzy on the footage of Patrick continued until every last angle had been chipped away, the story becoming round and constant, a fully formed memory in the country's psyche. The only positive was that she was old news now: the images of her and Patrick no longer held much interest in the face of his captured outburst.

With no chance of conversation with Azra, she decided to head into the office. But she walked the long way in, knowing she would only feel at ease once she'd stepped into the elevator, once she was closer to crossing things off her ever-growing to-do list in preparation for trial. Patrick could be fronting a judge or jury of peers who had now seen him bite the heads off reporters on a night out. They had to scrape together the evidence needed to counter that.

With the Goodalls acquisition nearing its close, she expected the office to be buzzing at noon on a Saturday. But when she opened the door she was faced with apocalyptic silence. Errant papers drifted across the floor, pizza boxes were left open in the kitchen, and folders were piled high in meeting rooms. There wasn't a soul in sight.

Treading tentatively to her office, she sniffed the air for smoke. Maybe a fire alarm had just gone off, or there had been a gas leak. But if that had happened, she would surely have passed a group of exasperated lawyers stuck on the street outside the building.

Still uneasy, she turned on her computer and sat down, ignoring for a moment the flashing light on her office phone. With her computer booting up, she almost didn't hear the papers shuffle behind her. The hair stood up on her arms, before a timid voice eased her nerves: 'Did you hear?'

Gretchen stood in the doorway, clutching a pile of papers. Her tired face was crestfallen. She looked like a child after her first sleepover.

'Hear what?'

Gretchen lowered her voice. 'Goodalls pulled out of the deal. It's pens down. Malcolm's gone bananas.'

Maybe it was the mention of bananas, but Romola started to giggle – stifled at first, then full-bellied, out-of-breath laughter. This was very bad news for the firm. Payne Corp was one of its biggest clients. But for some reason she found the thought of Malcolm's precious deal falling through hilarious.

Gretchen gawped, horrified.

'Sorry.' Romola composed herself. 'I know it's not funny. Tell me

– what happened?' She leaned forward, suddenly anxious for details.

'Apparently they had concerns about Payne Corp's image, with Patrick and all. They say they need to appeal to families, that any connection with Patrick would be bad for the brand.'

'Oh …' Her light-heartedness completely vanished. Malcolm had lost his deal, and it was all Patrick's fault. 'This is not good. So everyone's just … gone home?'

'Derek had Malcolm on speaker in his office. We all knew something was up – you could hear the yelling a mile away. Then he came out and told everyone to leave. He said we're not charging anymore, so everyone should go home. No one's had any sleep so they all just, like, evacuated.'

Romola's mind tracked through the consequences for Patrick's trial. Could he add the financial loss of the Goodalls Supermarkets deal to the damages claim against Rabbit Hole? Unlikely, given the deal was still going ahead after the publication of the Rabbit Hole stories; rather, it was Patrick's public drunk and disorderly conduct that had pushed them over the edge. What if, on top of that, he lost the defamation case? What if he was found to be as bad as Rabbit Hole had suggested? Would Malcolm be prepared to sue his own son for the loss of the deal?

Tears began falling down Gretchen's face. She wiped her nose clumsily with her shirtsleeve. Her normally perfect blonde hair had fallen over her face.

'Oh, Gretchen,' Romola said gently, feeling equal parts sympathy and irritation at the sight of tears. 'There's no need to be upset. Things happen. Look at the positives – now you get to go home for some rest.'

'I'm sorry.' Gretchen sniffed. 'I know I'm being silly. It's just … Derek didn't seem very happy with my work, and I thought if I'd been able to do things quicker maybe we could have got all the documents signed before this happened.'

Romola stood up and walked over, clasping Gretchen's shoulders. The women were the same height, so Romola could meet her eyes head on. 'You're officially being ridiculous. You are overworked. I guarantee you that nothing you did, or possibly could have done, would have changed this outcome. I don't mean to take away from the work you were doing, but in the scheme of things it probably wasn't all that important. Okay?'

Gretchen's eyes started to clear. 'I know you're right. I guess I always wonder what I could have done differently, you know?'

Romola was reminded of something she'd read years ago about the difference between male and female professionals: imposter syndrome. Successful women thought of themselves as imposters, assuming that one day they would be exposed for their failings. Men had no such doubts – even those who actually were imposters didn't realise it. Emmett wouldn't have given the firm's dumping a second thought; he was probably drinking beer with friends right now, patting himself on the back for having worked on Malcolm's matter in the first place.

Still holding Gretchen by the shoulders, Romola gently turned and pointed her towards the door. 'You're better than all of them, Gretchen. In so many ways. Now go home and sleep.'

The young woman shuffled slowly out of the office, her tiredness presenting as a limp, her body crumpled.

Unsettled, Romola noticed again the flashing light of her desk phone. She began playing her messages. The first was from Imogen, stuck in traffic yesterday morning, livid about something insignificant. The second message was from an unknown number.

'Hello. It's Jason Reznak here. I'm returning your calls from a few days ago. Sorry I've been hard to catch – I've had some issues with my phone, and work's been crazy, you know. I'm happy to talk to you, though. I've been giving this a lot of thought, and, well, I think you're going to want to hear what I have to say. Call me back.'

Jason Reznak – Tilly's surfer boyfriend. Romola had left three messages for him and all but given up hope of him providing any useful information. She jotted down his number and rang him back immediately, frustrated when it was once again diverted to voicemail.

She spent the next couple of hours going over Tilly's statement, adding to her detailed notes as to what she wanted to ask Jason about. It was slow going. Her previously well-formed trains of thought were now scattered and frayed by the trifecta of new developments: the collapse of the Goodalls deal, Patrick's public drunken tirade, and

Jason's mysterious intimation that he had something important to say. By 2 p.m. Romola couldn't restrain herself from calling Jason again, but as soon as she picked up the phone it buzzed in her hand, making her jump.

She recognised Imogen's number. It was hard to imagine a time when she hadn't, but her mind flashed to ten weeks earlier, when an unfamiliar number had appeared on her screen as she sat in Cliffy's kitchen on a Sunday night. It seemed an age ago.

'Imogen,' Romola answered. 'I'm at the office. I just heard –'

'You're at the office? I need you to stop working now.'

'Is this about the Goodalls deal?'

'Sort of. Listen – can you come to my place? Normally I'd come into the office, but Mitch is out and I don't have a babysitter. I want to talk with you in person. How soon can you be here?'

Chapter Twenty-Five
At Home with Imogen

Imogen's house was as hard-edged as the woman herself, all bright white render, shadows and glass. There was no sign of a bell on the enormous steel door, and it seemed improbable that a simple knock would stir anyone inside. Romola thought of the contrast with her childhood home. The front door was mostly left unlocked and often completely open behind the flyscreen, with the light at the end of a long corridor visible to all. The house had a 'welcome' doormat and climbing roses, and visitors would signal their arrival with a 'yoo hoo' as they came up the hall.

Romola was about to take out her phone when the heavy door swung open and Imogen appeared. She was wearing a lacy black cocktail dress and was perfectly made up, with her fine lips ruby-red. At her feet stood a screaming red-faced child, pulling on her hem. 'Come in!' she said. '*Quick*, before the other one gets out.'

As Romola obeyed, she noticed another, slightly bigger, child running back and forth across a light-filled living room. Wearing a torn Elsa costume, the child was dangling a spoon laden with chocolate custard perilously close to white leather couches while giggling like a maniac. 'They're so cute,' Romola offered.

'Don't humour me,' Imogen said flatly. 'Mitch gave them juice boxes and then left the building. One ounce of sugar and it's like they're possessed.' She dropped the smaller child into a beanbag next to her sister and pressed a button on a remote, bringing a larger-than-life yellow Wiggle onto the huge screen in front of them.

'Wiggies!' yelled the older child, clapping her grubby hands in glee.

Romola leaned in closer to the girl, who was now eagerly licking at the spoon, legs spread in front of her, eyes glued to the screen. 'What's *your* name?' Romola asked.

The child ignored her, mesmerised by the woman in yellow bouncing across the screen.

'Don't bother,' Imogen called over her shoulder. 'If you must know, the bigger one's Maude and the smaller one's Constance. Fifteen months apart. We were running out of time so got them both out of the way. I don't know what we were thinking.' She grabbed a bottle of white wine and a couple of glasses from a sparkling kitchen bench, then started backing out of the room through a set of sliding doors. 'Now if we're very quiet we can walk away without them noticing.'

Adjoining the lounge was an enormous dining room. An arrangement of mauve peony roses sat upon a round marble-topped table. Floor-to-ceiling windows faced out onto an aquamarine pool.

Imogen poured out two enormous glasses of wine, handing one to Romola without asking if she wanted it, and taking one for herself. 'I'm due at a function in half an hour. If Mitch doesn't get home soon I might just break out the Phenergan and put them to bed.'

Imogen stared at Romola expectantly, and it occurred to Romola how rarely she'd seen her boss tell a joke. It didn't suit her.

Imogen pointed her wineglass in the direction of her children in the lounge room. 'Now you know why I always look so happy to be at work. I'm escaping the madhouse.'

Romola glanced around the dining room. The place was immaculate, anything but a madhouse. And Imogen never, ever, seemed happy to be at work.

She seated herself at the table and put the glass to her lips, taking a small sip. The wine was the colour of straw and so dry it made her mouth purse, but it did calm her nerves. She felt utterly out of place and still had no idea what she was doing there, or whether Imogen was about to hit her with good or bad news. It was like playing the blindfold game as a child, told to open your mouth but unsure if you would be fed honey or vinegar. 'You wanted to see me?' she ventured.

Imogen set her own glass down and sat next to Romola. 'You've heard about the Goodalls deal?'

'I know they've pulled out.' Romola was conscious of revealing too much of what Gretchen had told her, not wanting to get her friend in trouble if she had overshared.

Imogen swirled wine around in her glass and fixed Romola with a sidelong stare, clearly savouring the moment before revelation. 'The Goodalls team are blaming Patrick,' she explained. 'His behaviour is apparently inconsistent with their brand, et cetera. They won't let their company be owned by a Payne. The community sentiment against Patrick is too strong. So they say.' She drew wine from her glass and sucked in her cheeks.

Romola feigned surprise. 'Hard to believe they would give up a deal worth so much because of Patrick's night out.'

'Like they're all so fucking squeaky clean,' Imogen spat, before peeking through the door at the children and lowering her voice. 'I suspect there's something else at play here, and Patrick's behaviour gave them an easy out. Idiot. What was he thinking?'

'He's lost,' Romola offered.

'If he thinks he's lost now, he's about to get dropped in the middle of the fucking Amazon.'

'How do you mean?'

Imogen swished wine about her mouth, still watching Romola carefully. 'Malcolm's had enough. He's cutting Patrick off. No more funding Patrick's lifestyle, no more funding his business, his charity … and, more importantly for us, no more paying his lawyers' bills. Patrick's going to have to fend for himself.'

Romola froze, and it seemed the world around her also stopped. A shiver ran across her body, and the skin on her arms puckered into goosebumps. She fixated on Imogen's ruby-red lips and what they would say next. 'So what does that mean for his case?'

'Well … ' Imogen drew out the word. 'I'm afraid the firm – well, Derek actually – has decided that, in the circumstances, we should cease acting for Patrick. We're giving him two weeks' notice of termination of the retainer. It's all over.' Imogen didn't make eye contact, offering no clue as to whether she'd been part of 'the firm's' decision.

Romola placed her glass down carefully on the marble surface, her first thoughts for her client. 'But what about Patrick? His trial starts in six weeks. On top of everything else, how will that look? People will put two and two together. If his own father doesn't believe in him, who else will? He's our client.' Romola just stopped short of reminding Imogen that they had a duty to act in Patrick's best interests – of course she would know that and wouldn't appreciate Romola suggesting otherwise.

Imogen shook her head. 'I have been through this already with Derek, and the fact is our retainer letter gives us the right –'

'Mama.' Constance entered the room, dragging a battered bunny toy behind her, thumb in mouth. 'Mama,' she whimpered again.

'Come here, bunny.' Imogen placed down her wineglass so she could hold out her arms, and Constance heaved herself up, curling into a ball, her head resting on Imogen's chest. A smile turned up the corner of the little girl's mouth. Imogen continued speaking, almost in a whisper now, over her child's head, rocking her gently back and forth. 'Our retainer letter allows either party to terminate on two weeks' notice. I've already called Patrick to break the news.'

'How did he take it?' In Romola's mind it could have gone one of two ways: despondency or rage.

Imogen shrugged. 'I think he might have been drinking again. I don't know if he fully understood. He's livid with Malcolm, as you can imagine. I'm less sure of his feelings about us. He seemed to accept that's the way it's going to be.'

Romola could picture Patrick miserably accepting his fate. 'What about you, Imogen? I thought you'd worked hard to get Patrick as your client. You're going to let him go, just like that?'

'I never said I was happy about it,' Imogen said calmly. 'Yes, I worked extremely hard to get Patrick as my client. Some people at the firm were not so happy about it either. But I didn't give up. It was once a big thing to say I was Patrick Payne's lawyer.'

'So why give him up without a fight?' asked Romola, feeling incredulous.

'There's so much you don't understand.' Imogen bent her head to smell her daughter's tangled hair. Constance stared into the middle distance as her eyelids began to droop. 'Do you know how much maternity leave I had with Connie?'

Romola shrugged.

'Four weeks.' Imogen scoffed. 'That's not even long enough for a baby to learn how to smile. Mitch's job is more flexible, so we decided he should take the time off to look after the girls. I'd seen what happened to women who took months of maternity leave. I was so bloody insistent it wouldn't be me.' She closed her eyes. 'I wanted the other partners to think I was like them. But I never will be. The irony of it is that when they see their worst qualities echoed back at them, they label those qualities as female – the bitchiness, the gossiping, the vindictiveness. Now I've learnt exactly when, and when not, to act like one of them. I've given up a lot to get where I am. I'm not going to kiss it goodbye this easily.'

'But isn't the alternative to sit back and lose one of your best clients?' Romola countered.

Imogen shook her head. 'If I stand up to them now, I won't be fighting for myself. I'll be committing suicide. Malcolm is the firm's biggest client – I have to protect that relationship. If Derek says we're not allowed to act for Patrick, then that's exactly what will happen. At least if I take it lying down I might get some sympathy, people might shoot some work my way. Patrick's had everything in life. Believe it or not, I haven't. He'll survive. I may not. I have to let him go.'

Romola had seen the firm in action and could believe every word of it. But still she felt angry. Her face and fingers were tingling with it, her lips fizzing with all the words she wanted to say, though she couldn't seem to get even the simplest ones out. She had stuck out her neck for Patrick's sake. She had lost her oldest and dearest friendship, damaged her tenuous relationship with her stepmother, and for the first and hopefully last time found her image plastered over the tabloid news. All because she was doing her job, acting in her client's interests. And now she was expected to abandon him because his daddy said so?

'What if I don't want to let it go?' Romola jutted out her chin, unsure exactly what her words meant but knowing she couldn't find it within herself to abandon her client as easily as Imogen had.

Imogen examined Romola's face closely. 'And why would you do something like that?'

'Because he needs someone who's going to represent his interests.

And we're his lawyers.' Now she couldn't stop herself from speaking her mind. 'It's what we're supposed to do.'

Raising her eyebrows, Imogen asked, 'So you believe him then?'

Romola clenched her teeth, exasperated to have a fellow lawyer ask this question. Imogen should know better than anyone that her beliefs were irrelevant. 'What does that matter? He's entitled to a lawyer who's going to see his case through to its conclusion.'

'If you want to try and change Derek's mind, then so be it. I'm not going to stop you.' She didn't seem altogether unhappy at Romola's perseverance, though her squirrel eyes were brimming with emotion. 'But you've been warned. They won't forget.'

Romola heard the front door open.

'At last – he arrives.' Imogen spoke with exasperation, but Romola saw her almost instantly relax with the arrival of her husband.

'Princess! Come and give Daddy a hug.'

Peering through the sliding doors to the lounge, Romola could see a stubbled man in a tracksuit squeeze the life out of little Maude, who giggled hysterically. He had an easy smile on his face as he sauntered into the dining room. Imogen held a finger to her lips, pointing at Constance, who had fallen sound asleep in her arms.

'She wouldn't take her nap,' Imogen whispered. 'She was beside herself. I figured I should let her sleep. Right?' Imogen was looking to her husband for his approval. Romola had never seen her so uncertain.

'You did the right thing,' Mitch said softly.

Imogen tilted her face to him, and he leaned over and kissed her forehead, stroking Connie's cheek with the back of his hand. Imogen's eyes shut with his touch, the office surely a million miles away. Romola wished for a moment that there was an alternate universe to which she could flee at the touch of a hand, a place that could somehow diminish the despair she felt at having to discard her one and only client. But the fact was, she had no one.

Chapter Twenty-Six
One Too Many

'Another gin and tonic, please.' Romola waved her credit card in the air.

She'd found the bar not far from Imogen's house, tucked in a side street close to the water, with a Prohibition vibe about it. Judith had always said gin was a depressant, but here, served in a heavy glass with lime and elderflower, it tasted anything but depressing.

A bartender stood drying glasses a few feet away. Romola supposed most people would have called him handsome. He had kind smiling eyes, and his hair was pulled back in a ponytail – like Johnny's. Romola winced.

The bartender nodded to the empty stool next to her. 'Are you waiting for someone?'

'Nope.' She had another gulp. 'I'm not from here. My friends are somewhat ... limited.'

'Just visiting?'

She held her glass out in front of her, poking at the beautiful big ice cube with the metal straw. 'Am I visiting? I mean, I moved here for work. But it's not going so well. Sort of a disaster, actually. So it might be more like a visit, after all – a terrible disastrous holiday.'

For the first time, she let herself contemplate calling the whole Bassett Brown endeavour a failed experiment and returning to Sydney for good. She didn't know what would be worse: Judith's satisfaction or Cliffy's disappointment. Romola's sense of failure would trump them both. Maybe she would head overseas again? Work in a bar in New York City, dry glasses and chat to people, like this guy was doing. He seemed happy enough.

'Melbourne's tough for outsiders,' he said. 'They're so damn parochial here.'

Nice as well as handsome. And he could use big words like 'parochial'. This was the type of man Louise would have tried to make Romola go home with.

'Do you enjoy working in a bar?' she asked, just as one of her dad's favourite songs began to play: 'Stuck in the Middle with You', by Stealers Wheel. That was how she felt, stuck between clowns and jokers. She felt naïve to be the only one looking after the interests of her client, while everyone else was looking after themselves. Always the goody-two-shoes. Maybe now was the time to be selfish for once.

'It's fine,' the bartender said. 'Pays the bills. How about you? Let me guess –' he gave her a once-over '– something corporate, high pressure, not very satisfying?' He grinned, reaching up to hang a glass on a rack above her head. He had not insignificant biceps, she noticed. And he smelled of firewood.

She was deflated that he'd picked her as 'corporate'. That was the last thing she wanted to be, but he must have sensed her hopelessness.

'Best not to talk about my job.' She shook her head enthusiastically as she spoke, and a moment later the room moved. Her vision was playing on delay. She remembered the wine she had consumed at Imogen's, and happily realised she was now getting drunk, her mind bubbling with its escape from the thoughts of Sober Romola. None of it really mattered now. She was giving herself a leave pass – permission to spend an evening being anything but serious. 'I'm thinking of becoming a bartender,' she said.

The barman laughed half-heartedly. 'I can see that. But you know it's not all it's cracked up to be. I only work here weekends and nights. I'm a social worker by trade, but it doesn't quite pay the bills.'

'I see … You, my friend, are a *good* person. I used to be one of those.' She bowed her head and lifted her drink. 'Cheers to you.'

He shook his head and laughed as he walked away to serve other customers. Just as she had been about to order another gin.

Chapter Twenty-Seven
Awakening

R omola had left the curtains open, and she woke to the sun on her pillow. She felt the pain in her head before she was conscious of being awake. Was a ball of lead crashing into the side of her skull with each movement? The pain intensified with every heartbeat's rush of blood.

She couldn't remember the previous night in chronological order, but foggy images montaged through her mind. She had danced – or at least there had been people dancing around her. A big man had stroked her shoulder and whispered in her ear how he loved the taste of chocolate. She had pushed him, and the friendly bartender had come to her aid. Had he taken her somewhere private, somewhere quiet? As she drifted back to sleep, she could only remember the quiet.

The muffled sound of her phone woke her a short time later. It took all her strength to heave herself to the side of the bed and rummage through her bag. She was relieved to see Louise's name, as she couldn't have faced anyone else. She answered with a groan.

'Hey,' Louise said softly, 'you okay?'

Romola managed another groan and pushed her face into the pillow.

'Geez, Romy – I've been worried about you.' Louise sounded genuinely concerned.

Romola propped herself up on the pillows and forced herself to face the sun, waiting for the black-and-orange glow behind her eyes to fade.

'Hello? Romy?'

'I'm here. Sorry. Okay. I'm okay. I mean, I think I could be dying but, I'm mostly okay. You know those times when nothing seems to go right …?' A memory suddenly came to her. She put her hand to her head. 'Oh shit, I tried to kiss the bartender last night.' He'd flinched, holding her at arm's length like a star-struck teenager.

'Was he cute?'

'Yes, he was.' Romola cringed, the embarrassment of the moonlit moment magnified in the light of day. 'And also married with twins.' Her face burned with the thought. No wonder he had so many bills to pay.

'It's not like all of us haven't done it a million times, Romy. It's just that you never have because you're always so damned unfriendly to boys.'

'Hmph.' Romola rested her head back on the pillow, knowing she'd been right all along to be unfriendly. Look where friendliness had got her. 'Hey – you're calling me,' she said, only then remembering they weren't actually on speaking terms. 'Does this mean I'm forgiven?'

Louise was silent for a long moment. 'I thought we covered that last night?'

The blood rushed quicker to Romola's head as the throbbing changed to a constant thrum of pain. 'Huh?'

'You called me last night. Remember?' Louise's voice grew louder, more serious.

'I did?' Romola searched her mind and briefly saw herself shouting – and possibly crying – into her phone.

'You wanted me to come out and dance with you,' Louise said matter-of-factly. 'Then you apologised about a million times. Then you said you were thinking of helping out at an orphanage in Cambodia? Is any of this ringing a bell?'

'Oh god, I don't remember any of that. Cambodia?' She managed a laugh at herself. 'Well, I am sorry – that bit's true. I should have said something to you a lot earlier about acting for Patrick.' Romola felt lighter, the air clearing at the prospect of having Lou back in her life.

'It's okay. I'm over it. And none of that matters now anyway, does it?'

Sore head and all, Romola sat up straight. 'What do you mean?'

'I mean, you said you're not acting for him anymore. Daddy's not paying his fees. So it doesn't matter anymore, does it? We can all carry on like normal, you and Johnny can get along et cetera?'

'I told you that? I said the words "we're not acting for him"?'

'Yep. And you didn't seem all that happy about it either.'

Romola began to sweat. She stood up unsteadily and closed the brocade curtains. 'Listen, Louise, I really shouldn't have told you that. It's not something I'm allowed to say. What the fuck was I thinking? You didn't tell Johnny, did you?'

The silence made Romola's stomach drop.

'You've told him.'

'I might have ... a little bit ... but listen, I'll tell him he is absolutely not to do anything with that info – it's completely off the record.'

'Oh god, but he's the defendant, Louise.' Romola put her hand to her head, leaning into the folds of the curtains. 'He'll tell his legal team. He has to.'

'I'm so sorry, Romy.' Louise sounded genuinely regretful. 'I didn't realise it was a secret. Honestly. Let me go speak to him now, and I'll see what I can do.'

Romola's mind raced while the room span around her.

'He owes me one anyway.' Louise kept chattering incessantly, though Romola was barely hearing the words. 'You know I discovered he's the one behind those photos of you and Patrick? He'd sent a photographer up there to get some more dirt on Patrick. Don't worry, I got proper furious with him about it. He's intent on bringing Patrick down, there's some deep-seated hatred there. I think Johnny's actually too principled sometimes, if there is such a thing. You know what I mean?'

Romola let Louise's words wash over her, her thoughts firmly planted in her own circumstances. The fury she felt at Johnny was instantly snuffed out by thoughts of her own wrongdoing, as she struggled to make sense of just how bad her indiscretion had been.

'Okay,' Romola said, in response to nothing in particular. She crawled back into bed, willing the world to disappear again. 'I need to go, I think.'

'I'll let you know what he says. Speak soon. And take care of yourself, you big boozer!'

Romola hung up, then checked Rabbit Hole, the other news sites and social media. Nothing new about Patrick – maybe Johnny would do the right thing and keep this to himself.

She peeled off last night's clothes, ready for a long, hot shower. But first she would lie on top of the covers for a moment. The linen felt so cool against her skin. Within minutes, she fell into a deep sleep.

*

Two hours later she found Cliffy in his library with a set of engineering plans spread out on the desk in front of him. He set down his magnifying glass and stretched. 'Please offer me some distraction, my dear. Professional negligence case against mining engineers. The detail is excruciating.'

Romola nodded, clutching a steaming cup of black tea, her headache having settled into a constant, low-frequency pain.

He regarded her with a sympathetic smile. 'You look like you've seen better days.'

'You could say that.' She lowered herself into a deep velvet armchair, lifting her tea to feel its steam on her face. Her glasses fogged. 'I've stuffed up, Cliffy.'

He scoffed. 'What is life without a monumental blunder every now and then? I'm sure it can't be that bad.'

This was one of the things she loved most about Cliffy: whatever she said to him, it was like he'd been expecting it. It was so comforting to feel incapable of surprising someone.

'Between you and me,' she said, 'we've been acting for Malcolm in a very sensitive, very important transaction. And it's just fallen through. As a consequence of which, for various reasons, the firm is going to stop acting for Patrick.'

'Let me guess. Malcolm won't pay his fees?'

'No comment.'

'I'm not surprised. For all his talk of philanthropy, Malcolm Payne is a beast of a man. I've seen him threaten to pull the pin on cases before, my dear. It's normally a lot of puff and whistle, and then he changes his mind.' Cliffy began methodically sharpening the pencils he'd been using to mark up the engineering plans. One by one he laid them next to each other.

'I think it's the real deal this time,' Romola said softly, feeling numb. And then, with no further introduction, she confessed all her sins to Cliffy.

'So that's why we haven't had the pleasure of Louise's company lately?'

Romola shut her eyes tight. 'It's hideous, isn't it? Do you think I'll still be able to practise?'

Cliffy laughed, though his heart wasn't in it. 'I'm not going to lie to you, my dear. It's not an ideal position to be in.' He propped his head to one side, crinkled his forehead and regarded her with a mixture of sympathy and sorrow. 'On a positive note, you haven't told the other side anything they won't find out shortly. You'll have to come clean to Imogen, of course, but she may not take it quite as badly as you might think.' He started tapping one of his pencils on the desk in a quick rhythm. 'In fact, you might be surprised by how all this turns out. Solutions have a way of presenting themselves in time.'

This was exactly the kind of non-specific Cliffy comment that she found comforting. He had a confidence in the universe that whatever happened would be enough – faith, of a kind.

She'd almost come to the end of her tea. 'I don't know if I made the right decision, moving down here. It doesn't seem to have gone terribly well.' Her voice began to break as, for the first time, she verbalised her sadness. With little warning, her eyes welled up and warm tears fell onto her cheeks. The pounding in her head returned.

'Oh, Romy, my dear. It's not as bad as it seems. Not every client will be a Patrick Payne,' Cliffy consoled. 'When they come along they are a challenge, no doubt, but that's how you become a better lawyer.'

Romola sniffed, wiping her face with the back of her hand.

Cliffy stood up and passed her a tissue from a box on the bookshelf behind him. He seemed to weigh up whether he ought to come out from behind his desk to comfort her, but instead started flicking to the back of the Sunday newspaper on his desk, apparently looking for something. 'So far you've never given up on Patrick. You've done well – I've been watching. What you need is some perspective. And I know just the thing.' He continued flicking through the paper, as Romola gradually controlled her tears, already feeling a little better.

After a few moments, Cliffy held up the newspaper. 'Aha!' He pointed at a black-and-white artsy photo of a sparse pine forest. 'Nordic cinema! There's a Norwegian film festival on today in Brunswick. Why don't we find the most noir movie we can, and wallow in your misery for the afternoon?'

She wanted nothing more than to curl up in bed and give in to her regret. But she never could say no to Cliffy. 'Give me ten minutes to make myself presentable.'

*

She sipped a large Coke with ice and waited for the cinema to darken. Cliffy sat next to her, munching eagerly on his popcorn – too loud, she thought, embarrassed. She checked her phone one last time before turning it to silent. A new email had appeared. Only then did she remember the phone message from Jason, Tilly's ex-boyfriend.

> Hi Romola,
>
> I left a message for you about Tilly. To be honest I'm not a great talker and I don't know if I'd get the words out right anyway. So I'm writing you this email instead.
>
> I've been thinking for a while about whether to say anything. I've only recently got my life back on track after Hurricane Tilly, and I'm worried this might start her up again. But at the same time I don't want anyone else to go through what I did.
>
> Tilly is a liar and she likes hurting people. I was with her for two years and you can trust me on this. I felt sorry for her because she said she had a bad childhood and was abused and neglected. She said her mum was a drug addict and her dad was in jail. After we broke up I found out from one of her friends that her family were 100% normal.
>
> I used to be a good surfer. I almost went pro, but I hurt my back while I was packing up my boards. She told me to say that I hurt myself at work so I could get compo.

The worst thing was when I tried to break up with her. She started telling people I hit her. She convinced my boss I had stolen from him. I lost a job that I loved.

I would be surprised if it was just me she's done this to. I've heard rumours over the years.

I feel sorry for Patrick Payne because I know she's made it up and I know what he's going through right now. If I can help him, I will.

Call me if you think any of this will help.

Jason Reznak

Romola read the email three times. It was almost too good to be real. She wondered what rumours he was referring to. Maybe there were other people she could speak to, beyond those she'd found from Tilly's public dating history. She forwarded the email to Imogen, her spirits lifting a little.

Imogen,

See below from TK's ex. Sounds promising? Could this change the firm's position?

R

She bounced her leg up and down, unable to focus on the screen as she waited for a reply. Within two minutes she had it.

No it won't change anything.

But this might:

www.newsdaily.com/news/2019/payne/familytiessevered.

Romola caught her breath as she opened the link to a *News Daily* story. The headline made her shudder.

Family ties severed: Malcolm Payne dumps son. Lawyers follow suit.

Johnny had talked. The story was out. And Romola alone was responsible for the leak. She alone had revealed her client's confidential information to the press.

As the cinema darkened, the pumping in her head started up again, the glow of her phone leaving a watery blue mark over her vision. She lifted her drink and wiped the cooling condensation across her forehead. The opening credits were playing out in black and white, the soundtrack an urgent monotone pulse. She felt vibrations against her ribs, uncertain if they were caused by her heart pumping or the cinema's surround-sound system. Her chest hurt. Fresh air would help. She inhaled deeply. Should she try to leave the cinema? She put two fingers to her neck, feeling for her pulse, needing to know if her heart really was racing like a cricket's trill.

Cliffy, who was staring straight ahead at the screen, gently placed his hand on her forearm. His touch was an anchor. 'You're okay,' he said in a low voice. 'It will all be okay, my dear.'

She closed her eyes and hoped that, as always, Cliffy knew better.

Chapter Twenty-Eight
Sacrifice

Dear Imogen,
As discussed, I'm writing to notify you of my resignation
from Bassett Brown. I am grateful for the opportunity
to have worked with you, and I have learnt an immense
amount in my short time at Bassett Brown. For now, I have
decided that I should take a break from the law. I plan to
spend some time travelling and considering my options
going forward.
Thanks again,
Romola Cross

She read the message ten times over before saving it to her drafts. She would speak to Imogen before sending it, confess her sins and bear the consequences. Most likely she would be fired anyway. Knowing about her connection with Johnny, her boss had probably figured out by now that she was the source of the leak.

Under her contract – which she had frantically read many times over the previous evening after returning from the movies – the firm could dismiss her either on two weeks' notice or immediately if her misconduct was serious enough. Revealing confidential client information was, she knew, on the more severe end of the spectrum. While she could argue that she'd merely disclosed the fact Bassett Brown no longer acted for a client, rather than any client information as such, she was acutely aware that she didn't want to get into an argument with the firm about just how bad her behaviour had been.

What she did want was for this chapter to be over – for the

bandaid to be ripped off and her fate to be known. She'd also spent a considerable part of the previous evening reviewing the lawyers' conduct rules, trying to establish whether, if Bassett Brown and the Paynes hated her enough, they would be able to make a complaint about her to the Legal Profession Conduct Commissioner, and if so whether the complaint would get any traction. At around midnight she'd decided it would be best for everyone if she gracefully exited stage left, in the hope that they would decide to leave it at that, and perhaps she'd be able to revisit legal practice one day after she returned from overseas. To that end, just after midnight she started researching South American hiking destinations, before finally shutting off her laptop at almost 2 a.m.

She'd now been at the office for an hour, and there had been no sign of either Imogen or Derek. The place was eerily quiet again; all the lawyers who had been working on Malcolm's deal enjoying a late start to the working week.

The wait was torturous. With no significant work to do, Romola couldn't avoid reading the online stories about the Paynes. Malcolm's decision to cut ties with Patrick hadn't been received well in the press. While some commentators saw it as damning of Patrick, far more saw it as damning of Malcolm. One had called him the kind of father who throws his only child to the wolves.

As Romola forced herself to sort through her emails, she saw a message from Patrick that had arrived on Saturday night. She must have received it about the time she'd been on the dance floor.

> Romola,
> Please accept my apology for the phone call last night. For whatever I may have said, I'm sorry.
> Thanks for all your help with my matter. Despite everything that's happened, I appreciate it.
> Regards,
> Patrick

She leaned back in her chair and stretched her arms above her head, taking a break from her fatalistic dive to at least smile at their respective fuck-ups. She only wished she wasn't supposed to be the responsible one.

'All okay in here?' Victoria had poked her head in the door, worry lines creasing her forehead. 'I didn't see you come in.'

Romola felt grateful for the chance to speak to someone without having to venture out of the room. 'You heard what happened with the Paynes?'

Victoria nodded, pointing her head towards the opposite side of the building. 'They're in there together.' She glanced at her watch. 'It's been over an hour now.'

'Who's in where?'

'Imogen, Derek, Malcolm, Patrick – they're all in Derek's office. I walked past about half an hour ago. It looked intense.' Derek's office was on the other side of the building to Romola's, a corner office that was sunny every afternoon.

'Oh god,' Romola said, hanging her head.

Victoria, staring at her quizzically, must have noticed her unmistakable despair. 'Cheer up. You know this is a job, right? It pays the bills. For me, it means I can send my sons to a better school. Your job's not your whole life, though.'

'Of course.' Romola felt slightly embarrassed.

Victoria seemed to read her mind. 'But you're different to me. You're lucky. You went to uni for years, right? And you must have done well if you've ended up here. So you clearly have options. You should like your job.'

Romola thought of her dad, who, other than his family, had loved his work more than anything and encouraged her to go into a profession she loved too. He'd always said that finding a profession you were dedicated to was the secret to a happy life. But she couldn't even keep her mouth shut about her client's business – that was Lawyering 101. Did she even deserve to keep practising?

Something grabbed Victoria's attention to her right. 'They're out,' she whispered, slowly backing away. She gave Romola an encouraging wink as she sank into her seat at her workstation.

Imogen and Derek didn't ask if Romola was free to speak before they strode into her office. Derek took up his usual position, leaning on the desk, glasses in hand. His perfectly coiffed hair was a little dishevelled, his face unshaved and pale. Imogen had her hands on her hips and was pacing the office even before the door had closed behind her. Romola spun her chair to face them and sat on her hands, having felt them begin to shake upon Derek and Imogen's entrance.

'We've been with Malcolm and Patrick for the past hour.' Derek loosened his tie. 'Neither of them are happy. You've seen what's happened – somewhere along the line there's been a royal screw-up. Malcolm was planning to spin the news about Patrick parting ways with the firm in a different way, as you can imagine. He was bordering on apoplectic.'

'Before you go on,' Romola cut in, 'I have to say something.' She couldn't stand Derek and Imogen dragging it out any longer.

Imogen gave a slight shake of her head. 'Let Derek finish first.'

This wrong-footed Romola, who closed her mouth again, wondering what on earth Imogen was trying to convey to her.

'But, touch wood –' Derek flattened his palm against her desk, a smile glancing across his face '– we may have just figured out a way forward. It's not ideal, but it could work for us in the long run.'

Romola held her breath, allowing herself the faintest of hopes.

'Malcolm blames us for the leak – he's threatened to report the firm to the conduct commissioner and pull all of his work. I have no idea how this thing got out.'

'Well –' Romola began, but Imogen shut her down with a single look. Romola now thought she understood what Imogen was doing – protecting her.

Derek continued on unperturbed. 'Lucky for us, if there's one thing Malcolm hates more than bad publicity about Patrick, it's bad publicity about himself. He can't stand being portrayed as a bad father.'

Imogen muttered something inaudible.

'So he's agreed for us to keep acting for Patrick,' Derek said.

'That's good news, isn't it?' Romola said, feeling lighter, like a valve had been released that allowed her to breathe again. The future she'd conjured for herself over the course of the past day started to dissipate in her mind's eye.

Derek help up a hand. 'There's a condition.'

'A huge fucker of a condition,' Imogen chimed in, as Romola paused.

'They won't pay us,' Derek said bluntly. 'We've agreed to do Patrick's trial for no charge, on account of the leak. Otherwise we risk losing all of Payne Corp's work. Which is … I don't know, around twenty per cent of the firm's revenue.'

Romola felt like a teenager who had just crashed her parents' car.

'In the circumstances, we're going to work this lean from now on. Malcolm's not worried about how we get this done, or frankly even *if* we get this done – although let's keep that in this room, please. Between you and me, Malcolm just wants us to stay on the record and that's it. He's livid with Patrick – says he's done being let down by him and that he can clean up his own messes from now on.' Derek fixed his eyes on Romola. 'You're the one who'll have to bear the load though, Romola, I'm afraid. And of course you should do your best – Patrick's still our client, after all.'

When combined with his obvious happiness at retaining Malcolm as a client, Derek's words of concern for Romola and Patrick seemed to her to be empty at best. 'What about counsel?' she ventured to ask.

'The firm will be footing the counsel bill as well as our own costs,' Imogen said, arms folded in front of her. 'But Patrick's not happy with Neville anyway, as it turns out. We all knew his heart wasn't in it. We'll need to think about another option for senior counsel.'

Leaving Romola's lingering guilt aside, this scenario was oddly perfect: she would have control of the case, with no more micromanaging from Imogen, and no more Slug and Hare. She bit her lip, knowing she was about to throw a grenade into the paradise presented to her on a silver platter. She knew she couldn't carry the weight of her drunken disclosure on her conscience. 'The workload doesn't bother me,' she said tentatively. 'But I should say one thing before we go on.'

Imogen interrupted casually. 'I know you're probably wondering how the leak got out, Romola.' As she spoke, she pointedly met Romola's eyes. 'But nobody knows. Derek and I are *assuming* it's the same source as the original story. Some disgruntled Payne Corp employee, probably.' She shrugged and turned to Derek, who was plainly clueless.

Romola held back her words, in that moment feeling more allegiance to Imogen than to Derek.

'Well, that's that,' he said. 'You'd best be getting on with things now, I guess.' He awkwardly patted Romola on the shoulder. 'You'll be great. And you let me know if it gets too much. I'm always here to help.' He gave her a patronising smile and bounced out of her office.

Imogen watched him leave, then closed the door and waited a second before turning, her squirrel eyes suddenly wild with anger. Romola realised with a shudder that Imogen was probably only protecting her from Derek for her own sake – and that Romola wasn't going to be spared her wrath. 'Tell me exactly what happened. Now.'

Romola steeled herself. 'I'm sorry, Imogen. I went out on Saturday night and had a few too many drinks. Louise called me, and I let it slip about us pulling out of the case. Don't worry, I have my resignation letter all ready to go.'

Imogen stood there, fuming and tapping her foot. Romola could see the flash of a red sole beneath her black stiletto. 'You're not going to get out of it that easily. This is a *huge* fuck-up, Romola. You have single-handedly almost cost the firm its largest client, for Christ's sake. However ... ' Imogen paused, fixing Romola with a puzzled stare, as though even she couldn't figure out why she wasn't firing her instantly. Romola felt she was on a rollercoaster. 'Crazy or otherwise,' Imogen continued, 'I want to give you a chance to fix this. So the case is yours now. If you manage to win it, the firm will gladly take the glory. But I want nothing to fucking do with it. I'm done with them.' She went to open the door but turned back one last time. 'And if you don't win, you can hand me that resignation letter. There won't be much of a future for you here if I have anything to do with it.'

Romola nodded. 'Of course.' She was embarrassed at her lack of fight but grateful for Imogen's mercy, if that was the right word, and for the end of the rollercoaster ride.

'And you better get on with it,' Imogen called as she walked out. 'Your client's waiting in the boardroom.'

Chapter Twenty-Nine
The Client Revisited

Romola felt light. Imogen had been spot on – it was a huge fuck-up. To have it acknowledged, at least by one person, felt strangely cleansing, and for the first time in days she felt clear-headed. As she entered the meeting room to see Patrick, it was as though she were meeting her first client all those years ago, with only grateful anticipation as to the task that lay ahead.

Patrick looked the opposite of how she felt. The first thing she noticed was that he wore saggy grey tracksuit pants. They seemed to make him slouch more than usual as he sat at the meeting table – he reminded her of a prisoner waiting for his legal aid solicitor to show up at the city watchhouse. 'You must have drawn the short straw then.' He offered a half-hearted smile as she entered. His tired eyes were red rimmed. 'You're stuck with me, and you can't even get your billable units up for it.'

Victoria had handed her a plate of blueberry muffins on her way in, and Romola plonked them on the table in front of Patrick. 'Fresh baked. You look like you could use some sustenance.'

He waved them away.

She sat down opposite him. 'I like a good challenge,' she said.

At this he laughed, shaking his head at the absurdity of their position. 'Apparently I'm too challenging even for my dad after all these years.'

'I'm sure it's only the heat of the moment. He'll come around.' Romola didn't really believe this, but she figured that what Patrick needed was reassurance rather than confirmation that he'd been mistreated.

'No, I don't think so,' he said sadly. 'The unescapable fact is, I'm not the type of son he wants me to be. I never have been. I keep remembering his face when I used to stammer as a kid. It's the same way he looks at me now – unabashed disappointment.' Patrick exhaled slowly and loudly, then sat up and moved his shoulders in slow circles, like he was warming up for a workout. Whatever demons he was fighting, it seemed to Romola that he was attempting to put them aside. He sat still for a moment before grabbing a muffin, eating it in two bites and reaching for another. 'Sorry again about Friday night,' he said with his mouth full, 'and that phone call. To be completely honest, I don't even remember what I said, but I'm sure it wasn't all that clever.' He met her eyes. He wasn't only saying he was sorry, but also that he wanted to start afresh.

'I've got my own apologies to make.' Romola held her breath, knowing that as her client he was the only person who really needed her confession right now. 'I've just told Imogen about this, but I'm not sure if she'll pass it on, and it's something you need to know ...'

Patrick raised his eyebrows and swallowed the last bite of his muffin as he waited expectantly.

'One of my good friends started dating Johnny Wise. Well, they're now living together – it moved very fast – they'd only just started seeing each other when I moved to Melbourne, and I only found out about it after I'd already started working on your file. I've had nothing to do with him, nothing at all. My friend and I have actually had a bit of a falling-out over it. I'm confident that, moving forward, it won't conflict with my duties to you.'

Patrick's face gave nothing away; he just ran his fingers over his bristly jaw. Some reaction would have made it easier for her to go on.

'However ... after I heard the news about the firm dropping you as a client on Saturday, I had a big night of my own. *Way* too many gin and tonics.' She closed her eyes, remembering the gin's bitter taste. 'This friend of mine called me – and in my state, I told her that we had stopped acting for you. I can't be certain, but there's a chance that's how the story about your dad dropping you got out.'

Patrick regarded her for a moment, then a smile began to emerge on his face, a smile broad enough for her to see the gap in his teeth. 'You're even worse than me after a few drinks.' He almost seemed proud of her, or perhaps it was a smile of companionship, of knowing relief that he wasn't alone in his foolishness.

'I would completely understand if you don't want me acting for you after all –'

He continued smiling.

'It really was very unprofessional of me.'

'I understand.'

'You should probably report me.'

'Maybe. My dad would in a heartbeat, no doubt about it. But I won't tell him. I need your help.'

They regarded each other, knowing they were moving forward.

'Right,' Romola said, picking up her pen, 'so let's figure out what's next. How we're going to win this thing.'

'I don't want to win.'

'No?' Her enthusiasm was brought down a notch. Did he mean he wanted to drop the case entirely? If so, she would need to figure out how they could extract him without paying Rabbit Hole's costs – surely Eddie and Johnny would still be happy to settle on a walk-away basis like they'd put forward at the mediation.

'Like you've always been saying,' Patrick continued, 'I don't want to go to trial. Now that Dad's not paying for the lawyers, I can make my own decisions. I want you to try and settle this. I don't care about how much we get, if anything. I don't care about losing the preselection – let's face it, I would have been terrible in politics. But I do want them to apologise – to say sorry – and to print a retraction. You're going to convince them to do that.'

She'd never heard him be so decisive. 'I agree that should be the strategy, and I will absolutely do all I can to get a settlement back on the table. But we need to do that from a place of strength. We need to be prepared to go to trial and show them we're confident about your chances of winning. We can bring together all of your strongest evidence and put it to them – point out their own weaknesses. That's the best time to go in with another offer. Or, even better, they'll waver first and come back to us with a better position, if nothing else, in order to protect themselves on costs.'

Patrick nodded enthusiastically.

'But ...'

'There's always a but,' he said, a little deflated.

'Sorry. The "but" is that the decision not to go to trial isn't entirely in your hands. Unless you want to completely capitulate – discontinue and pay all of their costs – which means no apology. I'm assuming you don't want to go down that road.'

Patrick nodded.

'So we still need to be ready for trial in case you end up having no other option, but we can use all our work to try and draw Rabbit Hole and Johnny to settle. The key is making them understand they're at risk too.'

'Understood.' He brightened. 'So let's do this.'

Romola switched focus to what would need to be done next, remembering the email she'd received the day before as if it were an age ago. 'I almost forgot to say – I have good news. Tilly's ex-boyfriend, Jason Reznak, finally got back to me.'

She found the email on her phone and handed it to Patrick. He read it with a broadening grin.

'I'll go and speak to him,' she said. 'Find out who his contacts are.'

'Tilly always did like to burn people. I think I only escaped it at the time because of who I am ... or who I was.'

Romola, anxious for Patrick not to slip into another mood, tried to bring him back to the case at hand. 'So, speaking very generally, Tilly is looking more positive, with Jason and potentially other supporting witnesses. Rabbit Hole will be worried by that. For Beth we have her parents, although Rabbit Hole will disregard them because of the connection with your dad. But the fact is, our opponents don't appear to have any direct evidence of any mistreatment of her. They'll know that Lara could be problematic for them in the witness box– most of what she can testify about is either hearsay or supposition, as she didn't actually witness anything firsthand.'

Patrick nodded again, looking less glum.

She went on. 'That leaves Hana – and this is where they seem the most confident, Patrick. If you want an apology, we're going to have to find something that makes them rethink the allegations about her. Where is Emir? How can you be sure he's not speaking to

Rabbit Hole? Do whatever you need to get him back here.' Romola realised how much she was sounding like Imogen, but continued regardless. 'Is there anyone else you can possibly think of?' She felt like this was an equation she'd gone over a thousand times, never calculating the right answer.

Patrick held his phone between his hands on the tabletop, flipping it over and over. 'I wonder …'

'Yes?' she urged, wondering if he secretly held the answer to her equation.

'I wonder if you should speak to Sonia after all,' he said sheepishly.

Romola wasn't following. 'But you and Imogen have told me hundreds of times not to do that.' Was he saying that Sonia might know something specific, or just that, despite everything, he now suspected his ex-wife would be a supporter?

'I guess I just thought, with her addiction, and all the animosity during the divorce, that it wasn't worth even trying with Sonia. But when I think more about it … She knew Hana, and she sees Max regularly. Sonia knows I was good to her, and that I'm not the type to hurt anyone. She *has* to know that, in her heart of hearts. So maybe we shouldn't rule out the possibility that she'll give you something you could use to extract an apology from Rabbit Hole. Maybe I'm underestimating her – she seems to have her act together lately, so she might have changed. And after all, we did love each other enough to get married at one point.'

Romola noted down his words. Her truth antennae were on high alert about this backflip, but the fact was she'd wanted to speak to Sonia since the beginning. Romola knew she would be crazy not to take the chance Patrick was offering now. Two of his ex-girlfriends had overdosed, and his ex-wife had a substance problem during their marriage. Same, same but different – but Sonia was able to talk, and hopefully to explain herself. Was it too much to hope that she would place the blame elsewhere?

Patrick seemed to read Romola's thoughts. 'I'm not sure if this will help?'

'We can only try.' She put it to the back of her mind as she went on. 'Another thing: if we do end up going to trial – and we should for all intents and purposes look like that's what we're doing – we'll need a new barrister. We can't use Neville anymore.'

'Good. He's a creep.'

'I have someone in mind. He's very experienced – close to retirement, actually. But I suspect he'll give us a good rate. And I don't think your father likes him very much.' She remembered Cliffy's stories, the vision of Malcolm Payne tucking into a hog's head. Malcolm's final words to him: *You will never see a brief from me again.*

Patrick grinned. 'Sounds perfect.'

Chapter Thirty
The Ex

Media Release from Mr Malcolm Payne OAM
In reference to recent reports that Malcolm Payne OAM
has cut familial and financial ties with his son Patrick Payne,
Mr Payne OAM wholly denies such reports. Patrick Payne
continues to have his father's full support at this difficult time.
Reports to the contrary are egregious and incorrect. Insofar as
it has been reported that there is a change in legal team acting
for Patrick Payne in the pending defamation proceedings
against Rabbit Hole and Jonathan Wise, it is confirmed that
Neville Desmond QC will no longer be appearing as counsel
for Patrick Payne due to a timetabling conflict. Heathcliff
Garner QC has accepted the brief in his place. Patrick Payne
continues to deny the outrageous, baseless, and incorrect
allegations that have been made against him and is confident
of succeeding in his upcoming trial.

Romola had known Cliffy would say yes – he always liked to back
an underdog. And despite Patrick's life of privilege, that's what he
had become: a man with his back against the wall. His only real asset
had been his reputation, and without that he had nothing left to lose.

She rang Cliffy after Patrick left the office that Monday. Before
leaving, Patrick had promised to dig up every last skerrick of evidence
about what Hana had been up to, in the time since their romantic
relationship had commenced and also in the weeks immediately
before her death. They needed to understand, as much as possible,
what had led to her suicide.

Romola had folders of documents prepared and sent to Cliffy the very same afternoon, and by the evening they were discussing the evidence that needed to be compiled before trial – and how much they would reveal in advance of trial to Rabbit Hole's lawyers in a last-ditch attempt to avoid having a trial at all.

Over the coming days there were phone calls that Romola answered and phone calls that she systematically rejected. Louise was trying to contact her again, calling and texting daily, and Judith remained persistent. But Romola didn't have room for mending relationships; she didn't have the energy for anything beyond work. The calls she answered were from people who could help her – from Jason Reznak and the others who had been wronged by Tilly. Jason put her onto two other men with similar stories of Tilly's damaging lies. Romola hadn't been able to find them sooner because after dealing with Tilly they'd all but erased any online profiles they'd once had. Romola met them all in person and obtained careful statements that she added to her brief.

She went to see Beth's parents again, this time at their research institute, and took second, more detailed statements from them. She spoke to doctors at the rehabilitation facility that Beth had attended, who agreed that she was essentially beyond hope by the time she had her overdose. No one knew what drove her there, but no one said it was Patrick.

And then there was Sonia Kirk.

*

The vegan café seemed to have been constructed from pieces of driftwood. To all appearances it had washed up on the pavement of its trendy suburb, smack bang next to Sonia's regular yoga studio.

'Are you waiting for someone?' The waitress's hair was wrapped turban-like in a colourful fabric. A silver stud was embedded in the side of her nose.

Romola looked up. 'Yes, sorry. Do you want me to order something?'

'That's sort of the point.' The girl pointed a pen at the brown paper menu in front of Romola.

'Let me see.' She attempted to decipher the menu. 'I'll just have a flat white, please.'

'Almond, coconut, soy?' asked the girl in a bored monotone.

'Normal milk is fine.'

'We only sell plant-based products. If you want "normal" milk you'll have to go over the road.' The waitress pointed disapprovingly at a slick-looking coffee shop full of mums in activewear with heavy-duty strollers.

'I'm meeting someone here. I'll have a juice, please. Orange.'

'Just orange? No powders?'

'Plain orange juice.' Romola smiled. 'Call me old-fashioned.'

'Yeah, okay.' The girl scratched her head with her pencil before jotting something on her notepad and turning away.

Romola gazed across the street, longing for her regular coffee order. It had now been a little over a week since that day in the office when she'd been given a second chance. Working late every night, she'd become even more dependent on a steady stream of caffeine to resuscitate her brain.

'You must be Romola.' A tall woman had appeared in front of her, one whose appearance was nothing like that of the Sonia Kirk she'd been expecting. The Sonia in her head wore Chanel and Balenciaga, and kept her hair in a perennial blonde ponytail, like in the pictures from before the divorce. This Sonia was dressed in a kaftan, her long hair now a natural mousy brown, let down in loose waves held back by aviator sunglasses, her wrists covered in jangly jade bangles. Romola was expecting some reticence, but Sonia had a broad smile on her face as she lowered herself to her seat, dumping a floppy woven handbag on the floor next to her. 'Before you start talking, you should know that I am determined to be calm.' Now Romola could see that her teeth were clenched. 'I will not let that family ruin my serenity now, but I'm prepared to listen to whatever it is you want to say.'

'I appreciate you taking the time, Sonia. As I tried to explain on the phone –'

'I don't like to speak on the phone. All those rays.' Sonia fluttered her fingers in front of her face. That explained why she'd been so short during their call the previous week. Despite Imogen's warning that there 'wasn't a chance' Sonia would help, she had almost immediately agreed to meet Romola – without an explanation as to what they would be talking about.

'It's about Hana Vukovic,' said Romola. 'And Patrick – I'm acting for him in his defamation proceedings.'

'How's that going then? Does he have a good case?' She raised an eyebrow and floated long bony fingers as she summoned the turbaned waitress, who was all smiles as Sonia ordered a drink with a very long name.

'I can't say,' Romola was hoping to nip in the bud any idea that today's meeting would involve an exchange of information, as opposed to being a one-way street. 'I just have a few background-type questions for you, about when Hana was living with you.'

Sonia winced. 'I don't like to think of that part of my life. I've turned a page. I am revived.' She placed her hands as though in prayer and balanced her chin on them. 'But isn't it the case that I couldn't say anything about it, even if I wanted to? Contractually obliged? If I'm not mistaken, the agreement I signed says I must not disclose anything about the circumstances surrounding the marriage or how it ended, or else the Payne family will unleash almighty hell against me. Something along those lines, anyway.' She shrugged.

Romola had prepared for this response. 'This is a separate matter to your divorce, Sonia. And Patrick's quite happy for you to speak to me about it. I can get him on the phone now to confirm that if you like.' Romola started taking out her phone.

The waitress returned with Sonia's tall green drink and Romola's orange juice. Sonia waited for her to leave before speaking again. 'You might want to double-check that he's happy for me to talk to you about everything.' She stirred her drink with a bamboo straw.

Romola didn't know exactly what Sonia was suggesting, but hated that recurring feeling of being in the dark. She fished out her pen and notepad from the bag at her feet, making out that she had ignored Sonia's comment. 'Maybe we can start with some basics. Like Hana – your impressions of her. She wasn't a part of your marriage.'

Sonia's left eye had begun to tic, flickering up and down like a broken streetlight. 'What can I say? Hana was sweet. Everyone knew Hana was sweet. But she ruined my marriage, so my praise for her is limited. Max loved her very deeply, and for that I am grateful. It helps me in some ways to know she was there for him. A female influence can be important.'

'Patrick says he wasn't in a relationship with Hana when you two separated.'

'I don't think there's any point going back over that old ground.'

'Did you see the two of them together?'

'As I said I've moved on from all of that. I have a new life. I have my yoga, and my meditation. I am mindful.'

Romola was doing her best to admire Sonia's healthy lifestyle change, but the obfuscation was infuriating. She tasted her orange juice, which was so sour she squinted involuntarily and pushed the drink to one side. 'What exactly did you feel you had to move on from?'

Sonia rolled her eyes. 'The list is endless. The spotlight. Keeping up the pretence. Feeling miserable but having to appear otherwise.' She didn't make eye contact with Romola, sipping her drink as her gaze darted around the cafe. 'Of course it was Patrick too. I divorced him, didn't I?' She looked Romola up and down. 'If what you're trying to ask me is whether Patrick abused me, whether what they're saying about him is true, just come out and ask me. After all, I'm in the best position to know if it's true. I imagine I could be quite a help – or an enormous hindrance – which is what Rabbit Hole's lawyers clearly hoped when they contacted me.'

Sonia met Romola's eyes then, focused and no longer twitching. She must have been expecting that her news would come as a rude shock, when in fact Romola had anticipated Rabbit Hole would have beat them to Sonia. 'And what did you tell them?' Romola asked, hoping Sonia might just be cocky enough to give herself away.

'Well ... I said I wasn't in a position to assist them at that time.'

'Right,' said Romola, happy to move on from discussion of her opponents. 'You've already guessed my next question. Was Patrick good to you?'

Sonia gathered her mess of hair up above her shoulder before letting it fall to one side. 'Good? What a word. He basically ignored me for the last six months of our marriage. I could have fallen off the face of the planet and he wouldn't have noticed. He only had eyes for Hana by then. So no, he was not good to me in that sense. Did he abuse me, hurt me, control me? Now that is a different question. My answer to that –' she paused for effect '– is no. For all his faults, Patrick wasn't bad to me in that way. I never felt unsafe with him. He never threatened me. He never controlled me.' Sonia poked at her drink as she spoke, gazing at it like a fortune-teller looking into a crystal ball. It was as if she could see into her and Patrick's past in the green haze.

Romola's instinct was that Sonia's words were too good to be true. She found it hard to believe that if her evidence was going to be this positive, both Patrick and Imogen had been reluctant to approach her before. 'Would you be prepared to testify to that? To sign a witness statement about it?' Romola asked, pen poised to note down Sonia's answer.

'Possibly.' Sonia lifted a napkin and dabbed at her face, then bent over and retrieved a brown jar from her bag; she smoothed the balm over her lips before smacking them together. 'It depends,' she said once she was done.

Here's the catch, thought Romola, exasperated that Sonia was dragging this out. It was clear by now that the woman was going to propose some sort of quid pro quo. But what exactly was she expecting from Patrick in return for her cooperation?

'Depends on what?' Romola asked.

Sonia returned her lip balm to her bag, removed her sunglasses from her head and began smoothing the front of her hair. She did all this while looking just beyond Romola, as though into an invisible mirror. 'On Patrick.'

'What about him?' Romola tapped her pen on her pad in frustration and attempted to move her head a little to catch Sonia's eye.

The woman continued tending to her hair, then finally shifted her gaze back to Romola. She seemed ready to lay it on the line. 'You see,' she said in a strained voice, 'it's so difficult at the moment. The arrangements we have in place, I mean. Patrick has Max most of the time. I have him one weekend a month. I could live with that while Hana was around, not that I liked it, but she and Max had a good connection. I wasn't in a good place, and I knew there was simply no point in fighting with the Paynes. But now things have changed – I've changed. And Hana's not here anymore. It makes sense for Max to spend more time with me now. No – it's more than that – I *need* to see Max more. I really need this, Romola.' She held her hands to her heart. 'If Patrick is prepared to revisit our arrangements, then I'll help him out with his case.' Keeping her hands to her chest, she waited for a response, her face a picture of desperation.

'I'll speak to Patrick,' Romola said, careful not to give Sonia – who, despite her faults, really did appear desperate for more time with her son – false hope. Romola was thinking of Max's chubby face and clever eyes, and how fiercely Patrick loved him. 'But I'm not hopeful that's going to work, because the defamation case and Max's custody are separate issues.'

'Are they, though?' Sonia asked pointedly.

Romola was unsure if she was reading too much into Sonia's words, but got the distinct impression that Patrick was being threatened. It seemed Sonia was saying she had the power to make Patrick's trial impact the custody arrangements, possibly by ensuring that he came off badly enough at trial to ensure she would be granted more time with Max. Romola knew she had to tread carefully – if she rejected Sonia outright, the woman might run off to Rabbit Hole straight away. But if Romola led her on too much, she was at risk of compromising Sonia's testimony if she did eventually give evidence for Patrick; her credibility as a witness would be ruined if her evidence was dependent on her having custody of Max.

Romola spent a moment choosing her words. 'Yes, they are separate, Sonia. And you would, of course, need to think carefully about treating them as if they depend on one another – if you do want your evidence to be worthwhile to either party, that is.'

Sonia flinched, considering Romola. 'You don't have children?'

'No.' Romola stiffened at the suggestion that her childlessness could be relevant here, wondering if Sonia's conclusion was drawn from her age or something else in her demeanour.

'Well, if you did, you might show a touch more sympathy to my situation. I'm not proud of how I behaved in the past, and it hasn't been easy, but I think it's bloody impressive what I've overcome.' Sonia's chin was wobbling, her face red with the effort of holding back tears. 'There's someone missing, though. I got clean for Max, and now I can't even see him. It's not fair. Without him, what's the point? I'm very prepared to sacrifice whatever integrity I have left to get him back. If you can go back to Patrick and ask him about Max, that would be appreciated.'

Romola nodded, and Sonia lifted her bag and stood to leave, picking up her used napkin and wiping away the tears that had escaped.

'Do you know how Hana may have got her hands on fentanyl, Sonia?' Romola asked quickly. She knew that if Patrick wasn't prepared to cooperate with Sonia, this might be Romola's only opportunity to speak to her – and Romola wanted to understand precisely what might come out if the woman ended up testifying for the other side. Plus, Romola still hadn't managed to work out how Hana had got the fentanyl, there being no prescription for it in her medical records. While the Rabbit Hole articles didn't suggest that Patrick had supplied her with the drug, Romola wanted to be satisfied that he wouldn't be accused at trial of not only giving Hana the motivation to take her life but also the means.

Sonia stopped. Her eye tic returned, but it was more pronounced now, almost a wink. 'I couldn't say.'

'Did you used to take it? You said you had some addiction issues.'

'As though you didn't already know that.' Sonia glanced around the café, saw that all the nearby tables were empty, put on her sunglasses and sat back down. She kept her big straw bag close to her chest, as though she was ready to flee. And she'd gone back to clenching her teeth; it appeared she would sooner explode than speak a word. But eventually she replied, almost in a whisper. 'As I said, I was in a bad place back then. I don't think you could understand. I'm not proud of it, but I did get carried away, not only with alcohol but with painkillers too. They're incredibly addictive. There's a lawsuit about it in the US, you know.'

'Fentanyl?'

'Yes – it's horrific what you read about it. I had very little power over myself. I have an addictive personality, so was susceptible to it.

But as you can see I've never been healthier. You can pass that on to Patrick as well.'

'Can I ask where you got your supply from?'

Sonia stood up again and slung her bag to her back. 'Sorry, I've really got to get to my yoga class. This conversation hasn't helped my anxiety levels. It's important that I go.'

'It's my last question, Sonia.' Romola held out a steadying hand, willing the woman to stay a moment longer. 'I'd just like to know who supplied you with the fentanyl. Was it anyone Hana would have known?'

'I would have thought so.' Sonia was emu-like, peering down at her.

Romola stiffened, hoping she wasn't about to say Patrick's name. 'Why is that?'

Sonia glanced over each shoulder, again surveying the café for spying eyes. 'Because it was her brother Emir.'

Chapter Thirty-One
Growing

'I'm not bringing Max into this.'

Romola was sitting on a stool in Patrick's kitchen as he angrily threw smoothie ingredients into the blender. The kitchen was a serene space combining golden-syrup timber and black marble, every surface glossy and unmarred by either handles or fingerprints. An enormous arrangement of eucalyptus leaves and yellow proteas softened the space, and the garden framed in the window to the left glowed even greener in contrast to the dark palette of the cabinets. A door through to a scullery kitchen revealed where the real action happened: there were stainless-steel appliances, knives stuck to the walls, and cooking implements hanging from beams. The blender, fruits and milk in front of Patrick seemed out of place amid the elegance of this show kitchen.

He peeled a banana and dropped it whole into the blender with a splash. 'What sort of person does that? I knew I was right to begin with. She hasn't changed at all. She should be helping to clear my name for Max's sake, not putting him right in the middle of this bloody mess. The poor kid's getting teased at school because of what they say about me on the news.'

Patrick spooned in a sprinkle of chia seeds, closed the lid and turned the blender on. Unnecessarily, he continued pressing firmly on the lid as it powered up, his shoulder shaking with the machine's vibrations. He was wearing a faded T-shirt, with dirt stains across the front, and what looked like original '90s jeans. His face was red and sweaty, and she could smell his saltiness over the kitchen counter.

'I agree with you it's completely unreasonable,' she said. 'On the one hand there's a possibility she could be an incredibly effective witness for you, because she knows what you're like in a relationship better than anyone. On the other hand she's desperate and obviously has been unpredictable in the past, so I feel as though we could never be completely confident as to what she might do on the stand.'

'"Unpredictable" is a nice way of putting it.'

'But if you don't go forward with this, there's a possibility of her agreeing to testify for Rabbit Hole. Do you think she's capable of lying on the stand?'

'I don't know if she'd go that far. I guess she'd be capable of embellishment, exaggeration ... but telling lies under oath would be another thing.' He poured his drink and glugged it noisily as he gazed out of his perfectly clean window at his perfectly manicured lawn. 'No, I'm not even going to think about it. I can't let her hold me hostage over Max.'

Romola nodded and for the third time crossed Sonia's name off her list of potential witnesses, though in her head there was a lingering question mark. She would speak to Cliffy about it. Sonia might be their only hope of countering Rabbit Hole's truth defence.

Patrick picked up a tea towel and wiped the sweat from his face, then threw it over his shoulder and met her eyes. 'Sonia was a different person when I married her. I'd never been with an older woman before. She charmed me.' He shrugged and gave Romola a sideways smile.

'People do that,' Romola said, thinking of how Judith had charmed her father. Don had somehow loved her enough to bring her into their home, to ask Romola to call her Mum. He'd seen something in Judith that drew him to her inexplicably. But Romola had never experienced the feeling that she had to be with someone no matter what. She was still sceptical that relationships actually ever worked like that – more likely it was what people told themselves when everything went wrong.

As for Sonia, Romola wavered as to whether she was so terrible. Whatever demons she'd once fought had been admirably staved off, and Romola – despite her childlessness – actually did appreciate the impact of Max's absence from her life. Romola knew what a great kid he was. If he was her son, she would want to be part of his life every day.

'So she's really clean?' asked Patrick. 'Or is she still pretending like she didn't have a problem?'

'From what I could see, she's clean. And she conceded she had a problem.'

Patrick nodded, still staring out at the garden.

'There's one other thing she said,' said Romola tentatively, having no idea how Patrick would react to the news about Emir, or if he'd known all along that Hana's brother might have something to answer for. Since her conversation with Sonia, Romola had gone over in her mind everything Patrick had said about Emir's trip – how he'd gone 'off-grid'. Had Patrick been trying to protect him?

Romola had been taken aback when Sonia named Emir. But then she'd thought of those sad green eyes – perhaps there was guilt in them too. If Hana had overdosed using drugs once intended for Sonia, then he would likely feel responsible. And it seemed, from the remainder of Romola's conversation with Sonia, that this was possible.

Shaken by Romola's questions, Sonia had ended up ditching her yoga class. The two of them had briefly conversed in Sonia's car, where they couldn't be overheard. Sonia had revealed that Emir had run a slick operation: whenever her supply ran out, she left coded messages for him. A day later, she would find a package in one of her dressing-table drawers, the second drawer down with the crack in its corner. At the end of that month, she would pay an 'employee bonus' into Emir's bank account alongside his salary.

'You told me Sonia had a substance abuse problem, that it always started with alcohol, but you weren't exactly sure what she was taking in the end.' Romola repeated Patrick's words back to him. 'Sonia confirmed that she used to take fentanyl, which was one of the substances that Hana had taken when she died.'

'Right,' Patrick said slowly, holding his glass suspended in midair as though he'd forgotten why he was holding it. 'So you think there's a connection?'

'I don't know.' Romola was being honest. 'There was a long break between when Hana and Sonia were living in the same house. It could be that the two instances of fentanyl abuse are completely unconnected. Only … there's this one thing tying them together …'

'One thing?' Patrick asked, urging her on with a nod.

'Sonia's supplier. It was Emir.'

'Wait a second.' Patrick took a step towards her then paused, as she carefully watched his reaction. 'As in my Emir? As in Hana's Emir?'

'Yes. I'm afraid so.'

Patrick's sweaty brow furrowed in confusion. 'She's not suggesting he supplied Hana though, is she? His own sister? There must be a mistake.' Patrick reached for his phone, shaking his head in disbelief.

'Please don't say anything yet. I want to talk to him first.' Romola had to stop herself from grabbing the phone off him. Then she remembered. 'I thought Emir was uncontactable anyway? Off-grid?' She had a sinking feeling – after all they'd been through, was Patrick still being dishonest with her?

He glanced up from his phone and said, as though it were nothing, 'I forgot to tell you, he got back yesterday.' Patrick tucked his phone into the back pocket of his jeans, seemingly oblivious to the shock that had passed across Romola's face.

'He's back? Where is he?' She was thrown; she tried to settle her racing heart. A moment ago she could have sworn she'd caught Patrick in a lie, but his explanation was plausible, and she didn't want to risk losing what trust she had established by accusing him of misleading her now.

'He's having a few more days at home before he gets back to work.' Patrick walked to the kitchen counter and began taking his smoothie paraphernalia back to the scullery kitchen. He called over to her. 'I hear what you're saying, but I find it hard to believe Emir had anything to do with whatever ended up in Hana's system.' He returned and stood with his hands on the benchtop. 'They were so close – he wouldn't be able to live with himself. Maybe Sonia's got the wrong end of the stick somehow.'

Romola would have said how unlikely that was. She would have explained how much detail Sonia had provided to support her claims. She would have explained how she had already checked Emir's criminal record, and that he'd done time – six months for the supply of methamphetamine – so the shoe fit. But she held her tongue, as Patrick had held his. Now that Emir was back, she wanted to speak to him as soon as possible; to understand his perspective before she tested Patrick's any further. Maybe one or other of them would be caught out.

She caught Patrick's eye. 'Just be careful around him for now. You don't know that he hasn't been in contact with Johnny Wise.'

Patrick seemed sceptical. 'Sure. If you say so. But I genuinely believe he's only dealing with his grief at the moment. I keep remembering that night after our dinner at Costello's, he dropped us out the front of the house, then sped off without saying anything. I remember thinking he was driving too fast. Actually, I've been thinking about how that must be hard for him now, that the last time he saw her he didn't even say goodbye.'

Romola's mind travelled to a winter's day a little over a year ago. She and her father had arranged to meet for dinner at one of their favourite restaurants, a small South Indian place run by a couple from Kerala. It had been full of vibrant university students that night. At first she thought her father must be caught up with one of his fellow academics – he always did struggle to extract himself from conversations – but as time wore on and with each unanswered call she grew nervous. The noise of the restaurant began closing in on her.

And then Judith called. She didn't even ask if Romola was alone, or if she was sitting down, like they did in the movies. She just blurted it out frantically: 'Don's dead!'

Romola felt weightless. The nice Indian couple guided her to a room out the back and spoke in whispers. They brought her a cup of tea and watched her from the corner.

Louise eventually came to pick her up. Held her tight.

Her last text to her dad had been 'c u there' – not even proper English.

'You okay?' Patrick stood up, frowning with concern. He had rounded the kitchen benchtop and was coming towards her, tentatively extending a hand.

She hadn't noticed that her eyes had started to well. Suddenly she was aware of how quiet she'd been, gazing at the oven ahead of her but looking at nothing. 'Sorry. Yes, I'm fine.' She shook her head and sipped her coffee as Patrick dropped his hand to his side. 'Emir will remember everything from that night. It's not easy to forget.'

'However much you try,' Patrick replied, his eyes downcast. They stood quietly for a moment before he picked up his sunglasses and headed for the door to the garden. 'Let me show you something.'

He was met in the doorway by Jessie the golden retriever, a worn tennis ball in her jaw. Patrick threw the ball across the garden and led Romola, followed by Jessie, to a corner of the block that was hidden behind the pool house, a part of the garden she hadn't seen before in her other visits to Patrick's house. An old oak tree stood beside a basically constructed garden shed. Next to the shed was a pile of mulch, a spade stuck in the top like a flag upon conquered land. As she and Patrick stepped inside, she saw that it wasn't a shed but a greenhouse.

'My new project,' he said with a grin.

The greenhouse was warmer than outside. There were orchids along one wall and green veggies along the other – neat lines of spinach, runner beans, lettuce and broad beans.

'I've found a new way to spend my time.' Patrick beamed. 'I love it. I've been carting mulch all morning.' He picked two snow peas and handed one to her, before crunching into the other. Here, with his faded clothes and untended hair, he was like a different person; it was as though he had shed an uncomfortable skin to reveal the man beneath. 'Taste,' he urged, leading by example and crunching into the green shell.

She bit into the pea's skin and was surprised by the intense sweetness. 'I'm truly amazed. I've never been able to grow a thing.'

'Well, I always enjoyed it but never had the time until now.' He began turning his fingers through a patch of dark, moist soil. 'I think this might be something I can do – *really* do. I don't need to impress anyone. I'm sure it sounds insignificant, but I find it quite satisfying to watch things grow. I've also been looking at landscape designs, and there's a patch near the pool that I'm playing with.'

'Good on you,' she said, smiling. She perched on a wooden stool and gnawed on her snow pea. She supposed she should have been reflecting on her client's happy change in attitude – and she was glad his life was taking a turn for the better. But mainly she was thinking about how this hobby could be used to his advantage in the case. Could she and Cliffy weave it into Patrick's evidence if, despite her best attempts, they were left with no option but to go to trial?

'You should taste the broad beans.' Patrick gave off the innocent air of an excited child. 'A bit of oil, salt, lemon – incredible!'

Yes, she decided, laughing at his enthusiasm, this was surely something they could use.

Chapter Thirty-Two
A Brother's Love

'Refreshments or good news – which one first?' Gretchen stood in the doorway, balancing a box of doughnuts, a tray of takeaway coffees and a folder of documents. A huge smile lit up her face, which had fattened and regained its colour in the two weeks since the collapse of the Goodalls deal she'd been working on.

'No contest.' Romola stood up, accepted the doughnuts and cleared a space on Cliffy's wide antique lacquered table, shoving aside piles of papers laid out in preparation for the trial they were all hoping to avoid but had to be ready for.

Over the past week Romola had taken to working from Cliffy's dining room, sick of Imogen's glares from across the office and Derek's nervous visits. Cliffy was charging reduced rates on the basis that Romola would do the bulk of the work, so he made contributions in the evening, fastidiously tidying the piles of paper she scattered over the room during the day. Gretchen had also become something of a faithful offsider, realising that the detailed investigative work required in the lead-up to a trial was much more interesting than the due diligence she'd been consumed by in the Goodalls deal.

Romola closed her laptop and took a glazed doughnut from the box. She was grateful for the distraction of Gretchen's arrival, having spent the morning writing submissions for the argument they would have in court later that week.

Rabbit Hole and Johnny, as was their right, had elected for a jury trial. Bassett Brown, on Patrick's behalf, had objected, on the basis that the trial must be heard by judge alone because Patrick would suffer irreparable prejudice from a jury trial. In argument before Justice Debenham, who seemed to relish each interlocutory hearing in the matter, Cliffy would submit that the extent of media coverage about Patrick made it impossible for him to receive a truly impartial jury. Cliffy would argue that the trial should instead be decided by Justice Debenham.

'So?' Romola asked Gretchen. 'What's this good news?'

Gretchen remained standing. She'd told Romola that she had been a star of high school debating, which explained why she had a habit of conducting conversations as if she was gesticulating in front of a lectern. 'Tilly's been outstagrammed!'

Romola laughed. 'Since when is that a thing?'

'Since I coined the phrase. It means the outing of an Insta influencer, aka social death by Instagram.'

Romola talked with her mouth full. 'Well done to you. What's happened?'

'You remember how I was looking into those beauty slash empowerment seminars offered by Tilly in Byron earlier in the year, after her Patrick claims came out?'

'Yep.'

'Well, I spoke to a few people who signed up. They say the whole thing was a complete mess – three hundred dollars on a ticket, and they were left with a couple of tea bags and some quotes from Oprah. Apparently Tilly promised a whole load of guest speakers, speaking coaches, mindfulness people, that type of thing, but her and a friend just turned up with a couple of yoga mats on a public beach. There were about twenty people in each session, so she would have made a fair amount of cash over the week. One third of the fee was supposedly going to a women's refuge, but some people got upset and checked with the refuge, which received nothing. So then others did some more digging, and it turns out Tilly's lifted parts of her Insta profile from other people – as in, taken whole Insta stories and posted them as her own. To top it off, some other ex-friends have piped up with tales similar to Jason Reznak's. They're all comparing details on the socials as we speak.'

Gretchen pulled out her phone, which showed Jason's Instagram, his handle photo a curling beach wave, his followers up from a couple of hundred to twenty thousand. Romola grabbed the phone and started scrolling through the mounting lists of comments. Some of them were disbelieving, others were hateful, but most of them were angry. She was reminded of the flood of comments on Patrick's social media when Johnny's story had first broken.

'It's a witch-hunt,' Romola murmured without thinking, remembering the words Malcolm had used at the mediation.

'I thought this would be a good development.' Gretchen shoulders dropped, her face crestfallen.

'I know it is.' Romola handed the phone back. 'I'm just lamenting. What happened to the days when this stuff came out in court, when truth was tested in front of a judge or jury rather than on bloody social media?'

'Well, you can go on lamenting, but I really think we should be getting in contact with some of the people who've had direct dealings with her, to see whether they'll testify for Patrick.'

Romola gestured for Gretchen to sit down, her comment reminding her that she was just a clerk, still new to practice so not yet accustomed to examining a piece of information from all perspectives before making a decision. 'Think it through first. These people who are speaking out now –' Romola pointed towards Gretchen's phone '– their evidence won't be directly relevant to any of the allegations Tilly has made against Patrick, because they didn't witness anything. If Tilly gives evidence, we can possibly call some of them as witnesses going to her credibility, depending upon what exactly she says, but we'd need to make sure they're real live people who are prepared to speak the words they write. She'll go to ground now anyway, I suspect. I can't see Rabbit Hole or Johnny wanting to rely on her evidence after all of this.'

'Right. So I shouldn't contact them?'

'Not yet. Make a list of the main people who appear to have stories discrediting her. I'll work out where to from here with Cliffy.' Romola glanced down at her phone. 'Shit, is that the time?' She started sifting through the mess of papers. 'I'm meeting Emir in five.' She found the handwritten list she'd been searching for – her talking points. 'Can you pack up here once you're done?'

Gretchen lifted the box of doughnuts from a pile of papers and surveyed the state of the table wide-eyed, as though it had just occurred to her what an untidy boss Romola was. 'Leave it with me. And good luck!'

'I'll need it!' Romola called from the hallway, before closing Cliffy's big blue door behind her.

*

Azra was making coffee at the counter. She raised an eyebrow when Romola walked in, then pointed to the back. 'You have a gentleman waiting for you.' He'd taken her favourite table. 'Such a big man?' Azra whispered. 'You so small.' She shaped her hands around a space the size of a shoebox.

Romola smiled at Azra's interest in her love life. 'He's just a colleague.'

Emir stood to greet her. He wore a black baseball cap, which he removed as she approached, neatening his hair and shuffling his feet. He looked like he was preparing for a job interview. His sage-green eyes were drawn down at the edges, reminding her of a sad seal.

She shook his hand firmly. 'Thanks for meeting me, Emir.'

He sat down and put his hat on the table next to his coffee. 'I was gonna call you anyway – when I got back.' He picked up his mug, which appeared tiny cradled in his huge hands. 'Sorry I didn't get you one. I didn't know what you'd want.'

Romola shook her head to indicate there was no need for apologies. She'd called Emir after leaving Patrick's house last week on Tuesday. It was now Monday of the following week – Emir's first day back at work for Patrick and also the first day he'd said he was available to meet, offering no explanation of what he'd be doing in between. 'Emir, is there anything you'd like to ask me before I ask you some questions?' She took out her notepad.

He hesitated, his eyes darting to the front of the café where Azra was reading a magazine and shooting glances at their table. 'Not really.' His voice was dull, and he rubbed his eyes with his knuckles. 'You go on.'

She felt sorry for Emir. How could anyone not feel the pain of a grieving person sitting across from them? But was his grief compounded by guilt, the pain of loss made sharp-edged by the knowledge that he'd supplied at least some of the poison that killed his sister?

He wore two gold chains, one hanging underneath and one sitting atop his round-necked black T-shirt, over which hung his black puffer jacket. His right leg bumped up and down as he spoke. She was well aware of the size difference between them. His legs, wide open, extended to her side of the table. Feeling all the smaller, she was conscious of where she placed her feet, not wanting to knock knees with him. She was aware of the fine line such men walked in the minds of women. He was the right size to secure, to protect, to shield, but he could also crush her while barely moving a muscle. Her clients from her practice in criminal law had taught her that such a thing was entirely irrelevant to a person's guilt; still, she sat up a little straighter in her chair when faced with this massive man.

Romola wasn't sure if there was anything remotely consoling she could say to him – and she needed to learn as much as she could while she had him in front of her. 'So, Emir, you know I'm helping Patrick with his defamation case. Obviously Rabbit Hole has claimed that Patrick treated Hana very badly, and Patrick's saying that's not true. The trial is going to start soon – in around four weeks' time, in fact – and we're looking to call witnesses who will be able to help Patrick show that the story was false. Given you're Hana's brother, and also obviously around the two of them a lot as part of your work for Patrick, you're one of the main people who could help – if you agree that the claims are false, that is.'

Emir's pained eyes met hers. He placed a hand between them and began tapping his fingers lightly on the tabletop. He looked as though he would rather be anywhere than sitting with her.

'I'm sorry if this is difficult,' she said. 'Patrick says he loved your sister very much.'

Emir stopped tapping. He nodded in resignation, but neither explicitly accepted nor declined Romola's request for help.

'Do you think you could tell me how you and Hana came to be working for Patrick?'

Emir breathed in a lungful of air and exhaled slowly before he answered. 'Hana started first. She moved in with them after a couple months. I'd been out of work for a while, had a break from things cos I was having a hard time. Hana was worried about me … Well, she was always worried about me. She'd said something to them about me having done security work before – they wanted to step up security after a few close calls. I was happy, cos I wanted to be close to Hana again. And to make sure they treated her right.'

'You and Hana were close?' Romola had been told by everyone that it was so, but she wanted to start with questions that were easy for him to answer.

'She was my only sibling, my only family.' Emir shuddered. 'She was younger than me, but we'd always been tight. Our parents escaped Bosnia during the war. I was born after they arrived here – as refugees – and Hana a couple of years after. But my mother, god bless her soul, never adjusted, you know? She passed away suddenly, when Hana was eleven.' He pulled out the second gold chain and kissed the gold cross that had been hanging under his T-shirt, then held it skyward. Romola remembered the photographs she'd seen of Hana's body in her final repose: the gold chain she had been wearing was similar to the one Emir held close.

'I'm so sorry,' Romola said, feeling for Hana and Emir, and wondering how much of a mark their mother's early death had left on Hana. Romola knew how it felt to grow up without a real mother, but she had never known another way. Now that she had also lost her father, she saw how precious her years with him were.

Emir continued. 'Hana was brought up by Dad and me … More me than Dad. He was a hard guy, worse after Mum died. He wasn't easy to live with, but I tried to make things better for Hana. Dad was really proud when she got qualified, but he was sick by then. He died not long after. Lucky he wasn't around to find out she was pregnant.'

'It wouldn't have been culturally acceptable?' Romola asked, taking in what Emir had said about his father and underlining the words 'hard man' in her notebook. It sounded as if Hana had more scars than she had known about.

'I don't know about culture,' Emir baulked, 'but he would've hated it. Our little Hana-Bee.'

She examined Emir, questioning if he was a hard man too. For all his talk of loving his sister, had he learned from his father how she was to be treated? Romola thought back to what Storm had said: Emir had been Hana's protector, had taken himself a bit too seriously, and Hana had been the opposite.

Emir's voice grew more assured as he explained. 'When Dad died, he made me promise I would look after her, but he had it all wrong. *She* was the one looking after me. She was always sending me messages or leaving me notes – *go to the dentist, service my car* – and always with a smiley face.' He bit his lip, holding his fists together on the table.

'She sounds like she was a good sister to you. It must be hard without her. Do you have someone you can talk to now, Emir?' It had become a habit of hers, since her father's death, to try to work out if people had support and company. Lately, she'd suspected she was actually searching out others like her: people with only themselves to rely upon.

Emir smiled for the first time, warmly. 'My girlfriend – Tamara, Tam. We've been together a year.' Though his smile was wide, his eyes began to well. 'This is a pretty weird thing to tell a total stranger.' He assessed her, and she tried to look reassuring. 'We're having a baby. Tam's ten weeks. We're trying to save up for a place of our own, and her folks are over the moon.' He wiped away the tears with his thumb, blinking.

'Congratulations, Emir. That's wonderful news.'

'If it's a girl we're going to call her Hana. My sister would've made a great aunty – and mum. They would have been the same age, our babies, like brother and sister.' He clenched his jaw. 'Hana had always wanted to be a mum, you know.'

The mention of Hana's dreams caused Romola's mind to flash again to those pictures of her body, her dead hand held out in her last expression of surrender, all hopes and dreams given up on despite the life growing within her. Romola thought back to her conversation with Patrick on the yacht – his shock that Hana had wanted to terminate the pregnancy.

'Hard to believe she'd just give up on it, hey?' Emir said, as if following her train of thought.

'Yes – it is.' When she met his eyes, she could have sworn she saw him flinch. She pondered whether he was telling the whole truth, or whether he was actually acutely aware of some reasons Hana may have felt compelled to take her own life: a childhood marred by the death of her mother and possibly abuse by her father for a start.

'Did you see much of her and Patrick together?' she asked.

Peering towards the front of the café again, Emir rubbed at his unshaven face. 'I saw them all the time.' He avoided returning her gaze and put his baseball cap back on, squeezing its visor a few times.

'You knew her best. Do you think she was happy with him?'

He shrugged. 'Yeah, I'd say so. I mean – she never complained, so …' He trailed off as he focused on the exit beyond Romola.

It wasn't exactly the confident endorsement that she'd been hoping for, and she was left with the distinct impression that there was much that Emir wasn't saying. But Patrick was his employer, and Emir would be providing for a family soon with the income the job provided. Unfortunately he had every reason not to be open about his real feelings, something Rabbit Hole and Johnny would make everything of at trial were Emir to testify.

She tried another tack. 'Did you ever feel like she was scared, even if she didn't say it?'

'Nah, not scared or anything.' He shook his head. 'She was quieter than usual at the end, but I thought it was morning sickness.'

Romola jotted down his answers as she searched for a question that would cause him to divulge whatever was on his mind. 'What was Patrick like with her? Did you ever see him angry?'

'Nah – he was okay. You know – just the usual moods.' His head sank down so she could only see the top of his cap

'What about the night before she died? I understand you drove them home from dinner? Can you tell me what happened?'

She waited an age for some reaction. When he looked up his sad seal eyes were wet but strangely resolute in the face of the uncertainty of his previous answers. He shifted in his seat before he spoke. 'You're right – I drove them home. They'd obviously been fighting – they would normally hold hands in the back, but they didn't want anything to do with each other. I was waiting for Hana to speak to me, but she just stared out the window. When I left it was like she wanted to say something, but … I don't know. I was late home for Tam so I drove off … but a couple minutes later I had second thoughts, I don't know why … I turned around and came back by the house, watched them go in.'

'Did you see anything else then?' Romola prompted, too absorbed by Emir's account to bother with her notes. She wondered if he was on the verge of finally delivering her the missing piece of the jigsaw, while she hoped that the completed picture was one that her client would want a judge or jury to see.

'Hana was standing at the door, like she wasn't going to go in. It was cold out that night, and she just had this little gold dress on. Patrick had put his coat over her, but still, she was standing there in the cold. He grabbed her by the arm, just to bring her inside, I think. There was probably nothing in it. She would've been too cold out there, I guess.'

'Could you show me?' Romola held out her arm for him to demonstrate, wanting to understand, thinking perhaps Emir would show her what he seemed reluctant to explain in words. She wondered where that reluctance had been when he'd told his secrets to Johnny Wise, as she was now almost certain he must have done.

As he moved closer, she suddenly became aware of the silence around them. Azra had turned off the music, and there were no other customers. Romola remembered that Azra closed early on Mondays to pick Mohammed up from school and take him to soccer practice. It was getting close to 4 p.m. – her friend would be preparing to leave.

Emir slowly reached across the table. His fingers were warm and heavy; they enclosed Romola's wrist entirely. He stared into her eyes, unflinching, and she didn't look away. She couldn't have moved if she'd tried. White noise filled her head as she tried to decipher Emir's message, told not through words but through his grip and his eyes. He wanted to tell her something else – Romola was sure of it – he just didn't want to come out and say it.

'Can I get you anything else before I close up?'

Azra's voice came from beside Romola. She turned her head and realised that her friend was standing beside the table, staring at them with concern.

Emir released his grip. Romola glanced down at her wrist, lighter where his fingers had been, before the blood came flooding back. 'Thanks, Azra, but we're fine.'

Her friend seemed dubious, but nodded and walked away.

'Sorry,' Emir whispered, and his hands retreated under the table. 'I never saw anything other than that.' His words were casual, but he spoke with such intensity that Romola had to look away, shaken. She lifted her pen to note what had been communicated but then abandoned the task, knowing she would remember. Just then she remembered Patrick's words on the yacht when she'd asked him whether he had grabbed Hana: *Not that I can remember. I didn't want to lose her or our baby, but I would never have threatened her, never would have hurt her.*

Her eyes searched her notes for something else to ask about, and she found there was only one thing left – and there wasn't an easy way to bring it up. 'Sorry to have to go here, Emir, but I've been doing some looking into Sonia, Patrick's ex-wife. You worked for Patrick when Sonia was still living there, right?'

'Yeah …' Emir muttered, distracted, as though his mind was still caught up in the last moment he'd seen his sister.

'I understand Sonia had a substance abuse problem, including using fentanyl?'

Emir froze, his attention obviously pulled back into the moment. He started jiggling his leg again, and he crossed his arms in front of him. 'Right. What's that got to do with me?'

In Romola's mind, his defensiveness immediately confirmed what Sonia had alleged.

'There's no easy way to say this, Emir, but I've been told you were the one who supplied her with the drug.'

He recoiled. 'I wonder who would've told you that.' He scoffed. 'There's only one person I can think of.' He shifted forward in his seat. 'You've been speaking with Sonia, right? She swore she'd never talk.'

Emir had obviously forgotten himself, every other emotion overtaken by his contempt for Sonia. Romola held off asking anything further in the hope more information would spill out of him in anger.

'So yeah, I knew some people. I don't have anything to do with them anymore, though.' He uncrossed his arms to hold out a hand, pleading to be believed. 'Through them I had access to painkillers, oxycontin mainly, but also fentanyl. Sonia found out by accident – overheard a phone call. She said she'd tell Hana and Patrick, and, you know, my parole officer, if I didn't supply her. She was already hooked. She thought no one noticed.' He let out a bitter laugh. 'As if.'

Romola now wanted to understand whether there was any bridge between Sonia and Hana. She wanted to rule out any possibility that at trial there could be a suggestion that Patrick was somehow involved, or even just knew, of how Hana could get her hands on her weapon of choice. Romola decided there was no way for it but to ask directly. 'You know, Hana had some fentanyl in her system when she died, Emir. Do you think there could have been any left in the house after Sonia left? Or would Hana have any other way of getting it that you're aware of?'

His right fist came down on the table, its legs whining as they scraped the floor. Romola winced. 'I'm sure there was none left after Sonia had gone. It was a long time ago, but I specifically remember I checked the spot where she kept it, plus everywhere else she could have hid it in the house. And I would've noticed too if Hana had been taking any. There are signs. And I would have seen them, especially with Mum and everything.'

Romola was conscious of Azra floating near their table, busying herself as she kept half an eye on them, the shutters already having been pulled down and the signs taken in from outside.

Romola almost didn't register Emir's last remark. 'Sorry, what about your mum?'

'I thought you already knew?' he said, sounding surprised.

Romola put her pen down, her heart skipping a beat. 'Knew what?'

Emir sat perfectly still, his green eyes welling once again. 'Suicide. Mum overdosed.' He didn't take his eyes off Romola as tears rolled down his bristled cheeks. 'We never saw it coming.'

Chapter Thirty-Three
Same Same but Different

After her meeting with Emir, Romola took a long walk to clear her head. She walked through the residential streets of East Melbourne and Richmond, before taking a slow stroll along Bridge Road, checking out shops she had never bothered to discover. She passed a trendy-looking whole foods store and remembered she hadn't made any contribution to Cliffy's groceries in the past two weeks, so she spent a further half-hour lazily trawling crowded shelves, trying to select things that Cliffy, the resident chef, would find useful. It was close to dark by the time she arrived back at the house, carrying a calico bag filled with an odd assortment of items, from spelt flour to cashew butter to leafy greens.

Romola heard Lou's voice before she saw her giggling in the kitchen with Cliffy. Pausing for a moment at the doorway, Romola steeled herself to see her oldest friend again. They'd spoken only once since their hazy conversation the morning after Romola's big night out. That had been a short polite conversation over the phone, guided by an unspoken rule not to speak about Johnny, the ponytailed elephant in the room.

Romola knocked on the kitchen door like a stranger. 'Hello?'

Louise turned, stretching her arms and fingers wide. 'It's me! I thought I'd pop in to say hi. Is that okay?' She hesitated. 'Cliffy was saying maybe I could stay for dinner?'

He shrugged and held up a bottle of red. 'I was just making a risotto. There'll be plenty to go around.'

Romola awkwardly kissed Louise on the cheek and set the bag of groceries down on the counter before pouring herself a large glass.

Cliffy gasped. 'Is that fruit and vegetables I see? Why thank you,

Romy my dear.' He pulled out the jar of cashew butter and shot Romola a curious look, before pushing the bag into a corner near the sink and returning to the kitchen island. 'Now given neither of you are going to come out and say it, I will lay some ground rules for this evening.' Cliffy planted his hands palm down on the kitchen bench between the women. 'No discussion about these men – no Johnny, no Patrick. And that goes for me too now, given I'm involved. Let's make it no discussion about work at all, shall we? There must be more interesting subject matters that can occupy three brilliant minds like ours.'

Romola wondered why she hadn't simply approached the matter like this in the first place, calm and to the point. She wondered if she would have got a similar reaction from Louise, who laughed and touched Cliffy's shoulder. It was so remarkably strange seeing her friend be playful like in old times. Louise seemed intimately familiar but entirely new, like a once-loved but long-forgotten pair of shoes found at the back of the wardrobe.

Cliffy spent the next hour holding court in his kitchen, topping up wineglasses and whipping up a tarte Tatin. Romola got the sense he was reeling out his very best stories, desperate to keep the conversational ball in the air: the quirky anecdotes he used in speeches at art openings and stuffy legal conferences, and the more risqué tales saved for his famous dinner parties. She was exhausted just listening to him. It was almost a relief when, after they'd eaten, he started fastidiously wiping the benchtops. 'Well, work awaits me as always, ladies. Time for tomorrow's reading.' He flung a wet tea towel over the oven door, then patted them each on the head as he left, like he was counting small children. He closed the door behind him.

Louise and Romola fell into fits of giggles.

'Oh my god, I'd forgotten how much he can talk,' said Louise, red-faced with laughter. 'How can you stand it?'

Romola managed to settle herself, then stood up to turn on the electric kettle. She put an Earl Grey tea bag in a mug for Louise. 'He was putting on a bit of a show for us – nice of him, really. He's normally much more sedate these days.'

The kettle hissed to life, and Romola leaned against the bench. She could listen to a cup of tea being made forever.

'Do you have any peppermint?' Louise asked over her shoulder.

'But you always have Earl Grey.'

Her friend's face crinkled apologetically. 'I'm actually caffeine free at the moment. It's a thing Johnny and I are doing together.'

'You? No coffee?' Romola was floored. She held Louise solely responsible for her coffee addiction. When she was fourteen she hated the stuff, but Louise, sophisticated for her age, drank a flat white every morning with her mum at a café overlooking the Bronte Baths. Romola started drinking weak lattes just so she could become a part of those mornings. In the hour before school started, the girls would talk with Louise's mum Helen, a local GP, about everything from boys, to schoolteachers, to periods, to future aspirations. Helen still had an Irish accent and would soothe their teenage worries with sweet Irish expressions or else tell them to just 'feck it off anyways'. Louise's parents had long ago divorced.

When they were sixteen, Romola's dad started joining them, which slightly altered the tone of the conversation. Don, who loved high school gossip, would always start off with a goofy 'What's up, gals?' before offering a completely unhelpful perspective on their problems. One time he suggested Louise go right up to Joseph Barinello and say that she was in love him, because boys were always the ones doing the chasing and maybe he would appreciate the sentiment. Louise was brave enough to follow Don's advice; in response, Joseph had checked her cleavage and then said, 'You'll do. Shall we do it now behind the sheds?' Louise recounted her shock to Don. 'Holy Moses,' he said, and never again offered advice about boys.

Romola and Louise harboured *Parent Trap*-style fantasies that Helen would fall in love with Don and that he would ditch Judith. Then the friends would become proper sisters. On the bus to school after each coffee date, they would analyse the way Don and Helen had spoken to each other over their long blacks.

'I know, me without coffee is inconceivable, right?' Louise said, snapping Romola back to the present. 'I had withdrawal at first, but now I feel a lot better for it. You should give it a go. We could do it together?'

But you're already doing it 'together' with Johnny, thought Romola. Louise had become one of those people, part of an 'us'. Soon she and Johnny would be doing fad diets together, training for half-marathons together, going to Bunnings on the weekend to buy things for DIY projects together.

'Caffeine is too important to me right now,' Romola said as politely as she could. 'But I'm glad it's working out for you.' She reached high into the cupboard in search of peppermint tea bags.

The revelation that her coffee-loving friend had ditched caffeine raised so many questions that she longed to ask. What was it like living with Johnny? Was he messy? Did they fight? Did he snore? Could he cook? Was it everything Louise had expected and more – or, as Romola hoped, much less?

'How's work?' Romola asked instead, taking two steaming mugs to the table and sitting opposite Louise. Cliffy had turned off the main light just before he left, the room now illuminated by two pendulum lights that cast warm yellow circles over the kitchen island: one for Louise, one for her.

'Same old same old,' Louise said, looking downcast. For years she'd been hoping for a promotion in the magazine ranks but was convinced her editor had it in for her. 'I'd ask about your work, but ...'

'That's okay,' said Romola, while wishing that Louise had never met Johnny, that she could have her best friend back, and that she could tell her best friend that she was tired and wanted to go to bed at a reasonable hour on a Monday night, instead of sitting in the kitchen having an awkward conversation as if they were acquaintances who were both too polite to end the evening.

'I still feel awful about telling Johnny what you said that night,' Louise confessed. 'I guess we shouldn't talk about that either, though, hey?' She shrugged. 'How are you going living with Cliffy anyway? Are you looking for your own place yet?'

Romola felt flat. She'd pushed aside her guilt about overstaying with Cliffy, because she had too much on her plate right now to look for a rental. And trying to make a home for herself in this city outside of her godfather's place felt inconceivable. 'I'm waiting to see how things pan out.'

Cliffy had made it seem so easy not to talk about Patrick or Johnny; he'd fooled them into false a sense of security. The reality, Romola now saw, was that it was almost impossible to talk about other things. For better or worse, Johnny had become an integral part of Louise's life, and at least for now, Patrick had become an integral part of hers.

'How's your family?' Romola asked.

'Fine, all fine. Mum's thinking of retiring. Dad's Dad. You know how it is.'

'Not really,' Romola said without thinking.

'No. Of course. Sorry.'

She hadn't intended to make Louise feel bad, though she immediately realised that she had. Nevertheless, she was too tired to correct her mistake, to engage in an exchange of polite apologies. Instead she offered a sad smile.

'How are you going, with your dad, I mean?' Louise asked. 'Is it getting any better?'

'Not especially.' Romola felt the pull of tears, both of sadness and exhaustion. Again, she simply could not be bothered trying to explain; even if she'd been free to speak about everything on her mind, Patrick included, she didn't have the energy.

'You know, Judith's really worried about you, Romy.'

'Judith? How do you know that?' The mention of her stepmother jolted Romola like a pinprick, but the thought of Louise speaking to her hurt even more. She felt both embarrassed and infuriated, imagining the two of them scheming about her behind her back.

'She calls me,' Louise answered. 'She calls a lot, actually – sort of almost at stalker level, to be honest with you. She wants to know if I've seen you, and if I think you're, you know, sleeping with Patrick et cetera. That conversation always gets a little weird. She said you haven't been returning her calls … which I completely understand, by the way.'

Romola sipped her tea, considering her friend. Maybe she was wrong to think that Louise and Judith had been bonding over their mutual concern. Maybe Louise had actually visited tonight just to get Judith off her back – to handball back to Romola the burden of a stepmother who didn't belong to her. 'Sorry about her. I just find her exhausting, you know? Dad would have understood.'

Louise let out a sigh of irritation. 'So you think you're doing the right thing at work do you? With Patrick?'

'What's that supposed to mean?' Romola willed herself not to get too angry. She couldn't help thinking that Louise had only come to do Judith's bidding and to lighten her own load. And now she was asking about Patrick again?

Suddenly all Romola wanted was her bed. She had a big day tomorrow: she and Cliffy and Gretchen were meeting with Patrick at Cliffy's chambers to take him through his evidence. The trial was only four weeks away, and they had the jury argument to prepare for later in the week. Romola needed to get some sleep – she didn't have time for another fight with Louise.

'This isn't going to work, is it?' Romola said abruptly. 'You and me pretending like everything is normal, acting like we're friends when actually you don't agree with anything I'm doing. It's just … silly.'

Louise flushed pink, but Romola couldn't tell if it was from anger or embarrassment. Her friend put down her tea mug and stood up. 'I was only trying to be nice, Romy. Some people still care about you, after all. If this is what you want to be doing with your life, if this is what you think lawyers should be proud to do, then good on you. Don't come crying to me when it all goes horribly wrong again.' She picked up her bag and turned for the door.

Romola marched after her, any remaining hope that they wouldn't fight now lost. 'Thanks for the support,' she snapped. 'And same to you, when you find out Johnny's not all he's cracked up to be either.'

Louise turned back, her bag strap tangling around her with the movement. Her face was now full-blown red. 'You don't know the first thing about him. You've never even done him the courtesy of having a proper conversation with him. And that's your loss, by the way – he's a good guy. Who are you to talk to me about relationships, anyway? When was your last relationship, hey? Face it, you're romantically moribund, Romola. Until you get the guts to take a chance on someone, I don't know why I should listen to anything you have to say!' Louise waited for a moment, but when Romola remained silent and fuming, she left with a loud slam of the door. A sunhat fell off the coat rack.

As Romola faced the door, still full of rage, she thought of all the things she should have told Louise. How she would rather be 'romantically moribund' than perpetually date dirtbags. And how she couldn't think of anything worse than living with a self-aggrandising wanker like Johnny. But as the rage subsided, most of all Romola was stung to learn what her friend really thought of her. She didn't see how she could ever forget it.

After taking a few deep breaths she walked to the kitchen, slower than she needed to. She rinsed the tea mugs, trying to control her breathing as the warm water flowed over her hands. If Louise was an old pair of shoes, they weren't comfortable anymore. Romola's feet had grown, and the leather was cracked and stiff. She rubbed at the mark Louise's red lipstick had made on her mug, wishing her friend had never come over at all.

Chapter Thirty-Four
Preparing for Plan B

They'd been sitting in the meeting room at Cliffy's chambers with Patrick for three hours. In his later years of practice, Cliffy had moved from busy chambers on Lonsdale Street to a smaller space on William Street. The meeting room here was similar to the Slug's: shelves filled with old volumes of law reports and textbooks acquired from an old law library that had moved online. But in this room there was a single window, with a view over Flagstaff Gardens, perfectly positioned to capture the westerly sun. Patrick sat at the head of the table and was framed within the light, a halo forming over his head whenever the dusty rays appeared.

Gretchen had already spilt her water three times. Each time she'd glanced at him and profusely apologised.

'Fourth time lucky, eh?' Cliffy said with a smile as he refilled her glass from the jug. 'Now, where were we?'

'You used to buy her flowers,' Romola said to Patrick.

Gretchen giggled. 'Sounds like the name of a song.'

'Yes. I used to buy her flowers. She used to leave me notes. We were always accused of being too soppy, if anything.'

After much toing-and-froing, they'd decided Patrick would testify if, despite their best efforts to elicit a settlement offer, they had to go through with the trial. Cliffy and Romola had considered leaving it to Rabbit Hole to prove the truth of the imputations in the articles, and allowing their client to stay silent. But if there was to be a jury, Romola agreed with Cliffy that Patrick needed to face them. Otherwise there would be too many unanswered questions; too many inferences could be drawn from the evidence of Rabbit Hole's witnesses. While Tilly was not likely to be relied upon any longer, they anticipated Rabbit

Hole would call Lara, former friends and acquaintances of Lisbeth and of Hana who had observed a change in their behaviour, possibly Sonia, and now, Romola suspected, Emir.

She had recounted her meeting with Emir to Cliffy, and they agreed there was little doubt he had already turned against Patrick. His recent disappearing act had most likely been brought about by an inability to stomach being close to the man he held responsible, in some way, for the loss of his sister, and he was likely the source who Johnny had on the record saying Patrick had forcefully grabbed her that night.

To succeed, Patrick would have to credibly counter that, and Cliffy was now taking him, in painstaking detail, through what he would say on the witness stand. He needed to recount what his relationship with Hana had been like, from beginning to end. This involved delving into details that wouldn't normally have been shared with a group of three relative strangers, but which Cliffy drew out from Patrick gently, like a teacher urging a child to participate in show-and-tell. Romola could see that her godfather was trying to come from every conceivable perspective that a judge or jury member might have.

'Tell us about what you would describe as your high point as couple,' said Cliffy. 'When were you both at your happiest?'

Patrick smiled. 'My favourite times were when we had Max on the weekends, with no plans, nowhere to be. Hana would play in the garden with him or spend all day cooking us a Bosnian meal. One day in the middle of winter, all three of us spent a Sunday in our pyjamas. Max was into Harry Potter, so we watched the first three movies in a row. Yeah, those were the best times, when we didn't have to bother getting out and making an appearance.'

'Okay,' Cliffy said, like he'd been hoping for something more insightful, 'and what about the reverse? We all have moments where if we had the ability to press replay and watch ourselves back, we would not be proud. We would rewind and delete the scene if we could. Can you tell us about any times like that?'

Patrick rested his elbows on the table and examined his hands, his hair falling into his eyes. 'What used to drive Hana mad was when I went quiet. Sometimes I can't bear to talk anymore – I tend to dwell on things. Hana was the opposite. She was high energy. And she was like that in anger too, going a million miles an hour. I guess when I was angry I'd just stonewall her until I was ready to talk … which could sometimes be a while.'

'What is a while, would you say?' Cliffy asked.

'Hours, maybe a day or two. I'd sometimes disappear for the day, leave my phone at home and everything.'

'How often would that happen?'

'I don't know, maybe every few weeks, or once a month. On average, that is – not every month.'

'What types of things would make you angry like that?'

Patrick cast a fleeting look at Romola and Gretchen. 'Sometimes it would be when Hana kept going on at me. She was like a dog with a bone when she got excited about something. It could be tiring.'

'Examples?'

Patrick sighed, swivelled his chair and stared out the window to the parklands across the road. A mothers' group was meeting, picnic rugs were laid out, and toddlers chased bubbles against a grey sky. He turned back to the conversation. 'A recurring one was that she wanted me to be on her blog – she wanted to have a father's perspective. It probably wouldn't have been a bad PR exercise for me either, but … I don't know … I couldn't presume that anything I had to say on parenting would be useful to people, you know? It felt stupid when I tried to do it. And then she thought I was criticising her because she obviously felt comfortable giving people advice.' He paused. 'Another one was travel. She wanted to travel a lot. But like I said, I preferred being at home with her and Max. She was always trying to get me to go somewhere or other – Italy most recently, Positano. I got sick of hearing about it, so I agreed. Then when we were there it was all about getting the right Insta shot. It was infuriating.'

Romola glanced down at her phone, which had buzzed in her lap with an unknown number. She rejected the call without thinking, her mind occupied instead by the memory of those shots on Hana's Instagram: timber cruisers on turquoise seas, suntans, sunlit breakfasts, Patrick in linen shirts and Hana in flimsy floral dresses, terracotta tiles and wrought-iron balconies. It was strange to think Patrick had hated it all along, that he'd been dragged there.

'We got some new information from Emir yesterday, Patrick.' Cliffy started, and Romola braced herself.

'Yes?' Patrick asked, with no hint of concern.

'He said that, after he dropped you and Hana home the night of her death, he turned his car around, and when he came back he saw you grabbing her arm – with some force. The likelihood is that he's the one who's told Jonathan Wise about it.' Cliffy didn't sugarcoat the news, which Romola supposed was the best way to deliver it.

Patrick's reaction was the polar opposite of what she'd been expecting. His grey eyes grew wide as he jolted up in his seat, then he let out a disbelieving laugh, one in which she thought she detected a note of relief. When he spoke, his voice had travelled up an octave. 'Are you serious? It was Emir who said that to them? If that's true then maybe this is just a huge misunderstanding. I remember that exact moment like it was yesterday. It was bloody freezing outside, and Hana was insisting that she wanted to go for a walk. She was completely determined, even though she was wearing next to nothing. She wasn't making any sense. I've already told you about the argument at dinner. It was more of the same – that she needed to think, be by herself, that kind of thing. I was worried about her, and the baby. So I pulled her inside. I mean, I wasn't rough with her at all – more like I was guiding her, you know?'

'I see,' said Cliffy. 'So there's nothing in the suggestion you were in any way violent with her then? How do you think it would have appeared to an onlooker?'

'Well, if that onlooker is outside on the street in his car, like Emir says he was, then I don't think he's in a position to say how it appeared at all. You wouldn't be able to see what was going on from there, especially at night. He must have got the wrong end of the stick. Can't you talk to him again – I'm sure once I explain he can go back to Rabbit Hole and tell them he was wrong after all?'

'Perhaps.' Romola didn't want to agree to anything just yet. She knew there was still a finely balanced judgement to be made as to whether to attempt to convince Emir of anything now, or whether the points Patrick had made were better saved until Hana's brother was on the stand in cross-examination, without any prior notice or opportunity to find his way around them.

Cliffy leaned back in his chair and contemplated the ceiling. Romola wondered if, like her, he was carefully constructing images in his mind, both of Hana, and of Patrick and Hana together; whether he was piecing together Patrick's recollections like a director in an editing suite, sorting through footage to create the vision that would play best in front of a courtroom. 'You seem to be painting a picture of Hana being fairly highly strung, yes?'

'I guess that's right.'

'And was she always like that, or did she have down times too? Quiet times, perhaps.'

Patrick spoke tentatively, his enthusiasm of a moment ago now fading. 'Yes, she had quiet times. Sometimes they were darker times. Before she died she had a tendency to stare off into space. We'd be watching television together and I'd make a comment about the show, and she would be taken off guard, like she hadn't been watching at all ... Sometimes I'd find her sitting at the kitchen bench, and I'd realise she'd been stirring her tea for literally fifteen minutes. The tea wouldn't even be hot anymore.'

Cliffy lifted off his reading glasses and began sucking on one of the arms like a pipe. 'Did those darker times coincide with anything?'

'Not that I know of.'

'But she was having one that evening – before she died? You just said you were worried about her?'

'Oh right.' Patrick exhaled, clearly following Cliffy's train of thought. Any hope he had garnered a moment a go seemed to evaporate. 'Yes, that's right. I was worried.' He didn't explain any further, placing his hand over his mouth in contemplation.

Sitting forward and putting his glasses back on, Cliffy jotted down a note in his book. He'd filled pages already and started going back over them. Romola could see that he was seeking out where further information was required, probably thinking of which areas were susceptible to questioning from the Bulldog and to unknown answers from Patrick. They wanted to avoid the worst nightmare of every lawyer: new information coming out on the stand.

Romola noticed her phone screen lighting up again – the third call in half an hour from an unknown number. She clasped it between her hands and held it firmly under the desk, focusing back on the meeting.

'Can I ask you something?' Patrick asked Cliffy quietly.

'Go ahead.' Cliffy removed his glasses once more, his face a gentle smile.

Patrick hesitated. For a moment the sun came out from behind the clouds and illuminated him. The lines on his face had become more prominent over the past few weeks, and the strands of white in his thick dark hair seemed to have multiplied. 'Would it be better or worse if I knew she was unwell – mentally, that is? I mean, the fact is I knew something wasn't right, I didn't do anything about it, and then she took her life and that of our child. Isn't that just as bad as what they're accusing me of? Aren't I just as much to blame for what happened?' Patrick's face contorted with grief. He was clearly willing Cliffy to give him some relief from his guilt, which until now he'd kept hidden from Romola. It had obviously been lurking in the background, tapping at Patrick's conscience like a clock.

Cliffy's face fell. He placed his pen down in front of him. 'No, my boy. I would argue that's a very different thing indeed. Failing to accept or to act is not the same thing as being the cause of Hana's unhappiness. And the latter is what this journalist is inferring – that you were the *cause*. If that were true, then this case would indeed be difficult to win.' Cliffy smiled gently. 'But a lack of foresight is different... people can understand that, and they can forgive it.'

'You might misjudge what people think of me.'

'As might you, my boy.'

Patrick bent forward, cradling his head, a gesture Romola had become all too familiar with. His hair poked through the gaps in his fingers.

'Shall we have a ten-minute break?' Cliffy asked softly. 'I'll get some coffee brought in.'

Romola excused herself and headed for the door. She stood in a nearby stairwell as she dialled the unknown number, thinking about the potential witnesses she'd been trying to reach over the past few days. Would whoever was calling be a help or a hindrance?

A woman answered, her officious voice softening when Romola introduced herself. 'I've been trying to get hold of you,' the woman said. 'I'm the manager of the surgical unit at St Vincent's Private Hospital in Sydney. I'm afraid there's been an accident.'

*

Ten minutes later Romola returned to the meeting room to find the others had started without her. Cliffy and Gretchen didn't look up, and Romola sat down, swivelled to face Patrick and picked up her pen.

He caught her eye. 'You okay, Romola?' His look of concern made her want to disappear.

'I'm fine,' she said.

Cliffy glanced across at her, pointing his nose down and focusing his clear blue eyes on hers above the frames of his glasses. He would normally have noticed that everything wasn't okay, but he was clearly consumed with his next line of questioning. She couldn't tell him now, she decided.

'I'm fine,' she insisted. 'It's nothing. Let's carry on.'

It wasn't nothing; it was Judith. She'd had a fall from a ladder onto her outdoor paving. She'd broken bones and possibly had internal injuries as well. She was in surgery getting put back together.

If Romola was perfectly honest with herself, her immediate reaction was that she didn't have time for falls. Why would her stepmother go and make herself fall at such an inconvenient time? Typical Judith. Heartless Romola. But she had to admit she was feeling uneasy. Her arms seemed to have turned to jelly, her hands shook, and her tummy flipped over every time she thought of the nurse saying 'internal injuries'.

Urged on by a look from Romola, Cliffy continued. His questions led Patrick to the moment he'd awoken one morning to his house cleaner's screams. Patrick said that he had run up the hallway and seen a look of panic on the old lady's face. He'd then seen Hana's outstretched hand, white fingers poised like those of a ballerina. Her face puzzled him – her downturned mouth was all wrong for the girl who was usually smiling. He placed a hand on her head and felt the cold of her skin; it was so cold she couldn't have been alive, but still, against the old lady's protestations, he tried to shake her awake. The gold cross fell off her chin, and the coat opened, his coat. He could see Hana properly then, her body under her flimsy cocktail dress. He put his hand on the place where their baby had been growing. The size of a raspberry, the doctor had said, not yet big enough to feel or see. He'd tortured himself by contemplating whether it would have made a difference to Hana if the baby had been kicking. Patrick couldn't remember if he'd spoken any words in that moment.

'That's all we need for today,' Cliffy announced, once it was clear Patrick had nothing left to say. 'We can talk about Beth tomorrow.'

Patrick stood and faced the window, and Romola followed his gaze. It was close to 4 p.m. and the mothers in the park had been replaced with city workers making an early exit, earbuds in, immune to the broken man watching from the window. The days were beginning to stretch a little longer, and the sun had made appearances throughout the afternoon, but it looked cold out there. Strangers' hands were dug deep into coat pockets, and breath came in clouds.

'Do you think it will be enough?' Patrick asked the room, without turning.

Cliffy cleared his throat and crossed his arms. 'That depends. Jury trials, if that's what we end up getting, are funny things, Patrick. It partly depends on whether you get good people on the jury who truly assess the evidence dispassionately. Tragically Rabbit Hole and Jonathan Wise have two young women on their side who died in the prime of their lives. Those women cannot speak for themselves, and a jury will want to fill in the gaps. You're the one who will need to give them the story to plug those spaces.' Cliffy rubbed at his grey stubble, grown longer by the end of the day. 'If we get to that point – which we're all hoping we won't – tell it to them like you told it to us today, and you might win this.'

*

By 5 p.m., Cliffy and Romola were finally alone in the meeting room at his chambers. He poured two cognacs from a hidden bar before she could stop him. His bow tie, paisley today, had been sitting crooked for the latter part of the afternoon; he removed it and laid it in a straight line on the drinks table, unbuttoning his shirt collar. His thick white hair, which had started the day in a smooth curl, was an erratic mess, and weed-like stubble darkened his jaw. He started to hum to himself, something that sounded vaguely like the French national anthem.

Romola felt especially cold-hearted telling him the news about Judith now that he was winding down, ready to dissect the interview with Patrick, to discuss their client's strengths and weaknesses. She longed to have that conversation instead of the one she was about to have.

'What do you make of Patrick?' Cliffy asked.

'He seems sincere. But he's omitted important things in the past.'

Cliffy sipped his drink and flipped through his notes, highlighting passages, underlining others. She sat watching him until his pen stopped moving. 'What is it?'

'That call I had today was from a hospital up in Sydney. Judith's had a fall. She's broken a few bones. I think she's going to be fine, but –'

Cliffy's jaw dropped. His mouth opened and closed, but he seemed unable to speak.

'She's still in recovery. I just spoke with the nurse again, and she said the surgery went well. It's nothing … life-threatening or anything.'

Cliffy nodded, his lips pursed. His nostrils ballooned out, and his chest heaved with the effort of containing his emotions. She hadn't seen him this way before, but Cliffy was angry with her. He steadied himself by holding on to the back of the nearest chair, while Romola stayed seated, feeling like a child in the principal's office. 'For goodness sake, Romola, why didn't you say something sooner? You just let me go on working like an idiot.'

'I didn't want to distract you. We only have limited time with Patrick, and we're so close to the end. There's nothing that can be done to help Judith right now, anyway. The nurse said she would call if anything changes.'

Cliffy was staring at her incredulously. 'Shouldn't you be getting yourself on a plane up there, right now?'

Romola hadn't even considered flying up to Sydney. A phone call and some flowers would surely suffice, she'd thought. 'But we have so much to do here.'

'Where are your priorities, Romola?!' Cliffy pressed down hard on the chair until it slipped out from under him; he fell off balance before righting himself on the table. 'Why worry about work now? Family *must* come first, or you'll end up with nothing *but* work. Believe me, I've firsthand experience with that.' Cliffy didn't look at Romola as he confessed this unhappiness. 'You're her daughter. You should go and make sure she's okay.'

'Stepdaughter,' said Romola without thinking, accustomed to making the correction.

Cliffy shook his head in disappointment. 'It's the same thing to her, and you know it. It hurts her that, despite everything, you still won't accept her as a mother. She's been there almost your whole life. Why do you still treat her like an evil storybook stepmother? Why not let her in now that it's just the two of you?'

Romola realised in that moment that she had divided her life into two: a 'before Judith' and a 'with Judith'. The realisation dawned on her that she'd always thought there would be an 'after Judith', a time when she and her father would reunite as the dynamic duo of her primary school days. But there had been an unforeseeable plot twist: there would never be an 'after Judith', only an 'after Don'.

Romola caught her breath as her renewed grief smacked her in the face. She felt the heat of her tears before she knew they were falling. 'I don't want it to be just the two of us. It can't be me and Judith. It's the wrong two.' She wiped at her eyes with the backs of her hands, beyond embarrassment. 'It was supposed to be me and Dad.'

Cliffy relaxed the hand that had been clutching the table. He turned to open a cupboard behind him, where he found a tissue box and silently handed it to Romola before leaving the room. She barely noticed his absence until he returned five minutes later with a stack of A4 pages in hand. He placed them on the table in front of her. 'Read this.'

The pages were still warm from the printer. According to the title, they contained sentencing remarks from the District Court of Queensland, dated July 1992. The defendant was named Raymond McClusky. He had been convicted of attempted murder, two separate counts of assault, and stalking offences. The judge described him as 'narcissistic', 'egocentric', 'domineering' and 'monstrous'. His victim was his wife. He had beaten her with an iron, so severely that she'd lost the child she had been carrying. Her pregnancy had been six months along. The damage from her injuries was irreversible – she would never be able to conceive again. The judge said McClusky was remorseful, but the seriousness of his offending could not be ignored, nor the impact of his actions on his victim's life. He had been sentenced to twelve years in prison, with a non-parole period of ten. Not long enough, thought Romola.

She wiped her nose. 'Horrible. Why are you showing me this?'

With his back to her, Cliffy said, 'Raymond McClusky's wife was Judith.'

Romola froze, unable to follow the threads that her godfather was using to guide her. 'Judith? *Our* Judith? But she wasn't married.'

'Yes she was, I'm afraid.'

'To this man?' Romola pointed at the pages, feeling agitated. 'This was her?'

Cliffy turned to her, his face still flushed. 'The fact is, you have made judgements about Judith that simply are not correct, my dear. She is a survivor. The year I met her was the same year her ex-husband was released from prison. He tried to come back for her, but she wouldn't have a bar of it. I represented her in the Family Court proceedings and then made submissions on her behalf before the Parole Board. McClusky was sent back to prison. She had too much to live for then.'

'How do you mean?'

'She had *you*, silly, plus your dad. But she loved you as much as she loved Don. From the moment she met you, she was entranced. She may be overbearing, but she knows what this world can be.'

Romola bent her head, reading more of the judge's remarks. After McClusky had beaten Judith with the iron, he had wrapped its cord around her neck. He was still holding it tight when he was interrupted by a visit from a neighbouring farmer, who had come about a fence. The man had run inside when he'd heard Judith's screams. She lost consciousness as he rushed into the room and the cord loosened. Romola felt her own throat constricting at the thought and held a hand to her abdomen.

'Why didn't they ever tell me?' Romola whispered, her tears completely dried up, shocked into retreat.

'She doesn't like to think about it. And she was so happy in her new life – she wouldn't have wanted you to think any differently about her.'

'To think she's survived this.' Romola kept her finger on the paper in front of her. 'How could she not think about it every single day?'

Cliffy didn't respond. Instead he tidied papers from Patrick's case and slotted books back onto the shelves. After a few minutes, he spoke again. 'So you'll go and see her?'

Romola knew her answer must be yes, even though her insides knotted at the thought of facing Judith with this new information. The knots formed with the guilt she suddenly felt, and with the utter certainty that she would be at a loss for words when faced with her stepmother, as though meeting her for the very first time. Then her eyes fell on the folders covering the table. 'But what about tomorrow? We're meant to be meeting with Patrick again. And then the jury argument on Thursday?'

'We'll cope without you. That's what they pay me the big bucks for.'

Romola stood up like an elderly person would have, slow and steady, as she braced herself for the coming hours. For getting herself to the airport in peak hour. For joining the tired east coast commuters on their journey home. For explaining to anyone who asked that she must get to Sydney as soon as possible because there had been an accident and her mother needed help.

Chapter Thirty-Five
Perspective

'She likes to talk, doesn't she?' The nurse must have seen the embarrassment, or panic, in Romola's eyes. It was 10.30 p.m. and she had come straight from the airport then sweet-talked her way into Judith's ward. The nurse gave a sympathetic smile as she led her down the corridor. 'Mine's exactly the same. God help me if she's ever a patient here.' Romola laughed nervously, and the nurse paused. She examined Romola's face, her eyes travelling to the top of her head. 'You look exactly like she said.'

'She's been talking about me?'

The nurse rolled her eyes. 'Nonstop, love. We know everything there is to know about you. Apparently you're a very high-powered lawyer.' She winked, and Romola felt self-conscious about her charcoal pinstriped suit, wishing she'd had time to change. The nurse stopped outside a door marked '18' and pointed her clipboard inside. 'This is her. She was lucky – it's our last private room.'

Romola stood frozen, then finally asked what ought to have been her first question: 'How is she?'

The nurse offered the hint of a smile. 'Don't worry, she's not on her way out just yet.'

Something dissolved inside of Romola with those words. All of a sudden she knew she had been terrified, ever since she'd left Cliffy's chambers, that she wouldn't get the chance to make amends.

'Your mum's leg was fractured quite badly. They've wired her up in surgery. And her pelvis is cracked. Lucky she didn't land on her head, or it would have been a different story. I'd say another week in here and then off to rehab – she's at that age where they need a bit of help getting back on their feet. After that, she's all yours.'

The nurse swung open the door. Judith lay with her leg suspended in the air and her hands neatly placed on top of the folded sheet, a tray of food pushed to one side. She wore a light-blue hospital gown, and her hair, which had been let down, framed her pale and rested face. Free from her usual adornments, she no longer seemed to be an ageing fortune teller. Her eyes, in a drug-induced wonder, moved from the television hung high above her head to her visitor. She caught her breath as though she'd received an unexpected birthday present. 'You came!' she exclaimed in a croaky voice, her eyes bright. 'I didn't think you would.'

Romola moved closer to the bed, dumping her bag on the floor. She felt warm, and slightly embarrassed that her presence had induced such happiness. To think, she wasn't going to come at all. 'I was worried about you. And Cliffy was beside himself. He insisted I come.'

Judith's face fell a little.

'I would have come anyway.' Romola took in the cannula in Judith's arm, the clear bag dripping medicine into her bloodstream.

'Sorry to cause a fuss. It's been an ordeal.' Judith almost looked embarrassed.

'Does it hurt?'

'They have given me the most *magnificent* drugs. I can't feel a thing! When I fell – well, that was something else. I cried like an injured bear. When Barry from next door finally arrived, he must have thought I'd been a crime victim. He came along with his cricket bat, all ready to rescue the damsel in distress. Honestly, that man –'

'You must have been terrified.'

'I'm tougher than I look.' Judith winked.

'I know you are.' Romola went to stand next to the bed, picking up a plastic bag that been placed there and briefly peering inside: denim, with the unmistakable dark brown stain of dried blood.

Judith followed her eyes. 'My favourite gardening pants! I asked them to keep them in case I can sew them back together. They had to cut them off me, you see. Can you imagine? It was an open fracture. Do you know what that means?'

'Afraid so.'

Judith closed her eyes, and Romola hoped she might fall asleep. Now that she knew her stepmother would be fine, she was longing to sneak back to Judith's place to grab a few hours of her own.

A beep came over the hospital intercom, followed by a monotone voice: 'Resuscitation team to Emergency Two. Resuscitation Team to Emergency Two.' Romola imagined the doctors and nurses running; a poor family at the bedside hearing the call.

'That happens more than I would like,' Judith said, opening one of her eyes. 'It's driving me up the wall. I don't know why it's necessary to broadcast to the entire hospital that someone is being resuscitated. It hardly lifts the spirits.'

Romola didn't respond – only Judith could think of herself when hearing that message. Then she chastised herself for being judgemental; she wouldn't do that anymore.

'I hate hospitals,' Judith muttered, scrunching her face as she propped herself up on her pillows, attempting a shift of position.

'Need a hand?' Romola asked uncertainly.

'I'm hot. It's insufferable. And my hair is irritating me, so I'm going to cut it off again. These curls are ridiculous. Would you mind grabbing that hair tie over there?'

Romola grabbed the elastic from the cabinet next to the bed and dug her own hairbrush from the bag that she had packed in a hurry before leaving for the airport, then perched on the edge of Judith's pillows. She gathered her stepmother's hair in her left hand and pulled the brush through the soft silver curls, holding a fistful of hair firmly near the scalp so as not to cause any pain as she brushed out the knots. She used broad strokes until the strands started to shine.

Judith's head gently rocked back and forth with each brush. 'Thank you, honey. That's lovely.'

'You're welcome.' Romola continued the brushing for longer than was necessary.

'I'm sorry, Romola,' Judith murmured, almost too quietly to be heard.

'Sorry for what?'

'You know very well,' Judith admonished. 'I'm sorry for judging your new job. And for jumping to conclusions about you and that

Payne man. It's your business.' She paused, perhaps contemplating if she should stop at an apology, but she couldn't help herself. 'It's only that I worry for you. I don't want you getting into something that's hard to get out of.'

'It's fine,' Romola responded quietly. 'I'm sorry too. I guess I've been pretty dismissive of your concerns.'

They sat in silence for a moment. Two nurses stood outside the door, having a loud conversation about their weekend plans. Romola gathered Judith's hair into a high ponytail and laid it on the pillow above her head. But before Romola could move to stand up, Judith reached out and grasped her hand. As Romola felt the bones in her stepmother's fingers, it occurred to her that she couldn't remember ever having held Judith's hand before. She supposed she must have as a child – when she was twelve years old, already too old for hand-holding, but Judith had been attempting to win her affection. Then she became a teenager and would have none of it, and they weren't the type to hold hands in adulthood, even while grieving the death of the man who linked them. Judith's skin was much softer than she had expected, and the woman smelled of hospital-grade sanitiser. It had been so long since Romola had held anyone's hand; the gesture reminded her of all that she was missing and made her want to cry.

'Are you listening to me, Romy? I really am sorry. There are so many things I should have told you about – maybe you would have even liked me more if I had. You were so innocent. But now I can see there was never really any protecting you.'

She tugged at Romola's arm as she spoke. Romola could see that her stepmother was on the verge of telling her everything, of revealing the secret that had always been too big for words. She didn't want to hear Judith wrestle with the monster that no doubt still lived within her, so Romola saved her the effort. 'I know about your first marriage.'

Judith's breath caught in her throat.

'I came across the sentencing remarks when I was doing some research. I saw your name.'

Judith peered back towards Romola, suddenly a scared old woman – but one who still had fight in her. 'There was never any need for you to know. Your father was such a good man. Why tell you about the other kind of men who exist in the world?'

'It's okay. I understand.'

'And you were so insistent that you weren't interested in boys anyway. When you went into criminal law, I thought to myself, It's okay, she'll see the worst of it through those clever lawyer's eyes of hers; she will learn how to see a man for what he is. But this Patrick Payne, he worries me. I thought maybe if he was charming enough, you could fall into the same trap I did. You might never know what to look for until it was too late.'

'You must have been terrified.'

Judith nodded, and Romola could see that she had closed her eyes. 'The worst of it was being both uncertain and certain. After the third time, I knew he would do it again. I knew that each time would be worse than the last, but I didn't know when it would happen. I was very vulnerable.'

'Surely someone must have noticed?'

'We lived in a farmhouse miles from anywhere. He could yell, scream, hit – no one had the chance to notice. And it wasn't like I had black eyes or anything.' She extracted her hand from Romola's and began massaging her fingers. 'He liked to hurt my fingers at first. He would jam them in doors, drawers, give them a burn here and there. Maximum pain for minimum effort, easily dismissed as a self-inflicted accident. Or pinches – my thighs were covered in marks. They were the minor things; the bigger ones were harder to cover up. He would always feel so guilty afterwards. He would put me into bed and nurse me back to health. He'd always been angry, but in the end he was downright sadistic.'

Romola shuddered. Just as she had before in Cliffy's chambers, she felt prickles in the places that Judith was describing, her fingers and thighs burning with the thought of her stepmother's injuries. 'Did you think of telling anyone?'

'It's difficult to explain, but I couldn't find the words. It felt like confessing something I had done to myself. It seemed such a strange, unwelcome thing to verbalise. Who would want to be lumped with that knowledge? I really just desperately wanted to be normal, like the rest of my friends. They'd all married and had children. When I got pregnant I thought it might finally happen, but instead he got much worse. I'll never understand why.'

Romola rose from the edge of the bed and drew up a nearby chair so she could face her stepmother. 'There must have been some signs people should have picked up on. Your parents were living nearby, weren't they?'

Judith shook her head firmly. 'Country towns are funny places. Everyone likes to think they know everyone else's business, but it's all a facade. The distance between people makes it easier to pretend. Ray was always first to help out in a crisis – a country firefighter, one of the boys. No one would have known what he was doing to me unless they'd really and truly got to know *me*.'

Romola wondered when Judith had last told anyone about this. She seemed relieved to be speaking the words.

'I wrote a letter, you know, to the coroner, to be opened in the event of my death. I know it all sounds very dramatic, but I truly believed my husband would eventually kill me. And I didn't want him to get away with it, which I knew he probably would with the cops being as they were in that town. So I hid the note in the drawer where I kept my tampons. I knew he would never look there. I thought of that note as my black box. It would be a silver lining – I would be gone, but the truth would come out. Everyone would know what he truly was. I hated him by then; it was like poison to me when people said he was a good man. How I wished someone would accidentally find that note. I would dream of someone coming into our house when we weren't home and putting two and two together, to save me from telling.' Judith sighed and began patting the sheets that were draped over her, pushing away invisible dust, flattening out the crinkles. 'I always thought if someone could just be present in our home for a while, they would know. It would sit in the atmosphere, what he did to me. Maybe they would see some of the marks on the walls or notice how meticulous the place was – his sock drawer, for goodness sake! I kept waiting for that person, that saviour. But of course it was too late by the time it finally happened. I'd lost her.'

'Your baby.' Romola couldn't help herself from speaking the words, though they emerged as a gasp. It was perfectly clear who Judith had lost. All of Romola's thoughts over the years about the childless Judith attempting to hijack her family took on a new, hurtful, form.

Judith closed her eyes again.

'And he left you alone once you married Dad?'

'When I'd married him yes, but before that, when I first started seeing your father, he found me. Luckily Cliffy helped me in court, and after another stint in prison Ray eventually got the message. I never saw or heard from him again. He might be dead – or married again, god forbid.'

Romola shuddered at the thought. 'I don't know how you did it.' She grasped Judith's hand again and gave it a squeeze.

Her stepmother squeezed back. 'I had no choice in the matter, my love. It was life or death.'

They sat in silence a while longer, until Judith began to shift her body under the sheet to make herself comfortable. 'Would you mind putting the bed down for me? I feel utterly exhausted all of a sudden. I think I might drift off. Don't mind me.'

Romola stood up and instinctively pulled Judith's cover to her shoulders, tucking her in safely. Then Romola pressed the button to lower the bed head. 'I'll wait here until you fall asleep. And I'll come back in the morning.'

Judith's eyes were already shut, but she lifted her hand and gave a thumbs up.

Chapter Thirty-Six
Home

The house smelled exactly as Romola remembered. She hadn't been aware of it having a smell before she moved out at age eighteen; now it hit her every time she walked in the door: open books, Indian spices, and fresh roses from Judith's shop.

The kitchen was just as Judith had left it when she'd stepped outside for some gardening that morning. A tea mug sat next to an open women's magazine on the bench. A piece of half-eaten peach tart was sitting on a Blue Willow china plate. A fat fly perched on a small piece of fish left defrosting on the sink.

Since her dad's death, all Romola had seen when she'd come home was him – or the absence of him. His creased black Danish leather chair. The shelves filled with the textbooks he'd had to find space for when his university offices had turned open plan, something that had infuriated him. The coffee maker he would put on the stove every time she visited, and the brown '70s cups they would drink from. His vinyl collection sitting too neatly in its glass cabinet, next to his record player.

But as she familiarised herself with the house again, all she saw was Judith – all the things about her stepmother that she'd been ignoring or downright hating ever since Judith came into her life. The fresh flowers in every room; the dried flowers hanging from the ceiling. The old-fashioned dresser in Judith's bedroom, where costume jewellery flowed from bowls and hung from every corner. The lotions and potions. The kitchen cupboards stocked like those of a health food shop, crammed with every conceivable oil and vitamin. Romola checked the pantry and saw that it was still stocked with her favourite staples: a tin of Milo and jar of peanut butter, which

Judith would surely never touch now that she lived on her own.

On a side table stood Don's old chessboard. Romola and her dad would play games that could last for days, moving pieces only when the mood struck them. Judith had always complained about that board, but she had kept it there, still waiting for the next move.

Romola now realised the extent of her mistake. She had liked to pretend Judith didn't even exist, while Judith had been carrying on living regardless. Romola regretted all the energy she had spent on hatred when she could have used it to see some good. She could have been spending time with a mother during all those years she had been pining for one.

Romola opened the door to her old bedroom, which had been her refuge from Judith. It was like a shrine to her teenage self – not a thing had been changed since she'd moved out. But the absence of dust suggested it was vacuumed often, and there were fresh sheets on the bed in case she came to stay.

After changing into one of Judith's nighties, realising she'd forgotten to pack her own, Romola lay down in the darkness and felt for the familiar grooves in the bookshelf next to her bed. She had secretly carved 'Jacob' there, the name of her high school crush, a boy with cool blue eyes and a reckless attitude. She'd been so straight-laced, at the time no one would have understood her belief that Jacob was destined for her. She was too embarrassed to confess it, even to Louise.

Romola closed her eyes. The smell and feel of the covers brought her back to those nights in high school when her biggest problem was that she didn't have enough friends. Then she remembered the joy of finding Louise, and the sleepovers they had in this room, staring at the glow of the Milky Way stickers on the ceiling, talking until the early hours. They spoke about what they dreamed for themselves. Louise would write for the *New Yorker*, and Romola would be a human rights lawyer at The Hague. At uni they'd each started on the right path but had been blown off track by the reality of making a living. Louise was now writing stories about celebrity gossip, while Romola was defending billionaires. How had they come to this?

As Romola fell asleep, she pretended Louise was there again, on the trundle mattress beside her. Louise would have gushed about Johnny, and she would have listened. Despite the day she'd just had, she fell asleep smiling.

*

Romola decided to spend as much time as she feasibly could caring for her stepmother in hospital before returning to Melbourne. They continued their discussion of Judith's first marriage; it was cleansing, Romola suspected, for Judith to divulge all the gory details. The secrets would flow out of her until, every hour or so, she fell asleep, the drugs working their magic. Romola would sit there quietly, catching up on work and awaiting updates from Gretchen.

Halfway through the second day, Thursday, Gretchen sent a short text:

> We lost the argument. We're going to a jury. Cliffy says it's not as bad as it seems.

Romola took in this news in the same way she might have acknowledged news of an earthquake on the other side of the world. She hadn't heard from Patrick in a couple of days, and Judith's need for help seemed much more immediate than the defence of his reputation.

By the end of the third day it was clear Judith had turned a corner. She stopped telling stories of her abuse and started to talk about the years after she'd met Don. Her face brightened, and the doctors found her a place in a rehabilitation clinic a short distance from home. She would need a couple of weeks there, then would likely have to walk with a frame and a moonboot for eight weeks. Barry from next door, who had proved very helpful, promised to visit Judith in rehab every couple of days. He was a widower with an empty nest, and Romola suspected he saw in Judith the opportunity for companionship, maybe more.

On the morning of the fourth day, which was a Saturday, Romola received a call from Patrick that jolted her back to the reality awaiting her in Melbourne.

'Have you heard from Sonia?' he asked.

'Not recently. Why?'

'She keeps leaving messages asking if I've thought about her proposal – asking for more time with Max. I thought you'd dealt with that?'

Romola had thought so too. Cliffy had agreed that it was too risky to call Sonia as a witness with the conditions she'd attached to her testimony. Romola had phoned Sonia a few days after she'd met with her, explaining that they wouldn't need her to give evidence and that Patrick wouldn't negotiate any change to the custody arrangements in exchange for her evidence. Sonia had hung up without hearing her out, and Romola had felt grateful for the brevity of the conversation.

'I told her you weren't interested,' Romola said. 'I'll call her again. Did Cliffy speak to you about Debenham's decision on the jury?'

'He seems relaxed about it – says to be myself, tell the truth, listen to each question carefully, only answer the questions I'm asked. The standard advice he reels out for all the poor suckers on the stand, I suppose. In the meantime I continue to be persona non grata in this damned city. God knows how I'm supposed to get an impartial jury if we get there. Speaking of that, we haven't talked settlement strategy lately – when are we going to reach out? I thought you and Cliffy were waiting for the perfect time. All this talk of evidence and juries is making me worried it's not going to happen.'

Romola clutched her phone and nodded, though Patrick couldn't see her. She'd been expecting this question. She had meant to discuss the settlement strategy again with Patrick in their second interview, which she hadn't ended up attending. Gretchen had reported that Cliffy hadn't brought it up, and Patrick must now be getting jumpy. 'We were hoping that Finnigan would reach out to us first to discuss settlement – we don't necessarily want to be the ones blinking first. But Cliffy and I think it's important that, if we do make the first approach, it's on the basis that you're raring to go to trial but we've managed to talk you into making in a last-ditch attempt to settle on a commercial basis. We want to have compiled as much evidence as possible before the approach so that, as we discussed, they're left on the back foot, wondering if their case is as strong as Finnigan has made out all along.'

Patrick was slow to respond. 'Right ... so aren't we at that point now? I feel like we're beginning to cut it pretty fine here.' A note of aggravation had crept into his voice, and though Romola managed to reassure him for the remainder of the conversation, she knew it was time for her to head back to Melbourne – and time to finally risk their hands by making a call to Finnigan Price.

There wasn't a teary goodbye when she left Judith that afternoon, for which Romola was grateful. They hugged and agreed she would visit again once the trial was over.

'See you soon, Mum,' she said warmly as she left the room, noting that although she felt happy, it wasn't because she was leaving Judith; it was because she had been there at all.

Judith glanced up from her crossword. Romola thought she saw tears welling, but Judith simply wished her luck and returned to her page. For once, Romola thought, like a normal parent.

*

A storm had come in, and the plane landed with an uncomfortable bang. Romola lurched forward and grabbed the seat in front of her. Horizontal rain smacked the plane's windows.

At the terminal she broke her golden rule yet again – with a jolt of nerves, she jumped straight into a cab to Cliffy's. An accident on the M1 had traffic at a standstill, and the cab's heater was broken. Shivering, she covered her fingertips with her coat. A few seconds later she fumbled with her phone when it rang, showing an unfamiliar number. 'Hello?'

'Oh,' a man said. He sounded surprised to hear a voice on the other end of the line. 'It's Piers Janssen here.' His voice cracked, and there was a constant low hum in the background.

Cliffy and Romola had arranged that, if they were to go to trial, Piers would be their fifth witness. First they would call the sergeant who had investigated Hana's death; he would testify that there was no suggestion of foul play and no suspicious circumstances. Then Patrick would testify, becoming a real person in the minds of the jury. He would be followed by Hana's friend Storm, then the expert psychologist, then Piers and Carol Janssen, then a friend of Beth's who had known her during the time of her drug spiral. They had tried recommending to Patrick that Max also be called as a witness – to testify as to the lack of any abuse in the household – but Patrick still flatly refused to involve his son, which they could hardly argue with. Finally they would present the evidence of loss, meaning evidence of the damage to Patrick's reputation; this included evidence from people within the Liberal party who had previously supported him and had withdrawn that support following publication of the articles.

Piers cleared his throat. 'We've had some bad news in the family,' he muttered. 'I'm at the hospital now. I'll have to be quick.'

Romola's mind instantly turned to Lara, who must have overdosed or been committed, and her heart sank to think of that damaged family suffering yet another tragedy.

'It's Carol.' His voice cracked again.

Romola rearranged her thoughts. She erased her mental image of Carol and Piers at Lara's bedside, replacing it with one of an anxious Piers standing alone in the hospital corridor.

'She's unwell,' he said, before clearing his throat again. 'It's all become too much for her. She'd been suffering in silence. She's going to spend a little while in hospital, until she's feeling more … herself.'

'Are your daughters there with you?'

'Lara's gone. She could be anywhere. Peta is on her way back home as we speak.'

'Is there anything I can do to help?' Romola offered, though she keenly felt her status as a stranger to the family.

'What could you possibly do to help?' Piers snapped. 'I'm only calling to tell you that Carol won't be testifying – and nor will I. We won't be involved any longer. It's not feasible. This all has to finish, for Carol's sake. Malcolm will have to deal with it, whatever that might mean for us.'

Romola shuddered. Piers had just confirmed what she had been worried about all along: he and his wife had only been in it to please Malcolm. Better they not testify anyway then, she thought, feeling a creeping sense of shame.

So she didn't try to convince Piers otherwise. She went to say her goodbyes, but he'd already hung up.

Romola sat in the cold cab, contemplating the line of vehicles leading her to the city. At last her taxi passed the emergency services personnel and crushed cars at the scene of the accident. Though not religious, she made a sign of the cross for the sake of the casualties – and for poor Carol Janssen, who was lost forever without her daughters.

Chapter Thirty-Seven
Light in the Dark

Saturday night and the lights were out at Cliffy's. In fact, there was no electricity at all – on her approach to the house, Romola saw that a powerline had fallen across the next street over, with repair crew trucks blocking the road. Cliffy was sitting alone in the candlelit kitchen, while something simmered on the gas stove behind him. He hummed to himself as he attempted to read documents laid out on the kitchen island, leaning in close to the fine print. 'This is impossible,' he muttered upon Romola's arrival. 'Ruddy weather.' He closed his folder. 'Welcome home. Now tell me, how is Judith today?'

Over the past four days Romola had called Cliffy every evening. He was always anxious to hear the day's report, and he would reciprocate with updates on Patrick's case.

'I'm happy to report she is still recovering well.' Romola sat down and poured herself a glass from the bottle of cabernet sitting open next to Cliffy. 'Thank you for telling me about her. It's changed everything.'

'Well, something needed to change, didn't it, my dear? I only wish I'd said something sooner.' He stood up and lifted two bowls from the drawer. 'Some soup for the soul? Plain old vegetable, but delicious nonetheless.'

'Perfect.' She sat listening to the howl of the wind and rain. She still had her coat on and was rubbing her hands together, unable to leach the cold from her bones. 'She was actually fine about me coming back. It was the right time too – with Patrick's matter, that is. We're going to have to think about opening up discussions. There have been a couple of developments.'

'Mmm?' Cliffy mumbled from his place at the stove.

'Firstly, Piers Janssen called on my way from the airport. Carol is in the hospital. Neither she nor Piers will testify. I think it's for the best, though – he basically came out and said they were only ever helping because of Malcolm.'

Cliffy continued spooning out the soup. In the dark she could only see the outline of his back and hear the splash of liquid being ladled. 'Bugger,' he muttered. 'If they had been genuine, even with their relationship with Malcolm they would have thrown some doubt over the claims about Patrick's treatment of Lisbeth.' Cliffy brought the bowls and spoons over and sat down, the candlelight glowing warmly on his red face and bushy eyebrows. Romola was used to his classical music playing as they ate together, but tonight they were accompanied by the heavy rain and the occasional slosh of a passing car.

Cliffy handed a spoon to Romola and then held his out to her in a gesture of cheers. After clinking hers against his, she dipped it into her bowl and blew on the steaming liquid before savouring its home-cooked goodness after her last four days of takeaway and hospital cafeteria food.

'And the second thing?' Cliffy prompted.

'Oh yes.' Romola had lost her train of thought in the soup. 'The second thing is that Patrick gave me a call this morning. Sonia's been hounding him about her offer to testify in exchange for a change to their custody arrangements.'

Cliffy slurped a spoonful, then patted his mouth dry with a handkerchief. 'Abhorrent proposal. Imagine if it came out while she was on the stand that a deal had been made about Max. It would completely discredit her, and it would make Patrick look all the worse for agreeing to it.'

Romola nodded before filling him in on her conversation with Sonia earlier that day. Patrick's ex-wife had been harried and breathless, in the middle of a workout. 'Tell him I'm prepared to do this for him!' she had shouted. 'You must let him know that! It could change *everything*. Say those exact words to him. All he has to do is let me have more time with Max. I'm desperate. He's almost nine, and I'm going to miss him growing up! What's so hard about giving me that time, considering what's on the line here?'

Romola and Cliffy sat talking about the case as they finished the their meal, until he began to yawn. In the candlelight she saw the lines under his eyes, the slight unsteadiness of the spoon in his hand, a spill every now and then. It struck her that he was becoming an old man.

'I don't think this electricity's coming back on any time soon,' he said. 'For once I will have to go against my obsessive tendencies and leave the dishes out for the night, until we have hot water.'

'I'll give them a rinse,' Romola offered. 'You go up to bed.'

'I'll see you bright and early then.' He stood and turned towards the door.

'Take a candle with you,' she called after him. 'Or where's your phone? You can put the torch on.'

He waved her away. 'I've lived here for thirty years, my dear. I could walk the route from kitchen to bed blindfolded if I had to.'

She listened as he slowly but steadily made his way up the stairs, making sure he'd arrived safely at his bedroom before moving the candle to the sink and beginning to rinse the bowls. The freezing water stung her hands, undoing the warming effects of the soup.

Cliffy's parting words reminded her of the time she'd just spent in her childhood home. Her body remembered that place without her even having to open an eye. Over the years the house had become a part of her, not just a backdrop but a character in the play that was her life.

Judith had said something along those lines as well, about the house she'd shared with her violent first husband. Propped up in the hospital bed, she'd told Romola that she wished someone had come to sit in that house for a while, because she was sure what had happened there must sit in the atmosphere. The silent witness would have revealed all the secrets.

Romola's mind turned to Patrick's Toorak home, and the atmosphere between Patrick and Hana. Aside from Max, who might have noticed marks on walls, if there had been any, or witnessed the aftermath of their arguments?

Romola was hardly registering the cold stream across her hands; it could have run hot, and she wouldn't have noticed. She suddenly recalled that there was such a person, alive and well – the housekeeper who had found Hana. She had come every morning, except on Tuesdays, without fail.

Chapter Thirty-Eight
Mrs Forsyth

' I wondered when someone would come.' Mrs Mary Forsyth, Patrick's former housekeeper, had half a smile on her face and a tea towel in her hand as she opened her front screen door. The glint in her eye said that she'd been relishing the thought of this day.

Romola spoke louder than she normally did. 'Thank you for seeing me at such short notice, Mrs Forsyth.' Patrick had given her Mrs Forsyth's contact details on Sunday, and Romola had called her first thing Monday morning. Mrs Forsyth had said she would check her calendar and waited a brief moment before agreeing that Tuesday morning would be 'perfectly fine' for a visit.

The elderly woman had striking violet eyes, like Elizabeth Taylor's, and they travelled over Romola from head to toe. 'You look too young for this sort of thing.'

Romola would have guessed Mrs Forsyth to be at least seventy, although she dressed as though she were older, in a plain smock of a dress and floral slippers. Her hair was cut in a functional grey bob, those violet eyes were bright, and her skin was clear.

Mrs Forsyth held the door open, standing to one side to make way. She was sucking on a lozenge, clacking it about in her mouth as Romola shimmied through the doorway. The house smelled of Vicks VapoRub and pickled vegetables. 'If you wouldn't mind.' Mrs Forsyth pointed to a small shoe rack on which sat a pair of brown leather sandals.

'Of course.' Romola slid off her stilettos and bent to place them on the rack. She hated being barefoot, as she was insecure about her height; she felt annoyed that the elderly woman was now taller than her.

She followed Mrs Forsyth down a dark hallway, along which ran an ornate dado. The house was a 1940s weatherboard, the last one standing on a street now lined with apartments and semidetached houses, an ageing rose amid the thorns. The hallway walls were hung with bronzed religious scenes and crocheted landscapes.

They came to a neat, compact sitting room with simple pine furniture and a pair of two-seaters. Mrs Forsyth gestured to them. 'I bought these sofas fifteen years ago now. You wouldn't know it, would you? Never had a stain.'

'What a good idea to put those sheets over the top,' Romola said, wondering what the point was of having decent furniture only to cover it up. A photo frame on the mantel showed a smiling round man with three little girls. 'Your son?' asked Romola, for something to say.

'My nephew. I leave it out for when he visits. Sometimes he gives me no notice, you see. He thinks I need supervision.'

'You don't look like you need supervision to me, Mrs Forsyth.' Romola smiled and saw another twinkle in the old lady's eyes.

She went to fetch them some tea. Romola felt the nephew staring at her from his photo frame. Knick-knacks were everywhere, placed precisely on top of white doilies. Boxes and tins had been stacked carefully against the walls and under the side tables. It was all very tidy, but the quantity of containers made Romola wonder what Mrs Forsyth was gathering and why.

Romola jumped as Mrs Forsyth entered the room with a rose-coloured melamine tea tray in hand, upon which were balanced two retro lime-green teacups, bronzed inside, and a matching teapot. She placed it on the coffee table between the sofas. 'Do you mind if I ask what your heritage is? My church has quite a large Indian community, you see. Perhaps you know some of them?' Those violet eyes stared hard at Romola, the lozenge clacking from side to side as the old lady waited for an answer.

'I'm from Sydney. My mother was Sri Lankan, but I was raised here in Australia. My father was from Brisbane originally.' Romola was accustomed to trotting out the basic facts, only feeling a small pang this time at the mention of her father.

Mrs Forsyth appeared disappointed. 'I see. So difficult to tell nowadays, isn't it? Where people are from, I mean. I'm always putting my foot in it one way or another.'

Romola poured herself a cup of tea. 'I'm hoping not to take up too much of your time today, Mrs Forsyth. I really just wanted to speak to you about your work at Patrick Payne's house – what you may have seen there, including when you found Hana and in the lead-up to that morning.'

Mrs Forsyth lowered herself onto her seat, making a show of it as she trained her eyes on Romola. 'And what will you do with my answers, young lady? I know all about this court case of yours. Will you need me to testify?' She raised her eyebrows knowingly as she poured her tea.

'It's possible that you'll need to come and give evidence,' Romola said calmly, 'if what you say is relevant to the dispute, that is. Have you spoken to anyone else about this, perhaps other lawyers?'

Mrs Forsyth shook her head and clicked her tongue, eyes wide. 'I spoke with the police briefly when it happened. I expected them to have some follow-up questions, but I haven't had so much as a phone call.' She winked. 'You're the first to come.'

Romola silently breathed a sigh of relief. Whatever Mrs Forsyth told her today, good or bad, at least Finnigan Price hadn't heard it first.

Mrs Forsyth pressed her smock dress flat on her knees. 'Do you know hers was the second dead body I'd seen, after my husband's. At least I was expecting it when he passed. He'd been very sick, you see – in a home for a long time, then palliative care. When he left us, it was almost a release. If you've ever nursed a dying person, you might understand.'

Her violet eyes searched Romola's. She was happy to let Mrs Forsyth keep talking in the hope something useful would fall out.

'But the girl came as a shock. Before I knew it, Patrick was right there next to me. Completely and utterly beside himself, he was. I told him it was best not to touch a thing – evidence, you know – but he wasn't listening. We stayed there like that for what must have been a good fifteen minutes, Patrick holding her and me trying to peel him off of her. Can you imagine? Little old me? Then the ambulance people came and realised there was nothing to be done, and the police officer came and asked me a few paltry questions, nothing very pressing. They ushered me out like I was chopped liver – a no one. I haven't been able to go back since. As if I wouldn't be affected by seeing something like that?' The elderly woman regarded Romola over her nose. She had a habit of sucking in her cheeks in between words. She was a cunning fox, this Mrs Forsyth.

Romola noted everything down. The old lady glanced at the pen every time she finished a sentence, apparently wanting to make sure it was all being recorded. 'It must have been awful for you, Mrs Forsyth. Can we go back a step first? Did you know Hana when she was alive?'

Mrs Forsyth shook her head firmly. 'Never met the girl. Can you imagine? I picked up her dirty clothes on a daily basis, but I never so much as said a word to her. What an odd thing that was.'

'And Patrick?'

'I only bumped into him once or twice, and he scurried off as if he'd seen a ghost. I spoke to someone else who worked for him over the telephone before I started the job.' She crunched her lozenge, swallowed, then lifted her cup of tea to her chest. 'I always suspected he didn't want to meet me – embarrassed, most likely.'

'What did he and Hana have to be embarrassed of?'

'How would I know? We're all as filthy as one another when it comes down to it.' Mrs Forsyth dusted imaginary dirt off her shoulder.

'How long had you been cleaning the house before Hana's death?'

'Around a year.'

'You wouldn't have worked for Patrick's ex-wife, then?'

'No. There's nothing I could say about her, I'm afraid. I've never seen her either – in the flesh, anyway.' Mrs Forsyth's eyes darted to a pile of women's magazines neatly stacked under the coffee table. Perhaps she had intended to remove them before Romola's arrival, not meaning to reveal herself as a creature of gossip.

'Did you ever come across anything untoward in their house? Anything that concerned you? I'm just trying to understand what life was like for Hana before she died. As you know, Patrick denies what has been reported in the media about him.'

'Of course he does. And it certainly surprises me, what they're saying about him.'

'Why is that?'

Mrs Forsyth put down her cup and leaned back into her seat. 'Well, I only mean that I got the impression they were in love. Just a feeling I had – I'm good at picking up on things like that. Don't ask me why.' She looked away, seeming slightly embarrassed.

Romola put her notebook to one side. Time to try a different tack, she thought. 'I'm sorry to hear about your husband, Mrs Forsyth. Was it very long ago that he passed away?'

'Going on fifteen years. I've adjusted to it now – I'm very independent, and regularly involved with my local parish.'

'That's very generous of you to donate your time. Everyone seems too busy these days, don't they?'

'You're absolutely right about that. Our parishioners often assume Mass will organise itself!'

Romola pointed to the photograph on the mantel. 'And do you see much of your nephew?'

'He likes to think he's responsible for my wellbeing.' She sucked in her cheeks. 'He's a pain.'

Romola nodded knowingly. 'Men are like that,' she said. 'Sometimes it's just about making them feel important, don't you agree? We all know who's really running the show.'

Mrs Forsyth cackled, slapping her thigh. 'That's a good one.' She pointed a crooked finger at Romola. 'I think I like you!'

Romola grinned, the rapport she had been searching for now established.

Mrs Forsyth composed herself and took up her tea, slurping it through her thin lips while peering over at Romola. 'I'll tell you something.'

'Yes?'

'The reason I think that couple were in love.'

'Hmm?' Romola tried to sound casual, but she was on the edge of her seat.

'She would write him little love notes. She'd leave them all over the house for him.'

Romola held her breath, steadying herself before she asked, 'What did they say?'

Mrs Forsyth sat still for a moment, then with a sigh she put her hands on her knees and heaved herself up from the lounge. She waved a hand behind her as she left the room. 'Hang on a minute. I might just have kept a few of them.'

Romola couldn't help but smile to herself in the silent lounge room.

A minute later Mrs Forsyth returned holding a deep rectangular white box printed with the Chanel label. She held it close to her chest as she explained. 'Hana would just throw the boxes out like they were rubbish, but to me ... well, to me they seemed lovely little things that I could make use of.' The old lady placed the box on Romola's lap. It was heavier than she had expected. 'This one ... this one I brought home without realising what was inside.' Mrs Forsyth pointed to the lid. 'Go on. Open it.'

Romola pulled off the lid and set it beside her. The box was filled to bursting with folded scraps of paper in a variety of colours and sizes. She stared up at Mrs Forsyth and widened her eyes. 'You took this?'

'I cleaned it up.' Mrs Forsyth said, bristling. 'As I said, Hana used to leave these boxes all over the place, mostly in the bin. What a waste! I didn't open this one until after her death.'

Romola struggled not to let her disbelief show. 'Have you told Patrick?'

The old lady held up her hands, all innocence. 'Don't you worry, I was going to. But then, as I said, no one made any contact with me. If anyone had asked, I would have gladly given this over.'

Romola began reading the notes. There was something shocking about seeing Hana's handwritten messages as opposed to her contrived social media posts. She wrote in a teenage hand, with circles hanging above her 'i's rather than dots. Some notes just said, *I love you*, while some made Romola blush to read them in company. Others were cutesy and addressed not from Hana but from 'Mr Scruff'.

Mrs Forsyth read the note in Romola's hand and laughed. 'I think that must be Patrick's teddy bear. He kept it on the bed, tucked underneath the covers where he thinks no one will notice.'

Romola started refolding the notes, closing up the window into Hana and Patrick's world. 'Did he ever reply to her?'

Mrs Forsyth seized the box and started scrounging through. 'Only a few times. A man of few words, as they say.' Her bony fingers found what she was looking for – a thick piece of cream card, heavier than the others. She handed it to Romola.

Patrick wrote in a slanted, curling cursive in striking black ink. *Hana, you must stop this note-writing at once. We might get in trouble with Mrs F. XXX*

Mrs Forsyth cackled again. 'When I saw that, I thought he must have a sense of humour after all.'

'Do you mind if I take these with me?' asked Romola. 'I think Patrick would like to see them again.'

Mrs Forsyth grimaced, clearly reluctant to part with her treasure. 'I guess I can't refuse, can I?'

'I guess not,' Romola agreed, taking back the box. She shifted in her seat. 'Funny how she didn't leave one at the end. A goodbye.'

'Well, the poor dear did try.' Mrs Forsyth shrugged. 'Patrick found a piece of notepaper on the floor next to her. But it was blank. I remember it as clear as day.'

'Why is that?'

'Because I'd opened the blinds before I realised Hana had died, and Patrick held it up to the sunlight. His hands were shaking like my late husband's used to. And then he wailed and wailed. It's not something you can forget, a grown man setting up a wail like that.'

'Did he say anything?'

Mrs Forsyth's violet eyes shone. 'He said, "I'm sorry." Over and over until he went hoarse.'

'And then?'

'And then I heard the sirens.'

Chapter Thirty-Nine
Blinking First

Patrick was by the pool, which reminded Romola of their first meeting. He was standing at the edge and holding a pole, slowly drawing a net across the water to catch leaves blown in by the storm – green leaves, because it was almost spring. Jessie stood by his side, poised to grab whatever might leap from the blue.

Romola had called him, on the tram from Mrs Forsyth's house, to let him know she was coming over. 'Don't you have someone to do that for you?' she asked between breaths as she made her way across the terrace, feet sore from having walked at far too quick a pace from the tram.

Patrick laughed. 'Have you been catching public transport again? I told you it will kill you.'

His eyes moved to the Chanel box in her hand. She'd planned what to do with the pilfered notes, but she wanted to show Patrick first.

'Been shopping?' he asked.

She shook her head. 'Can we sit?'

He didn't ask any questions as they wandered up to the verandah and sat on a wooden bench.

'I've just come from Mary Forsyth's house,' Romola said.

'Right.' He furrowed his brow. Jessie, tail wagging, placed her chin on his lap.

'As I said, she was here that morning, and before that she was regularly in your house, so I was hoping she might tell me something helpful. No one else had spoken to her.'

'And?'

'And I was right. She was helpful.' Romola opened the box's lid, its contents popping up like a jack-in-the-box. 'She is also something of a thief.'

Patrick made a small noise of surprise. He began picking up the notes and slowly reading each one. 'The cleaning lady took these?'

'I'm afraid so.'

'I figured Hana must have thrown them out. I was going to mention them to you, but ... I don't know ... I was embarrassed, I guess. I thought it sounded childish to tell you about her love notes. And I had no proof.' For a few moments he kept picking through the notes and reading them, shaking his head and smiling. 'I can't believe the cleaner stole them. I always got the impression she was a bit batty. There was something about the way she would handle our stuff. Sometimes we would purposely leave the shelves a little off kilter to see if she would notice – next day, perfectly straight. We used to joke about it. It was like she was telling us off.'

'I guess that's want you want in a cleaner – an obsessive attention to detail.'

'That's what we thought too,' he murmured, still focused on the notes.

Romola let him look at them for a couple more minutes before she went on, speaking gently. 'Mrs Forsyth told me about the blank paper Hana was holding. That must have been hard for you.'

Patrick paused. His hand closed around a square of pink paper. When he faced her again, his eyes were damp. Then he was crying in earnest, tears falling between his fingers onto the verandah. Two clear rivulets streamed from his nose. Jessie repositioned herself to be further onto Patrick's lap and peered up at him with sorrowful eyes. 'I'm sorry ... after all of this –' he gestured to the notes '– no goodbye, no explanation.'

'Maybe she just couldn't find the words.' Romola felt the hopelessness of her consolation, knowing how little comfort could be taken from the notes.

She offered a tissue from the small pack in her bag, then sat with him as his tears stopped flowing and he dried his eyes. He shot her a grateful smile and picked up a bunch of notes, running his fingers over the coarse paper.

'I think …' she said, getting his attention. 'Now that we have it in Hana's words, we should show Rabbit Hole how good you and Hana were together. Don't you?'

'Give these to them?'

'Yes.'

'When?'

'As soon as I can. I'll make copies of everything, and send them to Finnigan Price. I'll ask him for a meeting. No barristers this time, just Finnigan and me. Then I'll do my best to convince him that his clients shouldn't go to trial – and that they must apologise to you. I know that's all you want right now.'

Patrick fleetingly held a note to his lips and closed his eyes, then he placed it back in the Chanel box and closed the lid. He handed the box to Romola. 'Do what you need to do.'

*

Two letters were sent to Finnigan Price by email that Tuesday night. The first was an open letter enclosing copies of all of Hana's notes and the limited number of Patrick's responses. The second was without prejudice.

Romola kept it simple: she referred to the recent disclosure of the notes, as well as Tilly Klein's unreliability as a witness, and said that although Patrick's prospects of success at trial were strong, both parties' interests would be served by avoiding a costly trial. She gave Finnigan Price until the end of the week to agree to a meeting – solicitors only – to 'explore the possibility of a commercial resolution'.

Chapter Forty
The Deadline

Romola was hunkered down in her office when, with fifteen minutes to spare before 5 p.m. on Friday, she received a short response from Finnigan Price. He agreed to a meeting at his offices the following Monday, precisely two weeks before the trial was due to start. Romola, who had been on edge all week, sighed with relief and stretched, feeling her spine loosen. She'd been expecting the worst: that her letter would get no traction, and that she had been wrong to recommend a meeting with Finnigan as opposed to openly putting up the white flag with a low offer.

Over the week she'd continued preparing for trial. She had engaged a handwriting expert to give an opinion on the authenticity of Hana's notes, and she'd sent copies to the psychologist for her views on whether someone in an abusive relationship would have been likely to write them. Romola had continued the search for a substitute for the Janssens' evidence, although the best she could find was Lisbeth's school rowing coach. He was prepared to testify that before Lisbeth had started dating Patrick, she was prone to high stress about her sporting performances, that her moods were up and down, and that he'd often wondered whether she might be depressed but had done nothing about it. His evidence would hardly have the impact of the Janssens', but it was something.

Romola was glad that Finnigan had agreed to meet on the Monday, as this gave her the weekend to prepare what she would say. She was about to call Patrick when she was stopped in her tracks by Imogen hollering, 'Romola, I need you in here now!'

Buoyed by the good news of the meeting with Finnigan, Romola straightened her skirt, grabbed a notepad, and dutifully crossed in front of Victoria's desk into Imogen's office.

Imogen's eyes were trained on her computer screen. 'Close the door and take a seat,' she said calmly, and Romola obeyed. Imogen turned to face her, those squirrel eyes shining bright in anticipation. 'Two weeks from trial now?'

'Two weeks on Monday.'

'And how would you say preparation is going?'

'Good. We found some useful documents earlier in the week and –'

'I just got off the phone with Sonia. After we finalised that horrific divorce, I thought I would never hear from the woman again. Let me tell you, she must be pretty fucking desperate to be calling *me*.'

'What did she have to say?'

'She was all over the place, about the deal she's proposed?'

Romola nodded, wanting to show Imogen she was on top of this. 'It's totally unacceptable. She said she'll testify in exchange for more time with Max, but we can't take the risk, let alone be blackmailed into it.'

'Well, she's just raised the stakes. She says she's going to see Finnigan.'

'Shit. That was always the concern. She told us she'd rejected his advances once, and we were hoping that with the non-disclosure agreement she wouldn't talk. Patrick at least seems to think she won't go so far as giving false evidence.'

'You should be more than fucking concerned, Romola. Sonia is completely without scruples.' Romola was taken aback by the fierceness of Imogen's reaction to Sonia, particularly given her boss had, until this moment, wiped her hands of the case. Over the past few weeks she had offered Romola only scowls as she'd gone about preparing the matter for trial. Perhaps it was because Imogen had dealt with Sonia before in relation to Max; perhaps things were harder to forgive, mother to mother, when kids were involved ...?

'Did she give any idea of what she would say?' Romola asked.

'Yes, in fact, she did.' Imogen read a scribbled note on her desk. 'She told me that she gave a stash of her pills to Hana when she left Patrick. She instructed Hana to use them in case of emergency to soften the blow. Sonia said she knew Hana was bound to need them.'

Romola shuddered. 'But that won't paint Sonia in a particularly good light, given she wants to get Max back.'

'I guess not, but she figures it makes Patrick look even worse. And it supports Rabbit Hole's reports that he is a fucking nightmare.' Imogen began cracking her knuckles, one by one.

'So she's not worried about the non-disclosure agreement either?' asked Romola.

Imogen settled her hands in her lap with a huff. 'She's clearly figured out that it won't apply if Rabbit Hole subpoenas her to give evidence, which no doubt Finnigan will have told her. The court can order her to talk – about anything. So it's fucking skeletons out of the closet time. These two have a history, and it seems she's intent on bringing him down. She says she'll go to Rabbit Hole next week – she's given us until Wednesday. Apparently it's her weekend with Max, and then she wants a couple of days to clear her head before she fucks Patrick over.'

Imogen leaned in and placed a hand over Romola's notepad. The office door was closed, but she still spoke quietly. 'You need to close this thing down. Now.'

Romola was silent. Not because she disagreed with Imogen, but because something her boss had said had caused a tiny niggle of familiarity to flicker at the back of her mind. She had half a mind on Imogen's rant while the other half was trying to pin down a memory.

'Are you with me here?' Imogen clicked her fingers, eyes wide. 'I don't care what you need to do to get it over the line, but you need to settle – for anything. There can be no trial here. Do whatever it takes. Do you understand?'

'Sure.' Romola still remembered Imogen's scorn at the walk-away offer put forward by Rabbit Hole at the mediation. The stakes had obviously been raised, but Romola had more important things on her mind.

'Better get on with it.' Imogen ushered Romola out of her office with a hand on her shoulder. She gave it a little squeeze, like that of a boa constrictor.

*

Back in her cramped office, Romola sat thinking for a long time, then began typing out everything she would put to Finnigan Price in aid of extracting a settlement offer. The time had come to pull out all the stops. As good as Hana's notes had initially seemed, Rabbit Hole's legal team might spin them as nothing more than the flirtatious words of a woman trying to stay on her partner's good side. If Romola was to extract an apology as Patrick wanted, she needed to use everything at her disposal – including information that she'd only just realised she had been given.

Initially she was unsure if she had dreamt it. She had only been semiconscious at the time, and she'd been so concerned about her own misdemeanours that she had almost missed it entirely. But Imogen's words had brought the memory back into focus, and Romola was certain now that, despite some fuzziness around the edges, the words 'intent on bringing him down' had been spoken to her before – by her best friend in an offer of consolation.

She sought out Gretchen in the photocopier room and told her that she had urgent research to be prioritised over everything. Romola didn't even pause for thought. Eventually, when she reflected back on this as an old lady, she'd be able to convince herself that betraying her best friend in the interests of justice – and in the interests of her client – had been the right thing to do. Even if it didn't feel that way now.

Chapter Forty-One
The Pitch

The offices of Rabbit Hole's solicitor, Finnigan Price, were like a cross between a subway station and a nightclub. Romola had expected a two-room operation with an elderly secretary out front and Finnigan in a back room with a gold nameplate in front of him. Instead Romola and Gretchen walked into a sparse exposed-brick foyer, with Price & Co emblazoned in pink fluorescent signwriting behind a receptionist with an undercut and a nose piercing.

On Monday morning they arrived five minutes before the agreed time of ten, and Finnigan met them almost immediately. After two long discussions over the weekend, Patrick had agreed with her recommended strategy, but carrying it out felt like another thing altogether. The situation called for a bravado she wasn't sure she had in her. But when she saw Finnigan, she mentally put on her armour. She would become a different person for this meeting.

'Not one but two lovely ladies!' he exclaimed. 'What a nice surprise for a Monday morning.' He ushered them into a small meeting room with three chairs around a circular table. A large abstract painting hung on the wall behind Finnigan – not abstract enough to disguise the fact that it portrayed a pair of huge breasts. Finnigan's head, with purple-framed glasses and mad-professor grin, sat smack between two enormous blue nipples. 'How about this for a gender gap?' he said jauntily as he looked from Romola to Gretchen. 'I'm feeling slightly outnumbered here.'

Gretchen let out a feeble laugh, clutching onto a slim folder, but Romola ignored him. 'You agree this meeting is without prejudice?'

'Of course. Don't worry, I've had a few of these meetings before in my time. But I'm happy for you to proceed formally if you wish. I'm sure that's what Imogen has told you to do.'

Romola smiled through gritted teeth. 'I wanted to speak to you in person, in order to give your clients an opportunity,' she said, more confidently than she felt. 'As you will have seen from our client's additional discovery last week, a witness was able to provide correspondence between Hana Vukovic and my client Mr Payne that makes it perfectly clear she was very much in love with him. She made a choice to take her own life, but she did it despite her relationship with Mr Payne, not because of it. Our handwriting expert will testify that these were written by Ms Vukovic, and our expert psychologist will testify as to her frame of mind. I'm not sure if you've had much experience with domestic violence cases, but these are not the notes that a victim would write to her abuser.' Romola thought briefly of Judith and her black box. 'How can you possibly show that Ms Vukovic was scared of Mr Payne, that he mistreated her, drove her to death, when her own words say otherwise?'

Finnigan still didn't move.

'We also have Ms Vukovic's friends as witnesses, none of whom witnessed any ounce of wrongdoing by Mr Payne. We also have witnesses who can testify as to Lisbeth's depressive tendencies during high school, before she met Patrick. It's also not apparent what if any reliable witnesses you will be able to call to give evidence about Beth and Patrick.' What Piers had said about Lara hadn't escaped Romola – that she 'could be anywhere'. 'We also have numerous witnesses who will discredit Tilly Klein which surely you're aware of by now. I don't think you will need convincing on that score. And we have Mr Payne, who will be giving evidence. He will testify as to his love for Hana and his complete devastation upon finding her body.'

Finnigan listened with a smug smile, glancing from Romola to Gretchen as she carried on.

'And of course we'll be calling witnesses who will testify as to the damage this has caused Mr Payne's reputation – the preselection lost, the charities that have broken ties, the speaking engagements gone. The man has become a pariah. And it sounds out in dollar terms, in the millions.'

Romola paused. She didn't dare look at Gretchen, who she knew would offer an encouraging smile. She couldn't crack her armour now.

'Finally – but most importantly – there's the conduct of the journalist, Jonathan Wise.' Romola took a sip of water. 'As you know, if he was motivated by malice to write those articles, then your reasonable journalist's defence will be defeated, no matter what. With that in mind, I would invite you to do some background checking on Mr Wise.'

Romola motioned towards Gretchen and, as planned, she slid the slim folder onto the desk between them.

'If you look hard enough, you will discover that around fifteen years ago, when Mr Wise was still a teenager, his father owned an old pub down in St Kilda. The family lived upstairs, and the place was his parents' life. But it was getting decrepit – the family were served with a steady stream of health and safety notices from authorities. The family didn't have the funds to fix these issues. Payne Corp then mysteriously appeared and made them an offer for the place they couldn't refuse, assuring them that the company would lease it back to the family – which of course never happened. The pub was bulldozed ten weeks later. Jonathan's father didn't work again. Since then, Mr Wise has had something of a vendetta against the Paynes.'

Gretchen opened the folder and began handing over pages to Finnigan. He accepted them with a raised eyebrow.

'With some forensic IT work, we were able to discover that Mr Wise uses a couple of Twitter handles, and then there are his Facebook accounts under different pseudonyms, but I think you'll agree the language is disgusting whichever way you look at it. Not what you would expect from a credible journalist. It turns out Mr Wise was one of the first to comment on his own story. The hashtag #Paynemustpay was one of his efforts, for example.'

Finnigan rubbed his chin as he read the documents. It had taken some IT genius to make the connection between Johnny and the numerous Payne hatred tweets – but as it turned out, IT was Gretchen's second degree. She was a whiz.

'I am also reliably informed that Mr Wise, outside of his work with Rabbit Hole, has been arranging for Mr Payne to be followed by a photographer – and that Mr Wise is responsible for some of the more colourful photos of Mr Payne being distributed to the media, including photos of myself in circumstances under which Mr Wise was aware that I was Mr Payne's lawyer.'

Finnigan clasped his hands in front of him. He had obviously read enough.

Romola continued. 'So I'm sure you'll agree that even if your clients do, as you allege, manage to establish that the public has an interest in receiving information as to Mr Payne's alleged conduct, which seems unlikely on the evidence – then we will be in a strong position to show that Mr Wise was motivated by malice to write those articles. The reasonable journalist's defence won't work. You'll then be left with the truth defence alone, and given Tilly's unreliability, plus the direct evidence we now have of Hana's feelings towards Patrick, your clients are unlikely to succeed.'

Finnigan puffed out his chest and exhaled. He took his time before peering up at Romola again over the top of his glasses. His tie was slightly crooked, and his glasses were smudged. After everything he'd just heard, Finnigan Price still couldn't wipe off his stupid condescending grin. 'And …?'

'And I'm giving you an opportunity, right now, to retreat without losing face. To save your clients the time, cost and embarrassment of a trial.'

His grin turned to a smirk. 'How thoughtful of you.'

Frustration flared in her. She wanted to feel like she had made a mark, but the heaviest stones she threw were skimming the surface rather than taking flesh. She continued, even though saying any more was against her better judgement when Finnigan had said so little. 'Both our clients have spent a lot on this case to date. Over the next few weeks, as we go to trial, it's only going to skyrocket. And if Mr Payne wins, which you *must* see he will, not only will your client have to pay our costs, but imagine the reputational damage as well. How bad will Rabbit Hole look when they can't even get an exclusive story like this right? And when they have to pay up – to Patrick Payne, of all people?'

She savoured another long sip of water, feeling it cool her right down to her sternum.

'On the flipside,' she said, 'what happens if Rabbit Hole wins? We have to concede that it's at least a possibility. So what? The damage has already been done. Have you seen what's been written about our client? Do you know of the opportunities he's lost? Your clients can feel vindicated whether they win this case or not – it's all downside risk from here on for them. If Rabbit Hole settles, everyone will know it was a question of money and risk, simple as that. It's what the lawyers said to do. Is settlement at this point really so different from winning?'

Finnigan tapped his pen on the desk between them, like a metronome. 'That depends, doesn't it?' The tapping grew louder.

'On what?'

'On what the settlement is. My clients would disagree with absolutely everything you've said about the evidence, by the way. We have more than enough on your client. But I'm not going to go into chapter and verse about that now. It won't get us anywhere. So Johnny may not have particularly liked the Paynes, but who does? Any compromise, if there is to be one –' Finnigan raised his eyebrows '– would need to reflect the strength of my clients' position.' His tapping stopped.

Romola relaxed a little, knowing she had him. He was willing to talk. This thing could get settled without Patrick having to testify, and without her having to expose Louise's boyfriend as the less-than-ethical journalist that he was. For she knew now, without a doubt, that her friendship with Louise would not survive a trial: on Romola's instructions, Cliffy would have to tear Johnny to pieces on the stand, and Louise would never forgive her.

'A settlement doesn't have to be a loss,' she said to Finnigan. 'It simply reflects the risks both parties face going forward. I'm sure we'd both agree on that.' She shot him her most gorgeous smile, the one her dad had said could break a man's heart.

'That may be something we could agree on, Miss Cross.' Finnigan's gaze shifted again from Romola, to Gretchen, then back to Romola. 'So what do you have in mind?'

'As you will recall, our client's last offer at the mediation was $1 million.'

'I remember,' he said with an unmistakable air of condescension.

She swallowed, uncertain even as she said the words of the strategy they had agreed upon, knowing Patrick would take anything. She kept her voice steady. 'Mr Payne wants $1.2 million now. Things have changed because of the new information. In the circumstances a $200,000 increase in any settlement is better than your clients could expect.' Her stomach flipped with the risk of it. She held her hands firmly in her lap so Finnigan wouldn't see them shaking.

He scoffed. 'What – and he thinks our clients are suddenly going to accept that, after they've offered him a big fat nothing at mediation? We're supposed to be closing the gap here, Miss Cross, not widening it to a frigging freeway.'

'I had to talk him down to this, Finnigan.' One white lie wouldn't hurt – in the spirit of gamesmanship. 'In light of what we've discovered about Jonathan Wise, my client is very confident in his case. And he's angry, as he should be. But I've convinced him that there's merit in settling this on the right terms. Patrick's listening to me right now. If you can work with me, perhaps we can settle this thing together.' Again she used the smile.

Finnigan swung back in his chair and stared at the ceiling for a long moment. Then he shrugged. 'All I can do is get some instructions.'

'One more thing.'

'Oh, there's more? This will be good.' He seemed pained.

'The offer's only open until 9 a.m. tomorrow. We need some certainty. Both sides need to stop haemorrhaging legal costs. Either it settles now or we go to trial.'

Finnigan blew out his cheeks before throwing up his arms in surrender. 'If you want to do it that way. I'll be in touch – even if it's a no.'

Romola stood to leave. Gretchen followed, flashing Romola a quick smile with her back to Finnigan.

As he opened the door for them, he paused. 'What's happened to Imogen, anyway?'

'She's still on the file. I'm just handling the day-to-day conduct.'

'I see.' He gave a wry smile. 'Well, it makes a nice change dealing with you. If Imogen were here, I'd be up against the wall getting skewered by now.' He laughed.

'I have a different way of doing things,' Romola said plainly as they waited for the lift doors to open.

'Something tells me you're just as lethal,' Finnigan said, reaching out his sweaty paw to shake their hands as the lift arrived.

Once inside, Romola and Gretchen waited for the doors to close. Then they turned to each other and Gretchen screeched in triumph, practically jumping out of her skin. 'That was brilliant!'

Romola's face felt flushed. She stretched out her aching fingers; she must have had her fists clenched the whole time. Her legs wobbled. 'Hold off on your praise,' she said. 'If they don't take the bait, we're screwed.'

'Oh, they'll take the bait. They'll choke on the stuff.'

Chapter Forty-Two
Holding Breath

C liffy had cooked again: spaghetti with cockles. Aromas of the sea, garlic and chilli floated through the room. The full bowl in front of her steamed up her glasses, but as Romola lifted a forkful to her mouth she could hardly taste the flavours, other than a tingle of chilli after each bite. All she could think about was her phone, staring up at her silently, determined not to ring. Finnigan had said he would call before the offer expired, one way or another. It was now closing in on 8 p.m.

Her heart had leapt earlier when her phone sounded as she was leaving the office. She'd answered too quickly, before realising it was Louise.

'You're keen.' Louise sounded surprised.

'I was right by the phone.'

'I just wanted to let you know that my family's coming down – well, just Frankie and Mum. Johnny and I are having a barbecue, sort of a housewarming, next Sunday, and Mum really wants to see you. So I thought, if you're free, you could make an appearance so they know you're alive and all.'

Romola's mind turned to the following Sunday. If she managed to settle the case, she would be free to see Louise again. She could go to the barbecue, chat with Louise's mum Helen, and get things back to normal – or as normal as possible with Johnny still lurking in the background. But unless that phone of hers rang soon, none of that would happen. The case wouldn't settle. Instead, Sonia Kirk would go to Rabbit Hole on Wednesday and say all sorts of horrible things about Patrick. By next Sunday, Romola, Cliffy and Gretchen would be in full swing getting ready for trial – one that would forever put an end to barbecues with Louise. But how to explain all that to Louise without getting herself into more trouble?

'Thanks for thinking of me,' Romola said. 'It depends a bit on work. It's complicated. I think I'll probably be too busy to make it.' She bit her lip. 'Sorry.'

Louise's voice became muffled. 'Okay. I just wanted to give you the option. Let me know if you change your mind. I'd better go.'

The phone went dead before Romola could apologise. With a groan, she dropped her head perilously close to her keyboard.

Imogen walked past her office. 'Was that Finnigan on the phone?'

'No. It was Louise. My friend.'

Imogen did a double-take. 'She's still around? I thought you'd moved on.'

'I have.' Romola glowered.

'For the best. Carry on.' Imogen disappeared back to her office.

Now, sitting in Cliffy's kitchen, Romola twirled spaghetti on her fork until the amount was far too large. She shook it off and began again.

'Would you care to consume the food that I've so lovingly cooked for you rather than playing with it like a three-year-old?' Cliffy said. 'And don't you waste those vongole, either. They gave their little lives for you.' He reached across and tapped his fork on the side of her bowl, a gesture that would have seemed like an intrusion if made by anyone else.

She swallowed a mouthful like it was a ball of playdough.

'Have you thought about what you're going to do?' Cliffy asked casually. 'Long term, I mean.'

. Romola glanced up from her bowl, feeling as though she'd been hit by a brick. She had been so focused on work that she hadn't thought about the fact she was still living at Cliffy's, months longer than planned. She'd become a dependent again without realising it. 'I'm so sorry. I haven't managed to properly look for a rental yet. As soon as the trial is over, I promise –'

'I don't mean to throw you out, my dear. You know very well you can stay here for as long as you like. It's no skin off my nose – in fact,

I rather like it. Who else would I be able to share my fabulous food with?' He glanced down at her still full bowl with a frown. 'No, my query is directed at your career. It seems you've had a challenging few months.'

Romola laid down her fork, giving up on eating entirely. She closed her eyes and massaged the bags beneath them. 'I haven't even thought about it, to be honest. I'll wait for this trial to be over, and then everything will become clear.'

'You're expecting to have an epiphany?' He pointed his fork in her direction, as though he had seen this before.

'Yes – or very much hoping for one.' She opened her eyes. 'Oh god, why did I increase the offer? What was I thinking?'

Cliffy laughed, spilling a drop of his wine over his belly. 'Look what you've made me do. I'll have to go and change. Now stop thinking about this ruddy settlement at once!'

As he stood, Romola's phone sprang to life, vibrating and ringing, about to shimmy off the bench. She jumped.

'Good luck!' Cliffy called as he headed upstairs.

'Thanks!' she called back. When she answered the phone, she tried to keep her voice calm as her heart raced. 'Romola Cross speaking.'

'It's Finnigan. I've spoken to my clients about your offer.' He was all business, though she could hear a clattering of glasses in the background.

'Yes.'

'It's not acceptable.'

She saw her fingers shaking as she placed them on the edge of the kitchen bench.

'It's a fanciful offer,' Finnigan said. 'Your client is dreaming.'

She waited, her breath caught in her throat.

'However, our clients are commercial people. They run a business. They know they have to approach litigation sensibly and commercially. For that reason, and for that reason only, they're prepared to make an offer to your client.'

Romola grabbed for a notepad.

'The offer is $375k. I expect it will go towards a reasonable part of your client's costs to date – no more. And it's on a without admissions basis, with a deed releasing our client from all liability arising from the article.'

Romola scribbled down the offer on the corner of a newspaper that had been left out, just as Cliffy walked in wearing a fresh shirt. She pushed over the paper so he could see; he raised an eyebrow and began to smile.

'Obviously,' she said in a stern voice into the phone, 'that's a lot less than what my client wants – and frankly what he deserves.' She bit her lip, stood up and started doing a little dance around the kitchen.

'Let's just cut the self-serving statements and deal with the numbers, shall we? The question is, what is your client willing to accept to make the whole thing go away?'

'But it won't go away, will it? Your clients have published these things and money alone isn't going to fix that.'

He audibly sighed. 'Then why the fuck are we even having this conversation?'

'Look, I think I can bring my client down, even to the types of numbers your clients are talking about. But first he's going to need an apology, and it needs to be posted to the Rabbit Hole website. Something that says your clients got it wrong about Mr Payne, and that they are sorry for the offence caused et cetera. Even if the deed of release says your clients don't admit liability to my client at law, he'll want the public record to be corrected.'

'Fine.' He sounded dismissive. 'I'll speak to my clients. I don't think it will be an issue, provided your client agrees on the dollars.'

'And I'll speak to my client about that,' she said quickly.

'Sounds like we'll be in touch again soon then.'

'I'll call you.' She hung up.

Cliffy met her eyes across the kitchen bench, a toothy grin on his face. 'Nicely played, my dear. Nicely played indeed.'

Romola sat back down, her head swirling. She felt as though she'd been dumped by a wave and – having feared the worst amid the toss and turn of the current – had finally reached the surface, gasping for air but knowing that everything would be okay.

*

Patrick was silent for what must have been thirty seconds after Romola relayed the offer to him. When he finally spoke, his voice faltered, and he had to start again. 'This could all be over? No trial? No evidence?'

'We could play with them some more,' Romola said, conscious that she should advise Patrick of his options. 'I think they'll probably split the difference – this is a first offer, after all. I think they'll publish an apology. You'll need to sign a release, they'll transfer the money, then the proceedings can be discontinued without any of us having to step into that courtroom again.'

'I can't even ... Sorry, I'm so relieved. That's all.'

'So shall we go back to them with, say, $800k?'

'No. I want to accept this now – with the apology.'

'You don't want to push them up?'

'I would have accepted nothing if they were willing to apologise.'

'Best not to repeat that. Please.'

'You're a gun. Thank you.'

Along with her immense relief, Romola felt the first flush of a warm satisfaction. 'So I'll call them back and accept, provided they apologise?'

It had been almost four months exactly since she had begun at Bassett Brown; since she had received that call from Imogen. To be a phone call away from the end was surreal. She couldn't conceive of her life in Melbourne without the all-encompassing tension of representing Patrick.

'Yes. Please. Now.' He was almost yelling with excitement. 'Before they change their minds, the bastards.'

She laughed as she hung up.

*

Retraction and Apology – Patrick Payne

Earlier this year, on 18 May and 7 June 2019, Rabbit Hole published two articles written by Jonathan B Wise regarding Patrick Payne and his former romantic partners Hana Vukovic, Lisbeth Janssen and Matilda 'Tilly' Klein.

Rabbit Hole and Mr Wise wholly retract the statements made in the articles concerning the circumstances of Patrick

Payne's relationships. Rabbit Hole did not intend to infer that the actions or omissions of Patrick Payne led to the deaths of either Ms Vukovic or Ms Janssen, or caused any harm to Ms Klein, Ms Vukovic or Ms Janssen, and Rabbit Hole and Mr Wise acknowledge that Mr Payne played no role in the tragedies.

The articles were incorrect and inaccurate, and Rabbit Hole and Mr Wise apologise to Mr Payne for any hurt caused by those errors and inaccuracies.

– Jonathan B Wise and the Rabbit Hole editorial team

Chapter Forty-Three
Sunshine and Barbecues

It was a Saturday, and the sky was a proper springtime blue. The air smelled moist, but green rather than grey. Romola could feel the beginnings of a hayfever scratch in the back of her nose, unpleasant but welcome. The winter, and the war, was over: the Deed of Settlement had been signed, the settlement monies had been paid, and the proceedings were finished. Romola was on her way to Louise's place, a short walk from the tram stop, for the family barbecue.

Romola stopped outside a narrow sandstone terrace house with roses climbing all over. There was surely a courtyard at the back, because she could hear echoing laughter and guitar music. The smell of the barbecue matched the brightness of the sunshine. She steeled herself, held her breath and knocked.

Louise answered the door. 'You came,' she said flatly. She held a corncob aloft in one hand and a bottle of beer in the other, propping the door open with her bottom.

Romola felt like she was back at school and had turned up to a cooler girl's party. She awkwardly held a bunch of blue delphiniums, a gift for her former best friend, and she wore a stupid emerald green dress like she was going to a formal. But it seemed there was no way to retreat from this doorstep. 'Is it still okay ... for me to have come?' Romola tilted her shoulder bag to reveal the bottle of wine. 'Non-alcoholic – for Johnny. I remembered.' She had been so proud of herself at the bottle shop. 'I think it's organic too.'

Louise paused a moment longer, then waved her corncob dismissively. 'Oh, he's over that now. He's well and truly back on the booze. Come in.'

As Romola entered, they exchanged cheek kisses.

'Mum!' Louise called over her shoulder. 'Can you grab a vase? Romola's brought me the most beautiful roses.' She met Romola's eye.

'They're not roses. They're delphiniums.'

'If you say so.' Louise winked.

In that instant Romola knew she was forgiven, at least in part.

As teenagers, they had come up with a fun way to pass the time whenever they were forced to spend rainy afternoons in Judith's cold old florist shop. Louise would refer to every flower in sight as a rose, and Judith would insist on correcting her, unaware that the girls were giggling behind her back, hysterical at her deliberate pronunciation of flowers like delphiniums. Their favourite word was 'peonies', because Judith always made it sound like 'penis'.

Louise put her beer aside and grabbed hold of Romola's hand as she led her down the hall. The touch of warm fingers between her own made Romola flush with joy.

'Is that Romy I hear?' Louise's mum called from the kitchen. Romola would have recognised her Irish-accented voice anywhere.

Soon Helen appeared in the dark narrow hallway, sunlight from behind turning her to a silhouette at first. Up close she was just as she'd always been, red haired and coated in freckles like her daughter, with a glowing, welcoming smile and a comforting confidence – the kind of mum all the girls wanted to have.

'I was worried I might not see you,' Helen said, giving Romola a warm hug and then holding her out at arm's length. 'You've not changed. I was worried you'd be dressed in black and looking downcast like the rest of this Melbourne crowd. Before you do anything, come and help us put out these mountains of food my daughter has cooked. My daughter, cooking! Who'd have thought it?' She gave Louise's hand a squeeze. 'Then we can sit and you can tell me all about life in Melbourne. I saw Judith before I left – she's looking great. In fact, I think she might have a crush on that young physio of hers.'

Helen ushered Romola into a small kitchen at the back of the house. The room was filled with more people than the space comfortably allowed, most of whom Romola had never met. Guests manoeuvred around each other to transport platters of food outside into the sunshine.

Among the faces Romola spotted Louise's older brother. At school he'd been known as Frankie Fingers because he had broken his fingers so many times thumping guys or hitting walls. His poor face bore the brunt of his rugby-playing past, with a squished-sideways nose and a slightly overhanging right eyelid. But Romola knew that all the anger had seeped out of him with age, and now he was as gentle a soul as you could ever find.

He caught her eye across the kitchen and sidled over. 'Mate – you gotta help me,' he whispered conspiratorially. 'There's no meat. I mean *no* meat.'

'I think Johnny's a vegetarian,' Romola explained.

'He's only told me about a thousand times.' Frankie rolled his eyes. 'Fancies himself a bit, doesn't he? Bloody hipsters.'

Romola giggled. 'No comment.'

'Maybe you and I can sneak out later and grab a cheeky steak?' He nudged her with his elbow.

'I like the way you're thinking, but I suspect your sister might put a stop to it.' Romola glanced across at Louise, who stood at the back door telling people where to put the plates of salads and roast vegetables.

What Romola didn't say was that in a little over an hour she was expected at another party – a gathering at Patrick's house to celebrate the settlement. 'Just good friends and supporters,' he'd told her. She had refused at first, but he'd insisted. 'You can't *not* be there – you're the one who has to take most of the credit.' So she had promised to make an appearance, albeit late.

Louise was calling from the back door. 'Everyone out! You Sydneysiders may not understand, but sunshine like this does not come along very often, and I have never in my life cooked this amount of food. So get out there and stuff your beautiful faces!'

Romola headed for the door, half smiling at the men with beards and women with tattoos who were now Louise's friends.

The little garden was lovely, with a raised deck, hanging pots, a couch, a hammock and a small grassy area. Louise was standing in a group near the back fence, playing hostess. Romola spooned salad onto her compostable paper plate and slunk to a corner, looking towards the kitchen for a sign of Frankie or Helen. She hoped one of them would rescue her from being that person sitting by themselves at the party.

For a brief moment she was relieved when she felt someone at her shoulder. Then she saw it was Johnny standing beside her. It was the first time she'd seen him since the settlement. With his hair loose rather than pulled back, he had grown a five o'clock shadow to match the bags under his eyes. In a band T-shirt and ripped jeans, he couldn't have looked more different from the dapper gentleman who had eyeballed her across the boardroom table at the mediation. He smelled of an unappealing mix of chargrilled vegetables, sweat, beer and aftershave.

'Congratulations,' he said dully. 'You won.'

She swallowed a mouthful of lentils. 'I don't know about winning. Both sides compromised. That's often the best outcome for everyone in litigation.'

'If you say so.' Staring out into the crowd, he rolled his tongue around in his mouth. 'Except I had to publicly apologise to Patrick Payne.' He looked at her sideways. 'That hurt.'

Romola saw Louise peering above heads, seeking out the two of them across the garden. Her eyes latched on to Johnny rather than Romola – she was clearly checking if he was playing nice.

Romola stared at the ground, readying herself to swallow her pride. As much as she would have liked to never see Johnny again, she knew that for Louise's sake they would need to put aside their differences. 'I'm hoping we can start again,' Romola said, turning to him with a tentative smile. 'Pretend the last few months never happened. For Louise?'

'Sure. Sounds fine to me,' he said quickly, his voice was so low she could barely hear it. He didn't meet her eye. 'Are you going to keep working there. For Patrick?'

Romola had been mulling it over. Did she want to keep working for Bassett Brown? Did she want to work for Imogen, who had all but abandoned her until she'd settled the case in a blaze of glory, who now called her 'my protégé', and who had invited her out for coffee every day since the settlement and unloaded a multitude of files on her? Only 'the best' files, Imogen had said. Flattered though Romola was, she couldn't wrap her mind around whether this was what she wanted. The past few months had been horrible in so many ways, but exhilarating and challenging too. As Cliffy had said, not every client would be a Payne.

'I'm not planning any moves just yet,' said Romola, Johnny's obvious disdain for the firm helping her to make up her mind. She would give Bassett Brown more time to steep. She'd been so involved in Patrick's case that she still hardly knew anyone or anything else. 'I'm a lawyer. I represent people. That doesn't mean I necessarily agree with them.'

His journalist's eyes examined her; like a lawyer's eyes, they were trained to pick up the difference between truth and lie. 'Apology or not, he's a prick of a man.'

Despite her best efforts, she so despised his arrogance. She had come here in peace, even though his journalistic treatment of Patrick had been far from ethical. She had every reason to hate him but was willing to put that to one side for Louise's sake. But he had to have the last word. She filled her mouth with green leaves instead of proffering a response.

'All right, that's enough from me,' Johnny said, as she saw Louise begin to make her way over. 'Truce.' He quickly held out his hand.

Louise was practically running to them. Her freckled face was set in an awkward combination of horror and hope, her eyes on Johnny's outstretched hand. Romola thought her friend might force their hands together if she had to.

To save Louise the effort – and because Romola couldn't be bothered fighting anymore – she took Johnny's hand, which was rough but warm. 'Truce.'

Louise reached them, panting as though she'd run a marathon. 'You're friends! Thank Christ for that.' She gave Romola's shoulders a squeeze. 'Like the food? It's amazing, right?'

'I never knew lentils could taste so good.'

Louise elbowed Johnny. 'What do you think, J?'

'I think you're amazing.' He gave her a kiss. 'For a beginner.' He seemed unable to say anything nice without adding a squeeze of nasty.

He's a lost cause, thought Romola, plotting her exit.

Chapter Forty-Four
Seconds

With the paparazzi gone from the front of Patrick's house, it no longer stood out on the street lined with period mansions, manicured hedges and security cameras. Romola had become familiar with the place from her few visits, but today was different – for the first time, this was a social call. She would have to make polite chitchat with wealthy strangers as opposed to talking through the case with Patrick. It all felt beyond her as she pressed the intercom button. She adjusted her dress straps, making sure her bra wasn't showing beside the green silk.

A waitress in black and white, her hair in a tight bun, handed Romola a frosted glass of champagne and led her to the lawn. Patrick had said this would be a casual lunch with a few friends, but the lilting jazz and yelps of laughter from the lawn said otherwise.

The garden was like a wedding scene. Large bouquets of blue and white flowers ran the length of the white tablecloth, a row of waiters standing to one side, their arms tucked behind them. Beautiful people in sunglasses laughed and raised their glasses. A jazz quartet, accompanied by a velvet-voiced brunette, was positioned under a sprawling fig tree.

Romola noticed that the lawn was studded with daffodils, jonquils and bluebells. She remembered Patrick saying that Hana and Max had gone crazy in the autumn planting bulbs, and Romola thought that on this, the first day of spring, the flowers were beautiful – a glorious reminder of Hana.

Jessie spotted her first, bounding up in expectation of an ear rub, and Romola obliged. When she straightened, she saw Patrick approaching. 'You came,' he said quietly, just as Louise had. He placed a hand on her bare shoulder and kissed her cheek; he hadn't made either gesture before, and both seemed overly friendly. He smelled of red wine, and his cheek was hot.

She adjusted her straps again. 'Sorry I'm late.'

'Not at all.' Patrick guided her towards the table.

She searched for Cliffy's familiar mop of white hair among the guests, because he'd promised to save her a seat. But her eyes caught instead on the tall silver-haired man seated at the head of the table. 'Your dad's here.' She said the words before realising what they meant.

Malcolm Payne held Romola's gaze, though he was deep in conversation with Derek Russell, her managing partner, who sat next to him like a child sitting next to the birthday boy. A self-satisfied grin lay across Derek's face as he followed Malcolm's eyeline towards Romola. They were surely talking about her.

'Rabbit Hole and Johnny Wise aren't the only ones who apologised,' Patrick said, nodding towards his father. 'I think he genuinely regrets the way he acted.'

Romola was gobsmacked. 'But, Patrick,' she said under her breath, 'he cut you off entirely.'

He clasped her elbow and turned her subtly towards him. 'You don't have to remind me. I know ... *I know*. It's his temper – it gets the better of him every time. The truth is, if I wasn't forgiving, our relationship would have been over a long time ago. He's my only family, after all.' Patrick appeared defeated, his smile more of a grimace. But she also saw a little relief in his eyes – his life would be easier again.

She shrugged, uncertain. 'And what about turning a new page? Your idea to go into landscaping?'

'Sometimes family has to come first. And it takes all sorts. Right?'

'You're right,' she conceded, shaking away her doubts. Who was she to judge? If that was how the Paynes operated, that was their prerogative. She would have done anything to cling on to her own father.

Without further ado Patrick saw her settled next to Cliffy, who to her relief was seated at the end of the table furthest from Derek,

Malcolm and Patrick. Her godfather was surveying the scene with a bemused look. He wore a colourful scarf, and sweat was breaking through his shirt. 'The food is outstanding,' he said cheerily, scraping the last of a bright orange sauce from his plate. He leaned in closer to her ear. 'The company, on the other hand, not so much.' He inclined his head towards the beautiful blonde woman on the other side of Romola, who hadn't even bothered turning when she sat down.

Before Romola could begin to think about eating, she heard the ringing of cutlery striking crystal.

Cliffy nudged her arm. 'Hold on to your hat. I think the big man's about to speak.'

Patrick signalled for the band to stop playing. Malcolm stood up, a glass of mineral water in one hand and a small piece of paper in the other. He coughed three times before he spoke. 'Now that we're *all* here –' he glanced at Romola '– I hope you'll indulge me for a moment. I'd like to say a few words ... for a change.' He glanced up from the paper, waiting for laughs. A murmur ran down the table like a Mexican wave. 'All of you are here today because I think of you as close friends and supporters of our family. I want to thank you for that.' A few nods from the crowd. Romola wondered who all these people were, and where they had been when she'd been searching for character witnesses. 'Today, as you may be aware, is the first day of spring. And a fine day it is.' He lifted his glass towards the garden. 'Now, I wanted to talk a little about my son here.' He placed a hand on his son's shoulder.

Patrick slumped forward a little.

'Many of you would look at my son and think he is lucky. That he was born into wealth and privilege, with strong genes –' Malcolm paused for more laughter '– and has never had to want for a thing. But things have not been so easy. We lost his beautiful mother Martina when he was still a boy, and the kids were not kind to him at school. Do you remember, son, how you used to fumble over your words?' Malcolm laughed, and Patrick withdrew even further into his seat. 'But my son overcame all that, just as he has overcome the challenges that faced him this year. People wanted to tear us down with lies.

We had to fight hard. I'm proud of how I saw you fight, my son. And we prevailed. I would like to thank Derek here and his team at Bassett Brown for all their hard work.'

Malcolm raised a glass in Romola and Cliffy's direction. Her face grew warm.

'And so,' Malcolm continued, 'now is the time for us to come together, as the strong family that we are, and make Payne Corp better than ever. We have some new projects in the works that I'm excited to be announcing soon. And I'm happy to say that my son has decided not to pursue his political ambitions after all. We've all seen how fickle that business is. Instead Patrick will be beside me, in the family business. For that I thank you, son.'

Patrick's head was bowed, his eyes on the empty plate in front of him. Romola thought she could make out a smile on his face, though it could easily have been another grimace. He didn't look up at his father, nor return his thanks.

Malcolm lifted his mineral water. 'Please, everybody raise your glasses – to family!'

'To family!' came the resounding echo, before the glasses clinked. Romola switched from champagne to the red wine that Cliffy had poured. She took a grateful sip, thankful that Malcolm's speech had finished without any real attention being drawn to her.

Malcolm had not yet taken his seat when Patrick stood up. He was a little unsteady on his feet, as though he'd only just decided to speak. She observed that she hadn't seen him in a suit since the mediation and, seen from afar, this one didn't sit right on him. It took her back to the awkward, stilted, prickly Patrick she had first met, rather than the one she'd grown comfortable around. 'Please,' he began. 'Please, everybody, before you go back to lunch, I'd like to make another toast.' He glanced over at the daffodils. 'It has been just over four months now, since … since Hana died. And … with the way events transpired, I haven't been able to properly celebrate her life … or grieve her death. Hana was a beautiful person in every sense of the word … She brought joy to my life, to Max's life, to Emir's, and to the lives of every other person who met her. She left us far too early.' Patrick paused, covering his mouth with his hand. 'There's much more I could say. But for now, if I could ask you to please raise your glasses for one last toast – to Hana.'

'To Hana,' came the quiet response as sombre heads nodded.

Romola followed Patrick's line of sight and saw Emir standing under the verandah. Dressed in black as usual, he held a bottle of beer skyward to toast his lost sister. Romola was shocked and puzzled to see him there. The last she'd heard, Patrick had been planning to let him go immediately – and even if Patrick hadn't done so, Romola would have expected Emir to have left of his own accord after what he had seen (or thought he'd seen). But he seemed comfortable as he watched the festivities, as though he was going nowhere.

'Quite right, son,' said Malcolm, his glass raised. 'To Hana.' He patted Patrick on the back, then motioned to the jazz band. They struck up 'Mack the Knife', which, with its lyrical description of a murderer, seemed all wrong in the wake of Patrick's reflection on Hana's life. Patrick downed the remainder of his drink and closed his eyes.

'A turnaround for the ages from Malcolm, wouldn't you say?' Cliffy asked Romola, filling her glass with more red wine.

As she sipped, she noticed that Derek had got out of his seat and was coming their way. He sidled up behind them and placed a hand on the back of her seat. 'Romola, glad you could make it. Heathcliff, good to see you.' Romola turned, but Derek's face was obscured by the sun. 'I wanted to tell you what a stellar job you did on this case – truly. You had a lot thrown at you. Malcolm has been singing your praises over there. Now that we all know how good you are, you had better look out! Everybody will be throwing work your way.' Derek bounced on his toes as he tended to do.

Romola shielded her eyes from the sun. 'I thought Imogen would be here.'

Derek surveyed the table as if it had only just occurred to him that Imogen, the partner technically responsible for Patrick's file, was absent. He waved away a fly. 'I think one of her kids had something on. Shame she couldn't be here. Stunning day, absolutely stunning.' He glanced at the blonde beauty sitting next to Romola, then sank the last of his wine.

'If you'll excuse me, Derek.' Romola pushed back her chair and stood up. 'Bathroom.'

'Ask one of the staff up there and they'll show you where to go.'

'I know the way.'

'Of course.' He laughed. 'I keeping forgetting you've been here before.'

She smiled to herself as she walked to the house, starting to feel a little giddy. The champagne had sunk in, and the warm red wine was still savory on her lips. She floated her way past the busy kitchen, full of chefs crouched over plates, to the bathroom, which was dark and smelled of gardenias.

While washing her hands, she contemplated her reflection. She was tipsy enough to feel as though she were looking at a stranger. Her blackberry-coloured lipstick was still intact, and her hair had kept its shape, tied in a loose knot at the base of her neck. Her cheeks were a little flushed, but the sunshine was already working its magic on her skin, turning her face and shoulders a darker shade of brown.

She shook her hands loose and realised that she hadn't felt this relaxed in years. She still wasn't sure of her future, but she had time. Time to decide what to do with herself. Time to stay at Bassett Brown and see what it was really like. Time to find herself a place of her own. Time to try being friends with Louise again. She could face herself in the mirror and not feel like she had to turn away. She took a last look into her deep brown eyes, breathed in and exhaled. She was ready to face the sun again.

Chapter Forty-Five
Max

Romola was heading back to the party, along the sparse hallway towards the busy kitchen, when a voice, small and husky, stopped her in her tracks. The words were just loud enough for her to make them out above the sizzle of pans and the shouting of chefs: 'It's you again.'

She backtracked and craned her head through a half-open door.

Max was sitting on his bed, legs crossed, iPad balanced on his lap. 'Remember me? From the boat? And the tennis?'

'Of course I remember you – hi, Max,' she said lightly.

He offered a cheeky grin, sliding his headphones back from one ear.

'Can I come in?' she asked.

'Sure.' He removed his headphones and placed them on the bed next to a plate smeared with chocolate sauce. A smudge lingered above his lip. He followed her eyes and gave a guilty smile. 'Please don't tell Dad I was eating in here.'

'Your secret is safe with me.' Romola almost winked, then remembered kids found it creepy when adults did that. 'You like Lego?' She walked over to an expansive bookshelf upon which Lego constructions were displayed.

Max looked embarrassed. 'I pretty much only do ones that are for fourteen plus. Otherwise they're too easy, you know?'

She tried to remember at what age Lego had stopped being cool to her. 'I like this one best,' she said, pointing to a New York City skyline.

'Dad helped me do that one. It took three days.' Max's eyes were wide. 'My favourite's the haunted house.' He pointed to a purple-and-green castle, with ghoulish Lego men peering out the windows and a black cat sitting on a fence post.

Romola sat on the edge of the bed, examining the boy's other creations for a while. He had a queen bed and a big-screen TV. The carpet underfoot was clean and fluffy. She would have dreamt of such a luxurious bedroom as a child.

'How's school?' she asked casually. She remembered his crestfallen face the last time she'd asked that question.

'*Così-così*,' he said, his hand wavering in the air.

'You're learning Italian?'

'*Sì.*' He adjusted some of his Lego. 'Actually, a new kid's started – Ben. He's into Lego too. So, yeah, it's been okay.'

'A friend can make all the difference.'

'You need to go back to the lunch or what?' he asked. 'Looks pretty boring out there.'

'Nah.' She swatted her hand. By now Cliffy would be wondering where she was, but she was enjoying the comfort of the boy's room, of not having to deal with adult conversation. 'You're right. It can get a little dull.'

'Oh believe me, I know.' Max began looking around his room, searching for things to show her.

'What were you watching before?' she asked, trying to help him out.

He picked up his iPad from next to him and unplugged the headphones. 'YouTube.' He opened the screen with a thumbprint. 'I like watching kids do stuff, you know. There's kids making slime, playing games, building Lego, that sort of thing. There's this one kid who has seven million views. He's an unboxer.'

'Wow.' Romola wondered what an unboxer could possibly be.

'I want to start my own YouTube channel, but Dad won't let me. He says people will take advantage of me.'

'I think he's right about that.' Romola moved to stand up, feeling that their conversation was reaching its natural end. 'I should go back to the boring lunch, I guess.'

Max held his screen out to her. 'I've done some videos, though – just in case Dad changes his mind about the YouTube thing. I could show you some?' His big blue eyes conveyed such hope. 'They're quick. I promise.' Without waiting for an answer, he began deftly scrolling through videos. He had labelled them based on the type of Lego he'd constructed. 'I even use time lapse in some – it's pretty easy,' he said proudly.

'Oh look –' she pointed to one '– there's your favourite, the haunted house. Why don't you show me that one?' She hoped it was short.

Max beamed. 'Coming right up!' He sat next to her on the bed, awkwardly at first – then, as he became distracted by his screen, unconsciously squishing his leg against hers. He expanded the video to take up the whole screen before leaning over to hold it in front of her.

'Hi, this is Max Payne.' He was seated at Patrick's large dining table, the shiny black kitchen in view behind. He wore a short-sleeved school uniform and was red in the face – he must have raced to start making his video after arriving home. 'Today I'm going to be building this little beauty.' When he held the box in front of the screen, it blocked his face. 'It's special edition, to be released for Halloween in the US. But my dad managed to get me one early.' Max spoke as though he was sharing a secret. He showed the camera all six sides of the box, allowing the viewer time to appreciate its grandeur.

Romola realised the video went for twenty-two minutes. 'This is great, Max,' she said, beginning to think of exit strategies.

But then her attention was caught by movement in the kitchen behind Max's head. Like a ghost, there was Hana behind the counter. She lifted a quarter of watermelon out of the fridge and began cutting large chunks. Romola checked the date of the video: late February. Three months before Hana's death. The young woman seemed so healthy, in leggings and a crop top, a small smile on her face as she glanced over at Max.

'This one's a corner,' he told his viewers. 'They're really good joining pieces if you ever get stuck.'

Romola found herself transfixed by Hana. She'd seen her in countless Instagram posts, but it was different seeing her unguarded, in the midst of making an after-school snack for Max. 'Just another minute on that screen, Max,' she called, 'then you have to eat something.'

He ignored her, rolling his eyes conspiratorially at the camera.

A shadow passed along the back of the kitchen. Romola couldn't see who it was at first – Patrick or Emir? Hana's smile wavered, as though she'd heard the rumbling of an oncoming storm, and Romola's stomach began to churn.

The man grabbed a drink from the fridge like he owned the joint, before closing in on the centre of the frame until his features became clear – or clear enough for Romola to recognise that it was not Patrick or Emir in the kitchen with Hana. It was Malcolm.

Time seemed to stop as Romola watched him approach Hana from behind. She appeared to have suddenly become glued to the spot, utterly disarmed despite the enormous kitchen knife in her hand. Malcolm moved slowly but deliberately behind her. His long arms wrapped around her middle. His face nuzzled into her neck. His right hand breezed over the waistband of her leggings and brushed past the outer curve of her breast. He whispered something in her ear, and she adjusted her face, smiling. She turned to speak softly in response, then laughed.

Romola wished she could hear their words. She tried to say something to Max, wanting him to shut off the video, but she couldn't speak. He was still watching himself on the screen, a smile on his face as he proudly mouthed the words he had spoken months before. It was clear that from his point of view, nothing extraordinary was on display.

'Max,' Romola managed to say, keeping her voice light, 'is that your granddad back there?'

'Oh yeah, that's him,' Max said casually. 'He *always* used to come over.' He rolled his eyes, laughing at the thought, oblivious to what his words meant. 'Hana used to call him the tickle monster.'

Romola had so many questions that she couldn't ask an eight-year-old. The first one: Did your dad know?

As though on cue, Patrick sauntered into Max's room, a cheesy grin on his flushed face. 'Is this where the party's at?' His lips were stained with red wine from the glass in his hand. He kneeled on the bed and placed his hands on his son's shoulders. 'You're not trying to convince Romola here to set you up on YouTube, are you, Maxxy?'

Max paused the video and threw his iPad across the bed. 'Daaad,' he said in embarrassment, and Patrick playfully wrestled his son to the pillow, tickling him while he snorted with laughter.

Though Romola felt knocked off kilter, she seized the opportunity to grab the iPad. With a few deft strokes, she AirDropped the video to her phone.

Max wriggled to extricate himself from Patrick, who ruffled his son's hair as he was finally released, puffed out. His eyes crossed to Romola, and in that moment she knew that her face was betraying her. She couldn't think of a single thing to say, her mind occupied with the image of Hana and Malcolm in the kitchen together. She stood and instinctively headed for the door, and Patrick leaped off the bed. 'Wait.'

'See-ya,' she heard Max say. The poor kid – she knew she should offer him something, some goodbye, some compliment on his video, but a quiet, 'See you again, Max', was all she could muster as she walked up the hallway.

'Why don't you go grab some cake, buddy?' she heard Patrick say, before his footsteps came thumping up behind her. When he gently grabbed her arm, she wondered if he could feel her goosebumps. He led her by the elbow into the nearest room: his bedroom, with its king bed and walk-in wardrobe where Hana's clothes probably still hung. Romola wondered if Malcolm and Hana had been in here together.

Patrick released Romola's arm and gestured to two armchairs facing a bay window. They sat down, Romola right on the edge. The view was to the lawn, where the party was in full swing, everyone mingling. She spotted Derek still at Malcolm's side, arching his back with laughter. Cliffy remained seated, looking as though he had settled in for the day. A young man wearing a fedora had sat down next to him, hanging on his every word.

'Is everything okay?' Patrick's face was a picture of concern. 'You look sick.'

Horrified and embarrassed, she attempted to grapple sensibly with the issues that presented themselves. Malcolm and Hana had been together – intimately together. Hana's face and body language had told Romola that she'd been deeply uncomfortable about it, to say the least. But had that just been because she was torn between father and son, or had something more sinister been going on? Had Patrick known? If not, was Romola about to be the one to tell him of his father's betrayal? Or was this just the way things were in their world of privilege, and she was the last to know? How wholesome she felt to have never suspected anything of this sort.

'That video I was watching with Max ...'

'Yes?'

'I don't know how to say this.' She had to tell him – he'd decided to work with his father, so he needed to know the truth. But the right sentence wasn't presenting itself. 'I ... I saw them,' she finally murmured, 'I saw them together. Hana and –' She stopped, unable to say it.

Patrick closed his eyes. The muscles in his jaw pulsed. 'And Dad.' He nodded slowly.

Romola didn't need to say anything more. Her mind, still foggy from the champagne and red wine, understood that much at least. 'You knew?' she whispered.

He curled his hands into white-knuckled fists. 'I didn't *know* know. But I suspected. *Fuck*.' With deep, heaving breaths, he got himself under control. 'My father is a fucking vulture. He's done this to me my whole life. Anything good I have, he ruins it. No, that's not it – he has to have it for himself.' Patrick started rocking back and forth. 'It's like the more I love them, the more joy he takes in having them. I suspected about him and Hana. God, this makes me look terrible, but ... I didn't want to know for sure. I hoped I was wrong this time.'

'*This* time? Lisbeth too?' Romola's mind automatically turned to the youngest and most innocent of Patrick's girlfriends, and the first to lose her life. Feeling sick, Romola was repelled by the thought of Malcolm and Lisbeth together. Patrick had called him a vulture, and now she couldn't escape the image of a vulture preying on a baby bird.

'Poor Beth. She was only eighteen. She was the first one. I only found out afterwards. He even told me himself – trying to make me feel better when she dumped me. He called her a slut. I was furious. I even hit him – punched him right in the gut. He just stood there like I hadn't even touched him. I've never told anyone that.' Patrick heaved with effort as he spoke; it seemed he was about to retch, recounting his father's words.

Romola could hardly comprehend his words, but her eyes stung, and she felt a white-hot fury run through her veins. 'What about the others? Sonia, Tilly?

'There were more after Beth. Sometimes they were young women who'd started working for him, and other times I didn't know where he'd found them. But with Tilly I wasn't completely sure. I suspected … but then she disappeared – and anyway, she was so unpredictable that I guess I preferred to think the best …'

Romola thought back to how Patrick had suggested from the beginning that Tilly was unhinged; that she liked to tell lies. Anger rose in her at the hypocrisy.

'Sonia?' she asked.

'Not Sonia,' he said firmly. 'She was different. She was from money. And she was messed up already. I'm not sure why, but I'm sure Dad never touched her.' Patrick's rocking continued, the armchair was shaking with it.

'So it's all about power?'

Patrick turned to Romola and nodded, pain stretching his face. 'It's like he takes pleasure in knowing he's corrupting them. I wanted to protect them but didn't know how. And I didn't want to let them go either. This must all sound completely crazy to you.'

Yes, Romola wanted to say, completely and utterly crazy. She was shocked and horrified by Malcolm's conduct, but to learn that Patrick had failed to act was another thing. Romola had seen the sadness in Hana's eyes.

Then something occurred to her. 'Was it your baby?'

Patrick stopped rocking and stood up, turning his back on her to look out at the party. Romola watched too. His father had now sauntered over to the jazz band – it looked like he was requesting a song.

'I don't know,' said Patrick. 'If I'm honest with myself, I think it wasn't, judging by her reaction. I think some part of me realised it that night, at dinner, when …' When she'd rejected his marriage proposal, he didn't seem able to say.

Romola couldn't listen in good conscience any longer. 'I'm sorry, Patrick, but I don't understand how you can continue to have anything to do with your father. After all this, after losing Hana, you're going to work with him?'

Patrick remained facing the party on the lawn. He reminded her of Malcolm that day at the mediation; he'd stared out the window with his back to the room, unwilling even to pretend to be listening to others. But Patrick was responding to her, shaking his head and then saying quietly, 'I can see how it looks. And I know how it makes me feel. But he is all I have ever known. It's always been the two of us. And I know that's bad – probably insane, in fact. I don't know what I am without him.'

Romola stood, hands on hips. 'Are you kidding me? You're great without him. I haven't known you for very long, but even I could see how much happier you were without your dad around. Maybe there's someone you could speak to about it, someone who could help you make the break? Sometimes you just need to take a leap of faith.'

She couldn't see Patrick's face, but he started to laugh – a warped laugh that could have just as easily been a sob. 'You're one of the only ones who believed in me, Romola.'

Yes, perhaps she had been the only one, and now she wondered why. Was it just because he was her client, and she wanted to be a good lawyer? Or had she actually believed in his good character? Now, torn between pity and rage, she wondered how she could have. He'd known what his father was capable of, so he should have said something to Hana – maybe all that young woman had needed was an out.

Romola heard the door creak open. Max's face peered inside. He eyes shifted from Patrick to Romola and back. She offered him a soft smile, trying to convey that everything was fine; that they were just two adults having a normal conversation.

'Dad, that bossy lady from the kitchen wants you.'

Patrick didn't turn to his son. 'Okay, Maxxy, I'll be there in a minute.'

'I have to go anyway,' Romola said quickly, wanting fresh air and solitude.

Once Max had wandered off, she left the room without another word. As she swept past the kitchen, heaving with the family's servants, she suddenly saw the chefs in a new light. They were sweaty and red faced, slogging their guts out to serve the beautiful people outside – people who were laughing into the air as if they were responsible for making the sky blue.

Emir was standing just inside the door to the garden. She caught his gaze as she passed, her eyes starting to brim with tears of anger, and she bit down hard on the inside of her cheek to stop the flood from coming. She wished Emir wouldn't give her that doleful look, as though she was there to help him. Had he known the truth all along and kept the Paynes' dirty secret in exchange for money needed to support his new family? Had he been waiting for Romola to find out that he too had betrayed his sister with his inaction? Or had he been in the dark like her, knowing something wasn't right but clueless as to what or who had really pushed Hana over the edge?

Pushing open the door, Romola stepped into the sunshine like she was jumping into a public pool at the end of a hot day – expecting relief but finding herself immersed in soupy, tepid water. Everything seemed fuzzy. The music was too loud, and the laughter sickly sweet, along with the scent of those jonquils.

Walking as if she were balancing on a tightrope, she made her way to her seat and retrieved the bag she'd left there. A small group had joined the man in the fedora, gathering around Cliffy to listen intently to his stories. Romola turned in his direction without meeting his eyes. He knew her too well, and she didn't want to fill him in yet – not here.

'I'm leaving,' she said in a weak voice. 'I'm not feeling a hundred per cent. Must be the heat and the wine.' She started moving before he could respond, though she heard him calling something after her. Instead of turning back, she almost tripped over her feet as she sped up. Anyone would have thought she was being chased by a wild animal – a silver fox, perhaps.

Chapter Forty-Six
The End of the Day

At 4 p.m. on a Sunday, the Bassett Brown office was reassuringly quiet, with no sound but for the low hum of the air-conditioning system. Romola had taken the tram straight from Patrick's. She felt the need to look for clues, to understand how she'd overlooked the secret between father and son. In her poky office, she stood rummaging through file notes of phone calls, memoranda, articles, photos – all the detritus she had gathered about Patrick's life in her effort to prove him a good man. Whatever that was.

The door opened behind her. She jumped and dropped a bundle of paper.

'I didn't mean to startle you,' said Imogen. 'Just thought I'd say hello.'

'You're working?'

Imogen stood in the doorway, immaculate in a white linen T-shirt and blue jeans. Her pixie hair was more ruffled than usual, and she was wearing less make-up, making the lines under her eyes more obvious. 'What else would I be doing?'

'No. Nothing. It's –' Romola hesitated. 'To be honest, it's just that I saw Derek at the party the Paynes are having today. I asked after you, and he said you had something on with the kids.'

Imogen did not react immediately. Instead she checked her watch, then looked back to Romola. 'Almost five,' she said. 'Wait here.'

After ten minutes had passed, Romola assumed her boss's attention had been caught by something else. Romola had just got back to sorting through her notes, more calmly now, when Imogen returned with two crystal glasses in hand and a yellow envelope tucked under her arm. She placed one of the glasses and the envelope on Romola's desk. 'Gin.'

Romola lifted the glass to her lips. The smell hit her between the eyes, a reminder of that night at the bar. Despite her revulsion, she took a greedy sip, briefly letting herself forget about whatever new piece of work Imogen had passed to her in that envelope.

'You look like you needed that,' Imogen said.

Romola clasped the glass between her hands and wondered what she should say to this formidable woman. In the end, she didn't need to say anything.

'Derek has been bullshitting you, I'm afraid.' Imogen grimaced as she spoke, like the gin had burned through her. 'I wasn't with the kids this afternoon. I would dearly love to have been with my girls, but I have been sitting here doing my billing for the past two hours – as Derek well knows.' She swirled the ice in her drink. 'And, sadly, I didn't receive an invitation to the Payne shindig.' She smiled sadly at Romola. 'I think the Paynes might be done with me. But good for you – you're going places.'

Imogen lifted her glass in a sardonic toast, but Romola didn't reciprocate. She had done enough toasting for the day.

'I saw them,' she said.

'Hmmm?' Imogen didn't look up from her drink.

'I saw Malcolm and Hana, together.'

Imogen crossed her legs and Romola noticed her shoes, leopard-print suede ballet flats. She was of the class of people who appeared glamorous even when she was sitting in her office alone on a Sunday afternoon. Stretching her feet back and forth, she watched her pointy toes and swirled her ice. 'So I heard.' She drank the rest of her gin in one quick movement and clunked the glass down on Romola's desk. Then she picked up the yellow envelope and handed it to Romola. 'On instructions from Malcolm. Open it when you get home.' She stood and smoothed her jeans. 'I need to get some air. Shall we walk?'

*

Romola thought that a central business district late on a Sunday afternoon had to be one of the most morose places on earth. With the buzz of the working week long gone, the streets felt like a boarded-up theme park. A cold night, the first night of spring, was closing in. The skies were now a dull blue, and the two women, short and tall, walked in the grey shadows of black buildings. Both women had their arms crossed in front of them. As always when Romola walked with Imogen, the pace was far too quick for her to feel comfortable.

She remembered her father once telling her that if she ever needed to have a difficult conversation with someone, she should do it while driving or walking. 'Some place where you can look ahead, not into their eyes,' Don had told her. 'People feel more comfortable that way. They tell you more.'

The two women had walked a block before Imogen spoke. 'I never knew for sure – I only suspected it. Then at the mediation, you could practically see Malcolm's brain implode when he found out she'd been pregnant. After that, I was certain about what he had been up to.'

Imogen turned a corner suddenly, heading down one of the city's many small lanes. After a moment, Romola caught up again.

'When Hana killed herself,' Imogen said, 'Malcolm lost the chance at a second heir.'

Sore spots announced themselves on Romola's feet. She had chosen her shoes today for looks not comfort, excited at the prospect of strappy sandals. Now the skin behind her ankles was rubbed raw. 'How could that have possibly worked, though?' she asked. 'Patrick's girlfriend giving birth to his father's baby.'

'I'm not saying Malcolm would have told anyone about it. But *he* would have known – that he was still virile, capable of sowing his seeds. That's how a man like him would see it.'

They continued walking through small lanes until they reached Flinders Street. Streams of people were passing them now – the homeless who would be making their beds in the city streets tonight, and the shoppers and retail workers on their way to their warm homes. Romola wondered how they would react to the news about one of the richest men in the land.

If she and Imogen kept going at this pace, they would soon be at the muddy Yarra River, snaking its way through Melbourne like a king brown, wide and solemn. The sun was on the cusp of setting beyond the skyline, the proper cold sinking in.

'Patrick wasn't very clear on whether he did it to all of them,' Romola said. 'He seemed to think Sonia escaped untouched.'

She looked across to Imogen, but the older woman kept her gaze on the horizon. 'Sonia was raised with money, and her dad was a friend of Malcolm's. I get the impression he prefers girls who are powerless, those who have been raised with nothing and so are thankful for anything – whatever strings might be attached.'

'But Lisbeth didn't fall into that category. Patrick said he preyed on her too, and she had nice doctor parents.'

'Who knows? Maybe he had something against the Janssens. There's no telling what's going on in the twisted mind of Malcolm Payne.'

'How did you find out?' Romola asked. As much as Imogen had her faults, Romola would never have suspected her of harbouring a secret like this.

'It was during the divorce. Turned out Patrick had told Sonia about his father and Beth one night after he'd had too much to drink. She threatened to go public. But Malcolm stepped in and offered to pay her a handsome amount as part of the divorce settlement, in exchange for him not going public or to the police about her drug abuse.'

Romola soaked it all in, amazed that Imogen could recount these events with such nonchalance. She could barely grasp, let alone put in any logical order, all the questions that were circling. 'But why would Malcolm press Patrick to sue Rabbit Hole with all this going on? When he knew what could come out about him?'

Imogen shook her head as she walked. 'Malcolm was confident Sonia would stay quiet. We had the non-disclosure agreement, and he knew his payments were her main source of income. Plus Malcolm thinks he's indestructible; it might not have even occurred to him that he could be brought down by this. Again, that's men like Malcolm for you – the ego.' They walked past Federation Square, where a busker sat next to a standing piano on wheels. He played Billy Joel, and to Romola it sounded like the saddest music in the world. 'But as you got closer to trial, and Sonia started losing it over Max's custody arrangements, it became obvious to me that there was a real risk she would talk. I needed you to settle the case, whether Malcolm knew that or not.'

Romola's head was spinning, and she didn't think she could walk much further. Luckily Imogen finally seemed to be slowing as they approached the Princes Bridge.

'Just to defend myself here,' Imogen said, stopping as they reached the bridge, 'I thought carefully before taking on Patrick's case. Don't forget the words of that Rabbit Hole article. They said *Patrick* had mistreated those girls – abused them, even. That wasn't true. Yes, I suspected Malcolm had been involved, and I knew of what had happened with Beth, but that didn't make the article any less defamatory of Patrick. It didn't mean he didn't have a good case, or that what Malcolm had done was even relevant to that. I never put a case forward that had anything to do with Malcolm Payne. I never made any untrue claims about him, and Patrick knew about Beth and had instructed me not to use that information to his advantage. And you wouldn't have run the case any differently if you'd known either.'

Romola felt she'd been operating the whole time with half an eye closed. 'But if Patrick knew about Malcolm and Hana, he's hardly blameless. He's almost equally culpable.'

'*If* he knew. I never raised it with him.'

'How could he not have known?'

'A beautiful and a terrible thing about being a lawyer, as you're aware, is that you know things that others don't. It can be a curse. I had no obligation to raise it with Patrick. Sometimes I thought he must have known, while at others I believed he might really be that clueless.'

Romola held on to the bridge's balustrade, contemplating what to do next – both about her discovery this afternoon, and her future.

'You did a good job, Romola – a great job. It was better you didn't know, otherwise you would have grappled with that knowledge way too much. You needed to do your job representing Patrick without the distraction of Malcolm, and you did it well, despite everything. I'm sure you have a big future ahead of you at the firm.'

'That's what everyone keeps telling me.'

'Me, on the other hand.' Imogen's gaze followed a rowing eight who glided their way towards nearby boatsheds. 'I'm not so sure. I thought staying loyal to that family was the best thing to do – however many sleepless nights that gave me. There didn't seem to be another viable option. Fuck lot of good it did me, though. I think I've reached my end point – I can't stomach it any more. "The Trigger" has been pulled, so to speak.'

Romola gave her a quizzical glance. 'You know people say that about you?'

'Who do you think started it?' Imogen turned her head and smiled, then checked her watch again. 'Time to get back to the kids. If I'm home before six-thirty, there's a chance I'll be there for bathtime. Mitch will kill me otherwise. See you tomorrow?'

'Sure,' said Romola, not knowing if she would ever set foot in that office again.

*

Romola flagged down the nearest cab – this time without even a flutter of fear. The driver was a friendly Sri Lankan man who told her all about his young family and the difficulties of living in a new country. He must have noticed her heritage: Sri Lanka was in her eyes, her cheekbones, her skin. He would have assumed her to be a sympathetic listener, someone like him. Little did he know what she had become.

Although she had never known her birth mother, Romola was confident that the woman she had turned into was nothing like her. Her father used to say she'd been a nurturer, a gentle but fiery soul; the one who learned to speak English and then spoke on behalf of the whole village; the one who arranged delivery of medicines and school supplies. Both her mother and father had been protectors, and so was Judith. But what was she? Romola had thought she was doing the right thing – everyone was entitled to representation after all – but maybe she'd just been enabling the Paynes all along.

Cliffy's place was dark when she arrived, meaning he was probably still at Patrick's. She was glad not to have to face her godfather, unsure if she was going to tell him the truth she had uncovered. He had never liked Malcolm anyway. If she told him now, she would feel like a naïve child struck by the harsh realities of the world.

It reminded her of the time her father's car was broken into in their driveway. 'I can't believe there are *criminals* living near us,' seven-year-old Romola had said to Don in shock.

He had laughed gently. 'Well, what if they didn't have enough to eat? Perhaps they thought breaking into our car might be the least worst thing they could do. Maybe we should give them the benefit of the doubt?'

She'd crossed her arms and frowned. 'But it's obviously not the *least* worst thing they could do.' At that age, she hadn't doubted herself. 'They could have knocked on our door and asked us for some food. We would have given it to them, right?'

'That's right, love.' He'd tugged on her ponytail.

The memory made her chest hurt as she walked into Cliffy's dark entry hall. She went straight upstairs to her bedroom, put down her bag, kicked off her shoes and opened the curtains. She lay on her bed and stared at the ceiling for a moment, then remembered the yellow envelope that she had shoved in her bag before embarking upon her walk with Imogen. She had completely forgotten about it while Imogen had confessed all that she'd known.

Romola rolled over and grabbed it from her bag. She sliced a papercut across her index finger as she ripped open the envelope. The document had a sticky note on the front in Imogen's sprawling handwriting: *Malcolm called and asked me to give you this. Sign or don't sign. Up to you. – Imogen.*

It was a non-disclosure agreement, the parties to which were Malcolm Ernest Payne, Patrick Malcolm Payne, and Romola Ishanvi Cross. There were spaces for each of them to sign.

She realised Imogen must have found her middle name in her employment records. Seeing her birth mother's name, there within her own, reminded her of everything she had hoped to be and everything her mother had been.

The terms required her to agree not to disclose any confidential matters concerning the personal affairs of Malcolm Payne, Patrick Payne, Hana Vukovic, Lisbeth Janssen or Sonia Kirk, or any matter indirectly arising from those affairs. In return, Malcolm would pay her $375,000, the amount of the settlement sum.

The only surprise was how little she was surprised by this development. That Malcolm would require this of her was to be expected – she hadn't learnt about his treatment of Hana, Beth and the others under the cover of legal professional privilege, so she was free to tell anyone. If she didn't sign the NDA, her career at Bassett Brown would be over as quickly as it had taken off.

She stuffed the envelope in a drawer. The last thing she needed to do today was spend another moment thinking about the Paynes and their messed-up, cruel world. Instead, she picked up her phone.

'It's so nice to hear from you, my darling.' Judith sounded energised, but then she always did. 'Guess what – I managed to stand up by myself today! Ridiculous walking frame and all. I walked to the other side of the room, right into the arms of Sven the physio. His name's actually Paul, but I think of him as Sven. He's very Nordic.'

'That's fantastic news. Well done.' Romola adjusted herself on the pillow, staring out the window at the cloudless navy-blue sky. The night glowed with a rising full moon. Treetops cast black shadows, like fingertips reaching for the bright orb.

'Is everything okay with you, darling? You sound a little … flat?'

'I'm fine. I just wanted to see how you were. Thought you could tell me all the latest rehab gossip.'

Judith paused, but the opportunity to have a no-strings-attached chat with Romola was apparently too good to ruin with enquiries about her daughter's happiness. 'Oh darling – this place is like *Days of Our Lives*. Brian the nurse and Phillis the dinner lady went on a date last week, and Freda the other dinner lady has her nose right out of joint. The things I could tell you! I could talk all night.'

'That sounds … absolutely wonderful.' Romola closed her eyes and listened.

Chapter Forty-Seven
Three Weeks On

Romola stopped in her tracks as she rounded the corner and saw Patrick sitting on the steps to Cliffy's house. It had to be him, elbows on knees, with Jessie sitting loyally at his feet.

Her fifth run – she'd made it approximately three kilometres this time. She was heaving for air and deeply flushed with the sustained effort of kicking her feet off the ground. Hands on hips, she slowed to a walk as she approached him. 'I heard you'd gone AWOL?' she managed to say through laboured breaths.

He shot her a grin, as Jessie stood in greeting, wagging her shaggy tail. 'I'd heard the same about you. But here you are, running a marathon by the looks of it.'

'God help me, I'm trying.'

The day following 'the day of the barbecues' as she had come to know it, she had resigned from Bassett Brown. Her short resignation email to Imogen had still been saved to her drafts. Derek had called her several times, first leaving detailed messages about how disappointed he was, then begging her to reconsider. Suddenly the calls had stopped, and Romola wondered if Imogen had filled him in about Romola's discovery of Malcolm's secret. For Imogen's part, she had sent Romola a short reply: 'I understand. Good luck.' And that was that.

Since then Romola had been thinking carefully about her options, including leaving the law altogether. She still had savings from her Bassett Brown salary. The only thing she knew how to do was be a lawyer, and deep within her she knew she couldn't leave the profession altogether. Despite it all, she loved the challenge – but she wouldn't become an Imogen, of that she was sure. Perhaps a barrister, like Cliffy, away from the machinations of a firm.

She hadn't signed the non-disclosure agreement, but she hadn't thrown it out either. It had sat in her dressing-table drawer for three weeks, burning a hole next to her small collection of antique jewellery. She knew she wouldn't sign it but was perplexed as to what to do with the information she did have. Whatever had happened between Malcolm and those girls was murky at best, but she didn't know enough to assess whether it was also criminal – and as far Lisbeth was concerned, all she had was hearsay. She had tossed around the options in her head endlessly, but hadn't landed on an answer.

She'd heard from Gretchen that Patrick hadn't been seen since his celebration, and that he hadn't shown up to meetings with his father. He wasn't answering his phone or his door. Malcolm was furious – again.

Romola lowered herself onto the step next to Patrick. 'I thought maybe you were out on your boat?' she said to him, half in jest.

'I've been up the coast, thinking about things.'

'And?' She leaned back, resting on her elbows as her breathing returned to normal. A seagull flew overhead, and she wondered what it was doing so far from the sea.

Patrick grinned. 'Are you going to invite me in or what?' He pressed his thigh briefly to hers, like they were friends jostling over a joke.

Romola shook her head and moved her leg away. 'Here is fine.'

Patrick looked at her quizzically. This obviously wasn't how he had imagined their meeting going. He glanced around, no doubt conscious of the cars passing by, potential onlookers everywhere. 'I wanted you to know I've realised you were right. I've decided to disconnect from Dad and from the business. I'm going to do my own thing, whatever that may be.' He rubbed Jessie's ears and stared at Romola sideways, seeming almost embarrassed.

'I couldn't be happier for you.' She stood up and began to stretch.

'And I wanted to say thank you again. What you did for me was more than anyone else ever has.'

'No problem,' she said casually, folding an arm over her chest and pressing it down, feeling her shoulder muscle extend. Her face prickled with sweat. She felt an odd mix of gratitude that he had appreciated her, tinged with the shame that had unsettled her on and off since the day of the barbecues.

'I also wondered … if I could say thank you over dinner some time?' He glanced up at her, squinting in the sunlight, the gap in his tooth seeming more charming than awkward in this new, enlightened, version of Patrick.

A flicker in Romola's brain acknowledged that – up until that moment on the day of the barbecues – a part of her had found Patrick attractive. If events hadn't transpired as they had, maybe she would even have brought herself to say yes to his invitation. But that day had changed everything.

'Do you really think that's best, Patrick? I have a non-disclosure agreement sitting upstairs, which means I can't talk about your love life. And now you want me to be part of it?'

He sat up a little straighter. 'That agreement is all my dad. I couldn't care less if you sign it or not.'

Patrick stood up, coming closer to her, and she recoiled at the thought he might be about to take her hand.

Instead he put his hands in his pockets. 'I thought we got along well …? Dinner might be … nice?'

She stood up next to him, muscles aching, and touched his shoulder. 'You'll be great on your own for a bit, Patrick. You've thanked me enough. Dinner's really not necessary.' She began to gingerly walk up the steps to the front door. 'Good luck with whatever comes next. Stay away from that father of yours and keep up the gardening. I think there might be a future in that for you.'

Nodding in concession, Patrick leaned down to give Jessie's face a rub. 'If I ever need a good lawyer, at least I'll know who to call.'

Romola put her key in the lock, trying to think of a light-hearted way to tell him never to ask for her legal advice again. But by the time she turned around, he was walking away.

Chapter Forty-Eight
Four Weeks On

They'd booked a table at a small Japanese joint, but Louise cancelled at the last minute, saying she was coming down with the flu and would spend the night in bed. Romola texted that she would pop in at Louise's place anyway, bring some supplies. She'd been waiting for a chance like this.

She had spent a lot of time with Louise since the day of the barbecues. They'd had breakfast, gone for walks and grabbed coffee together, their meetings filled with chatter, both of them still unable to bear any awkward silences. Louise could now tell Romola all the gory details about living with Johnny. He was an early riser who would put on the Al Jazeera news channel at five-thirty every morning, make a pot of coffee and play his guitar, badly. He was madly trying to get Louise to drink green juices. He never closed cupboards, he forgot to put lids back on jars, and he ate Vegemite on roast potatoes but was horrified when she ate a sausage roll. Louise sounded endlessly frustrated with Johnny – but still, regrettably as far as Romola was concerned, completely in love with him.

And Romola filled Louise in about her plans for the future, even though they changed every other day. She'd decided to stay in Melbourne for now, to give the grey city another chance at winning her over. Judith had been fine about this – once Romola had quit her job at Bassett Brown, she could have said she was moving to Morocco and Judith wouldn't have cared. Romola was looking for a new place to live, a place to herself, maybe in the next-door suburb of Richmond – close enough to Cliffy so that he could make her dinner every once in a while. It was time for her to make her life about more than just work.

Johnny answered the door with a smile. Despite the time Romola had spent with Louise in the past four weeks, she'd seen him only once, and the conversation had been stilted. But today she needed him to be friendly, because it was really him she had come to see.

'Come in.' He held the door open. 'Lou's asleep, just drifted off. She actually seems quite sick. I'm starting to regret calling her a hypochondriac.'

Romola walked through to the small kitchen, where the smell of cooking hung in the muggy air. She could make out onions, chicken, and more onions.

Johnny walked over and turned off the stove. 'I'm making chicken soup.'

'I thought you were a vegetarian?'

'My mum's recipe – I always had it when I was sick as a kid. Mind you, it has been a while since I've cooked meat.' He pulled a ladle through the lumpy brown liquid.

Romola reached into her paper bag of supplies for Louise. 'I have vegetarian pies – spinach, I think, baked fresh – not by me – this afternoon, Panadol, butter menthols, and Portuguese custard tarts.'

'Brilliant.' Johnny glanced down at the sink – it seemed he still couldn't look at her when he paid her a compliment. She watched as he expertly navigated the small kitchen, finding a tray and putting the pies into the oven. It was the first warm night of the year, and he switched on the fairy lights that lit up the courtyard garden. James Taylor was playing 'Sweet Baby James'. 'There's beers in the fridge. Have one with me?'

'I can do better than that.' Romola reached into her handbag and pulled out a bottle of red wine. It had been delivered to Cliffy's house earlier that week with a card from Patrick:

Romola,

I've gathered it's a hard no to dinner. Please accept this instead. It was a gift to me from my father. He would hate that I'm giving it to you.

I can't thank you enough. Your loyalty was, and is, everything to me. If one day I meet you on the other side of a courtroom, I'm going

to settle immediately because I know how damn good you are. But if
you ever change your mind about dinner, I'm all yours.
Patrick

She held the bottle out to Johnny. If Patrick had passed the bottle to her to spite Malcolm, it seemed only fitting that she share it with Johnny. 'I don't think Lou will mind us having a drink together. For the sake of burying the hatchet, that is.'

Johnny dried his hands on a tea towel and took the bottle, turning it over to read the label. 'How did you get this? You do know it's like, crazy expensive.'

'A gift from an appreciative client. I know it's not exactly the weather for –'

He smiled at her conspiratorially. 'Let's open the bloody thing. I fucking deserve it.'

No, *I* fucking deserve it, she thought, but overlooked his self-absorption. She had come to expect it.

They sat at a small table on the deck. Crickets trilled. She could hear the clinking of cutlery and glass from the neighbours. It was unseasonably warm for October – a northerly bringing with it the heat from the country's centre.

'I hear you quit?' Johnny asked, eyebrows up.

The garden was dark. The candle between them lit his face from below, and she wasn't sure if it was beautiful or horrific. She remembered what Malcolm had said to Johnny at the mediation: *I know you. I know your secrets …* What did that mean coming from Malcolm, a man with enough secrets to bring down his empire? Was Johnny just as bad? Perhaps – she would need to keep her eye on him, for Louise's sake. But what Romola knew about Johnny was that he loved a good story and wouldn't let a good tip go to waste, and that he despised the Paynes with his whole being.

She held out her hands in mock surrender. 'Turns out Bassett Brown wasn't the place for me after all. Nothing against them, of course.'

'Of course.' He tipped his head back as he downed a mouthful of wine, then swallowed it and smacked his lips. 'Bloody hell, that's a smooth drop. I feel as though we should toast your old client – put it behind us?' He lifted his glass. 'To Patrick Payne.'

'No,' she said firmly, meeting his eye, 'we should toast Payne Senior instead. To Malcolm, the father who has it all – and the man behind it all.'

Johnny smiled through red-wine teeth, one eyebrow raised. 'As you wish. To Malcolm Payne –' he smoothed his curls back with one hand, continuing to point his glass in the air with the other '– the man who holds the purse strings.' After taking a sip, Johnny leaned forward on the table and began flicking his finger in and out of the candle's flame. 'It won't be the last time Daddy will have to come to Patrick's rescue, you know. I'm fucking certain there's more to it.'

Johnny was almost there – he just needed to be nudged in the right direction. The words were on the edge of her lips.

She was doing nothing wrong; she hadn't learnt the information in confidence, and she hadn't signed the non-disclosure agreement. She'd made a copy of it and scanned it into her Cloud, so she would always have a record of what he'd asked her to sign. She had been in contact with the police officer in charge of the coroner's investigation and forwarded him the copy of Max's video – he could take it from there.

But after much deliberation, she decided that she couldn't divulge what she'd learned about Lisbeth. She'd been told those details in a conversation with Patrick that was, among other things, about his case. Privilege was likely to apply, and she didn't feel she could ethically breach his confidence unless it was legally required. She just hoped the coroner's office would see fit to take their enquiries down a new path once they'd seen the video, and that it would lead them to Lisbeth.

The alternative was to put the information about Hana in the hands of someone who would use it to track down the truth. Someone who wouldn't be afraid of exposing Malcolm, whatever his influence. Someone like Johnny. Still, it felt sinful to be the giver, rather than the keeper, of information for once.

'Next time I'll get him.' Johnny stuck out his chest.

'Next time you'll need to get it right, then,' she said plainly, 'rather than put your foot in it.'

His fingers paused next to the flame. 'And how would I do that? Get it right, that is?'

She clutched the stem of her wineglass as he beseeched her for information. He was so greedy she could hardly bear to give it. She inhaled and peered up at the night sky filled with stars. Her dad had taught her that the apparent twinkling of the stars is caused by what the earth's atmosphere does to the light as it passes through; the stars themselves are stable and constant.

Perspective is everything, Romola thought. She could give Johnny the information, and he would lap it up. She could give him the tip and he could create the twinkle. And Malcolm would deserve whatever came his way. She wasn't sure whether that was the right or the just thing. Whether it was what Hana or Lisbeth would have truly wanted – to become the latest shiny distraction. But who was Romola to say? Surely they, along with Tilly, deserved the dignity of truth.

She snapped her gaze back to Johnny, making her decision. 'Lou tells me that, despite appearances, you're a pretty good journalist.' She flashed him that smile, the one her father had always talked about, and passed him a pen and notepad from her bag. 'You might want to take this down.'

December, Mrs Forsyth

Mrs Forsyth's nephew had come to visit. He walked his small dog to her house every Saturday morning, letting the terrier urinate freely in her back garden while he came in 'for a chat'. He normally had the weekend papers tucked under one arm and a tray of doughnuts in his hand. In his ghastly tracksuit pants, he would sit opposite her at the formica kitchen table, reading the headlines aloud as though she wasn't perfectly capable of doing so herself. His wife had him on a strict diet, but she never joined him for these visits. Nor did any of his three daughters, who he said were very busy with their extracurricular activities; they were very talented, he said. They had been due to perform in their school Christmas concert earlier that week. She would hear all about it from her nephew today, though he hadn't thought to invite her to the performance.

Mrs Forsyth knew his real worry was that she would sell the house. Prices in her suburb had boomed for a second time late last year. She was well aware that she was sitting on a gold mine and that her nephew was chief among the prospectors.

'How are you feeling this week?' he asked over the newspaper, barely looking at her as he stuffed a doughnut in his mouth.

'Fine. No different to usual.'

Her week had, in fact, been singularly dreadful. She could hardly move from kitchen to bedroom without the pain in her hip becoming insufferable. She had seen a new doctor on Monday – a new doctor with a new potential diagnosis. There was discolouration in the bone scan, a suspicious mass. She should prepare herself for bad news, he'd said. Good news for her nephew, she thought.

'Look, here's something interesting,' he said with his mouth full.

He pointed at a photo on the top of the front page, leaving a smudge of icing behind. He wiped at the page with the side of his hand, making it worse.

The photo behind the doughnut sprinkles was of Patrick's father, Malcolm Payne, with a smile on his face. He sat next to a handsome curly-haired bohemian; they wore tuxedos and were clinking champagne glasses. Interposed next to them was an old photo of Patrick during one of his political speeches, looking like a deer in the headlights.

Mrs Forsyth's heart gave a start.

'Your old employer's back in the news.'

She hadn't heard from Patrick since that young Indian solicitor had called to tell her she wouldn't be needed any further: there would be no trial. The girl had thanked her, said she'd been indispensable in securing a good outcome for Patrick. But still, Mrs Forsyth had been looking forward to attending court; she had already chosen an outfit.

After that she had scoured the papers each day for news of Patrick, but there wasn't a word. It was like the whole affair had never happened – as if she hadn't found that body lying prone before her.

She had not gone back to work at Patrick's house, even once she had recovered from the shock of discovering the body. Her hip couldn't take another summer's cleaning. If she was honest, she was also slightly embarrassed about those notes she had taken, even though she knew how important they had become. But she wished she could have met Patrick in person again so he could thank her.

What had he done wrong this time? she wondered.

Her nephew held his face closer to the paper. 'Not that interesting.' He sounded disappointed. 'Malcolm Payne has just bought something else. How's that for justice, hey? He's gone and bought that website they were suing, Rabbit Hole. Says he's diversifying. What goes around comes around, huh? Fifty million dollar purchase price.' He whistled through his teeth.

Mrs Forsyth's tea tasted sickly sweet. 'Who's that man there, next to Malcolm?'

'New editor – Jonathan Wise is his name. Apparently he received a cut of the money, lucky bastard.'

'Hmmm.' She dipped her biscuit into her tea, but the bottom had fallen out. She scooped it up, sucking the tea from the soggy end. She wished her nephew would leave her in peace.

'They didn't pay you enough, Aunty. They took advantage. Maybe we should be asking for some sort of compensation – for what you saw.'

'I will do no such thing.'

Why did he insist on calling her 'Aunty'? She was all too aware he was family, and that any money she made now would go straight to his pockets.

'Suit yourself.' Her nephew grunted, licked his thumb and turned the page.

January, Romola

Louise and Romola stood in a loft above a Vietnamese grocery store on Victoria Street, in Richmond. The woman who ran the store had given them each a steaming cup of coffee before they climbed the stairs. The place was basic, with raw timber floors made up for by the huge warehouse-style windows and the sweetness of the coffee. In the smoky summer sunshine, steam trails rose from their cups like lazy serpents.

'My desk will go there.' Romola pointed to a space opposite the window, where lettuce boxes were stacked against the wall. 'Fingers crossed I'll be able to afford an admin one day. They could sit near the door. I could get a partition to break up the room …?'

Louise turned in a circle, the sunlight tinting her orange hair gold. 'It's perfect.'

There was a constant hum and an occasional clang from the street, along with boxes being noisily stacked and instructions yelled in Vietnamese from the shop below. The sunshine was warming the space now, but its high ceilings would make it cold in the winter, which was about to arrive. But it was within Romola's price range, and she had signed the lease before she could give herself any more reasons not to.

She hadn't seen any more from Patrick since receiving that bottle of red, but she'd received emails from him every now and then, which she hadn't responded to. He was in Japan, learning more about gardens. He had left Max in Melbourne with Sonia while he sorted himself out. She had given up the meditation and, according to Patrick, had even been known to indulge Max with milkshakes and fries.

'Where did the flowers come from?' Louise pointed to the huge spray of pale pink hydrangeas on the windowsill.

'Judith. Who else would send flowers to an empty office?'

'They're lovely, though, aren't they?'

Until recently, Romola hadn't noticed how Louise had been subtly encouraging her to accept Judith. Everything seemed so much clearer now.

'I brought you a gift too.' Louise bent to reach into a cavernous straw bag. 'I don't even know if people put these things up anymore. It's probably daggy, but it might make the place look a bit more … official.' She pulled out a document mounted in a walnut-coloured frame. It was Romola's university parchment with its red wax stamp: Romola Ishanvi Cross, Bachelor of Laws, with Honours. A matching frame held her admission certificate.

'Are they too cheesy?' Louise asked with a wince. 'Judith dug them out and sent them down to me. I was going to get you some stationery, but I couldn't –'

'Lou – they're perfect. Thank you.' Romola balanced them against the windowsill next to the flowers in the sunlight. Her gift from Cliffy was there too: a gold fountain pen in its leather case and a pot of peacock-blue ink, the tableau for the next stage of her career as a barrister and solicitor. 'And what about you?' Romola asked her friend, who had moved to the window, holding the mug of sweet coffee under her chin as she peered down at the road. 'Everything okay?'

'Me?' Louise touched her chest. 'I *still* can't believe I finally managed to bag myself a millionaire, and then I let him go – poof! But …'

'But?'

'I admit he turned out to be a bit of a jerk. I mean, what kind of weirdo puts Vegemite on potatoes?'

A few weeks earlier, Johnny had moved out of Louise's place and into a South Yarra apartment purchased with his new-found wealth. Their relationship had ended amicably. The habits that had once seemed charming had begun to grate on Louise. According to her, although Johnny had justified his deal with Malcolm Payne to himself – his slogan was something like 'revolution begins with infiltration'

– the money had obviously talked. After belittling Louise's career in gossip magazines, Johnny was now doing Malcolm Payne's bidding at Rabbit Hole, where the reporting had become decidedly less controversial following Eddie Moss's departure. In the end, Louise couldn't get rid of Johnny fast enough.

Romola's phone began to buzz. She hadn't seen the number in a while, but the caller's name was still saved – and it was burned into her memory. 'Imogen?'

Louise turned, aghast, mouthing, 'What the fuck?!'

Romola shrugged, clueless.

'Romola, long time no see. How have you been?'

'Good, thanks. Really good.' Romola put her back to the window and appreciated the big empty space that was to be her very own office. She wouldn't let Imogen interrupt her happiness.

'A rumour's been circulating that you're setting up on your own?'

'That's right.' Romola wondered who had told. Maybe Victoria, who got coffee with her every now and then. Or Gretchen, who was still working at Bassett Brown but had sworn that she would work for Romola as soon as she had enough money to pay a wage. Gretchen had even offered to work for free, but Romola had refused, knowing the experience at Bassett Brown would serve the young woman well despite the firm's flaws.

'Good for you,' Imogen said lightly. Romola wished she would hurry up and get to the point. 'I have a matter for you if you want it, for one of my old schoolfriends. She's been royally fucked over by her ex-boyfriend. He's managed to transfer her house into his name, plus all her life savings. She doesn't fit Bassett Brown's client profile, but I thought, if you want, she'd probably fit yours? Can I give her your number …?'

Romola let out a silent sigh. As soon as she'd heard Imogen's voice, she'd been worried that she was calling on instructions from Malcolm to seek out a signature on the NDA again. 'Of course,' she said, 'that would be great. Thanks, Imogen.'

'Don't thank me yet. You haven't met her.' Imogen hung up, and Romola chuckled with relief.

'All okay?' Louise asked.

Romola stretched her hands high above her and brought them down in a rainbow arc, then did a little dance. 'I think I just got my first client.'

Acknowledgements

Thank you first to my agent, the brilliant Jeanne Ryckmans of Cameron's Management, for her belief in *She Too*, and for her graceful guidance and advocacy.

Thanks to Juliet Rogers from Echo, who with much patience and kindness has introduced me to the world of fiction publishing. Thanks also to Diana Hill for her hard work and skilful guiding of the ship, and to Lizzie Hayes for having to deal with my complete lack of public relations nous.

I would like to acknowledge the hard work of editor Kate Goldsworthy, whose wonderfully exacting and insightful editing made *She Too* into what I hoped it could be. Thank you, Kate.

Thanks also to everyone involved in transforming *She Too* from manuscript to book, including Lisa White for her beautiful cover design, and Shaun Jury for everything inside the cover.

I may never have had the fortitude to complete *She Too* without the guidance of Lisa O'Donnell from the opposite side of the world. Our late-night Skype sessions, which continued when the world changed around us in early 2020, kept me persisting. Thanks also to the team at Curtis Brown Creative in the UK for getting me started. Going even further back, I would like to take this chance (as it's not often one comes along) to thank Marcella O'Hare, my high school English and Drama teacher, who so valued and inspired creative writing.

She Too is about the practice of the law, and I consider myself lucky to have spent my career surrounded by good people who also happen to be great lawyers. I would especially like to thank for their support (of both my writing and my legal practice) Anthony Groom, Roxanne Smith, Magistrate Toni Vozzo, Paul Turner, Sam Johnson and Tony

Johnson. Special thanks also to Ben Renfrey and Kevin Lynch (the best media lawyer in the business) for reading the manuscript.

Thanks next to my friends for their encouragement, and particularly to those who were brave enough to read my writing and offer feedback. Thanks to Sue Agnew, Lillie Johnson and Jo Croser for being my first readers. A big thanks also to Marnie Wade, without whose enthusiasm and pep talks I may never have approached Jeanne. Thanks also to Natasha Stott-Despoja, for pointing me in the right direction.

Most importantly, thank you to my family. Thanks to my mum and dad, Marilyn and David Thomson, who always so steadfastly encouraged my writing efforts, and who will forever be my earliest and very best readers. Thanks to my sisters, Holly Clarke and Kathryn Thomson, for their friendship (and to Holly for her Riverland read), and to their families: Matt, James and Alfie, and Paul, Bea and Jules. Thanks also to my mother-in-law, Josephine Hillary, for her generous support.

To Anthony, your hard work gifted me the luxury of time to do what I had always wanted – to write a novel. Thank you for that, and for being a wonderful dad and my number one PR guy. And to our children, Mim and Frankie, thanks for never failing to cheer me on. You inspire me and make me happy and proud every day.

Book Club Questions

1. Why do you think the novel is named *She Too*? In your opinion, which 'she' does this refer to?

2. Romola experienced significant changes in her career, home, friendships and family. How do you think these changes affected her decision-making as a lawyer and in her personal life?

3. As *She Too* progressed, how did your impressions of Patrick Payne change? Did you ever think of him as a victim? Ultimately, do you think he was deserving of a fall from grace?

4. If this were a real-life scenario that you read about in the news, do you think you would believe that Patrick was a good man?

5. Do you find Malcolm's conduct explicable? What factors and characteristics do you think influenced his conduct? What role did ego play? By contrast, what role did ego play in Patrick's decision-making?

6. How much do you think Imogen's opinions and actions were influenced by the men in her life?

7. Romola and Louise's relationship was fractured throughout. Do you think Louise's treatment of Romola was fair?

8. What do you think would be the main obstacles for Romola succeeding at Bassett Brown in the future?

9. Why do you think Patrick remained loyal to his father for so long?

10. Do you think Romola would have accepted Patrick's dinner invitation if things had turned out differently?

11. What did you make of the ending? Would you have acted differently to Romola?

12. *She Too* examines the impact of power and wealth in the media today. What role do you think the Paynes' privileged position had on the ultimate outcome of how the media covered their story?

13. What have you taken from *She Too* about the state of Australian law firms? What difficulties do you think women might have in succeeding at these workplaces?

14. *She Too* explores the complexities in defamation law of proving the truth of a report or establishing that reporting was reasonable and justified. Often this is a very difficult threshold for media defendants to meet, and that can silence stories before they are printed. What do you think is more important: freedom of speech, or having laws that prohibit defamation and protect damage to reputation? Do you think journalists should be able to tell stories like this?